THE SHOALS OF HONOUR
and Early Stories

by Elisabeth Sanxay Holding

Introduction by Judith Rose Ardron

Stark House Press • Eureka California

THE SHOALS OF HONOUR / EARLY STORIES

Published by Stark House Press
1315 H Street
Eureka, CA 95501, USA
griffinskye3@sbcglobal.net
www.starkhousepress.com

ISBN: 978-1-951473-24-2

Book design by Mark Shepard, shepgraphics.com

First Stark House Press Edition:
December 2020

Elisabeth Sanxay Holding

I'm writing about someone I hardly met – my grandmother. I grew up with her daughters – my mother and my aunt – her darling girls. From them, I learned some of her myth as a mother and of her strength and struggles as a woman. She came from a dynasty of strong women who were independents spirits in a world that had rigid ideas of a woman's role and place in the economic order. From the depths of the Depression, she took responsibility for the economic survival of her family and harnessed her art, her craft, a questing mind and a social conscience to that goal. She was a free thinker; she loved to swim, at ease in the open sea.

When going through some family papers, I found two large cardboard boxes stacked high with lined foolscap sheets. Her small, close, uniform and intense writing covers sheet after sheet, ink now fading. These are her manuscripts. Hundreds of thousands of words, crafted by hand, bring her strength of will, her drive to produce into the room. What did it take to sustain that determination over those furlongs of faded foolscap? I want to put on record how hard won her achievements must have been.

She was a conscientious worker and craftswoman. She took her craft seriously, relying on deliberate thought, planning and hard work. She set herself the discipline of sitting down to write every morning. In the first seven months of 1928, she completely re-wrote a 90,000 word novel and wrote a 60,000 word serial and eleven short stories. Her day was organized into a routine that she strictly adhered to, not pausing for a cigarette or coffee until the appointed hour. Her daughters knew not to disturb her when she was working.

This was no hobby – it was an all consuming effort. She could not find peace without knowing she could provide for her mother, herself and her girls' future. The family fortunes were unpredictable, plagued by insecurity and lurching from the sale of one story to another. She experienced the misery of her writing getting stuck, while being tormented by a sense of haste to get working before she became penniless again. The Wall Street crash and the Depression left her penniless, unable to sell any work. Her family went without. Her sense of honour meant she agonized over the inevitable debts that accrued.

It was a wearing way to live. Her health was not good. In 1923, at the age of 34, she had pneumonia and was tormented by how she could continue to provide for her two little girls. By the time she was 39, she was experiencing extreme fatigue; her energy and confidence were low and she had trouble sleeping. Fatigue and depression continued to plague her but she strove to overcome all this by sheer force of will and strength of spirit driven by her fierce loyalty to her daughters. In spite of her ill health, her last novel was published in 1953, just two years before she died at the age of 65.

She rarely had the luxury of working without these financial pressures, of experiencing a sense of satisfaction from what she produced, of standing back and working on the big canvas of her novels. In her lifetime, she never reaped the benefits of great rewards or the critical acclaim that her work eventually came to attract. But her spirit and strength of character lives on in our family – six grandchildren, eight great grandchildren and four great great grandchildren. There is something of her in all of us. We are proud to celebrate this internationally esteemed writer as our own. I would wish for her to know that her work is still valued and enjoyed well into the 21st century. It's still out there engaging people's minds and intelligence. I would want her to rest reassured that her labour still bears fruit in her legacy to us, her family, and to her readers.

Judith Rose Ardron
Sheffield, England
October 2012

THE SHOALS OF HONOUR

by Elisabeth Sanxay Holding

CHAPTER ONE

THE NAUGHTY BOY

A cloud had come across the face of the April sun. The dining-room was dim and a little chilly; the napkins were cold to touch; the silver had a frosty gleam; the damask cloth was like a dazzling snow-field; the centre-piece of ferns might put you in mind of some early flora after the glacial age. And Mrs. Huested's words, too, were chilling to her guest.

"Hazeltine!" she said, "you're a naughty boy!"

"How can I help it?" he answered, promptly. This was without doubt the proper retort, and he made it with a gallant smile. After all, he had brought this upon himself; he had deliberately encouraged Mrs. Huested to call him a naughty boy, and now he had to be one. But with what an effort!

Still smiling, he looked across the table at her. She looked as she always looked, for she was the least variable of women, but Hazeltine, unfortunately, was not so stable. He had moods, fits of unwarrantable squeamishness, one was upon him now, and he was struggling in secret against an almost overpowering exasperation and restiveness. He wanted to get away—at once. And he could think of so many good excuses.

But that was impossible, of course. He must sit here, and he must smile, and he must look at her, though at this instant everything about her offended him, her stout and compact figure, her grim, copper-coloured face, her heavy black hair. She was, he thought, like an Indian squaw, and that air of dowdy respectability in no way concealed her native barbarousness. The soul of a savage was in that woman, he knew it very well.

The parlour-maid set before him a tall glass filled with some frozen mixture, and for a moment her small, blunt fingers came beneath his downcast glance. Not a pretty hand, not a pretty girl, yet he felt a sudden sort of affection toward her, because she was young, warm, cordially alive in this chilly room where he and Mrs. Huested sat facing each other, always on guard, always weighing and calculating, bent upon impressing each other. He dared not even allow himself the relief of silence, for Mrs. Huested distrusted his silences, she would not believe he was thinking of her, she wanted him to talk, she expected a certain measure of audacity from him, she required him to be a naughty boy.

"Making love like a travelling salesman," he reflected, in disgust. "Double meaning in everything—and no meaning at all."

He could see no other course, though. He was obliged to be elusive and cryptic, for the situation was one of extreme delicacy. The straightforward, manly tone was not possible; he could not make serious love to her. A handsome young fellow of twenty-eight, without a penny to bless himself with, and filled with a disinterested passion for this black-avised widow of forty-five? No; she could hardly swallow that. Great dramatic ability would be needed in order to convince her, and he was not good at drama. The first move would have to be made by her, and the best he could do was to wait with the sensitive air of one too honourable to speak. A difficult role, and, worst of all, he could not tell how much faith she had in this attitude; sometimes he had a disturbing suspicion that she understood everything....

And sometimes he did not care what she understood or what she felt. Reason told him that all depended upon Mrs. Huested, that here was probably his last chance, but sometimes he was rebellious against reason. There were moments when caution and diplomacy were nearly intolerable to him. Nearly intolerable, but never wholly so; a dangerous mutiny troubled his spirit, but he could keep it in hand. He argued with himself.

"After all," he thought, "she's been very decent to me."

After all, his affairs were in a bad way; no use in being a fool. He raised his eyes to her face again, and she was looking at him.

"What's the matter, Hazeltine?" she asked. "Worried?"

"No!" he answered. "No, thanks, I'm not!"

"Well, you're mighty quiet!" she said. "See here, Hazeltine! If you *are* worried about anything, you needn't mind telling me. I'm pretty practical; I dare say I could help you out."

He was silent for a moment, a grave expression on his face, and resentment in his heart. Her meaning was plain enough. She thought he was in financial difficulties, and she was ready to lend him money.

"Not much!" thought the prudent young man. "Then she'd feel she owned me, body and soul."

He had to make some sort of answer.

"It's nothing I could very well tell you about," he said, at last.

Mrs. Huested's black brows met in a fleeting scowl; she did not understand, and Hazeltine had meant her not to understand. This was his method.

"I can't make you out!" she reflected. "Sometimes I can't help thinking.... But no ...! That's all damned nonsense!"

She had heard and read about women of her age inspiring men with desperate passions; of course, she didn't expect that, and Hazeltine wasn't that sort of man, but still.... The thing which sometimes she couldn't help thinking was—that Hazeltine, with his superior discernment, might have seen in her the true Natalie Huested, invisible to others. The way he looked at her, the things he said.... Even if he were a little influenced by her money? Well, she too had moods, not suspected by Hazeltine, moods in which she was inclined to throw herself and her money at his handsome young head and, at the cost of all her pride, buy from him the falsest sort of ardour. She was accustomed to buying what she wanted, anyhow; she expected to pay for all she got.

Strange charm this graceless fellow had for her! In theory, he was everything she most despised—a man who either could not or would not earn his bread, who lived by exploiting his friends. And was not at all ashamed of it; on the contrary, he had more self-assurance and aplomb than any of the hard-working business men she knew, a polite effrontery which, in her eyes, somehow justified his shocking idleness. He "got away with it"; and she was obliged to admire that; he was, in his own way, successful, and she adored success. Try as she would, she could not really despise Hazeltine; she could not help a reluctant admiration for his cleverness, his nonchalant manner, his superb clothes. She had everything, and he had nothing; she was independent, worthy, self-respecting, and he was not; yet she felt a little afraid of him. His squeamishness was no secret to her; she knew very well that she sometimes offended him, and it hurt her to know it. She tried to be tactful with Hazeltine, according to her fashion. She had to encourage him.

"Something you can't very well tell me, eh?" she pursued, with grim playfulness. "Fallen in love, have you, Hazeltine?"

Here was a cue for a gallant speech, and exactly the right words came promptly to his mind. But he could not speak them. Not to save his life. He met her eyes for an instant and then glanced away....

And his silence seemed to ring through the room like a shout. Mrs. Huested sat downcast and quiet, the little servant in a dark corner by the sideboard did not stir; it was as if he had uttered words so momentous as to stun them.

Dismay seized him; he was almost ready to believe that he had spoken, said something irrevocable, and of immense significance. He started nervously as Mrs. Huested pushed back her chair. He fancied there was something hurried in her manner, that she was impatient to call him to account for those words he had not spoken.

But when they were in the drawing-room, she said nothing at all. He waited, walking up and down the long room, waited in dread, while she sat squarely in the middle of a great divan, staring before her with a faint frown.

"What did you mean, Hazeltine?" she asked, suddenly, "what was it you couldn't very well tell me?"

God knows what he had meant by that; nothing at all.

"I thought—" he began, and stopped. The less he said, the more meaning would she imagine, the more elusive he was, the more admirable would he appear to her.

"You do too much thinking, Hazeltine," she said, "and not enough acting."

"Very likely!" he agreed, with a sigh.

She looked down at her clasped hands, well adorned with jewels.

"That's not my way, Hazeltine," she said, "I'm not hasty, and I'm not rash, but I don't like shilly-shallying. I like plain speaking, Hazeltine!"

"Oh, do you?" he thought. "Not so much as you imagine! Not from other people.... I never noticed that you picked out plain-speakers for your friends. On the contrary! All that mob in London—the ones you liked were the ones who licked your boots." Aloud he said, briefly: "Plain speaking is a luxury I can't afford."

"You can—with me, Hazeltine," she said.

He realized with profound disquiet, what was happening. They were progressing toward an "understanding." She and her "plain-speaking." ... Never since they had first met, last summer in London, had there been one honest, careless word between them.

He had met her at a monster ball given for charity; someone had introduced him to her, and he had been very civil, as was his prudent habit with strangers. He had danced with her twice, and then he would have forgotten her, if his cousin, Charles Keyes, hadn't approached him.

"I see you've taken on Mrs. Huested," Charles had said, with his smile of pontifical subtlety. "Very intelligent of you!"

"Huested?" Hazeltine answered, "I didn't catch the name. Never heard of her, anyhow."

Charles had not believed this, he continued to smile. "The Pickle King's widow," he said, *"En avant, mon vieux!"*

This had displeased the fastidious Hazeltine; nevertheless, he had accepted Mrs. Huested's invitation to call at her hotel, and that was the beginning.

Her life had presented an appearance of great social activity; she was always going out, to lunch, to tea, to dinner, to plays, operas, and balls. But Hazeltine had soon discovered that she went almost nowhere without paying. Not twice in that season did she set foot in a private house. Stiff-necked, Mrs. Huested was; she would not angle for invitations, or buy them; she wished to be liked for her own sake, and saw no reason why she should not be.

At heart she was disappointed in London. She knew a good many Americans there, and went about with them, having very expensive good times, but they were not the sort of people she wanted. And Hazeltine was. Of his kind, he was perfect. She was proud to be seen in his company.

He had taken her out to dinner two or three times, and then Charles Keyes went home, and Hazeltine could no longer play the host. They both remembered that day; it was a little crisis; seven o'clock, in her hotel sitting-room.

She had hoped he would ask her to dine with him, but he said nothing about it, and when the clock struck, he prepared to take his leave.

"Going out with some of your friends, Hazeltine?" she had asked, with jealous curiosity.

"No," he had answered, smiling a little. "Dining alone—at a little Italian *table d'hôte*. I'd ask you to come with me, but I'm afraid you wouldn't like it."

It was Mrs. Huested who had flushed; Hazeltine had remained unperturbed.

"Now, see here, Hazeltine!" she had said, resolutely. "I don't like those cheap little restaurants, and that's a fact. But ... if you'll be my guest to-night ...?"

"Thank you," he had said, quietly, "but I'd rather not."

"That's damned nonsense, Hazeltine! I've been out with you lots of times ... if you're a bit hard up for the moment—"

"Rather a long moment," he had said, "I thought you knew...."

She had heard rumours that Hazeltine lived on nothing, but she hadn't really believed it. He was always so well-dressed; he went everywhere, did everything that anyone else did. It seemed impossible.... She had stared at him with a perplexed and troubled frown.

"Well ..." she had said, at last, "let's dine together to-night, anyhow."

But he had refused. For two weeks he had steadfastly declined her invitations, and when at last he surrendered, she had learned to appreciate his value. She had tried to be tactful. She had hired a motor by the month so that there should be no taxi fares to worry him, she arranged for their little dinners beforehand, so that no bills were presented. But there were, inevitably, some very awkward moments, which they both resented. Indeed, there was a continual undercurrent of resentment, of secret hostility, and when Hazeltine sailed for New York, they had parted with a curious sort of relief.

Yet they had both known that was not the end. Directly she got home, Mrs. Huested had telephoned to him, and he had come to her at once. It had begun all over again, but on a somewhat different footing. Mrs. Huested was on her own ground here; she was no longer a stranger, to whom Hazeltine's company could give prestige. She was in her own home, she was always the hostess now, and she had grown more autocratic. She liked him to come to lunch, for that seemed to her somehow more respectable than dinner; he was expected to arrive at one o'clock, and to "spend the afternoon," a form of entertainment hitherto unknown to him. Endless afternoons, exasperating and wearisome to both of them.

Of course, he had known all the time where this was leading him; hadn't he done his adroit and patient best to arrive at this moment? And yet, faced with the definite fact, he was panic-stricken.

"Hazeltine," she went on, with that incessant use of his name that so annoyed him, "you needn't be afraid to speak plainly to me. We've known each other a good while.... We ought to understand each other pretty well."

"A man can never understand a woman," said he. He was alarmed as soon as he had made this banal and flippant remark, but Mrs. Huested took it seriously.

"Well, I'm not—" she began, when the little parlour-maid entered, with a card on a tray. She picked up the card and looked at it, frowning.

"It's Mrs. Garvey," she observed, with a glance at Hazeltine.

"I see!" said he, politely, but she noticed, with disappointment, that the name meant nothing to him.

"Mrs. *Jewett* Garvey," she said.

Still he seemed unimpressed.

"Her name's been in the papers several times," Mrs. Huested continued, anxiously, "she does a lot of charitable work.... They live down on Long Island near where your cousin lives. She says she *met* your cousin once—at a bazaar!"

"I see!" said Hazeltine, again.

"Well!" she demanded, "do you want to see her, Hazeltine?"

"Any friend of yours ..." he said, mildly surprised.

"Bring her in!" said Mrs. Huested to the parlour-maid, and presently in came Mrs. Garvey. A curiously shaped little woman she was, very long-waisted, with a swan's neck, and a blonde head too large for her body.

"Natalie!" she cried, "Isn't this a simply *weird* time to call? But I simply had to see you about that 'Night in Stamboul' thing. I simply—"

Mrs. Huested interrupted, in a threatening voice.

"Let me introduce Mr. Hazeltine!" she said, "Mrs. Garvey!"

Now, the relations between Mrs. Huested and Mrs. Garvey were peculiar. They were not in any way rivals, they were very well-disposed toward each other, but they were confused, uneasy, not certain which was the superior. Mrs. Huested truly admired Annabelle for being—"smart," for her enterprise and zeal in persuading guests into her country house; she herself had merely rented a flat on Riverside Drive, in a region where Nobody lived, and made a brave show of not caring whether anyone came to her or not. Precious few did come, but even if Natalie was not popular, Mrs. Garvey felt a deep respect for her solidity. The Garveys were, after all, not yet rooted, and Mrs. Huested was; she had been rich twice as long as they had; she had lived abroad, she had contrived some sort of background for herself. And there was also her remarkable force of character.

What, then, was Annabelle to do about this Mr. Hazeltine? In him she saw something she wanted very badly for her country house, yet she could not tell whether Natalie would appreciate or resent her being nice to him. She had heard of him, often enough, but without a definite clue as to his standing with Natalie.

So, after an airy acknowledgment of the introduction, she thought it wiser to pay no more attention to him, but to go on talking to Natalie in her sprightly style.

"You must be in on this thing!" she said. "You'd be simply wonderful in an Oriental costume."

"I wouldn't make such a fool of myself," said Mrs. Huested, tersely. "But I'll come if you like. And I'll make a contribution. It's for orphans, isn't it?"

"My dear! I told you! It's for a scholarship fund for Turkish girls. You'll come out this week-end, won't you, and we'll talk it over?"

"All right!" said Mrs. Huested.

There was a moment's silence.

"If Mr. Hazeltine could come too ...?" Mrs. Garvey suggested.

"Thank you, but I'm engaged," he answered. "Very sorry!"

Neither he nor Mrs. Huested seemed annoyed by the invitation, so Mrs. Garvey went on, encouraged. "Next week-end, then?"

"I'm sorry, but I'm going out of town."

"Perhaps some time in the *middle* of the week would suit you better," said Mrs. Garvey. "We keep open house, you know."

Her hospitality suffered all things, endured all things; it was irresistible; in the end Hazeltine was solemnly pledged to telephone to her and tell her when he would come. In the excitement of the pursuit she had forgotten Mrs. Huested, but he had not. He took out his watch and looked at it.

"By Jove!" he said. "I must be getting along!"

"Going?" cried Mrs. Huested. "You didn't tell me you had an engagement!"

She was disappointed and angry; he knew it, and he didn't care. Nothing on earth could keep him here another minute. He went off, positively exalted by his escape, so happy to be free that he whistled as he went down the street.

Before he reached the corner, he remembered that he hadn't enough money for a decent dinner, and he stopped whistling and sighed, weary of this incessant hunt for food.

He knew where he could get what he wanted, though.

CHAPTER TWO

THREE MEN

Mac Donald sat at his desk by the window, bent over his work. But in spite of the best intentions in the world, his eyes would stray to the blue sky, and large, grave thoughts about Life and Destiny came into his head. He was ashamed of this; he had, in the past, considered himself a serious and substantial man, and his fondness for meditation a worthy trait; now, however, he saw that beneath his sober exterior lay a shocking frivolity. Nobody else in the office looked out of windows; only he. He was restless, couldn't put his heart into his work.

"Ah, well ...!" he said to himself, with a sigh. "It's a very peculiar thing.... Twenty-five years at sea—and now this! I've no aptitude for it. It is setting the old dog at new tricks."

But he could not feel so old as it was his duty to feel. Forty-two, he was; lean, hard as nails, with a dark, obstinate face, and an air of invincible composure. He wished to feel his years lying heavy upon him, but he could not; he felt altogether too light, too unburdened.

"It is a change," he reflected. "No doubt it's a change for the better—a step up, as you might say. But—ah, well!" He sighed again. "I must do the best I can."

What chiefly troubled him was, that his best in this place was not especially good. He was no longer master of the *George Rodman*, no longer a man of authority, able to smoke and meditate when he chose, and, worst, of all, no longer was he proudly, seriously conscious of his own perfect ability, his perfect fitness for his job. No; he was here in Mr. Martinsburgh's office because Mr. Martinsburgh had taken a fancy to him, and had tempted him with talk about "future prospects." He was making a good salary, and he could do, well enough, whatever work he was given to do. Only, he could do it no better than the next man; he was not necessary, not even important, and that humiliated him.

He stifled yet another sigh, and bent again to his task of preparing a statement to be sent to the insurance company. He picked up a document.

"At sea, on board the ship *Elmwood*, of New York, Frank Perley, master, bound from New York to New Orleans, Louisiana.

"We, the undersigned, master, officers, and mariners of the ship *Elmwood* of New York, do, after mature deliberation, enter this solemn protest."

Mac Donald's heart went out to the unknown Frank Perley, master, who after mature deliberation, held theoretically in a circle of conscientious mariners, had found it necessary to throw overboard a deck load of machinery. Owners never really understood these matters; they sat snug in their offices, and they always thought you might have done better. He had heard Mr. Quillen say, in respect to this case, that he feared Captain Perley hadn't shown very good judgment, and he had wished then that Mr. Quillen might spend just one night on board a ship straining and labouring in a gale, with a heavy deck load.... And yet, he ought now to be looking at such things from Mr. Quillen's point of view.

He glanced up at the sound of a footstep, and there was Mr. Martinsburgh coming back after two hours spent in lunching; he went by without raising his eyes or speaking to anyone, entered his little private room, and closed the door with a bang. But almost at once he popped out again, and came across the room to Mac Donald's desk.

"Mac Donald!" he said, in a whisper. "I ... See here, Mac Donald! I want ... You'd better come into my office."

"Very well, sir!" said Mac Donald, and rose at once.

The rest of the staff in the outer office did not fail to observe this.

"Old man's been hitting it up again," observed young Pennyman.

"Looks that way," said his colleague, young Williams. He glanced hastily about the room and then leaned across his desk to speak more confidentially.

"Mac Donald had to take him home in a taxi last night," he said; "waited until everyone had cleared out, but I had to come back after something, and I saw 'em. Old man was absolutely—"

The conversation stopped abruptly, because Mac Donald had appeared again. But instead of sitting down at his desk, he began putting his papers away; that done he took his hat from the rack and went over to the cashier.

"I'll be drawing my pay, if you please," he said.

"You want an advance, Mr. Mac Donald?"

"I do not. Only what's due me till the present time," he said.

His expression did not encourage questions, and the cashier retired, to investigate. Mac Donald waited, hat in hand, staring at the floor. And though everyone who had witnessed this scene believed that Mac Donald had been discharged without ceremony, it was impossible to feel either pity or amusement, so self-sufficing was the man.

Just then the door of the private office opened again, and Martinsburgh shouted:

"Mac Donald! What the devil are you doing?"

"I'm drawing my pay," answered the other, briefly.

"Come here!" said Martinsburgh, but Mac Donald did not stir. His face was an inexpressive one, nor did he have any great variety of emotions to express; he managed, though, by the set of his shoulders, to convey the idea that he had had enough. And Martinsburgh, the despot, knew not how to handle him. He stood in the doorway of his room, a remarkable figure of a man, tall, emaciated, with a sort of immortal youthfulness about him. Forty years had passed over his head, and he still had the look of a boy, a haggard, wasted boy, his hollow blue eyes luminous, his blonde hair curled thick on his head. His features were clear, delicate, unmarred; his was the austere and terrible beauty of a saint; he seemed infinitely remote from the world about him; his face was blank, as if he could not see or hear, lost in his own mystic thoughts.

What he really wanted to do, though, was to yell at Mac Donald, to break loose, to make a violent scene. He longed to do that.... But he stifled the longing; apparently without effort, a dreamy smile appeared on his lips, he crossed the office, and laid his hand on Mac Donald's shoulder.

"See here!" he said; "don't be a fool, man! Come along, and we'll talk this over."

"Very well!" said Mac Donald, stiffly, and once more they went into the private office. Martinsburgh slammed the door.

"Forget the whole thing, Mac Donald!" he said, in a kind and reasonable tone. "Put it out of your head."

"Very well, sir," answered Mac Donald. "I'll endeavor to do so."

And that was logically the end of it. Martinsburgh was sure that the fellow would never mention the affair again. Only, he *couldn't* let it alone, he couldn't keep still; he tried desperately, walking up and down the small room, his hands clenched in his pockets.

"The thing is ..." he burst out. "You—you .... I asked you as a friend, Mac Donald."

"Did you now?" said Mac Donald. "I understood you to say that you would pay me if I would do it."

"I know ! I did say that!" shouted Martinsburgh. "What if I did? You ought to be glad of the chance to help me. Don't you owe something to me?"

"No!" said Mac Donald, promptly, "I do not."

"You—damn you! You beggarly Scotch—"

"Mr. Martinsburgh!" interrupted the other sternly, "I am making allowances for you now, but I cannot say how long I'll be able to continue doing so."

"Get out!" cried Martinsburgh. "Get out—quick! No! No! Wait a minute! I didn't mean that ... I—see here, Mac Donald, I ... Who's that?"

For someone had rapped on the glass of the door.

"It's Hazeltine," answered a mild voice, and upon being told to come in, he opened the door.

"I say! I'm disturbing you—" he began, apologetically. "I'll wait—"

"No! Come in!" said Martinsburgh.

For the very sight of the nonchalant and elegant Hazeltine was soothing to him. Impossible to imagine a greater contrast to Mac Donald.... He hoped Mac Donald realized it, and felt shabby and humiliated. He turned toward him with a faint, indulgent smile.

"Very well, Mac Donald!" he said, kindly. "We'll say no more about the matter. Consider it closed. Let me see your statement of the

Elmwood claim when you get it in shape. That's all."

As the door closed behind him, Martinsburgh sank into his chair with a long sigh.

"Basil ..." he said, "I'm glad to see you.... Sit down! Good God!"

Hazeltine's quick glance rested upon the other with a moderate compassion.

"What's wrong, Lewis?" he asked.

"I'll tell you. Have a drink?"

"Let's talk first," Hazeltine suggested, but Martinsburgh took out a bottle and glasses from his desk and poured himself a stiff drink.

"I'm—worried," he said, "I'm—I'm upset, Basil."

His frail hands, extended on the desk before him, trembled pitiably, he raised his clear blue eyes to the ceiling, as if invoking aid against the worldly temptations assailing him; then he sighed again, and gave Hazeltine a quick sidelong glance.

"Anything I can do for you, Lewis?" asked the young man.

He was obliged to ask this, and, what is more, if there were anything he could do, he would have to do it. He and Martinsburgh were cousins, there was a strong likeness between them; they were both tall, both slenderly and neatly made, both fair, and much alike in face except that Hazeltine's features were somewhat blunt and debonair, and Lewis's incredibly rarefied, so that he was like the ghost of Hazeltine. Now, from his earliest years, Hazeltine had been taught the sacredness of family ties; there was not one of his prosperous or influential relations who could accuse him of neglect, no, not one. Because of the difference in their ages and their circumstances, he had not seen much of Lewis in his boyhood, but he never forgot him. And when his mother had died, some seven years ago, he had taken the small legacy she left him direct to Lewis.

"Look after it for me, won't you?" he had asked.

The paltriness of the sum was touching; the legitimate income from it would scarcely have paid for the poor boy's tobacco and hair-cuts. Lewis had accepted the trust, and saw to it that his cousin Basil got a monthly income of about twenty per cent on his capital, and Basil took it and asked no questions. He merely expressed an innocent admiration for Martinsburgh's business ability. And before many months had gone by, he had begun a course which he had now followed successfully for years; he would go to Lewis and ruefully admit that he was "cleaned out," and ask if he could draw a bit in advance, or, when he wanted a larger sum, whether some of his holdings couldn't be sold. This never failed.

But for all his intelligence, Hazeltine was under a delusion about this. He imagined that he gained all these benefits by his tact and skill, and it was not so. Lewis was more intelligent than he was; he saw through this chicane with ease; he did not give so lavishly because he was flattered into it or because he was generous, but because he badly wanted the friendship of this cool, good-tempered young fellow; he wanted—Heaven knows what he wanted, an impossible fealty, and, above all, compassion. Lewis cared nothing for respect or admiration; what he wanted was pity.

"It's about a woman," he said, "I know I was an ass, but—it's hard to explain.... And you're so damned cautious yourself. Never catch you in a mess like this!"

Hazeltine got up to take a cigar from a box which he could have reached without moving; he lighted it, and sat down in a corner, in shadow.

"Well, what about the woman?" he asked.

Lewis turned on the green-shaded desk-lamp, so that the light shone on his fine, austere face, and with an almost tearful vehemence, he told his little tale. Someone had introduced him to this woman; he had gone to see her two or three times, had taken her out to supper. He assured Basil upon his word of honour that that was all there was to it; he had simply taken this woman out to supper—and now she *bothered* him.

Hazeltine listened from his dark corner, glad to be unseen. Not that he was disconcerted by Lewis's story; he had no uncomfortable standards by which to judge others or himself; it was not concern for Lewis, either, which made him listen with pain in his heart. It was because Lewis was the husband of Jocelyn.

"What did you say to this woman, anyhow?" he asked.

"Say?" Lewis repeated, indignantly. "I said—what the devil does it matter what I said? You can't call a man to account for every fool thing he says. The thing is—she bothers me. She telephones.... It's—it's outrageous! I can't stand that sort of thing. I've got to be let alone. I ... no use my talking to her. She won't listen. But if you'd go to see her, Basil ...?"

There was a moment's silence, not pleasant for either of them.

"If you like," said Hazeltine, at last.

He was telling himself, very plausibly, that in helping Lewis he would also be helping Jocelyn. She wouldn't want Lewis to be mixed up in any sort of row. She would understand that—that he could not refuse this mission. And she wouldn't really care what he did; nothing could increase or diminish her gentle and nebulous affection for him. So, if she didn't care, why should he?

"Agree to anything she wants—in reason," Lewis went on. "It's money she's after, of course.... And naturally ... it's worth something to me, Basil, to get this thing settled. I don't want to bring a lawyer into it. If you'll settle the thing, I'll be glad to ..."

There followed another silence.

"I'll do what I can," said Hazeltine.

"There's a fellow here in the office," Lewis began, abruptly. "I've done a great deal for him. He was captain of one of our cargo ships—rotten little tub—and I gave him a good job here, with more money than he's worth. Sensible, level-headed sort of fellow. I thought he'd be just the one to—to handle this thing for me. But when I asked him—hanged if he didn't start to draw his pay and walk out of the office! I—that upset me ... damn it! I'm not a criminal. I've done nothing to be ashamed of.... I've told you. You can see for yourself that there's nothing."

"Rather!" said Hazeltine, absently.

"Here's the address. See her this evening, will you, Basil?"

Hazeltine took the slip of paper, and rose.

"I'll do my best," he said, "I'll let you know tomorrow—"

"All right! Wait a minute!" said Lewis, and went out of the room.

He had gone, of course, to interview the cashier on Hazeltine's behalf, and Hazeltine was perfectly willing to wait, even longer than a minute. He sat down on the edge of the desk, enjoying that excellent cigar, and thinking about nothing at all. He refused to think of this mission he had undertaken for Lewis, or to think of Mrs. Huested. Or of Jocelyn. He never thought of her. He would not. He made his mind quite blank, a useful art he had acquired, which was responsible for his fine poise. There he was, smoking, and not thinking, when the unlatched door was pushed open, and a man came in, to lay some papers on the desk.

Their eyes met for an instant.

"That's the fellow Lewis was talking to when I came in," thought Hazeltine. "Yelling at him.... Must be the fellow who—"

The fellow who had refused the task he had undertaken, who had been ready to walk out of the office and out of a good job.

"He's a fool, then," thought Hazeltine, with unwarrantable anger. "Dam' smug, self-satisfied prig.... Why shouldn't anyone be willing to help a poor devil out of a tight corner? ... If I were Lewis, I'd kick him out."

He looked again at Mac Donald, who was bending over the desk to make a correction on a paper, and his anger increased.

"You the chap who used to be a ship's captain?" he asked.

"I am," answered Mac Donald, equably.

It was by no means Hazeltine's custom to offend anyone, but he wanted to offend this man.

"What made you quit?" he asked, in an amused and condescending voice.

"Because I could get more money ashore," said Mac Donald.

"So you're like the rest of us ..." said Hazeltine, with a smile, "anything for money."

"I shouldn't go as far as to say that," answered Mac Donald. "Some men are like that, and some are not. I'd—"

"What d'you mean?" Hazeltine demanded. He had got up from the desk and stood facing the other with unmistakable hostility.

Mac Donald regarded him with surprise; for a moment they stared at each other in silence; then suddenly a realization of his own folly came over Hazeltine. He walked the length of the small room, amazed by his behaviour, by the unreasonable resentment he had felt toward this man. For a moment he had actually hated him. He turned, to say something civil, but Mac Donald had gone.

"What's the matter with me, anyhow?" he asked himself, bewildered.

CHAPTER THREE

A GIRL

The Hotel Sterbin was situated in the West Thirties, near Broadway. It was a very respectable hotel; "catering especially to private families," its advertisements declared, and there really were families living in it. Yet, for all its quiet and decorum, there was a sort of leer about the place; it had an air of being but lately reformed, and it was incongruous to see elderly ladies taking their afternoon tea in that naughty little tea-room, so dark, lighted by red-shaded electric candles, or to see mothers and young children dining in that sporting grill-room.

The family atmosphere had given a boarding-house flavour to the cuisine; there was a fine, long à la carte menu, but guests soon learned that the Club Dinner was what they were expected to take, and that otherwise they would be disappointed. Still, the rates were moderate and the address a fairly good one, and that was why Hazeltine had lived here for three years.

He came upstairs from the grill-room this evening and stopped at the desk to ask for his mail; he stood there for a few moments in the lounge, opening and glancing through his letters. Very magnificent he was, in his London-made dark grey suit, his made-to-order shoes, his soft grey hat, a light overcoat across his arm, yet the desk clerk was not impressed. He knew that Mr. Hazeltine had one of the worst rooms in the hotel, up on the top floor, on the same court as the kitchen. He knew that, secreted in this room, was an electric iron with which Mr. Hazeltine pressed his handkerchiefs and soft collars and, in very bad times, his trousers. Also, there was an outfit for making coffee, and in a mouse-proof tin box, various foodstuffs, so that Mr. Hazeltine could get his own breakfast, and even his dinner, if necessary.

Mr. Hazeltine did not get good service. Telephone messages for him were often forgotten; his summons were not answered with alacrity, and this was due not so much to the smallness of his tips as to the obvious fact that he could not afford to do better. Miserliness can be excused; it offers possibilities, but Mr. Hazeltine was simply poor, and the staff did not hold him in high esteem. He knew it, and cared not a whit. All he required was, that other people should make a decent pretence of respecting his pretences.

And as a rule, people did. He made it his business to avoid humiliations, and being quick-witted and very wary, and very civil, he was seldom molested. He had no enemies, bore no grudge against anyone; as he saw it, the world was a place of complete unreason, where some had a great deal, and others precious little; he accepted this fact philosophically, blaming no one, concerned only in adding to his own meagre store.

Toleration being another of those virtues which properly begin at home, it was natural that he should be no more severe with himself than with others. Indeed, he thought very little about himself but kept his mind upon the ends he had in view; he troubled Heaven with no questions as to whence and whither, he was calm—except when these occasional attacks of squeamishness came over him. And the one which had caused him to run away from Mrs. Huested that afternoon had not passed as such moods usually did; it lingered. He was vaguely uneasy; he was very reluctant to visit the adventuress on Lewis's behalf.

"It makes me sick!" he said to himself. "I wish to Heaven I could get out of it."

But he could see no sound reason for this reluctance, certainly no reason which he could offer to Lewis as an excuse. He had agreed to do it, and he couldn't just change his mind, couldn't afford to make

Lewis angry. He thought of the bills that had come in the mail.... He could always borrow a little here and there, and he had enough invitations to keep him fed and sheltered for the coming summer, but the source of all substantial benefits was Lewis. And Lewis needed careful handling.

"That fellow ..." he thought, with a frown.

It was Mac Donald he meant. He had not been able to forget the man.

"By Heaven, I'd have done the same thing myself!" he reflected, a little forlornly. "I'd have told Lewis I couldn't do it.... But after all, in the circumstances ..."

He shrugged his shoulders, looked at his watch, and set off. It was beginning to rain when he left the hotel, and when he came out of the Subway at Sheridan Square, a wild spring storm was at its height. The rain spattered down like hail, the road before him was like a shining black lake across which motor cars went rushing, with a splash of water and quivering reflections of light. The air was chilly, but it seemed to him that through the reek of gasolene and the evil smell of wet newspapers there was some furtive little hint of spring. He turned up the collar of his coat and pulled his hat down; then he hesitated, and at last, jumped into a taxi. It would be better, he thought, to appear before the adventuress quite neat and dry.

The cab stopped before a house on West Tenth Street, a narrow little house, dimly lit. He did not know if it was a boarding-house, a lodging-house or a private dwelling; he wished now that he had asked Lewis for a little useful information. He rang the bell, and waited; and presently the door was opened by an elderly woman.

"Miss Dennison?" he asked.

"Top floor," said the woman, and turning away went along the dim hall and vanished down the basement stairs. There was not a sound to be heard, and as Hazeltine ascended the stairs, he went into increasing darkness. No lights on the landings, nothing to guide his steps. And no clues for his nimble wits.

He had come to this interview with an open mind. He had no plan, for he knew that one could not make useful plans in which other people were concerned, because other people were in essence capricious and unstable. Fix your mind upon what you want, and be guided by circumstances—that was his way. It was a method flexible and very efficacious; it kept him free from dangerous preoccupations, from those perilous little phrases that come to schemers, and are too neat not to be used, whether prudent or not. No, he would deal with the adventuress when confronted with her, and not before.

He reached the top storey, and struck a match. There were four doors, all closed; he knocked upon each one, and got no response. The rain was drumming loud on the roof, and he could hear a window shade flapping somewhere, but there were no sounds of a more encouraging nature. Well, he had come, according to orders, and now he could go.

He was at the head of the stairs when a door slammed below and someone began coming up. He sighed patiently; it was his duty to wait to see if this was the adventuress, and, if it was not, to ask questions. He leaned over the railing and looked into the black abyss. Far below the dim light burned, but whoever was coming, came in darkness. The footsteps grew louder, he fancied they had passed the landing below him, and in order to advertise his presence, he struck another match and lit a cigarette.

"Who's that?" asked a ringing voice, a woman's voice.

"I wanted to see Miss Dennison," he answered.

"What for?"

"Well ..." said Hazeltine, in a polite, apologetic tone.

The unknown woman had reached his landing; she went past him, so close that her shoulder brushed his; then she snapped on a light and faced him. His eyes were dazzled by the sudden brightness; he had a fleeting impression of a pale, stern face under a wide hat-brim, before she turned and fitted a key into the lock.

"Come in!" she said.

He followed her into a room blazing with harsh light from an electrolier overhead; the door crashed behind him, blown to by the wind, and he stood just over the threshold, hat in hand.

"Are you a lawyer?" she demanded.

He smiled.

"No," he said. "Are you Miss Dennison?"

She did not answer. She was standing at the opposite side of the room, with her back to the mantelpiece; she was soaked with the rain, the water dripped off her wide hat-brim, and from the hem of her skirt, her dark dress clung to her tall, thin, young body. And she didn't care; dripping wet, pale, her tawny hair disordered by the wind, she had the air of one completely indifferent to any trifling considerations of health or comfort. Or manners. Her tone, her unwavering glance, were not courteous; she didn't even ask him to sit down....

"I'm not Miss Dennison," she said. "But I'm her friend. I know all about her affairs. You can tell me what you wanted to see her about."

"Thank you," said Hazeltine. "But I'm afraid I can't very well. If you could let me know when I'd be able to see Miss Dennison ...?"

"I won't!" said she. "I won't let her be bothered."

The rudeness of this speech was mitigated by the tremour in her voice; it was like the defiance of a child, it touched him. She was very, very young, he thought, and lovely, in an odd sort of way, she was immature and angular; her face was too thin, but she had what he had heard spoken of as "bone-beauty"—the imperishable beauty of true and fine structure. Let her be rude if she liked; he felt a great indulgence for her.

The lighted cigarette which he had forgotten was burning down now; he looked about for a place to put it, and doing so, his quick eye took in the details of the room. It was a large room, and comfortably furnished, in an inexpensive way—wicker armchairs with chintz cushions, a table covered with books, a piano. He saw a brass ash-tray on the table and he crossed the room to it and crushed out his cigarette. He was nearer to her now, their eyes met, and he fancied she was less hostile.

"Look here!" she said. "Have you come from Mr. Martinsburgh?"

He considered a moment.

"Yes," he answered. "I have."

She opened her handbag and took out a crushed package of cigarettes.

"Have one?" she said, with a brusque man-to-man air.

He could not refuse; he took one of the limp, shapeless things, and held a match for her to light another.

"Sit down, won't you?" she said. "I'd like to talk to you."

She sank down into an armchair, stretched out her long legs, and crossed her ankles; abruptly she sat up, took off her hat, and put it on the floor beside her, then lay back again, resting her bright head against the chair and staring at the ceiling as she smoked.

"Your shoes are very wet ..." said Hazeltine.

"I don't care," said she. "Just wait a moment, won't you? There were lots of things I've always meant to say to that man, if ever I got the chance.... I want to think."

Hazeltine was willing to wait, and while he did so, he meditated upon this girl. He found her singularly attractive, but that was quite beside the question. All that concerned him was her part in this dubious affair of Lewis's. Could she help him, or was she an obstacle?

"I've told Coralie all along that she ought to let me handle this for her," she began. "She can't. She's too emotional. And *he*—he takes advantage of that. They've got it all so muddled now. Gosh! I do hate a muddle!"

"So do I," said Hazeltine.

"*He* doesn't. She can't get a single plain, straightforward word out of him. He suddenly stopped seeing her. He said he was ill, but he wasn't. She wrote and he didn't answer; at last she got him on the telephone, and he said he'd come that evening and 'explain' and he just didn't come. That was two weeks ago, and she hasn't heard a word from him since."

Hazeltine was badly hampered by his lack of information; he had expected a far more obvious sort of affair, an interview with a more or less flamboyant lady, for which he would need tact but no great subtlety. But this ... There was an undercurrent here that disquieted him. The girl before him was not dubious, everything about her was clear and clean; either she did not understand the unsavoury position, or Lewis had led him astray. He would have to proceed carefully.

"It's a bit hard for me," he confessed. "You see, I don't know Miss Dennison; I do know Martinsburgh, though, pretty well, and—isn't it possible that she—misunderstood him?"

"Not much doubt about that!" said she, grimly. "Coralie thought he was honest. I *never* did. I never trusted him. I told Coralie, when he asked her to marry him—"

"Marry him?" cried Hazeltine. "But—what are you saying?"

"Didn't you know that?" she asked, startled by his tone. "Then why did you come? Wasn't it about that—about the letters?"

Hazeltine had risen, and stood looking down into her troubled face.

"Marry him?" he repeated. "That's not—possible."

"He did ask her, though! He said he'd get a divorce—"

"My God! I can't—" He turned away, shaken with pain and disgust. "No," he said. "I never imagined ... it's unspeakable. It's—I think, if you don't mind, I'll leave it at that. I'll say good night."

She got up from her chair and came nearer to him.

"But I don't understand!" she said. "Why did you come?"

"I didn't understand, either."

"But if he asked you to come, haven't you some message for Coralie?"

"No," he said, curtly.

"Oh, can't we do something—arrange something? Coralie's so miserable. He won't see her, or write. *If* you know what he means to do, won't you please tell me?"

"I don't know."

"Then why did you come? Just tell me that! Please!"

"I can't," he said, "It doesn't matter, anyhow."

"But it's got to be settled!"

This was true. He paused; struck by that unwelcome idea. It would have to be settled.

"Make him see her!" the girl went on. "Or write. But it would be much better if he'd see her. It's so cruel and cowardly, this way. Make him see her, just once. She'd give him back his letters if she thought it really was—was finished. But she can't believe it. She won't, until he tells her. I've tried and tried to make her see...."

She stopped suddenly, and glancing at her, he saw tears shining in her eyes. He could not feel sorry for her though, could not forgive her for the monstrous thing she had spoken of so casually; she had, he thought, pushed aside his darling phantom, and in doing so had hurt the fragile thing; she had somehow injured Jocelyn. She seemed to him crude and stupid, utterly unable to understand anything he might say.

"I'll see what can be done," he said. "And now—"

"Wait!" she said. "Won't you have a glass of sherry?"

The suggestion surprised him.

"Thanks," he said. "But—"

"Please do!" she insisted, earnestly. "It's awfully good! Please do!"

He could not very well refuse, so he thanked her again, and she hurried off into another room, and returned presently with a brimming glass. She watched him anxiously as he drank it. It was the worst sherry he had ever tasted.

"Thank you!" he said, again; "very kind of you...."

He smiled at her, but she had no smile for him. Her worn young face had an expression which he remembered afterward with disquiet, a look he never in all his life understood.

CHAPTER FOUR

HAZELTINE TO BE WEIGHED IN THE BALANCE

The night brings counsel. The trouble is, that the counsel comes from a badly prejudiced source; a voice speaks, perhaps, in the dark hours, but whose voice is it, after all?

Hazeltine awoke the next morning, quite himself again. The fit of squeamishness had passed; he felt able to deal with the complications ahead of him. In his mail there was a letter from Mrs. Huested, inviting him to lunch; he was pleased to get this invitation, proof that she had not been seriously offended by his running away yesterday, but he was not surprised. He felt pretty sure of Mrs. Huested.

Pretty sure of Lewis, too. Those letters must be bought back from the adventuress at any cost. Lewis would have to be frightened into taking some definite action, so that the whole disgraceful episode could be settled and finished. And forgotten. Hazeltine was in a hurry to forget it.

He decided to see Lewis as early as possible that morning. There was no use going to the office before half-past ten, though; he ate a leisurely breakfast in the grill room, read the newspaper, and then set out to walk downtown. It was a bright, windy morning, and Hazeltine was well-fed, and in splendid health; he had money in his pockets, his prospect was fair, he felt happy. He went out of the spring sunshine into the enormous office building where electric lights burned always, and the rapid footsteps of men and women made a confused echoing in the tiled arcade. All these people were bent upon making a living, and so was he; they were all slaves, and he too. Only he had discovered the secret of economy of effort.

He got into the lift and was carried upstairs, went down the corridor, pushed open the door, and the first person he met was Mac Donald. He recognized Hazeltine with a glimmer of a smile.

"I'll tell Mr. Martinsburgh you are here," he said, "If you'll wait."

He indicated a chair outside the labyrinth of low fences within which clerks and typists sat, but Hazeltine would have none of it. Anger rose in him against this fellow's presumption; long before Mac Donald had been salvaged from the sea, Hazeltine had been; long after Mac Donald should be jettisoned, Hazeltine would be; he was permanent, he had all possible rights and privileges in this office where Mac Donald was a fleeting shadow.

"That's all right!" he said, with a frown. "He's expecting me."

He started forward, but Mac Donald moved, so that he barred the entrance to the enclosure.

"I've Mr. Martinsburgh's orders," he said. "If you'll wait—"

Hazeltine was the least arrogant of men, not only because he was prudent, but because he was good-humoured. But Mac Donald had a peculiar effect upon him.

"Look here!" he said. "You're a bit officious, aren't you? I think you'll find your zeal's rather overdone, in this case."

He spoke with studied insolence; he smiled, looking steadily at the other. Mac Donald returned the look quite as steadily.

"I've no disposition to enter into an argument with you in this office, Mr. Hazeltine," he said, in his composed and careful fashion. "The odds are too much in your favour." He stood aside. "You must just do as you please," he said as he walked away.

"Damn you!" said Hazeltine, under his breath.

Then, with a shrug of his shoulders, he passed through the labyrinth to the private office.

"Come in!" called Lewis.

Hazeltine turned the knob, but the door was locked, and he was sorry; this habit of locking himself in was growing upon Lewis, and a bad habit it was, in the circumstances.

"Someday he'll go too far," reflected the temperate Hazeltine, "and make a rotten scene. Just the sort of thing he's most afraid of."

But when Lewis opened the door, he looked quite his usual self, bright and beautiful, like an archangel.

"Come in, my boy!" he said, cordially. "Sit down! Have a drink!"

Now, Hazeltine might have been the man who originated such amiable sayings as "Give him enough rope, and he'll hang himself"—"He's made his bed, let him lie on it." His rule in life was to mind his own business, so that it was a mark of genuine friendliness for him to say:

"Lewis, isn't it a bit risky—to drink in business hours?"

"No!" said Lewis. "If I don't—"

A curious change came over him, his body seemed to collapse inside his clothes, his well-fitting jacket was suddenly rumpled, the collar standing off from the nape of his neck as his head drooped; he was, in an instant, spineless, utterly dejected. It was a startling transformation, but Hazeltine had seen it happen before, and considered it only one more bad symptom; a prophetic vision of what Lewis might someday become.

"No ... see here, Basil! It's like this ..." he went on. "I—I'm ill.... It's not drinking that makes me ill. I drink because I *am* ill. Because I'm ... it's been coming on for a long time...."

"What has? What's wrong, Lewis?"

Lewis slipped lower in his chair.

"I—you know—I've always had these—these fits of—of depression.... But lately ... always been a sort of morbid streak in me ... but lately—lately, Basil, I've thought I'm—losing my mind! I mean that! I—I—I—I—" he ended in an incoherent stammer.

"You ought to see a doctor, old man."

"I will not!"

"No, because you know what any doctor would tell you. To stop—"

"Oh, all right! All right!" cried Lewis. "Have it your own way. I drink too much. Let it go at that. But let me tell you, my boy—" He stopped. "Don't talk about it anymore!" he said, wearily. He shut the whiskey bottle up in his desk, and lay back in his chair, and Hazeltine waited for a decent interval.

"About this Dennison girl," he said, at last.

"You settle it for me," said Lewis, in the same weary tone. "I leave it to you."

"You didn't tell me about those letters, you know, Lewis. I can't very well—"

"I don't want to talk about it," said Lewis. "You settle it. I leave the whole thing in your hands, my boy."

"That's all very well, but I've got to know a bit more about the case. What did you write to her, anyhow?"

"Oh, I don't know!" cried Lewis. "My God! *Can't* you let me alone, Basil? I asked you to arrange the thing—"

"I'm trying to. But I've got to know.... I'm afraid you'll have to pay a stiff price for those letters, Lewis. How far are you willing to go?"

"I don't care," said Lewis. "Use your own judgment. Only let me alone! I tell you I'm ill!"

"Give me some idea—"

"Anything!" shouted Lewis. "Every penny I've got! Anything—only let me alone! I—I can't stand this!"

He brought out the whiskey bottle again, and Hazeltine saw that he had got all the help he was going to get. He rose.

"I wish you'd talk it over," he said. "I could do better for you."

Lewis did not answer at all; he was sipping his whiskey delicately, as if it were a rich wine; he did not even turn his head as his faithful agent went away.

"Poor devil!" thought Hazeltine. "He can't last much longer, at this pace.... Bound to crash pretty soon."

He himself would be involved in that crash, too, unless....

He had allowed plenty of time for reaching Mrs. Huested's flat at the appointed hour, but there was a delay in the Subway and he was late. And Mrs. Huested was severe about it. He was brought directly into the chill dining-room where she sat alone at the table. She said, "Oh, you've come, have you?" and an iced half-grapefruit was at once set before him. There was no cocktail offered; there was no warmth of any sort in the greeting he got.

When she behaved like this, it was necessary to take a high hand; it would never do to bring forward the Subway as an excuse, like a belated clerk.

"Sorry," he said. "I was detained in Martinsburgh's office.... He looks after my affairs for me, you know."

Mrs. Huested smiled; he resented the smile, and fell silent. When he glanced up, he found her looking at him with an insufferable expression of benevolence.

"Hazeltine!" she said. "I wish you'd tell me something about your affairs."

He started nervously, amazed, affronted by this attack.

"Thanks," he said, stiffly; "nothing to tell."

"I might be able to put you in the way of a pretty good thing," she went on. "We've just declared an extra dividend—and by all indications this coming year ought to be the best yet. I've got some figures I'd like you to look at."

"Thanks. But that's not much in my line."

"See here, Hazeltine!" said Mrs. Huested, brusquely. "Don't be a fool! You want to make money, don't you?"

"No," said Hazeltine.

He was surprised at himself for saying that, but he did not regret it. Mrs. Huested's cool, efficient air, the implications beneath her words, roused him to active hostility; the very idea of his 'affairs' becoming known to her, being submitted to her domineering inspection, made his blood run cold. He thought of Lewis's charming vagueness and decent masculine reserve, and he imagined what life would be like under the rule of this lady. No! She might marry him if she liked, but his precious little 'income' she should never touch, not if she were to increase it a hundredfold.

"Now, Hazeltine!" she went on, in a reasonable tone, "don't be pigheaded! You're young, and you have brains. You ought to make something of your life. Now, just listen to me. You needn't make any investment. I only mentioned that because I thought you'd jump at the chance. You would, if you knew what you were talking about. But I'll tell you what. There is a good opening up at the plant for the right man. You can start in there, and after you've got the hang of the business—"

She had never seen an expression like this upon Hazeltine's bland face; she stared at him, perturbed; his eyes were cold, his blunt features seemed sharper.

"Thanks," he said, once more. "Very good of you. But I'm not interested in making money. And if you don't mind my saying so— I didn't come here to talk business with you. It's not quite my line."

He was really angry when he spoke, but it did not take him long to see that his impulse had served him well. There was a look almost of awe on Mrs. Huested's face. He was defying all her traditions, her principles; he was deliberately refusing what she believed to be the only honourable course for a man; he was preferring a useless, parasitical existence; he was a fool. Wasn't interested in making money ...! She felt a thrill of admiration for that superb blasphemy. Surely there was no one like him on earth!

She leaned across the table and slapped his hand.

"Hazeltine!" she said. "Aren't you ashamed of yourself!"

He was, because the little servant was watching them. It was not the first time he had noticed that shocking carelessness in Mrs. Huested; she had behaved like that in London, in restaurants, in the theatre, resting her hand on his shoulder, playfully slapping at him. And without ever losing her air of dowdy respectability.

"Come on!" said she. "You've finished."

He followed her into the drawing-room; she sat down in a corner of the divan, but instead of sitting beside her, Hazeltine walked up and down the room. She waited a moment, then from a box on a tabouret, she took one of her loathesome perfumed cigarettes. He struck a match and held it for her, and as she bent forward, the flame seemed to light her face with the strangest sort of gleam.... That copper-coloured face, those fierce white teeth, those glittering little black eyes.... Then a cloud of smoke veiled the vision. She was, he thought, like a bronze statue of Mammon, with incense ascending to her nostrils.

"Hazeltine!" she said. "Sit down here! I want to show you something."

She opened her leather hand-bag, that eternal handbag which so exasperated him. He had seen her at the opera, in evening toilette, carrying the thing, or one very like it. She went from room to room in her own flat with the thing dangling from her arm, kept it on her lap while she ate.

"What do you think of these?" she asked, and held out a case in which were a pair of cuff-links, gold, with sapphire-studded rims.

"Oh ... very nice ..." said Hazeltine, indifferently.

"They're for you, Hazeltine."

"I say!" he protested. "Really, you know ..."

"If they're not what you want," she went on, "don't hesitate to change them. I know you're pretty particular. But—well—it's a sort of little souvenir. I thought—"

Her hand fell on his shoulder, and turning, he saw her smiling at him with bright kindliness.

"Take care of yourself, Hazeltine," she said. "And be a good boy till I come back."

"Come back? You're going away?"

"Yes," she answered. "I guess I'll go out West for a while."

He found it difficult to hide his dismay. His nice scruples vanished at once; in his heart he cursed his captious folly.

"I just made up my mind last night," she continued. gravely. "There's something I want to think out—by myself."

That was plain enough. She was going off to think *him* out by herself, where she would not be disturbed by his engaging presence. She was going to consider him, coolly and soberly, like any other investment she might contemplate. She had offered him a chance to show what he was worth as a financial prospect, and he had refused it, saying he wasn't interested in making money. He had run away from her yesterday, when she had been in a mood to listen to him.

This, then, was what his undue coyness had brought upon him. Now all he could do was to wait at home while she analyzed him from a distance.

"In any case, Hazeltine," she said, "you've got a good friend in me. If there's anything I can do for you before I go ...?"

"Why, no, thanks!" he answered, as if surprised by such a question.

Somehow she had got the upper hand in this interview, with her air of indulgent but incorruptible judge. She was pitying him. It would never do for her to go away in this humour; he must recover his advantage. Her last impression must be of him smiling, gallant, inscrutable, a superior creature.

Smile he did, looking into her eyes, and he knew that this long, steady gaze troubled her. Her hand still rested on his shoulder; he covered it with one of his own.

"Don't forget me, Natalie!" he said.

"I won't ..." she said. "I won't."

For a moment she wavered, a little dazzled, then tears came into her eyes; she drew his head down and gave him a hasty kiss on his forehead.

"You poor boy!" she said. "I do so want you to have things.... You know, Hazeltine—I think a lot of you.... But—well! I never was one to act in haste. I like to take time, and think things out, and then when my mind's made up, it's made up."

There was nothing he could say. She had spoiled everything, broken his spell, robbed him of the last trace of superiority. There was no question of his deciding anything, or making up his mind; what he had to do was to wait. And she knew he would wait.

He returned her kiss in a gentle, melancholy way; then sat beside her for a while, holding her hand. His sadness was quite genuine, too.

CHAPTER FIVE

WHAT MRS. HUESTED DID NOT KNOW

Mrs. Huested was a woman of considerable intelligence, and had a practical sense of justice. What is more, she had a weakness for Hazeltine; she might be trusted to give him the benefit of every doubt, to make generous allowances for all his little failings. Yet, after all, what did she know of him? Properly to weigh him in the balance, she should have had the complete book of his life, and a knowledge of his hereditary tendencies, and of those things, inborn and acquired, which made up the body and the soul of him.

But he did not know these things himself. If he had had to stand before the judgment-seat of God, he could have offered in explanation of his imperfect state only certain memories. And that these memories might serve as an excuse never entered his head; he made no excuses to Heaven, to the world, or to himself.

There were a few confused little pictures of his very early days—of himself sitting on his mother's knee in a French garden—a little blonde, curly haired creature, vain as a peacock—and two ladies volubly adoring him. *'Beau comme un ange'*—that was what they said about him. 'Baba,' his mother called him. And he had been 'Baba,' and a baby, and *beau comme un ange*, and vain as a peacock until suddenly he had been taken 'home' to an America utterly foreign to him, and put into a boarding-school near Boston.

That was perhaps the supreme test of his life. He was only six, lonely, terrified, bewildered, but he had, without help or advice, abruptly ceased to be the angelic Baba, and had made himself into a boy creditably like the other boys. The scars of those first months still marked his spirit; he had been a joke, a butt—all the customs of boyhood were unknown to him; he even spoke his native tongue with a foreign accent. But he had conquered, he had won sufferance and a measure of immunity. He paid for this in blood and tears.

He remembered very well a visit his father had made to him at that school. His father was an Englishman who had been— 'naturalized'—extraordinary phrase!—a man of good family, but a black sheep of a very sheepish kind. A tall, weedy man, he was, with a foppish air and a strained, ghastly smile. He had insisted upon taking his small son rowing upon the lake; he had boasted of his prowess with the sculls, told tales of the marvels he had accomplished as a public-schoolboy 'at home.' But when he rolled up his sleeves his arms were like sticks, he coughed and sweated so, he could scarcely get round the lake.... And then, when they went down to the railway station, his hat blew off, and he made a dive for it, and came a cropper.... He jumped on the last car, just as the train was pulling out, and that was how his son remembered him, standing on the platform, waving good-bye, with his hat all bashed in, and mud on his forehead. That was the last time Basil ever saw him. He went out to Colorado for his health, but found death there instead.

Six times did Basil undergo the atrocious ordeal of entering a new school and always at a disadvantage. In France he was entirely foreign now; in England he was an American, in America he was a cosmopolitan suspect. And as soon as he had managed, by sedulous imitation and discreet flattery, to make some sort of place for himself, he was taken away and plunged into a new milieu, to begin all over again.

When holidays came, he was sent to make visits to relations or friends, wretched, indefinite visits; he was obliged to stay and stay, wherever he was sent, outwearing any welcome he got, waiting helplessly until his mother fetched him. And he had learned that, if life was to be tolerable to him, he must make people like him.

Until he met Jocelyn, he had never cared for anyone in his life. He was seventeen when he met her. He was visiting his aunt, Mrs. Bradley, down on Long Island, that summer, and Jocelyn came down from boarding-school with his cousin Sylvia.

Jocelyn was seventeen, too, a kid, with her hair down her back. But it seemed to him that, in all the years he knew her, she never had really changed. Even then, when he first saw her, she had had that same fragile, shadowy charm, that same insight, that sympathy beyond all measure. She developed according to some law of her own, no more influenced by the actions of other persons than a rose is perturbed by those who pass through the garden. She loved and she pitied, she did not judge, because she could not, knowing no measure. And she loved and pitied Basil as soon as she met him.

It had hurt her to see how indifferent the Bradleys were toward his efforts to please. Certainly, in those days he overdid it; he had just come from a month's holiday in Paris with his mother and he had, in several instances, been taken quite seriously there; he did not realize yet what a boy of seventeen meant to this household. He was growing up with artistic restraint; there was no youthful clumsiness about him; he was adroit, graceful, and so courteous, so eagerly attentive.... Later on, he acquired the proper tone of Anglo-Saxon calm, but at that time he was what his uncle privately called a 'young jackanapes,' with what his aunt called 'that *unfortunate* manner ...'

The younger Bradleys simply let him alone. They were an indulgent and amiable family, but Jocelyn thought them a little unkind to Basil.

"Don't you think your cousin Basil's an awfully nice boy?" she asked Sylvia.

"Of course I do!" answered Sylvia, in her tranquil, sensible fashion. "We're all very fond of him."

"But aren't you *sorry* for him?" asked Jocelyn.

Sylvia picked up the idea and examined it.

"Well ... yes," she said. "I suppose I am, in a way. It really is a shame. Aunt Julia's so selfish, and horrible to him, and poor Basil is so proud of her."

Jocelyn was the first one to discover that he was not proud of his mother and she found that out as soon as she saw them together. Julia Hazeltine stopped in at the Bradleys' one afternoon, *en route* for some other house—just to see my boy—she said. She sat on the veranda, with a plaintive and helpless air, while Basil ran up and down stairs and telephoned and fetched and carried for her, a most devoted son.

"Basil's so like you, Julia," said Mrs. Bradley. "Of course, he *looks* like Father, but in disposition he's so like you."

Jocelyn saw his face then with the strangest look on it, mutinous and yet frightened. She saw that he didn't want to be like his mother, and she looked at Mrs. Hazeltine to see why.... A dark and beautiful lady she was, exquisitely dressed, not lacking in any worldly allurement, yet with that helpless, appealing air....

"I don't think you are!" she whispered to Basil. "Not a bit!"

That won him. He had tried until then to resist Jocelyn, because he was afraid to make a friend, to be definitely committed to anyone; it was his policy never to take sides, always to avoid intimacy. But his mother's visit upset him, and in his troubled mood Jocelyn's sympathy seemed almost a miracle. That evening when they were alone together in the music room, he had talked to her in a fit of nervous volubility.

But not about his mother. His feeling for her was something he never spoke of, all his life long, to anyone, nor did he try to explain it to himself. Only, whenever he was with her, he suffered. He always fancied that people were staring at her, or whispering about her; soft-voiced, mild, discreet as she was, to him she seemed always horribly conspicuous. Whenever she came to visit him at school, he was in misery for two or three days afterward, expecting that one of the boys would say something about her for which Basil would have to punch his head. And he didn't know what anyone *could* say against her; he knew only that something was wrong, shamefully wrong.... They got on well together, for they were both good-tempered and diplomatic; they were jolly and friendly when they met, but in his heart Basil never forgave her. He was not exacting; he could have forgiven so much, her neglect, her shallowness, the caprices that made havoc of his life; but for that intangible wrongness which he had as a child vaguely and ignorantly discerned in her, he had no forgiveness and no mercy.

He told Jocelyn other things, though. He told her, for instance, about his last trip over from France, that spring.

"My mother's friends were jolly nice to me," he said. "Not like the people here. Not as if I were a silly kid. I don't look so young in a dinner-jacket, you know.... I played the piano in a concert they got up, and I used to take a hand at bridge now and then. But here ..." he flushed. "Well, I *am* here," he said, "and the only thing is—to make the best of it."

Jocelyn noticed how he did that. He watched the face of the person he was talking with, and his manner was a little different for each one in the household. He was so careful not to offend. When he observed that his piano-playing overshadowed Sylvia's, he ceased to play. When anyone else mispronounced a French word, so did he. He tried his best to be a nice boy, and indeed, in many ways, he was simply a nice boy, decent-minded, and well-behaved; but in other ways, he was not admirable. He was without affection or gratitude, he had no candour and precious little pride. He was cynically resigned to passive dependence upon his mother's whims, to a sort of beggary, cajoling what he wanted and needed from the people about him.

It did not occur to Jocelyn to inspire him to proud rebellion; all she could do was to pity him because there was not one human being he thought of with tenderness or regret, because there was nothing he valued in his life. It was as if he were sauntering through the world empty-handed, taking only what he needed from day to day; he had no pleasure in remembering the past, no interest in contemplating the future; he was never very happy or very unhappy. All this troubled Jocelyn. She had a dim conviction that he needed help, and with her blind and beautiful charity, she tried to give it. She would leave any of the others when Basil appeared; he was lazy and not fond of tennis or canoeing or swimming or any of the sports the young Bradleys liked, and Jocelyn would forego them, to talk to Basil. She was always anxious about him, afraid that he was lonely or neglected; she could not understand his remarkable detachment and self-sufficiency, any more than he could understand her limitless generosity. And out of this mutual lack of comprehension arose his disastrous error, for which she afterward so bitterly reproached herself. She did not see what she was doing to him. She wished to be his friend, and would not know what friendship meant to him. She had everyone about her for her friends, and he had no one but her. He gave her all the affection he had, and, if it were not a great thing, at least it *was* all he had.

Two months of that summer they had together, an innocent and beautiful time, never to be forgotten, for nothing so good ever came to him again. In August he received the staggering news that his mother had married a second time, and a little later she sent for 'her boy.' When he said good-bye to Jocelyn, he was white with despair, but he did not suggest writing to her, made no plans for seeing her again. He was, as usual, cynically resigned.

That was the end of his boyhood. He did not see Jocelyn again for nearly four years, and when they did meet again at the Bradleys' New York house, the old innocent intimacy was no longer possible. Jocelyn had been introduced to society under the auspices of her aunt, Mrs. Pugh, and Mrs. Pugh thought it better not to 'encourage' young Hazeltine. Maynard, his mother's second husband, kept him well supplied with money, and he had won the reputation of being 'wild.' There was talk of 'a married woman.'

This had no effect upon Jocelyn. She was still his friend, and he knew it, and they went to great trouble to secure an hour alone together now and then. Yet they were not happy together anymore. Basil was frank enough in expressing his affection for her, but he was frank in nothing else, and what distressed Jocelyn was his pretence of being so, his way of telling her so many details which seemed intimate and were only plausible. She grieved to see her dear friend so tarnished, but it was not her way to reproach him, and certainly not his way to make confessions. They let all that lie unspoken between them, both heavyhearted because the old beautiful friendship was gone. Both were incapable of making the small effort needed to recapture it—Jocelyn because of her sorry lack of spiritual energy; Basil because he was, as usual, cynically resigned. He took it for granted that he would never have Jocelyn. He had no money of his own, only what his step-father gave him, and there were already signs that his mother's ménage was close to disruption. He had no 'prospects,' either; he was to be graduated from Harvard, and then to study medicine, but he regarded the idea of his ever becoming a doctor as altogether whimsical. The advantage of the thing was, that it took a long time, and he trusted that something would turn up to interrupt the medical career.

Something did. The War. In the autumn of 1914 he came to say good-bye to Jocelyn; he told her he was going over to England to 'join up'; he was extraordinary cheerful about it, almost elated. And Jocelyn parted from him sadly, but without any great anxiety; she had seen nothing in him stronger than his self-interest, and she thought that he would take very good care of himself.

She did him less than justice. For all his wariness, there was not a trace of cowardice in Hazeltine; there was nothing he feared, because there was nothing for which his solitary spirit really cared; he had nothing to lose. And there was in him a cold zest for adventure. He saw his father's people and pulled wires, and got himself a commission in an infantry regiment; he made a debonair and gallant officer, he was wounded twice, and he was cited for 'conspicuous bravery.' That was, indeed, the sort of bravery he preferred, the conspicuous.

Jocelyn clung to the hope that he would come back changed. That vainest of earthly desires, which women cannot relinquish, that pitiful desire to go back, to be again what one has been, to have again what is gone, was strong in her. She thought, she hoped that then their old friendship could be restored.

Changed? Upon his return he came first to her, with a headlong eagerness new to him. He was so happy that she tried to smile with him through her tears and to hide her dismay and disappointment. He had dinner at the Pughs' that night, and they forgot all his past misdeeds, and were willing to adore him.

Mrs. Pugh spoke afterward of 'Basil's wonderful attitude—after all he's been through,' but to Jocelyn it was horrible, his amusing stories, his persistent dwelling upon the lighter side of his experience, his unruffled good-humour.... He had taken physical risks, but he had guarded his spirit with ignoble care; it had suffered nothing, learned nothing.

He had gained a new hardihood, though; much of his old fastidiousness was gone; indeed, he came close to being shameless in some matters, in regard to his mother, for instance.

Julia had resented the War.

"I'm not the right age for it," she complained. "It's such a *young* war. Women my age simply don't count."

She made a counter-demonstration by getting a divorce; but, after all, it was a feeble thing, merely the flicker of a candle against the monstrous glare across the sea. She did not receive her due of sympathy; no one understood her sufferings, no one cared to listen to her explanations. She made what she could out of being a War-Mother, with a son at the front, but in this role, too, she failed, because Basil would not play up to her. She wrote to him again and again, but he did not answer her letters; he did not even thank her for the packages she sent him.

When he came back, he went to see her. She was living in Marie Keyes' flat while Marie was at Southampton; all her friends were away, and doing very well without Julia. Somehow she had lost her hold upon those long-suffering friends of hers; she was left alone in the city, in midsummer, bored and restless, and struggling against a dim and dreadful fear.

In her plaintive way she reproached her son with his neglect. But this time he made no gallant response, he apologised in a manner so perfunctory that she began to weep. She told him that she was 'lonely and perfectly wretched.'

"Marie's coming back in September," she said, "and I don't know where I'll go. Baba, let's take a little flat together, you and I ..."

"Awfully sorry!" he said. "But I've made other plans."

He knew she had sufficient alimony from Maynard to live on; let her live on it, he wanted nothing more to do with her. He had never in his life felt toward anyone as he felt toward her this afternoon, such bitterness, such shame and anger filled him, that he could scarcely speak to her. This woman, wearing the jewels his father had given her, living on money another man gave her, this woman who must try her wistful coquetry even with him, was his mother ...

He did not believe that she suffered, that she was lonely and terror-stricken, famishing for even the simulacrum of devotion he had once given her. He did not believe her when she told him she was ill, did not believe her when she said she loved him. The time came when her first assertion was proved, for she died that winter, in France; but her second statement was not to be demonstrated. She had injured her son beyond remedy, and he did not forgive her.

Basil had changed and, in his eyes, Jocelyn was changed. The night of his home-coming at the Pughs' she saw that. With all her faith, she could not longer hope to go back, to know, ever again, the sweetness of their old friendship.

He went to see her the next afternoon, and they walked together in the Park. It was a grey April afternoon, windy, chill and damp; it seemed to him that she was too lightly dressed for such weather, he thought her terribly fragile, the wind fluttering her soft, dark dress, as if she were helpless, blown along at his side. He took hold of her arm in a sort of panic, so that she should not be driven past him, and she turned her head toward him, a little surprised ... He saw that she understood.

He tried to recapture the friendly manner.

"I'll have to be looking for a job now," he said. But it was not said in the light way he intended, his lips were dry, his voice unsteady.

She had grown very pale.

"Yes," she said. "You must.... We can't go on like this, can we, Basil?"

After a moment's silence, he began to talk to her of something else. He was sure that she did not love him, not in the way he loved her; but he thought that she would, that if he proved himself even a little worthy, she must love him.

So he did set about looking for a job, in his own fashion. There were ever so many people who liked him; he fancied he would have little difficulty in getting what he wanted. He went to everyone, and hinted or asked outright. He got several offers of small loans, he got more invitations than he could accept; one fellow offered to lend him his car for the summer, but no one offered him a job. This was not strange; he was earnest enough in his desire to find one, but it did not occur to him to offer anything in return; he mentioned no qualifications, never suggested that he might be useful. He did not see it that way. He was blandly aware of his own uselessness; he asked for a job as he would have asked for any other favour.

Then he got one. Or rather, Jocelyn got it for him. She did not say so, but he knew very well that Mrs. Pugh would not have sent for him otherwise. And he wasn't pleased that it had come about this way; he had to go and tell Jocelyn the news—which he was aware was no news to her—and he had to listen to her congratulations. But he was constrained and unhappy; he refused to show a spark of enthusiasm.

They were alone together in Mrs. Pugh's drawing-room. It was May then, a day unseasonably hot; the windows were open and a dry wind blew in, bringing the dust and the noise of the city into that characterless room.

"Shall we tell Aunt Marie?" Jocelyn asked, after a long silence.

A violent disgust for implications, for shadows, for half-truths, swept over him. He wanted, this once, to speak with harsh candour.

"Tell her what?" he demanded. "No …" He meant to go on, to say he knew she didn't love him, that the whole thing was a pitiful impossibility, but he could not; none of those vital words was ever spoken. She leaned across the tea-table and seized his hand.

"Basil!" she said, with a sort of anger. "You're not being kind to me. Don't make me unhappy …!"

"God knows I don't mean to do that," he said.

So Jocelyn and Basil were betrothed. They talked about their future; they made plans; he came and sat beside her on the sofa, and for the first time he took her in his arms and kissed her. She clung to him, laid her cheek against his, and he held her fast, in despair, in anguish, praying that the force of his own passion might touch her gentle heart, his kisses bring to life his Galatea.

She was herself dismayed. It was inhuman, base, treacherous, to love Basil in this way, to feel only a sorrowful bewilderment, only a profound longing to console his aloof and friendless spirit.

And she could not deceive him. He knew…. It had never even the illusion of reality, this engagement of theirs. They agreed that it should not be announced until Basil was somewhat more solidly established in the business world, and that time never came. Six months later he lost his precious job.

This surprised Hazeltine. He knew that Pugh liked him, that he was a general favourite, and as for ability, what was that? He observed no especial aptitude in Pugh for *his* post, no particular reason why he should be vice-president of a trust company. Simply, why shouldn't he be? As Basil saw it, one person was about as good as another; the necessary things got themselves done, if not by one, then by another. In the army there had been competent officers and incompetent; that was nature, and the war had been won. The thing was, to take the good with the bad, and strike an average. But the trust company thought otherwise, and Hazeltine was dismissed.

It was his first failure and, Jocelyn feared, his last. He was not likely to try again. She was at the opera, in the Sidells' box; he came in late, and sat down behind her, and when the curtain went down upon the second act of *Aida*, he told her the news. They sat there, a little withdrawn from the others, talking in undertones; then the music began again, the curtain rose; it was the strangest talk, interrupted, coloured by the polite barbarity of that music…. It was always so with these two, both homeless, like well-behaved visitors in this world, their own affairs forever broken into by the amazingly alien affairs of other people; no place of their own, no life of their own.

Jocelyn had never before seen him bitter, and it so distressed her that she grew bold.

"Do you mind if I walk home with Basil?" she asked Mrs. Sidell, in that apologetic way of hers. "It's such a nice evening...."

Of course, Mrs. Sidell didn't mind; Jocelyn was twenty-two and her own mistress and young Hazeltine a very old friend, so they set off together. It was, as she had said, 'such a nice evening,' a cool November night, dark, serene, with slow clouds trailing before the face of the stars. But they could not remain under the sky, walking the city streets. They went into a Child's restaurant for coffee and rolls, and there, at midnight, in the dazzling glare of the white-tiled room, enacted a scene of their shadowy drama.

"You'll soon find something else, Basil," she said.

He made no answer at all. They were both silent; Basil downcast and absent, Jocelyn with her fervent eyes on his face. He was so dear to her; he had been such a gallant and gentle lover, never exacting, never unreasonable, never tiresome, so grateful for the very little she had to give him.

"Basil!" she said. "It doesn't really matter.... Please try to see it my way.... Please! We've always been friends.... Let me be really your friend. Let me share what I have with you. No, no! Do please listen! Basil, dear, I have enough—"

It was as if she had struck him.

"No," he said. "No, thanks. You see ... I'm not much good—but—I'd like to keep up some sort of illusion—between us, anyhow...."

She said all she could think of about not judging a man's worth by the amount of money he made, and so on. He listened politely, but he was not impressed. Then she said she would wait, for years, forever.

"No," he said. "I'd rather you didn't."

He knew there was nothing for her to wait for, and he believed that he himself was cynically resigned. But it was not so. He went abroad with Charles Keyes, in a vaguely defined capacity, as secretary, courier, cousin, what you like. He lived in his usual fashion; he did not write Jocelyn, or she to him; what had they to say to each other? But all the time he thought of her; it was always in his mind that he would go back to her and find her unchanged, unalterably constant. Something would happen; one of his relations would die and leave him a little money, someone would tip him off to something really good in the stock market; not for an hour was he actually resigned to the loss of Jocelyn.

When he came to New York again, he found her engaged to his cousin Lewis.

It made no difference to him what man she had chosen. He saw nothing strange in her choice, nothing disastrous; it did not even occur to him—though it did to others—that she was drawn to Lewis, because he was like Basil. All he cared for was that he had lost her.

He behaved very well; he was almost her old friend again, affectionate, nonchalant, good-humoured, and he observed, with grim amusement, that this made her happy. It was his intention to let her keep on being happy, not so much because he was generous, but because he could not, just then, endure the thought of her compassion.

This fine gesture was a little beyond his ability, though. He failed, at their last meeting before her marriage; a June night, it was, and the first dance of the season at the Yacht Club. They danced together, his arm was clasped about her, he held her so, for the last time.... And she looked up into his face with a smile that was only friendly, only kind. He had never realized more clearly the hopelessness of his love for her, yet that was the very moment when he must speak. They left the club house, and were strolling across the lawn together, in the blessed dark.

"So you're going to be married ..." he said, in a strained, unsteady voice. "I'll ... it's finished now.... But I'll remember.... You're not easy to forget, Jocelyn."

"We don't want to forget, do we, Basil?" she asked, softly.

"I shouldn't mind. I'd like to forget—some of it." His voice had grown so uncertain that he could not go on; he took out his cigarette case, but his fingers could not open it. "You were—you were—I thought ... O God! Jocelyn, I can't bear this! I *can't* lose you!"

"But, Basil, my dear, dear Basil!" she cried. "You know you said—"

"I didn't think you *could!* After you'd told me you loved me—after you'd let me love you.... All that time, Jocelyn ... I never thought you *could* ..."

She listened downcast, as if burdened with guilt; she did not defend herself, she never could; she would listen to any accusation with a sort of doubtful wonder. "Have I really done this?" she would think. "I did not mean to, but perhaps it is true. I know so well that all things are possible. Only forgive me!"

"No one will ever take your place, Basil," she said, in tears.

"I shouldn't think anyone would want to," he answered, smiling to himself.

"Basil," she said, quietly, "I'll tell Lewis.... I'll go on waiting for you, my dear Basil."

That put an end to his reproaches; he turned away with something like a shudder.

"No ..." he said. "Forgive me. I'm a fool—and a brute." He smiled again. "I'd ask you to wait for me in Heaven," he said; "only I can't think of Heaven as a place where anyone has to wait. That belongs to Hell. No ... we've both done with waiting, haven't we? It's—finished."

They turned back toward the club house, where music was playing gently.

"Forgive me, dear girl," he said. "I was unjust and unkind.... I said I wanted to forget, but that's not true. I want to remember everything about you, as long as I live."

Their hands clasped in the dark.

"If I make anything out of my life," he said, "if I ever do anything worth doing—it will be done for you. I—I want you to know that."

Those were his last words to the only human creature he had ever loved.

But that was nearly five years ago.

CHAPTER SIX

DEMANDS ARE MADE UPON HAZELTINE

That had been nearly five years ago, and was dead and buried now. In order to live with any measure of tranquility, Hazeltine found it necessary to forget a good many things, and the memory of that scene at the Yacht Club had long since been dismissed. Sometimes he felt, with uneasiness, that it had not gone, but still existed in his mind, together with other pictures, terribly vivid; but, at least, he could always refuse to look at them.

And he had done a very clever thing; he had turned Jocelyn into a ghost, so that whenever he was obliged to remember her, there was no human quality left about her image to disturb him. She was a wraith, and her name was sacred; he would not admit that Lewis's affair with the adventuress was an affront to a living breathing woman; he preferred to think it was sacrilege committed against his saint.

This point of view rather exalted him. He went back to see the adventuress in a mood stern and almost heroic; he was going for Jocelyn's sake. To be sure, he would get a material reward from

Lewis, but he chose to forget that. And it is true that he would have gone anyhow.

He reached the house on West Tenth Street and rang the bell, the same woman opened the door, again he said "Miss Dennison?"; again she answered "Top floor" and vanished before he began to mount the stairs. But the atmosphere of the house had changed; it was alive to-night, on the first storey light shone from under a closed door, and he heard sounds of running water and dishes stirred about in a tin pan; the second floor was dark and still, but even there he could hear voices from upstairs, voices conversing in a fervent murmur.

As he set foot on the last flight, he saw two persons sitting on the top step; their earnest conversation ceased at once; they got up and stood waiting in silence, in the dark.

"Miss Dennison?" he asked once more.

"Oh! It's you!" cried a voice he recognised as that of the girl he had seen there before. Hazeltine could find nothing better to say than a polite "Good evening!" and he got no answer.

"Richard!" said the girl. "Go inside just a moment, will you?"

The door behind her was opened and, silhouetted against the light, Hazeltine had a glimpse of a young man with his hand on the knob; then he slammed the door after him.

"She's in there!" the girl whispered.

Hazeltine refused to whisper; this air of solemn mystery irritated him.

"Miss Dennison? Do you think she'll see me?" he asked.

The girl came nearer to him.

"I wish you hadn't come!" she whispered, with vehemence.

"It's not very agreeable for me, either, you know."

"You're the last person on earth.... You *never* could understand Coralie. Never!"

This surprised him.

"Why couldn't I?" he asked, mildly.

"She's been through hell!" said the girl.

He wanted to laugh. It was so correct; all adventuresses have 'gone through hell.' It is a necessary part of their equipment. And several other women, not adventuresses, had assured him they had undergone the same nerve-racking experience. So many Eurydices, and, apparently, so few Orpheuses....

"Of course," he said, "that makes it difficult. But

"You'll have to be careful," she interrupted. "You will, won't you? *Don't* hurt her!"

"I'll try not to be offensive."

She sighed, and for a moment he was sorry for her, and half-inclined to say something reassuring. But he did not, because the heroic mood persisted; he was stern, he felt that if it were possible to hurt a creature so hardy as Miss Dennison, he would very willingly do so. Probably he could not; it would be simply a matter of cautious bargaining, and very likely he would have to be extremely civil.

"You see," the girl began again, with obvious anxiety, "Coralie doesn't know anything about his wife. He just told her they'd been separated for a long time, and that—"

"Look here!" said Hazeltine, abruptly. "If you don't mind—we needn't discuss all that."

"But I want you to know! I want you to understand! If Coralie had thought she was doing any harm to anyone—"

"Exactly!" said Hazeltine. "May I see her now?"

For he thought that a more sophisticated adventuress would be a hundred times better to deal with than this crude and blundering young creature. Miss Dennison couldn't well have found a worse advocate; with every word she spoke his contempt and anger increased.

"May I see her now?" he asked, again.

The girl did not answer or move for a minute; then she opened the door, very slowly; it swung inward, and she went with it, holding the knob. The light shone upon her sorrowful and anxious face, her shoulders rested against the panels, she looked like a victim bound there.

Again pity stirred in him; their eyes met, hers full of entreaty; and, moved by a careless little impulse of compassion, he smiled down at her. It was his usual smile, quite unstudied, almost mechanical; it meant nothing at all, but it gave to his handsome face a grave and tender look which had often produced a gratifying effect. It was effective now. The girl sighed again, as if in great relief, as if she had read in his look something profoundly reassuring.

"All right!" she said. "Go on in!"

He passed by her, into the room, and he saw before him the most unwelcome figure his imagination could have evoked. He saw Mac Donald.

The effect of this encounter upon Hazeltine was extraordinary. The heroic mood vanished at once; he was still angry enough, but it was a hot, uneasy anger, from which all loftiness had gone. A sort of confusion came into that mind of his which was usually so clear and orderly; he thought of strange things, and he believed them. He thought that Mac Donald had come here to spy upon him to discredit him....

"Did you want to see me?" asked a soft voice at his elbow. "I'm Miss Dennison."

He realized then that he had been staring at Mac Donald far too long, and he turned to Miss Dennison with an apologetic air.

"I beg your pardon," he said.

And that was bad beginning. Miss Dennison was one of those persons who truly accept apologies, and embrace them, and never forget them; she loved them, she treasured them. She could tell you anecdotes about people who had apologized to her after prolonged struggles. She smiled.

"You must be the gentleman Agnes mentioned," she said.

This use of the word 'gentleman' gave Hazeltine his first clue, and he needed clues badly. He could not understand Miss Dennison; she was a type completely novel to him, and though he had tried not to have any preconceived ideas about Lewis's adventuress, he was surprised. Impossible to imagine this woman as the seller of compromising letters, impossible to imagine any man writing them to her, or wanting to write them. She was, Hazeltine thought, remarkably unattractive; she was a small woman of perhaps thirty-five, with a great quantity of brown hair dressed high on her head. She was pretty in a colourless, finicking sort of way, but he could see in her no hint of anything to cause madness. Moreover, she was genteel; she called him a 'gentleman.' She was dressed in a dainty and genteel style, somewhat outmoded, a thin white blouse and dark skirt, little ruffles at her neck and wrists. No; the secret of her charm for Lewis eluded him.

"I came yesterday—" he said.

"Agnes told me. And I'm sorry I wasn't home," she said. "Come over here won't you, where we can talk?"

Entirely self-possessed she was, and faintly condescending. She led the way to a couch of homemade appearance in a corner of the room.

"Sit down!" she said, graciously.

He obeyed, and there they sat, side by side. There was a flavour of the ridiculous about it. The girl was standing by the mantelpiece, talking to Mac Donald; the young man she had called Richard was moving restlessly about, all of them at the further end of the long room; it was as if no one else dared to be seated or to approach the couch where they sat enthroned.

"I'm sorry I didn't see you yesterday," said Miss Dennison. "I could have spared you this unnecessary trip."

"Thank you!" said Hazeltine. He was waiting for a better opening.

"Mr. Martinsburgh sent you, I believe?" she went on, and for all the affability of her tone and her glance, Hazeltine was aware that she meant to offend....

"Martinsburgh asked me to come," he corrected, blandly. "I'm his cousin you know." And he took a card from his pocket, and proffered it.

Miss Dennison looked and looked at it.

"Mr. Basil Hazeltine ..." she read, in her soft voice.

She was clever, no doubt about it, for without the least visible expression she managed to convey to him the idea that his name was absurdly 'highfalutin,' and that she was going to laugh at it when he had gone.

"What message did he send?" she asked.

"I'm sorry to say he didn't send any," answered Hazeltine, and with secret satisfaction he waited to see what she would make of that.

She did not like it. When she spoke, after a considerable pause, her voice had a note of genteel hauteur.

"Then may I enquire why you troubled to come here—twice?"

"I hoped you'd let me talk to you, Miss Dennison."

"About Mr. Martinsburgh?"

"I'm afraid, Miss Dennison—" He stopped. "I'm afraid," he said, gravely, "that you don't quite understand Lewis. A rather extraordinary character ..."

"I'm afraid," said Miss Dennison, "that you don't 'quite understand' me, Mr. Hazeltine."

"Unfortunately, I don't," he answered, politely. "But perhaps—"

"Because if you did," she went on, "you wouldn't have come. You'd have known that I wouldn't discuss this matter with anyone except Mr. Martinsburgh himself."

She spoke with dignity; sitting there beside him, with her little ruffles, her modestly long skirt, her unfashionable coiffure, she was a model of feminine refinement and decorum. Yet, looking at her, Hazeltine fancied he saw in her eyes a baleful glitter, and hers was, he thought, a beastly little mouth, spiteful and thin.

"I want to see Mr. Martinsburgh himself," she said. "I cannot talk to anyone else."

Her misty blue eyes were looking past him at some object across the room, and Hazeltine had a sudden conviction that she was looking at Mac Donald.

"He put her up to this!" he reflected. "He's advised her not to talk to me.... He's playing some game of his own, the damned sanctimonious humbug.... Told Lewis he wouldn't come ..."

He badly wanted to believe this, he felt that nothing would give him greater satisfaction than to prove this fellow a sanctimonious humbug; indeed, it was somehow necessary for him to believe that the man who would rather lose a good job than handle this little affair did not and could not exist.

"You might tell Mr. Martinsburgh," Miss Dennison went on, "that if he *won't* see me, he'll regret it."

Hazeltine rose.

"I shouldn't like to put it that way, though," he said, "it sounds— like a threat, you know."

"Oh, no!" said she, brightly. "Only a prophecy, Mr. Hazeltine!"

She rose too, and as he went toward the door, she went beside him, her high heels clattering smartly on the polished floor.

"*Good* night!" she said, holding out her hand.

There was greater condescension in her voice, in her gesture. Her last retort had gone to her head; she felt herself cleverer than Hazeltine, in addition to the natural superiority a lady has over a gentleman in genteel circles. And it seemed to Hazeltine fitting that he should bow low over her hand and lift it to his lips; he did this in mockery, with an exaggeration he thought she could not fail to resent. But to his surprise, it charmed her; a faint colour rose in her cheeks, and on her lips appeared a smile gay and naive.

"I've been an ass!" thought Hazeltine. "Homage—that's what she wants. If I'd waited—if that fellow hadn't been there ..." Aloud he said, with a hint of reproach: "You haven't given me much of a chance, Miss Dennison."

"Well ... no ..." she admitted. "Perhaps I haven't. But—"

"If you'd let me come once more—?"

She looked at him, and smiled again.

"Perhaps ...!" she said, enigmatically.

This pleased them both. She felt it to be a neat ending, the sort of thing that would make a good tale to tell. And Hazeltine felt encouraged.

He turned to take leave of the others, and he found them all regarding him with a curious earnestness—the girl, and the young man called Richard, and Mac Donald.

"Good night!" said Hazeltine.

"If you've no objection," said Mac Donald, "I'll go with you, Mr. Hazeltine."

Certainly, Hazeltine had no objection; on the contrary, he was well pleased at the prospect of a little talk with this fellow.

"Right you are!" he said. "I'll wait."

He descended the stairs, opened the door, and stepped out into the cool, fresh night. He lit a cigarette, and by that time the deliberate Mac Donald had appeared.

"Which way?" asked Hazeltine.

"I'll just step along with you, whatever way you're going."

"Mighty obliging, aren't you?" thought Hazeltine. "We'll see what you're after."

But Mac Donald was in no hurry. They walked across Tenth Street to Sixth Avenue and turned north, and they had reached the corner of Fourteenth Street before he spoke.

"I've no doubt you were surprised to see me there," he said.

"Not too much," answered Hazeltine, coolly.

"Eh? Well, maybe you're a philosopher," said Mac Donald, with good-humour. "And not surprised by anything. However ... you'll want to know what I was there for—"

"I rather think I do know. You changed your mind, didn't you?"

"Changed my mind?" the other repeated. "No. I did not!"

"I understood you'd refused to go."

Mac Donald was silent for a moment.

"I did not care to go on Mr. Martinsburgh's behalf," he said. "But I—"

"But you went on your own, eh? More profitable?"

"I don't know what you're talking about," said Mac Donald. "I wish you'd explain."

"That's for you to do."

"I've no objection. It was my purpose to do so. Because, when I saw you there, it came to my mind that I'd ask you for assistance—"

Hazeltine laughed.

"Go ahead!" he said. "Let's hear how I can assist you."

Mac Donald's good-temper seemed inexhaustible.

"You've no need to assist *me*," he said, in his equable way. "I'm very well as I am. It's Miss Brian."

"Never heard of her."

"You've seen her, though. The young woman who's living with Miss Dennison."

"All right! What does *she* want, then?"

"You'll understand, if you please, that she knows nothing about this. I'm acting upon my own responsibility, entirely. She came to the office this morning to see Mr. Martinsburgh, and—to be frank with you —he was in no condition to see her. I did not tell her that, but I persuaded her to wait." He paused a moment. "I entered into a conversation with her," he continued, solemnly, "and I don't mind telling you I was shocked."

"Shocked, were you?"

"It seems that Miss Dennison had been threatening suicide, and the poor young woman took it very seriously. She'd come to talk to Mr. Martinsburgh.... Well! You can see for yourself the folly of that! I tried to reassure her, but—well ... I've no talent for such things! She was very much upset.... She ... I persuaded her to step out into the corridor, where her—her upset condition would not be observed by the office, and I talked to her as best I could. And what she told me about the state of affairs shocked me. It seems there are financial difficulties...."

"All right!" said Hazeltine. "What about it?"

"It's obvious," Mac Donald went on, with a trace of severity, "what sort of girl she is. And it's equally obvious that this other woman is no fit companion for her. I'm asking you, Mr. Hazeltine, to help Miss Brian."

"Help her? I?" cried Hazeltine, astounded.

"She's involved in these difficulties through no fault of her own. If you'd help—"

"I?" cried Hazeltine, again.

"I was sure you'd be willing to do it. It's a matter of no more than six hundred dollars—"

Hazeltine stopped short in the street.

"I haven't six hundred pennies," he said. "Why, Good Lord, man! I'm next thing to a pauper!"

Mac Donald had stopped, too, but he said nothing. And Hazeltine was filled with an extraordinary desire to explain himself. He could not resist it; he meant to show this man, and to show himself, that he was in no way to be abashed by his own position in this world.

"I've no money of my own," he proceeded. "And I don't care about earning it by the sweat of my brow, either. You fellows who sit at desks think you're independent, God knows why! You're selling yourself, just as every poor man does. And it's a form of slavery that doesn't appeal to me. I'd rather use my wits. I can manage pretty well for myself, but I've nothing to spare for charity."

Still Mac Donald said nothing.

"Dam' self-righteous prig!" thought Hazeltine.

The violent dislike he had always felt for this man was growing beyond his control now.

"Why don't you tackle Martinsburgh?" he said. "You're the chief favourite, aren't you?"

His tone was unmistakable, but Mac Donald remained unperturbed.

"I doubt I'd be able to fill any such position," he answered; "I've not the qualifications."

"Too high-minded?"

"I'm not aware of any particular high-mindedness," answered the patient man.

Higher and higher rose Hazeltine's anger, he had no wish to check it now; he wanted only to hurt.

"You're prudent, anyhow," he said. "A bit too prudent to mind anything Martinsburgh's cousin says to you, aren't you?"

"I've no inclination to quarrel with you," said Mac Donald, briefly.

"Look here!" said Hazeltine. "I'm fed up with this! Ever since the first time I saw you, you've— you're—"

"Man!" cried Mac Donald. "What's wrong with you?"

The words, the tone, had a striking effect upon Hazeltine. The fine warmth of his anger fled, leaving him chill and a little dazed. The street was fairly quiet now. An elevated train had just passed, leaving a dull rumble in the air; people went by, yet he and this other man seemed quite alone, standing in an area of harsh white light from the windows of a confectioner's shop.

"What *is* wrong with me?" thought Hazeltine.

For no reason on earth he had insulted this man, and not for the first time, either. For no reason on earth.... And Mac Donald had borne with him so generously. There had not been a trace of resentment in his tone; only honest amazement. There he stood, neat and sober in his dark suit, his decent black tie with a decent little pearl pin in it, his derby hat, a typical shore-going outfit, offering the complete contrast to Hazeltine's superb nonchalance. A man of no brilliant qualities, no remarkable achievement, and a man who could not possibly count for anything in Hazeltine's scheme of existence. Yet from the beginning he had had a peculiar significance for Hazeltine. He knew that this scene was somehow of profound importance....

For a moment he contemplated making an apology—never a difficult matter for him—but he did not. He found it impossible to say anything at all, except a brief "good night" and he walked off, leaving Mac Donald standing there.

CHAPTER SEVEN

PRIVATE LIFE OF LEWIS MARTINSBURGH

Lewis Martinsburgh waked that morning with a sense of impending crisis upon him. He knew the mood well enough; so many times he had felt that now the turning-point of his life had come, now was the time for him to do some extraordinary and startling thing, to make a violent revolution in his manner of living. Everything must be changed; on how many mornings had he said this, in the course of how many tormented nights! And nothing ever was. Even his person seemed to him immutable; he would awaken, feeling himself to be desperately ill, ruined, and in the mirror always saw the same clear eyes, the same inhuman youthfulness....

This morning, however, he was very calm and resolute. This really was the turning-point. He got up for cigarettes and matches, and went back to bed to smoke while he decided his destiny.

"I can do anything I like," he reflected, serenely. "Absolutely anything. I can go where I please. I can find the sort of life that really suits me. There's nothing to stop me."

He lay back on the pillows, staring up at the ceiling; a tranquil joy flooded his soul, his fate rested in his own hands, and he felt himself superbly competent to direct it. What he wished to do, that he could do. He had, in the past, accomplished remarkable things; he could, in the future, do still greater things.

"Why not?" he asked himself, in a reasonable tone. "I'm at my best now, physically and mentally. I've made all the money I need for the rest of my life. I've provided for my family. I'm free now to choose my own way of living. I might write.... Why not? I've seen the world, I'm mature, I'm intelligent ..."

Suddenly his fine tranquility was shattered by a phrase which sprang up in his mind; bitterly aggrieved, he tried to ignore it.

"I'm intelligent ..." he repeated. And up sprang the phrase again, 'intelligent Mr. Toad!'

He remembered Jocelyn reading some verses to the children, from *The Wind in the Willows*.

> The clever men at Oxford
> Know all that there is to be knowed,
> But they none of them know one half as much
> As intelligent Mr. Toad!

Tears came into his eyes.

"Damn it!" he cried. "That's *too* much! I can't go on like this...."

Only, how to stop? He threw his lighted cigarette on the rug, and closed his eyes, not in peace now, but in wretched, nerveless apathy.

"I'm ill," he thought. "Very ill. I don't believe I can get up...."

But if he stopped in bed he would feel obliged not to eat, and he felt ravenously hungry. And lonely. He wanted to talk to someone. So he got up and dressed, slowly, crushed by fatigue. It was his habit to give his hair twenty-five strokes with the brushes every morning, exactly twenty-five; this morning, however, he was unequal to the effort; his arms were too weak; he counted eighteen, and then put on his jacket. But when he reached the door, great disquiet seized him because of that neglected duty.

"Rot!" he said. "I won't do it!"

Nevertheless, he went back to the chest of drawers, picked up the brushes, and with a groan gave to his hair seven rough strokes.

"But did I leave off at *eighteen* before?" he thought. "Or was it sixteen!"

Miserably he hesitated, trying to remember, and at last began all over again, from one to twenty-five. Then he opened his door, and stepped out. The house was very quiet, so he trod heavily going down the stairs, from a motive obscure yet familiar to him; he entered the dining-room and there was Mrs. Welley standing by the window, looking out into the bare, sunny little backyard where every spring she planted seeds in faith and reaped no reward.

"Mrs. Welley!" he called, sharply, and she spun round, with a little gasp.

"Yes, Mr. Lewis!" she said. "This very instant!" And going to the dumb-waiter, she called down to the cook, in a subdued, awe-stricken voice.

"Mr. *Lewis!*"

Mrs. Welley's entire life was dedicated to the service of Mr. Lewis. She had been his housekeeper for ten years before his marriage, and when that took place, he had insisted upon Mrs. Welley's being translated into his new existence. She had protested earnestly; he wouldn't need a housekeeper now; Mrs. Lewis wouldn't like it. But he would have it so, and so it was that Mrs. Welley was brought to the little house in the East Seventies, and to her amazement she found very little change in her status or duties. It was not the fault of Mrs. Lewis, it was because Mr. Lewis would not adapt himself. He wished to live in complete freedom, to come and go as he pleased, suddenly and violently to change his routine; he wished to make of his home a little private hotel maintained for his sole benefit. And poor Mrs. Lewis couldn't cope with that; she had tried, but she couldn't; and especially after the first baby was born Mrs. Welley was expected and required to devote herself exclusively to Mr. Lewis.

He never thanked Mrs. Welley; he noticed nothing except her rare mistakes; he was irritable, exacting, domineering. No matter; he could not alienate Mrs. Welley's affection. She had been fervently devoted in sequence, to her parents, to the late Mr. Welley, and to other employers, but no one else had ever had the mystic prestige of Mr. Lewis; perhaps because no one else had ever demanded such outrageous sacrifices. For fifteen years she had served him, and he was infinitely precious to her.

The only time he had really offended her was when he had told her, with immoderate laughter, that she was a 'fox in sheep's clothing.' Even that she forgave, unasked, and put it down as a bit of nonsense spoken when Mr. Lewis wasn't himself. But Lewis remembered the phrase; he thought it apt, and often repeated it to himself with secret delight. She had an alert, sensitive little face with a pointed nose, under a great crown of woolly white hair; she crept about so quickly in her trailing skirts; she had such a furtive, startled air.... There was nothing at all foxy in the poor old creature's nature, though; she was a most honest and scrupulous woman, and if she had a furtive, startled air, that was his doing, the way he'd fly out at her....

"Your mail, Mr. Lewis ..." she said.

She watched him anxiously as he opened one envelope after the other, leaving that one with the English stamp till the very last. His own wife's letter....

"But I dare say he's nervous-like," thought Mrs. Welley. She studied his face as he read that letter, but his was a face by no means easy to read. At last she ventured to speak.

"Mr. Lewis, sir," she said, "I do hope you have news of Master Lew."

He turned upon her that blank stare that always disconcerted her, and made no sort of answer. An installment of his breakfast was coming up then, and she had to attend to it. When she returned to the table, he was holding the newspaper up before his face, pretending to read. Mrs. Welley observed the trembling of his hands, his untouched grapefruit, his unfolded napkin.

"No one has any right to say he doesn't feel it!" she said to herself, indignantly. "Only he has his own way of showing it. He's just as upset over that poor child as ever could be.... A little more coffee, Mr. Lewis?" she asked, aloud, as if unaware that he had had none yet.

He made no reply. That was his way when he was what Mrs. Welley called 'nervous'; he would remain absolutely silent, or he might suddenly 'fly out' at you, or he might begin and talk your head off. Mrs. Welley was prepared for any of these contingencies, and no matter what happened, she meant to do her duty.

"Mr. Lewis!" she said. "You must eat!"

He threw the newspaper on the floor and glared at his plate with an affronted scowl; then he pushed it away so violently that the grapefruit spun across the table and was caught just in time by Mrs. Welley.

Then he lit a cigarette.

"Mr. Lewis!" said she, sternly, "you'll regret trifling with your health."

"I regret everything I've ever done since the day I was born," said Lewis.

Mrs. Welley was shocked, but compassionate. He did look so wretched! She sighed inaudibly; she regarded him as a loyal subject might regard a slightly mad king—not to be judged by ordinary standards.

"If I could get opium or hashish ..." he went on. "Good God! Anything...."

"If you'd take your nice hot coffee, you wouldn't feel like that," said she, but that only made him smile.

Because Mrs. Welley believed him to be suffering from a malady of comparatively recent origin; she had seen him very different from this and she believed him to be lamentably changed. And he knew it was not so; his disorder was not new; the insufferable fact was, not that he had changed, but that he could not change. It was that old, old Horror, climbing up into sight again from some monstrous black pit in his own brain....

And it was Jocelyn who had made this happen—Jocelyn with her accursed letters. Even Mrs. Welley, asking about the child, thinking about the child.... He remembered how it had been when the other child had been ill, three years ago. There had been two nurses in the house, the doctor forever coming and going, Jocelyn's friends, his own people, everyone so utterly absorbed in the child. Even Mrs. Welley.... No one thought of *him* at all. No one cared. The Horror came upon him night after night, when all these callous creatures were gathered together, concerned only with the unconscious little child.

It had been too much for Lewis. He had become violently ill one night, so that the day nurse had to be waked to attend to him, and the doctor called away from the baby. The doctor had decided that he was suffering from a severe, a dangerous attack of ptomaine poisoning. This had been a lesson for the selfish Mrs. Welley; she had at once forsaken all other matters and devoted herself entirely to Mr. Lewis. He too had had a nurse; he too was visited by the doctor. And Mrs. Welley had tried to conceal from him his child's inexorable progress toward death.

She hadn't succeeded. He had heard, he thought, every hurried footstep, every whisper in that house; he knew everything that went on. Everything.... That child had died, and now the other was ill. It was the same thing over again.... No matter that this time the thing was taking place three thousand miles away; he was again neglected, forgotten, abandoned.

He wanted somebody.... He must have somebody.... Somebody uniquely and passionately interested in himself. Just one person, among all the millions on this earth.... He couldn't bear this....

"Oh, Mrs. Welley ...!" he cried, in a pitiful, broken voice.

She came floating quickly round the table to his side.

"There, then, Mr. Lewis!" she said, laying her hand on his shoulder. "Don't take on so, Mr. Lewis! You'll do yourself an injury, sir, getting so worked up, and all.... If you could just take your nice hot coffee...."

He shook his head mutely, and held out before her a hand shaking like a leaf. And then an extraordinary scene took place. Mrs. Welley began to feed her Mr. Lewis with the coffee, spoonful by spoonful, and he sipped it, what time the tears ran down his haggard cheeks. Mrs. Welley wept also. It was preposterous.

But not to her. Zealous as if she were giving to a perishing hero the elixir of life, Mrs. Welley raised the spoon again and again. And attempted spiritual consolation as well.

"There, there, Mr. Lewis!" she said, in a quavering voice. "Now you'll feel better.... I know how it is, Mr. Lewis, I do indeed! I couldn't sleep last night myself, thinking of that dear little boy—"

The spoon flew out of her hand as he sprang to his feet.

"You damned old fool!" he shouted.

The silence in the house seemed almost terrible after he had gone. Mrs. Welley dried her eyes and fetched a long, trembling sigh; then she picked up the overturned chair, the newspaper on the floor, the broken cup, and opened one of the windows a little from the top. She felt better now, calmer, somehow stronger; the utterly unreasonable fury of Mr. Lewis had come like a thunderbolt of Zeus; it was a true catharsis; it aroused pity, terror, and wonder. But Mrs. Welley's thought was not classic, not pagan.

"He just doesn't realize ..." she thought.

That was the epitome of Mrs. Welley's sublime tradition.

Lewis was well known to be a business genius, brilliant, but sometimes a little unsafe. He was junior partner in the Quillen Steamship Line, and it was the combination of Martinsburgh's genius and James Quillen's sound common sense which had accomplished so notable a success. Both partners admitted this; Quillen had the greatest admiration for Martinsburgh's audacious projects, and Lewis always listened, or appeared to listen, with deference to his senior.

This morning when Lewis arrived at the office he found Quillen waiting for him.

"Lewis!" he said. "A word with you!"

"All you want," answered Lewis, pleasantly and together they entered the little room dedicated to Quillen's use. It was not austere, as Lewis's room was; it was a cosy cheerful little place, because Quillen was inclined that way; he liked what he called the 'human touch' in business.

"I don't want to interfere ..." he said. "We all have our—er—private troubles, so on and so forth. But after all, business is business, Lewis, business is business!"

"Is it?" said Lewis, vaguely.

Quillen, rather disconcerted, decided that this was a joke, and smiled.

"It's this ..." he said. "There was—a—er—a young lady ... Called here this morning, asking for you.... Said she'd tried to reach you on the telephone—"

"My God!" cried Lewis. He sank into a chair, and with a groan, buried his face in his hands.

Quillen was shocked by this theatrical emotion.

"I didn't mean to upset you so, old man," he said, honestly distressed. "Only—don't you see ...? It looks bad, you know. I thought if you could give her —er—a hint.... She—she cried—you know...."

"She's a blackmailer," said Lewis, briefly. "Nothing on God's earth can satisfy her, except to ruin me."

In the midst of his genuine concern for his friend, the pleasing thought came to Quillen that no living person could blackmail him. Never had he better appreciated the beauty of a fair and blameless life.

"That's tough luck!" he said, shaking his head. He suspected that the phrase was inadequate, but he was not experienced in any sort of emotion, a jolly sardonic, little red-faced chap, tightly buttoned into a blue-serge jacket; with his big nose and his wide grin he looked like Mr. Punch. But he had none of Mr. Punch's reprehensible traits, none of that shameless notion of humour, that flagrant disrespect for the law. On the contrary, he was a kind-hearted and highly respectable little man. Nor was he married, like his prototype; he was a bachelor.

"I'm mighty sorry, Lewis," he went on. "And that's the truth. But in—a case like this, m'boy—only course is—to be firm—grasp the nettle—d'you see? Face the thing, once and—"

"All right! All right!" Lewis interrupted, with a sigh. "Don't say anything more about it, James. I'll—do something...."

There was a short silence.

"And what news do you get about that boy of yours?" asked Quillen. "Going on well?"

"Yes," said Lewis.

"Fine manly little chap ..." said Quillen. "I'm very glad to hear his illness didn't amount to anything. Very glad! I suppose—"

Lewis suddenly began to talk of certain business matters, and Quillen was relieved to see that his private troubles had not impaired his remarkable grasp of detail. He complimented him upon this, and as they parted, looked after him with a somewhat reproachful admiration.

"Queer!" he thought. "Fellow who lives as he does—drinks—gets mixed up in an affair like this, and so on and so forth—never takes any wholesome exercise—doesn't play golf—and his mind's as clear as a bell!"

Without descending to envy, Quillen's admiration was tinged with a faint resentment at life's injustice. Here was Lewis with a charming wife, a fine boy, Lewis who had genius, who never grew old, whom beautiful young women came to the office to weep over.... After all, could one feel very sorry for Lewis?

Well, Lewis knew that no one did feel very sorry for him, or ever had. Not one soul would ever try to understand. 'Grasp the nettle'? 'Face the thing once and for all,' eh?

He began to think of his worthless emissary Basil with a furious hatred that made him sick. He hated Quillen, too, and everyone in the office, and everyone in the world. He didn't exactly hate Jocelyn, but he hated— His mind stopped there with a jerk like a nervous horse before a high fence. He was in no way ready for that leap.... He turned down another road.

"I'm about all in," he admitted, to the man who came in to see him about an expired charter. "My boy's ill, you know, over in England, with his mother. Nothing serious, but ... We lost our younger boy two years ago...."

He fell silent, and the broker, who hoped to renew the charter for the benefit of his own young family, respected his silence. Martinsburgh was staring at him blankly; the poor devil was probably thinking of that son of his.... As a matter of fact, Lewis was thinking of nothing except the knot in the other fellow's bootlace. How did he tie a knot like that? By accident or design? And how was he going to untie it? He had had a book about knots when he was a boy, and he had learned some twenty of them. The granny knot, that was the first one—granny—his own grandmother—dead now—death—the sick child over there—the child who filled the universe, crowding *him* out, so that no one remembered Lewis.... No one thought of *him*, no one was interested in his anguish.

As soon as the broker had gone, he locked the door and had a drink of whiskey. But the stuff didn't help him anymore. He had another drink.... There was a knock on the door, and he put away the bottle and glass, and turned the key. It was Mac Donald.

"A cable for you, Mr. Martinsburgh," said he. "Will you be wanting to send an answer?"

Lewis didn't answer; he took the envelope and laid it on the desk.

"Will there be an answer, Mr. Mar—?" Mac Donald began, but Lewis interrupted;

"No! Get out!" he said.

He knew what that message was. After a while he tore open the envelope and read the three words there; then he sat down at his desk and stretched out his hand toward the electric button which summoned his stenographer. But his eye fell upon his watch that, for some reason quite forgotten, he had laid on the desk. Half-past one? He couldn't remember whether he had had lunch or not. He fancied he was hungry, but he seemed to remember himself sitting at his usual table in the restaurant, even remembered what he had ordered. Or was that yesterday?

"This can't go on ..." he thought. "I'll have to see a doctor.... If I'm mad, I want to know it.... I *can't* go on like this...."

Quillen looked in at the half-open door.

"Better go out to lunch, Lewis!" he said, benevolently. "Can't run the old machine without fuel, you know. And you're not looking fit, Lewis. You—"

Lewis shoved forward some papers to hide the cable message.

"I'm a bit below par, James," he said, in a grave, low voice.

"What's wrong?" asked Quillen, anxiously.

"It's ..." said Lewis. He was fingering the edge of the hidden envelope. He hadn't noticed the address; had the message gone first to his home? If it had, Mrs. Welley would know.... In the course of time, Quillen would inevitably have to know. Everybody would.

He turned away to the window, and looked down at the street, far, far below, at the little square before the Customs House. More people hurrying about down there in the sunshine, brutally indifferent to him. Everybody in his especial world would have to know what that cable message contained. He would have to talk about it.

"I can't!" he thought, stifling a groan, "I can't ... O God!"

He turned back to Quillen.

"I believe I'll go down the docks after I've had lunch," he said, as if inspired. "I'd just like to see what those surveyors are doing on that rubber cargo business. They've been unusually slow...."

He took down his soft felt hat and put it on; then he remembered his watch lying on the desk, and pushed aside the papers to find it.

After he had gone out, Quillen saw a cable message lying there. He thought it was something Lewis had forgotten to tell him about, so he read it.

"But—Good Lord!" he cried, immeasurably startled.

"Son died yesterday."

The little man dropped into a chair, his red face grown quite pale. "But—never said a word!" he thought. "I—dashed queer, that is!"

CHAPTER EIGHT

QUIXOTISM

A steady rain had set in; it was falling past the window in straight fine lines, a curiously silent rain, Mac Donald thought, for the roof was so far above, the street so far below, that no sound of the downpour reached his ears. The green-shaded lamp on his desk was lighted; others like it glowed here and there in the long office. There were fifteen persons beside himself in this room, yet he could hear only mechanical sounds, the clicking of typewriters, telephone bells ringing, the long sigh of some patent silencer on the door near him.

"It is not human," he thought.

He was dispirited to-day. He was a patient man, never irritable; cheery, however, he was not, and had no desire to be. This job was irksome to him, he could endure it, and he would; but he did not attempt to delude his own soul.

"Ah, well!" he said to himself, "I must just do the best I can."

And that was the basis of the man's philosophy. Over his desk hung a card left by his predecessor: "Keep Smiling"; it admonished him; he left it there because he liked to look at it and to speculate upon the terror-stricken bewilderment of the spirit which had conceived so desperate a defence against life. To live upon this earth, to observe what was taking place upon it, and to keep smiling! To stand a watch in the quiet of a tropic night, to look up at the multitude of stars— and keep smiling! Shameless audacity of the notion! To be called upon deck, in an awful uproar of wind and rain.... No, the idiocy of the fancy ceased to amuse him. He pulled toward him the wire basket in which lay a pile of letters, typed after his dictation, and strangely altered in the process. Miss Hendricks had faithfully recorded his words, yet he was not satisfied; the letters seemed to him stilted and pompous.

"Ah, well!" he said to himself, "I doubt I'd be able to do better if—"

A tall figure in a rain-coat with a soft felt hat pulled low over his brow, went briskly past him. He jumped up, and followed to the door of the private office.

"Mr. Martinsburgh!" he said, "Mr. Peters telephoned—"

But it was not Martinsburgh, it was Hazeltine.

"Upon my word!" said Mac Donald, unreasonably startled. "I'd never observed how very like you are ..."

Hazeltine was not flattered. He did not believe that he was startlingly like Lewis, and he did not wish to be, either; his desire, naturally, was to be unique, to be the only one of his kind, no matter what the kind was. "Martinsburgh out?" he asked, briefly.

"It's extraordinary ...!" said Mac Donald absently, still looking at him. "Yes, he is out, and I cannot tell you when he'll return."

"He asked me to come in at half-past four," said Hazeltine. "I'd better wait."

He meant to wait in the private office, but he found the door locked.

"Will you not sit down over here?" asked Mac Donald, pulling up a chair beside his own desk. Hazeltine took it; Mac Donald sat down in his own swivel chair. They both smiled, as if this were the prelude to a friendly conversation. But neither of them had a word to say.

A considerable time went by; it was nearly five o'clock, and the office was growing restive. Presently Mr. Quillen came out of his little room, arm in arm with an important client; he waved his hat jauntily at Hazeltine. After he had gone, it was five o'clock, in effect, if not by Greenwich time.

"I doubt if Mr. Martinsburgh will be back this evening," said Mac Donald. "Good night, Miss Hendricks! Good night to you, Pennyman! I'll have these letters ready for the post directly, my lad."

This last was addressed to the office boy, and having spoken, Mac Donald turned to the reading and signing of the letters in the basket. Hazeltine watched him thoughtfully. The office had cleared rapidly; it was quiet now, empty, except for the office boy and one young fellow at the farther end of the room, bent over a ledger, the light of a lamp touching his bright, rough hair.

"Hanged if I see where the independence comes in!" said Hazeltine, as if continuing a conversation.

He had had a summons by telephone from Lewis, and he had obeyed it. Everyone else in the office had to obey summonses, like himself; they did as they were told, and got paid for it. Mac Donald, too ... What real difference was there, after all, between Mac Donald's position and his own—except that he managed better and made a greater profit?

"Well ..." said Mac Donald, with the careful attention he was wont to give to other people's words, "it is a matter of compromise. Human beings are interdependent; each man must contribute what he can to the common fund if—"

"Each man must get what he can for himself from the common fund," Hazeltine interrupted. "It's all rot to pretend that anyone works for the good of humanity. You're not going to tell me you're here every day from nine to five just to serve the public welfare, are you?"

"No," said Mac Donald. "That is not what I meant. To be independent, a man must feel that he is worth whatever he gets."

"I don't agree with you," said Hazeltine. "What I call independence is, having a bit more than you need, no matter how you get it. When you've got money, you're free. When you haven't you're obliged to knuckle under to the man who has."

He was in a singularly gloomy and dissatisfied mood. His antagonism toward Mac Donald had completely gone; in fact, he admitted that there was something very likeable in the man. But he was uneasy with him, he could not get rid of an unaccountable desire to explain to him.

"About this little job ..." he said, "I've agreed to help Martinsburgh out of this mess if I can."

"I hope you'll succeed," said Mac Donald.

"I mean to. But—look here! I wish you'd tell me what objection you had to doing it. It's simply lending a hand to a poor devil in a tight corner."

Mac Donald looked uncomfortable.

"Well ..." he said. "It's a matter of—personal inclination, as you might say."

But this was not enough. Hazeltine wanted to lead the man on to utter some priggish sentiment which would make him ridiculous.

"Doesn't it—" he began, when the door burst open and Lewis came in.

He did not so much as glance at the two who were waiting for him; he strode heavily past them to his own room, pulled out a jingling key-ring—but he could not unlock the door. He tried for some time, then suddenly he yelled:

"Come here! What the devil's the matter with you? Can't you *help* me?"

It was Hazeltine who came forward, and he had no trouble in unlocking the door: Lewis pushed by him and flung himself into a chair, in the dark, with a groan.

"Dear Lord!" he said, in a low voice, "this must be nearly the end. This can't go on."

Hazeltine turned on the light.

"Don't do that!" shouted Lewis.

But Hazeltine was very weary of the dramatic. He spoke in a brisk and cheerful voice.

"You said you wanted to see me about Miss Dennison," he began. "I went to see her—"

"No ... no ..." said Lewis. "No ... Look here, Basil, my boy, it's ... It's— d'you see—I—the ... the ..." He stopped, making an obvious effort to control himself. "Have a drink?" he asked.

"No, thanks. And, I say, Lewis! Don't you, either!"

"You think I'm drunk," said Lewis, wearily. "I wish to God I *could* get drunk. But lately—Basil, I'm ill!"

Hazeltine said he was sorry, but his tone lacked sincerity.

"I went to see—" he began, again.

"Now—this headache," Lewis went on. "It's not exactly a headache—not a pain—it's a sort of—I can't explain. Whether it's physical, or purely mental, I can't say. Question is, if a condition *can* be entirely mental—whether there's not always some obscure physical derangement at the bottom of such a—a condition. Who's to know which is cause, and which is effect? Physical symptoms—"

He stopped, and his face grew crimson, for he saw that Hazeltine was paying no attention to his words, was not disturbed by his suffering.

"I went to see Miss Dennison—" he began, for the third time.

"Ah!" said Lewis, with an odd smile.

"I had a talk with her. And she's agreed to see me again. I don't want to be too optimistic, but I hope I can settle it for you. She—"

"Basil, my boy, you're a marvel!"

Hazeltine did not like his tone.

"I'm doing my best," he said briefly.

"Well, it's a dam' poor best," said Lewis, with affability. "Because she came here, to the office, this morning, and made a scene."

"By Jove!" said Hazeltine, taken aback.

"And that doesn't suit me. You'll see her this evening, and you'll settle this thing, once and for all."

"I say, Lewis!" Hazeltine protested.

At heart he felt no particular anger against Lewis's savage insolence; he thought simply that Lewis was behaving more unpleasantly than ever before, and he wished that he could walk off and leave him. But, of course, he could not. While Mrs. Huested was absent, weighing him in the balance, he had only Lewis.

It was never his policy to be meek, though; he always made a point of resenting those things which a man of honour is presumed to resent. He knew his life would be intolerable if he did not exact a certain consideration from his various patrons.

"I'm glad to help you, and all that sort of thing," he continued; "but, after all, there's no occasion for speaking—"

"Oh, shut up!" said Lewis. "You make me sick! Help me—that what you call it?"

Even now Hazeltine was not angry; he could regard all this with philosophic detachment.

"Look here!" he said, with severity, "you're going a bit too far, Lewis, I'll clear out now, and see you later—when you're more yourself."

Such fury seized upon Martinsburgh that he could not speak. And speaking was the sole relief he had—the only outlet for this stifling passion would be a torrent of words. He had no impulse toward physical violence; his was the complicated civilized anger that is cruelly thwarted of any spontaneous reaction. This penniless beggar, this fellow who had lived so long on his bounty, daring to rebuke him, taking this highhanded attitude—toward him—when he was ill and in torment....

"I see!" he said, at last, with a contorted grin; "I forgot your pay...."

That's the trouble, eh? I promised you something—"

"That'll do," said Hazeltine, quietly. "I'll see you to-morrow, Lewis."

He opened the door, in a hurry to be gone before he was morally obliged to quarrel with Martinsburgh. Then he stopped on the threshold. He saw Mac Donald sitting at his desk, still busy with his letters. And at last anger came over him.

It was a strange sort of anger; it was not really against Lewis. Indeed it was more the spectacle of the sedate Mac Donald that aroused him. He did not, and he could not, object very much to anything Lewis said, but the idea of Mac Donald's overhearing....

"By Heaven!" he said to himself. "He's not the only one who can have 'personal inclinations.'"

He re-entered the room, closing the door after him. He knew very well what he was doing, and what the consequences might be. But it seemed to him that life would not be worth the living if he did not speak now.

"Lewis," he said. "I'm sorry—but you'll have to find someone else to do your dirty work for you. I've finished."

"What? What are you talking about?"

"I've had enough," said Hazeltine. "I've finished."

"You mean—" Lewis began. He looked up at Hazeltine, standing before him. "You won't *help* me?"

"Not this time."

"I'll—" said Lewis, and burst into tears, into convulsive sobs. He sank low in his chair and covered his face with his trembling hands. His thin body shook from head to foot.

"Oh!" he gasped. "I can't ... I can't ...!"

"Upon my word!" exclaimed Hazeltine, in disgust. "This is a bit *too* much!"

Once more he opened the door, and this time he went out.

"Finished!" he said to himself.

He did not fail to realize all that might now be finished. He was quite well aware of all that he might have shut in behind that door. But he was not sorry.

He glanced at Mac Donald; their eyes met. And Hazeltine smiled, a smile of immense and calm satisfaction. He imagined at that moment that he had triumphed somehow, over someone.

CHAPTER NINE

HAZELTINE IS IN A BAD WAY

"You don't see many like it nowadays," said the jeweller.

"It belonged to my grandfather," Hazeltine explained. He stood before the counter, gazing at the venerable watch with an expression which seemed to the jeweller rather sentimental. Quite right and proper for the young man to be sentimental about his grandfather's watch, and high time, too; he had brought the watch in here, six months ago, to be repaired; and he had had several notices sent him since then, announcing that the repairs were finished and that the charges were twenty-five dollars. But he had ignored those notices until this morning, when he had appeared early, and paid promptly. Still he lingered.

"What d'you think the thing is worth?" he enquired, casually.

"We-ell ...." said the jeweller, "the chief value, of course, is in the workmanship. That chasing—you don't see much work like that nowadays. Now, when I was a lad—"

Hazeltine appeared to listen with flattering attention to a lengthy discourse, but really he heard nothing; he was making calculations.

Two weeks had passed since his last conversation with Lewis, and he was feeling the effects of it. The first of May had come and gone, and brought no cheque; and Hazeltine's plan of living gave him no margin of safety. He lived from day to day, not gay and careless, like the ephemeral butterfly, but soberly and warily, in the manner of the greater carnivora. No more than a lion did Hazeltine have a store of bones; he hunted only when he was hungry. And now his chief hunting-ground was closed to him.

Still, like a superior Walt-Whitmanic animal, he did not sweat or whine over his condition. He had taken stock of his resources and they were these: a good supply of clothes, several invitations, three or four houses where he might visit without invitations, and a limited number of persons who would lend him small sums. An outlook precarious enough, yet with two great possibilities: one, that Lewis would send for him in such a manner that he could go; the other, that Mrs. Huested would make a favourable decision. So, altogether, he saw no cause for despair; he was going to be very uncomfortable for a time, but he had endured such periods before, and he could endure this. Food and shelter he could get without difficulty; the only really grave problem was that of ready cash.

The day before, when the last reproachful notice had come from the jeweller's, Hazeltine had been inspired to try a rather dangerous expedient. He had gone to Harold Coons, and had borrowed twenty-five dollars from him, to be repaid this day, by noon. For that was Harold's way; he would lend, but he required a note, or a still more offensive verbal promise, and he held you to this, not through avarice but because any other course, he asserted, was demoralizing. And if he were not repaid promptly, his very useful friendship would be forever forfeited.

Hazeltine's idea had been to pay for the repairing of the watch—taken to the jeweller's in a moment of prosperity—then to pawn it at a profit, reimburse Harold, and have enough left to pay his fare out to the Bradleys', where he could stop as long as might be necessary. But if the workmanship of the thing was its chief value, the prospect was bad.

He put it into his pocket and went out into the bright morning. He was calm, serious, intent only upon doing the best he could for himself. His attitude was not heroic, his fortitude had little that was high-minded in it; he would have made large concessions of his manly pride to Lewis or to Mrs. Huested, or to anyone else who would have helped him. And yet, he did not in the least regret what he had done; on the contrary, he recalled that moment of defiant independence with relish. He was willing to pay for that unique satisfaction; he earnestly hoped that he would not have to pay, but he was willing, if it could not be avoided. He knew he had been a complete ass, to quarrel with Lewis, but he fancied that the experience of being consciously and deliberately a complete ass was necessary to a well-rounded life. He treasured it.

But he continued to calculate. His pockets were empty, except for some small change. He would have to repay Harold and he needed at least ten dollars to get out to the Bradley's; he must therefore get thirty-five dollars for that watch. It was gold, and very heavy....

There came into his mind a memory of the first visit he had ever made to a pawnbroker. It was years ago; his mother had become involved in what her brother-in-law, Sam Bradley, called 'one of Julia's international complications'—a remittance hadn't come, or had been forestalled, something of the sort, and she had been temporarily estranged from her most useful friends. She and her son were marooned in a cheap little hotel for a week or so, and then, one morning, came a crisis.

"Basil!" she had said, in her helpless, pathetic way, "take my poor jewels and pawn them for what they'll bring."

Basil was at this time sixteen years of age, and a model of elegance and decorum. He had refused, nor had he been disturbed when his mother called him a nasty, selfish prig. But when she said she would have to go herself, alone, at once, he was defeated. Somehow he couldn't let her do that; he had been obliged to go with her.

He remembered the shame he had endured. The plaintive and lovely Julia Hazeltine was not a woman to pass unnoticed, and Basil, who was tall for his age, firmly believed that he looked a grown man, fully responsible, and capable of having prevented this disgraceful expedition. Heaven knows he had felt old enough; he had felt that he was now plumbing the depths of sordid knowledge. He had long before become pretty fully informed as to the more discreditable aspects of human nature, but whatever he was too young or too fastidious to relish he had been able secretly to disbelieve. It was the reality of this pawnshop episode that had so shocked him; he had had to believe it, he had to see his mother there, standing before the wicket, wistfully and helplessly driving a very good bargain....

Even now he could not smile at that recollection. Much water had flowed under the bridge since then, and he no longer considered pawnshops disgraceful or even embarrassing. All trace of priggishness had left him—and with it something he could less well afford to lose, some fugitive ideal, never quite comprehended, some little aspiration whose feeble life had been choked out that day.

He entered; the clerk knew him and smiled guardedly; it was in this shop that Mrs. Huested's gift of cuff-links now reposed. Hazeltine said he would like fifty dollars on the watch, and the clerk went off with it, to subject to an insulting scrutiny that timepiece presented to Francis Hazeltine, F.R.G.S. in 1882, by the members of some obsolete learned society. It had travelled far, that watch, up the Amazon and down the Nile, and it was now come into the hands of Mr. Weingelt, as a dishonoured hostage. It was never redeemed.

"We'll give you forty," said the clerk.

But Hazeltine managed to get forty-five.

So pleased was Harold Coons with Basil's promptness that he took him home to lunch. It was Saturday, and it was a proof of Harold's rectitude that he always went home to lunch on Saturday. He went home to dinner almost every night; indeed, he went home whenever he could, at any sacrifice. He was not yet married, but he was essentially a domestic man.

He and Hazeltine had been at school together, and both of them, according to the masculine convention, looked upon this as a more or less sacred bond. But they had not liked each other in their school-days and they did not like each other now; there was a profound distrust between them. That incident of the fountain-pen … whenever they met, Harold remembered that, and it caused him no little misery. Because virtue had not come easily to Harold, he was an honest and trustworthy man, but it was not easy for him to be so; not easy for him to be the admirable Harold Coons that he was. A lawyer, he was, and a reform politician, prepared to run for Assistant District Attorney this coming autumn on the Republican ticket; a young man socially and commercially impeccable, who had sternly conquered certain unworthinesses in his soul; all that he had done had been done with pain, and effort, and naturally the contemplation of the worthless Hazeltine, who could be honest and even generous without the slightest effort, was bitter to him.

"All right, Harold, take the dam' thing, if you're as keen on it as that. Only, for the Lord's sake, shut up about it."

That was what the sixteen-year-old Hazeltine had said about the fountain-pen when Harold had come to him, sick and shaken, after a night spent in making up his mind to confess. That was what Harold remembered.

Still they conversed affably enough as they went uptown to the Coons' nice little house in the East Seventies. Harold very serious, as was his way, a dark, severely handsome young man in eyeglasses, straight and soldierly in his bearing, and at his side the nonchalant and elegant Hazeltine. Harold had a cheque-book in his breast-pocket; Basil had a little bundle of pawn-tickets….

Scarcely had the parlour-maid admitted them when the telephone rang; it was a business call for the important Harold. So Basil went into the library alone.

This library enjoyed a sort of fame; it was an impressive room, panelled, running the length of the house, with a stained-glass window at one end and, in rows and rows upon open shelves, the collection of books left by the late Doctor Oswald Coons. It was a room designed to be taken for granted, and it generally was so taken, but not by Hazeltine. He had always had a cat-like curiosity about his surroundings; he liked to know where he was. Years and years ago he had perceived the faint flavour of mendacity here; he had examined the stained-glass window and found it to be of a clumsy and infantile design, and worst of all, he had really looked at the books.

Of all the available books in the world, Doctor Coons had

deliberately chosen and paid for the twenty-five hundred or so displayed here. First editions of writers with whom the first was likewise the last, poor, frowsty old poets, biographies of persons long ago forgotten, collections of letters from one nonentity to others, scientific works too old to be useful, yet not old enough to be curious. There were all the novels of Bulwer-Lytton and Disraeli, and George Eliot; there were eight volumes of *Medieval Castles in Southern Europe*; there was a fine set of *Mothers of Great Men*. You might take down a volume of the *History of the Court of Marie Antoinette*, with faint hope; you found it to be written by a Protestant lady as a bit of propaganda.

Basil had made interminable visits in this house. In this very library the first tears ever shed for him by feminine eyes had drenched the handkerchief of Dot Coons, because he was going back to England with his mother. He had promised to write to her, but he had not done so, for even at sixteen he had been aware that Mrs. Coons wouldn't like it and that Mrs. Coons was very much more useful to him than Dot could ever be. He had adopted a brotherly attitude toward Dot, and doggedly kept it up, and Mrs. Coons let him see that she appreciated it.

The unwavering fidelity of Dot failed to touch him; on the contrary, he found her wearisome beyond all others of her sex, and he was, moreover, in terror of her. He always tried to avoid a *tête-a-tête* with her; his heart sank as he heard her come galloping down the stairs now.

She burst into the room, a tall, robust girl, she was, with a head too small for her broad shoulders, and an honest, snub-faced little face, beaming with good-will.

"Basilisk!" she cried. "It's been ages and ages!"

At twenty-eight she was still girlish, full of naive enthusiasm, and alarmingly indiscreet. She always insisted upon talking about 'old times,' which invariably made her cry, and Hazeltine was always in dread that she would say something he couldn't ignore. Mrs. Coons and Harold didn't like that sort of thing....

He took her outstretched hand, and smiled at her, but with a trace of severity, for he saw tears in her eyes already. Whatever sympathy he might have felt for her was completely destroyed by her dress— her tragic dress of green foulard, with a sash tied in the back....

"Sit down!" said she, and herself flounced down upon the floor. Reluctant as he was, he could not very well sit elsewhere than in the chair nearest her.

"Give me a cigarette!" said she. "Harold'll be furious, but *I* don't care."

Basil did, however. Still, he held out his case; she took one, and as he lighted it for her, she looked up mischievously into his face. But she soon grew reminiscent.

"Basilisk!" she said, "do you remember that day we went out to White Plains to buy Petey? Harold's just bought another Irish terrier—but I'll never feel the same for *any* other dog.... Poor old Petey! He simply adored you, didn't he, Basilisk?"

"Oh, rather!" answered Hazeltine, vaguely. He was thinking of Mrs. Huested. She wasn't so bad, after all.

"Basilisk!" said Dot, laying her hand on his knee, "*why* haven't you come to see us for such an awfully long time?"

She was unmistakably tearful now, and Hazeltine stifled a sigh. He glanced down at her hand, lying on his knee, a stubby, innocent sort of hand, decorated only by a boyish seal ring, and he gave it a brotherly pat.

"Well, you see, Dot—" he began, when in came Harold, holding his mother firmly by the arm. I am the only son of this widow, he seemed to say, and I am a good son. Well, so he was, although that too was difficult, because Mrs. Coons was not quite up to the situation. She did not cling to her son; not only did she keep a firm control over her private income, without even consulting him, but there was something aloof and self-sufficing about her which he could not help deploring in a mother and a widow. She was a sallow, red-haired little woman who had never been good looking, but always trim and smart and attractive. She was a wise woman, too; she had a gift for witty repartee which she never used. Her quick mind found amusement in somewhat malicious reflections, but she never uttered them. She was busy, and she was interested in life, but she was secretly taken aback by what her fate had bestowed upon her. And it may be that she found in Julia Hazeltine's son something which her own children lacked, and which she valued; anyhow, she had always been very kind to Basil, and he was as fond of her as he knew how to be.

"I've come to borrow a book ..." he murmured.

She frowned at him, with smiling eyes. For he was perhaps the one living person who knew what she really thought of the Coons library. One rainy afternoon, long, long ago, when her own children were at school and Basil—a boy of sixteen—had been kept at home by a sore throat, she had found him in the library, looking pathetic. She had briskly recommended him to read a good book, and he had asked if she wouldn't help him to pick out one. And he had said such funny, outrageous things about the sacrosanct volumes.... She had laughed until she was weary, and afterward they had had tea together, cosily, before the open fire, talking cheerfully and lightly. How greatly did she appreciate that charming lightness in Basil, his tact, his obligingness, his debonair good-humour! Of course, she knew he was not to be compared with her own son—well, to be sure, she was very careful to avoid comparing them.

She saw such an awful expression on poor Harold's face now. He did not relish the spectacle of his sister sitting at Hazeltine's feet, smoking a cigarette, gazing tearfully into Hazeltine's face. She was glad he did not visit them often.

That was lunch. Walking back to his hotel, Hazeltine devoted his thoughts to the problem of dinner. He was expert in this matter; he never went where he was not honestly welcome; indeed, he was almost morbidly sensitive on that score. His art lay in making himself honestly welcome in many quarters; he was able to think of a considerable list of possibilities, and at last he decided upon the Wildings. They dined early, and if he dropped in there late for tea, they would surely ask him to stop.

He had a good deal of time to kill, though, before he could be late enough, and he meant to use it in reading a book somebody had lent him, a book he felt it was necessary for him to be able to talk about. He entered the hotel, and was going toward the lift, when a tall young woman sprang up from a chair in the lounge and stopped him.

"Mr. Hazeltine!" she cried.

It was the crude young creature who lived with the adventuress; he could not recall the name by which Mac Donald had spoken of her, but her face he remembered very well. A fine face, somehow haunting in its clean, strong lines, its expression of proud and ignorant recklessness. He liked her, he was glad to see her again, but he thought it better not to express any great pleasure until he knew what she wanted.

So he said, "Upon my word!" and smiled; but she did not smile. He observed, with dismay, that she had a tragic look.

"Mr. Hazeltine!" she said, again. "I'm awfully sorry.... But I thought you'd want to know ..."

"Sit down, won't you?" he said. "Here."

Some men, observing the quiver of her lips, would have sought in a panic for some place where they might talk unobserved. But not Hazeltine. He preferred to stay in the middle of the lounge, in a conspicuous position.

She took the chair he indicated, and he pulled up another, opposite her.

"Now!" he said, with the impersonal kindliness of a doctor with a large practice.

"Mr. Hazeltine," she said, slowly, "I've had a very bad time with Coralie."

"I'm sorry," said he.

He really was, but his sympathy was impaired by troubling memories of what Mac Donald had said. "Financial difficulties...." She was certainly shabby, disdainfully so, as if she wouldn't make the least effort to conceal it. She was wearing a felt hat—in May— a scuffed little black hat that came low over her face like a helmet. Her shoes were dusty, her hands bare, and for adornment she wore, over her dark dress, a string of meretricious green beads.

Yet, even to his fastidious eyes, she was admirable. She was touching, but she was not pitiable. There was strength and energy and fortitude in her, and good blood; she was a gentlewoman, and well aware of it. He was convinced that, whatever her financial difficulties, he would hear nothing of them.

"I can't make her see," she said; "she doesn't realize.... I didn't either, until you came, that time."

She raised her candid eyes to his face, and he was conscious of an odd qualm.

"I didn't care how much trouble she made for *him*," she went on, "after the way he'd behaved. I didn't think about there being— another person—who'd be hurt by it. But after you came"—she paused—"then I saw. I've tried to stop her, but I can't. She's desperate. She doesn't care what she does.... And I thought you ought to know."

He did not want to know. He did not want to understand her, or to hear anymore. She didn't realize how much she was saying ... "But after you came—"

"Yes," he said, with a sort of haste. "But—I saw some time ago that there was nothing I could do. I—I've dropped out."

"No! You don't understand. She's going to take those letters to Mrs. Martinsburgh."

A silence followed that name.

"There's nothing I can do," he said, at last.

"But I thought—" she began.

He waited a long time for her to go on; then he looked at her, and he saw on her face such a strange and wonderful look.... He could not bear it.

"No!" he said. "I can't do anything. It's up to Martinsburgh. I—I've finished."

She rose, and he too.

"Thank you!" he said.

He wanted to say more than that, but he could not, or dared not. He was very much moved, and he showed it, more than he knew. She glanced for a moment at his half-averted face.

"Here's my card," she said, gently. "I'd be glad to see you, any time."

He took the card, and was glad to look at it, so that he need not look at her. "Miss Agnes Brian," it read.

"Thank you, Miss Brian," he said, again.

She held out her hand; he took it, in a grasp firm enough, yet after she had gone, he felt as if he had rejected it. He felt as if he had turned his back upon her. He crossed the lounge with her, stood for a moment in the doorway, looking after her. She did not seem shabby now, walking in the sunlight; she seemed a tall and strong and splendid figure. And he regretted her. He did not feel very proud or very fine just then.

CHAPTER TEN

LEWIS SEEKS ADVICE

Mrs. Welley was sitting in the dining-room, reading the newspaper, and wondering however people could be so foolish, with all these murders and robberies and accidents. In the back of her mind was the pleasing consciousness of a baked ham in the icebox, and two chickens all ready to broil, and a noble Cabinet pudding with sherry sauce. Potatoes were pared and sliced and soaking in cold water, prepared for frying; mushrooms were peeled and sprinkled with salt; a tomato salad was waiting—everything so contrived that Mr. Lewis could be fed at short notice, alone, or with one or two friends, and if he didn't come home to dinner, it would keep. If everyone would look ahead as she did, there would be none of this nonsense in the newspapers.

She turned the page and continued to read of many catastrophes. She was a kindly and compassionate woman, but not imaginative, and these remote sufferings aroused in her only a self-righteous sort of cosiness. She liked to ask—whatever is the world coming to? But wherever it was bound, she certainly did not believe herself to be going along with it. No; she sat comfortable and sheltered in Mr. Lewis's house; she was old and done with the world, and the world very properly let her alone.

She read the list of passengers on an incoming steamer; sometimes she found in such lists a name familiar to her, some friend of Martinsburgh's or of one of her former employers, and that was delightful....

The front door was thrown open, crashing against the wall; she rose, hid the newspaper behind the sideboard, and stood waiting, looking really like a fox in her alert attentiveness.

"Alone!" she observed, with satisfaction, and hastened to the door of the sitting-room.... Mr. Lewis had flung himself into a chair; his hat was still on the back of his head and his light overcoat still buttoned about him.

"Shall I serve dinner, Mr. Lewis?" she asked.

He didn't answer, but stared at her so fixedly, with such an unreasonable malignity, that she was abashed.

"A nice little broiled chicken ..." she murmured.

Still staring at her, he began to grope in his pockets, and with growing agitation, Mrs. Welley waited for him to produce some bill to confront her with, some incriminating document. He muttered something between his teeth, sprang up, unbuttoned his overcoat and cast it off, and continued searching in his jacket pockets. Then suddenly out flashed some bright metal object and Mrs. Welley screamed.

"What the devil's the matter with you?" he cried. She had seen by this time that it was only his silver cigarette case, and she was overwhelmed with shame at her folly.

"I—it ..." she began, but he had walked off across the room, to strike a match on the nice fawn-coloured wallpaper.

"Shall I serve dinner, sir?" she asked, very softly.

Still he didn't answer, and Mrs. Welley went downstairs into the kitchen. She decided to get his dinner ready, anyhow, and tempt him with it; she left the kitchen door open, partly so that the appetizing smells might rise to him, and partly so that she might hear if he went upstairs to wash. But such a long time went by without a sound that at last she crept upstairs again. Not a sound from the sitting-room; so she stole along the passage and looked in. What she saw did not reassure her. He was standing before the mantelpiece, glass in hand, hat still on the back of his head; he had a rowdy look that shocked her; moreover, he was staring at his own face in the mirror, smiling—at himself. She withdrew in haste.

"I don't know, I'm sure ..." she reflected, in great distress. "Mrs. Lewis ought to be here with him—in his trouble—but—I don't know, and that's the truth!"

For she believed it was the recent illness and death of his little son that had so upset him. He had always been—'nervous,' but never so bad as this, and she thought it was due to the shock. And what so horrified Lewis was the knowledge that he could feel no shock. It was only the old disorder, come back, stronger than ever.

He had in his mind a perfectly clear graph of his life, a heavy black line, on white paper, which he often contemplated when lying awake in the dark. The nadir was during his eighth year. He suffered now, but it was in no way comparable to that torment of his childhood, no agony of his mature mind could rival what had been endured in silence by the child.

He had heard that the first six years of life were of unique importance, but he remembered nothing of them; his conscious existence began for him, on that winter afternoon, when he had been playing with his lead soldiers on the floor of his grandmother's room. He had the most vivid picture of that scene—the drowsy old lady, the warm, bright room, the snow falling outside, the tranquillity of the old house in Waverly Place, a tranquillity pleasantly alive, permeated by silent and invisible domestic activities.

The small boy had just finished a battle, and was counting the enemy dead, before they should be set up, to fight again, when, without warning, the fear of death came upon him, seized him by the throat, so that he could not breathe, could not stir. He sat there among his toys, in a paralysis of body and mind, while wave after wave of nauseating fear swept over him; he could feel the tide of it rise from the pit of his stomach, into his throat, and then flood his brain. Then it ebbed; he had just time to catch a breath, and then it came again. He believed that he was dying, and he believed he knew what death meant. His father had told him that up in the sky, where the stars were, there was neither beginning nor end, simply space, an idea, he had said, which the human mind cannot grasp. But this small boy did comprehend it in an instant's vision. He saw space. He understood nothingness. He was annihilated, for the time of one held breath. That was death, black, undimensioned space.

For two years moments like this had recurred to him at intervals. He never spoke of them, made no resistance; at the first sickening premonition, despair made him utterly passive; all he could do was to wait for the black flood to overwhelm him. Sometimes it came when he was in a room full of people, sometimes in the street, but most often when he was in bed at night. He would feel it rushing upon him; rigid with horror, he would close his eyes and begin to breathe fast, and then, as if a door had opened in his mind, he saw space, black, cold space, with his formless self lost in it.

And each time that he suffered so, he was further alienated from everyone about him. He knew that no one could understand or help him. He felt himself to be alone, the victim of peculiar and unspeakable torments. He was not like other people.

The next year, when he went to school, these attacks grew less and less frequent, and finally ceased altogether. The fear of death left him, though at no time in his life could he look up at the sky at night without quailing, and instead of fear he cherished a monstrous grievance. In school and in college he was a conspicuous figure, an erratic, brilliant fellow fervently hated by many and loyally befriended by others. And always he cherished his grievance. It was not that people did not like him, they did; the trouble was that he couldn't find anyone to like, he couldn't find the perfect friend he needed.

When he had influenza, at twenty-four or so, he began to hate women. He lay in sullen apathy, hating the nurse because she did only what she was paid to do, hating his sister-in-law and all other women who came to see him, because they so obviously regarded their visits merely as episodes in the day. He saw how unjust, how cruel it was that there was no woman especially attached to him, to whom his illness would be of supreme importance. He saw then once and for all how selfish women are.

Unfortunately, he was extremely susceptible to feminine charms, and fell in love often, and each time the same thing happened. He discovered suddenly that this was not the right woman after all; the woman he ardently admired one day he found repellent the next. And this inevitably made trouble for him. It was difficult to explain.

Still in spite of all this, the curve led steadily upward until he was twenty-seven, and then dropped suddenly. His father died then and young Lewis collapsed. This did not seem too extraordinary to other people, but to himself it was amazing, for he had had precious little affection for his father and certainly didn't miss him. Yet he broke down, he could not face the details of the funeral, he could not discuss the settling of the estate; he became ill, helpless, unable to eat or sleep; one arm was paralyzed; his eyes gave him endless trouble. The doctor had ordered him off to a sanitorium; he was there for three months, and made no improvement. Because he was determined not to improve. All his life he had needed this care and attention, this great interest shown in his sufferings, but never before had he been able to get it. He wished to stay in the sanitorium forever.

When at last the doctor told him he would be better off at home leading his ordinary life, he made no protest. He had hated the doctor, though, and never called him in again. Home he went, to suffer for three years.

And gradually that phase ended and he entered upon the most vigorous and satisfactory period of his life. He became filled with ambition; he went into business with James Ouillen, and made a spectacular success of it. He took a flat and furnished it and he found Mrs. Welley. And after two excellent years he was able to make up his mind that he wanted Jocelyn Deering, was able to ask her to marry him and to love her with great ardour for months and months. He had begun to feel safe.

Yes, he had felt safe. There he was, a married man, with two sons; he was making a great deal of money and he was reputed to be a business genius. This domestic life was not what he wanted, but he didn't really care about that, he pretended to Jocelyn that he was cruelly disappointed in her, but as a matter of fact he had been indifferent until the younger child had fallen ill. Then it had all begun again, worse that time than ever before, for he really wanted to recover now, and could not. Somehow he had got outside of life and could not get into it again; he felt with terror that he wasn't real. A horrible insensibility was growing upon him; he couldn't feel. All he could do was to think and think and think, with a sort of fury. He had struggled so patiently, so desperately to get back into life again and he almost had done so when this other child died.

When Mrs. Welley saw him looking into his own eyes in the mirror, he was considering the question of his own sanity. That was, he thought, a lunatic grin. The very fact that no one observed anything wrong about him simply proved his lunatic cunning. Someday he would stop grinning, and begin to laugh, yet with laughter at nothing at all, and then everyone would know.

"Dinner, Mr. Martinsburgh," came Mrs. Welley's voice from the doorway.

"Oh, my God," he shouted, "you and your dinner! Get out! Let me alone!"

Mrs. Welley did get out, and in the bright little kitchen she wept; she could shed honest tears over his incomprehensible troubles, but the man in torment could not even realise the existence of Mrs. Welley. A misfortune, this was. If she had known how to speak, or if he had known how to listen, she might have told him something. She understood more than he did; she understood how to live in peace and innocence. She could have told him that the sin of worshipping false gods is punishable by death.

But no such conversation ever took place. There was no one to point out to him that the god he was worshipping was the falsest and cruellest ever fashioned.

He awakened in the morning very weary, but quite calm and resolute. This could not go on, this should not go on; he was going to put an end to all this to-day.

"Set my house in order," he reflected.

A sort of Spartan sternness filled him. He felt that he had already begun this new life.

"I got rid of that damned Basil," he thought with satisfaction. "And I got rid of that woman."

So he had. He had gone to see her; he had broken down, telling her of the loss of his little son. She, too, had wept, had agreed that this great sorrow must, of course, alter everything. She had really been very kind to him; everyone had—Quillen....

This put him in mind of the fact that there was to be an important conference on freight rates this morning, at ten o'clock, which he must attend.

He could not. The realisation appalled him, but there was no help for it. He could not go to that conference. He went down to breakfast in his dressing-gown, which frightened Mrs. Welley.

"Aren't you feeling so well this morning, sir?" she asked.

"No ..." he said, with a sigh. "I'm—it's indigestion, that's what it is. Indigestion." He suppressed a smile at Mrs. Welley's earnest acceptance of this statement.

"I do hope you won't neglect it, Mr. Lewis," said she. And seeing him in an accessible humour, she went on; she told him about the peculiar and sinister indigestion of old Mr. Depuy, for whom she had once been housekeeper; she was charmed to see that Mr. Lewis was listening to her.

"I'll get rid of her, too," thought Lewis. "I'll make a clean sweep, start all over again."

At ten o'clock he telephoned to Quillen.

"I may be late to that conference, James," he said solemnly. "Don't wait for me. I've got to see a doctor.... Well, I can't tell, James.... Of course it may be nothing much, but—I'll let you know. Thanks, old man."

He got back into bed and lay there, smoking, for an hour or so; then he rose, bathed, dressed, left the house and at the corner hailed a taxi. He gave the driver the address of Doctor Percival on Madison Avenue, descended when they arrived there, and was shown into the waiting room.

The clock was ticking too fast, beating out its life in an insane race against nothing at all. He looked at it with pity.

"A clock," he thought, "should have dignity. It's a sublime instrument for measuring something which doesn't exist. We say the minutes are flying; no sense to that. Nothing is flying, nothing's passing." An alarming idea shattered his languid meditation. "No. But I'm here," he said to himself. "Why did I come here? What do I know about this fellow? Where did I hear of him? I can't remember. Suppose he's an oculist, or a throat specialist? Suppose he's a quack? Suppose he's an alienist?"

A cold sweat broke out on his forehead; he made up his mind to get away at once, upon some pretext. But he could not.

The waiting room was cool, filled with a dusty grey light. There were five or six persons in it, but they made no human sounds; they rustled like dry leaves. The rustle of a skirt, the rustle of a magazine page stealthily turned, a choked rustling cough, a faint, faint sigh, the horrible rustle of a child's bandaged hand moving on its knee.

Then a stiff rustle as a nurse came across the room to him.

"Dr. Percival will see you now," she whispered.

He rose and followed her down a short passage into a room startlingly bright and gay. He stood still, confused as if by a loud noise; the sun dazzled him, glittering on the glass top of the desk, on a bowl of goldfish in the window, on the framed pictures. He imagined that a strong fresh wind was blowing, carrying a perfume of lilacs.

He sat down before the desk and raised his eyes to the doctor. He was a dark, bearded man, tall and emaciated, sitting there downcast, not smiling, testing the point of a pen on a little pad. What was the matter?

"Well?" asked the doctor, looking up; now he smiled tragically, forlornly; their eyes met.

"My God!" thought Lewis. "He's just like me!" And he made a strong effort to speak in a calm and pleasant way, to reassure the poor devil. "I'm a bit below par," he said. "Nothing serious, but my nerves ..."

"Do you sleep well?"

"Yes," said Lewis, boldly. "Very well."

"Appetite good?"

"Very."

The doctor picked up the pen again and examined it. "Poor devil," thought Lewis. "He's afraid of me. Doesn't know what to say."

"Suppose you tell me as definitely as you can just what troubles you," said the doctor, suddenly. His voice had changed, his face too. He was looking at Lewis fixedly; there was a crafty glitter in his eyes.

"He's mad," thought Lewis, shocked and compassionate.

And then such terror seized him that he groaned. That was a symptom, an incontrovertible symptom of a disordered mind, to imagine that other persons were mad. He must at any cost conceal this; the doctor was speaking and he must answer.

He began, with a pained frown, to relate his sufferings. They were exactly those of old Mr. Depuy, as told by Mrs. Welley. Lewis was careful to add nothing, to invent nothing, but simply to repeat the safe facts, with his own peculiar fervour. Mr. Depuy's martyrdom had begun after eating an iced cantaloupe. Lewis said that he had had an iced cantaloupe for breakfast yesterday morning and had not been the same man since.

The doctor gave him a prescription, wrote him a diet list, advised a reduction in cigarettes and more exercise in the open air, and Lewis went away in haste, because he wanted to laugh. He had never felt so vigorously well in his life. He walked down to the Plaza and ate a hearty lunch, beginning with an iced cantaloupe.

Mac Donald was embarrassed; he wanted to get away, but every time he hinted at it Lewis asked him questions which he felt obliged to answer. He heard people in the outer office walking about with sudden freedom, calling 'good night' to one another, even laughing. The day was definitely done; the little room in which he was imprisoned was dark in the rainy twilight.

"Well," he observed, judicially, "I'm thinking it's about time—"

"Wait a minute," said Lewis. "Have another drink before you go."

"I'm very much obliged to you, Mr. Martinsburgh," said Mac Donald seriously. "It is very good whiskey. But I'll take no more to-night, thank you. I'll just be stepping...."

"No," said Lewis. "No. Look here, Mac Donald. I—I want to speak to you. I'm—I'm ill, very ill; I've been to see a doctor to-day, but ... Anyhow, it's not that. I—if I could find someone—if you'd listen to me. You might be able to advise me...."

Mac Donald's voice came cool and deliberate from the darkness.

"I'm no great hand at giving advice, Mr. Martinsburgh."

"Your opinion then," said Lewis impatiently. "Anything you like to call it. I want a disinterested, impersonal point of view. I—I've got to have that. I—I—the thing is, Mac Donald, I think—I think my mind's affected."

"Ah!" said Mac Donald. Nothing but that.

Lewis was aghast. It was as if he had shouted for help, and the fellow hadn't troubled to turn his head. He snapped on the light and stared at him, and Mac Donald endured his scrutiny with a sort of demure modesty, looking down at his boots. A discreet and trustworthy man, he had long been marked by Quillen as one of the most competent masters in their service, a man with something singularly agreeable in his personality, a cool and honest friendliness, a fastidious sense of decorum. But Quillen would have left him to rove the seas as was fitting for him; it was Lewis who had decoyed him here. Lewis had made a trip to New Orleans on Mac Donald's ship and after that he would not let him go. Like the Ancient Mariner, he had known the man predestined to hear his tale. Mac Donald was that man and this was the hour. He must shift his intolerable burden to some other shoulders for at least a little time while his exhausted spirit drew breath; very well; here was the burden-bearer.

"Doesn't interest you, eh, that I'm going mad?" he demanded with a smile.

"It was not lack of interest," Mac Donald explained carefully, "but lack of words in which to express myself, as you might say. But I'm inclined to think you're wrong."

"Are you? Then listen to this." And in a rapid monotone Lewis related the long story of his torment, all the details of his terror, his despair. Sitting on the edge of the desk, clasping one knee in his frail hands, he looked, with his clear and delicate features, his luminous eyes, like a creature immortally young, sent early to a hell which could never mar him.

"And there's no *reason* for all this," he ended. "Physically, I believe I'm all right. And I've nothing to worry about, nothing—that is, except this, this...."

"Nothing to trouble you except this unfortunate condition of mind, as you might say?"

"That's it," said Lewis. "And that's what no one understands. When I say I'm nervous and so on, they all have some dam' fool reason ready-made. I'm overworked. I smoke too much, drink too much, something of that sort."

"Ah, well," said Mac Donald, equably, "that's natural. In a manner of speaking, it is human nature to look for a cause. 'As the bird by wandering, as the swallow by flying, so the curse causeless shall not come.'"

Lewis was silent for a time.

"What d'you mean by that?" he asked angrily. "What are you talking about, anyhow? What cause d'you find for my case? Who's been telling you anything?"

"I'd not be likely to listen," Mac Donald began, stiffly, but Lewis wanted to hear no more.

"All right," he said. "I shan't keep you any longer, Mac Donald. Good night!" He wanted to be rid of Mac Donald now; he was disgusted with him.

"Stolid, thick-headed brute," he thought, contemptuously.

Alone in the office he poured himself another drink and lit another cigarette. A bitter sort of strength filled him. There was no one on earth who could help him; he must stand or fall alone. And he could stand if he wished. His head was clear, all confusion and trouble had vanished, he was not helpless, not in the least, he was in reality stronger and more adaptable than the rock-like Mac Donald, because he was so much more subtle and flexible. Helpless? Not he! There wasn't one symptom of his strange malady which he could not summon or dismiss as he wished.

He rose to his feet, overwhelmed by a new and astounding conviction. He could do what he pleased. He was standing at a crossroad; he could continue along his present road to some unimaginable inferno or he could turn his back on all that and go another way, facing life. He could.

"By Heaven," he said to himself awe-stricken, "I can; I can!" And he didn't have to do anything, needed to make no material changes in his existence; all that was necessary was to turn his eyes from the old things that tortured him toward the new thoughts he had never yet contemplated. He didn't need to be cured; he needed only to wish honestly not to be ill.

He heard a solid footstep in the outer office. Mac Donald. Let him go. He didn't need him or anyone else. The little arrow pointing his destiny quivered toward the new direction. Then panic seized him. He opened the door.

"Mac Donald," he called. Then he fell into his chair, covered his face with his hands. "My God," he groaned. "I—I can't ... I'm ill...."

Mac Donald could not attend to his own affairs that evening. He had to listen to Martinsburgh and later, to take him home in a taxi. As he saw it, this was his duty toward his employer and he performed it faithfully. Fortunately, he did not realize what he was being called upon to do; he did not know that his sturdy arm was supporting this man down the wrong road. Lewis had chosen, after all, to go that way. It was simpler.

CHAPTER ELEVEN

HOPE

Evelyn Bradley sat alone in the breakfast room, enjoying a perfect cup of coffee; the most exquisite moment of her day, this was, sheer joy and indulgence. Later, she would have to sit through other persons' breakfasts and be vigilant and be solicitous, and almost certainly be afflicted with the minor anxieties of the conscientious housekeeper; this moment, however, was her own.

From the window she could look out at the dripping garden, only a strip of it visible in the mist, like a smudged charcoal sketch, wet, with black trunks of trees running up into a blurred margin. The fog horns hooted dismally, but she liked to hear those sounds, suggestive of strange perils at sea and enhancing the comfort of her own pleasant room. She had desired a farm-like atmosphere here; there was an old oak dresser with pewter on it, Windsor chairs, rag rugs. The square table was covered with a fringed cloth of red and white checked cotton, and set out with gay, quaint china and old plate, all twinkling in the light of electric candles; the rich aroma of coffee warmed the soul.

Mrs. Bradley quite appreciated all this. Hers was a ruminative nature, taking its pleasure in the contemplation of this insubstantial pageant. She had affably declined Life's invitation to join the dance, and sat back to look on instead. Naturally, not having tried a measure herself, she had little appreciation of skill in others, nor could she always understand what she saw; but, in compensation, she had never been jostled or trodden on, had never become giddy or weary, so that her excellent disposition remained unimpaired. She was a benign and handsome woman, grey-haired, a little stout, with the negative and unassailable dignity of a family portrait; you might study her and discover any number of fine qualities which would never be tested.

The fog-horns put her in mind of the sea that rolled between herself and her husband, who was in England on business. She wondered casually what he might be doing. She thought of those six linen towels which were so oddly missing. The laundress ...? No, no one ever really stole, nothing ever really happened. Her thoughts went by with muffled step and veiled faces. She did not care to stop or question them; she let them go their way.

Someone was running down the stairs.

"Sillinger," said she. "Mr. Drake's Virginia ham!"

A subdued sort of bustle began; everything was ready for the breakfast of their son and heir, but Mrs. Bradley found it necessary to move about cups, spoons, and plates on the table, and old Sillinger in his soft dully-gleaming boots moved about springily.

Appeared young Drake Bradley in the doorway, a handsome fellow with a dark and sulky face. There was an early morning neatness about him, but he was pale and somewhat irritable. This was not unusual; he might have been up too late the night before; he might have eaten something which didn't agree with him; he might even have had a little too much to drink. Such things did not unduly trouble his mother; she knew this handsome son of hers to be indestructible.

"Morning, Mother," said he, bestowing a hurried kiss. "I'm late." She poured his coffee, smiling indulgently. Drake was plainly out of sorts this morning, but she could not take that seriously, and didn't imagine his having any but infantile and trivial worries.

"I shan't be home to dinner," he said. "I'm going to ... I'm going out."

He wasn't eating much.

"Do try the blackberries," said his mother. "Fresh from the garden— the very first ones."

"No," he answered, with a frown. "No, thanks. They look rotten. I'm going now."

He pushed his chair back and rose, giving his mother the best sort of smile he could manage just then and went out, almost running into Basil in the hall.

"Look here," said Basil. "Got a cigarette, Drake? I've run out of them."

"Plenty up in my room," answered his cousin, still frowning. "Help yourself; I'm in a hurry."

He hastened out of the front door, neglected to close it after him, and Basil stood watching him as he ran down the steps and jumped into the waiting car.

"I'm in a bit of a hurry myself," thought Basil. "But God knows where I'm going."

His aunt greeted him with her usual amiability. He had been here six weeks now, and he might stay here forever without finding any change in her, or in any other member of the family. They had long ago ceased to expect anything else from Basil; they took him for granted, were not impatient, not disdainful, not even sorry for him.

Perhaps Mrs. Bradley would have been sorry for him if she had known that he took good care she should not know. Like everyone else, she knew that Julia had left him something; she knew it was very little, but he was able to dress well, he went about everywhere, he seemed to have whatever other people had. And if he chose to waste his life in idleness, instead of being a financial marvel like Drake or a student of bacteriology like young Sam, well, that was no doubt due to his having been brought up more or less in foreign countries where the American tradition did not prevail.

Never for an instant did she imagine how precarious his situation was; it could not occur to her that he was actually in want.

He was, though. He had at last reached the end of his resources; all possible persons had been exploited. His tailor had grown menacing, the chap at the club who had obligingly got hold of a case of whiskey for him months ago was frankly resentful now at not being reimbursed, and rather public about it; he owed a garage for taxis, he owed the haberdasher, the florist, even the poor devil of a stationer who had supplied him with newspapers in town. He hadn't tipped any of the servants here.

He had nothing left now—nothing at all. He had done all he knew. He had gone about looking for a job, perfectly certain that he would not get one, and the knowledge of his own incapacity was writ on his brow. He had lived on his wits too long; he was like a fox asking for work in a vineyard; he hadn't the faintest notion of working for the good of an enterprise, only for the good of Basil Hazeltine; and this was manifest.

One man though, an old friend of his father's, had gone so far as to say, "Nothing doing now. Come back in October, November, later in the year, if you haven't found anything by that time, and we'll talk it over." And this Basil used as the basis for a lie. He was not given to lies. They were risky, and, moreover, he had a squeamish distaste for them, but this one he told readily, without hoping to gain anything by it. The spectacle of Drake going off every morning to his job was too much for him, so he said he too had a job but wasn't to begin until the autumn.

This made him seem more respectable, but it still further prevented anyone from suspecting his really desperate plight. Well, he didn't want sympathy, certainly not pity; if he was done for, he wanted to be let alone. With his own sort of gallantry he went his solitary way wherever it might lead, alert and ready to seize any advantage, but asking no quarter when hard beset. Indeed, he didn't believe that quarter was ever given. Life, as he saw it, was an affair of sheer caprice. He was simply out of luck; he blamed nobody, not even himself. Lewis had abandoned him. Very well, he had already had as much as he could reasonably expect from Lewis, and that lode was exhausted. Mrs. Huested kept silent; very well, he had lost on that throw, too. He had lost pretty well everything and had small ground for reasonable hopes.

There he sat, talking affably with his aunt; he appeared better dressed than her own sons, because it was his business to look so. He seemed quite cheerful and unperturbed, because it was his pleasure to seem so. It was his quite unresentful belief that nobody cared what happened to him, and he didn't see why anyone should care; so he held his tongue.

With his attentive glance on his aunt's face, what time he responded politely to all she said, he was miles away, in a little inferno of his own. Above all, he wanted to smoke. He had slept badly that night and while meditating upon his prospects he had absent-mindedly smoked his last cigarette. He hadn't one left, and if he bought any he would have to break his last ten dollar bill. He had a superstitious dread of doing that; while he kept the bill, he could hope, he could pay his fare into the city, he could ... Well, there wasn't much he could do with it, yet while it remained intact he could face life undismayed.

He felt a sick qualm at the sight of the food before him; all he wanted was a cup of coffee and a cigarette—and to escape, to be out of hearing of his aunt's voice, to be alone where he could make calculations and smoke. This was the last day; he had decided that when he came to that solitary bill it would be the last day, and the evening before he had had to stand drinks over at the Country Club.

He waited, he talked, he smiled, he waited. Then at last his aunt pushed back her chair and after a decent interval he went upstairs, leisurely, mastering an impulse to run. He opened the door of Drake's room and entered. That room was a storehouse of the things Basil most coveted and needed; it was in wild disorder, as if turned upside down the better to display the possessions of that lucky fellow and his arrogant disregard of them. Basil's neatness was ex-treme; he always put away his own belongings as if he were hiding them; he couldn't afford to lose or to be careless of anything. But Drake had left his desk open, the wardrobe, the bureau drawers; what cared he? Wherever Basil looked, he saw something he wanted. On the top of the desk there was a pile of change, one or two crumpled bills and a gold pencil, evidently forgotten in the process of transference from one pocket to another. Piles of handkerchiefs and silk socks were visible in a half-open drawer, a row of beautiful boots and shoes stood on the floor of the wardrobe; a very magnificent purple dressing-gown was flung across a chair. Hazeltine's dressing-gown was so shabby that he put it into his bureau every morning so that the house-maid shouldn't see it.

He smiled faintly, and crossed the room to the mantelpiece where stood a cedar-wood box, the key in the lock. This box was divided into compartments and filled with Virginia, Turkish, and Russian cigarettes. Basil took one and lighted it immediately, with a sigh of relief. Then, smiling still and not cheerfully, he brought out the pig-skin case Mrs. Huested had given him and filled it. It did not please him to do this. He had no more shaving soap; he had no more writing paper; he lacked a great many small conveniences. Yet he had never borrowed things of that sort; it was against his principles. He had always been extremely scrupulous in minor matters; until this moment. But the case held but twenty cigarettes, and he had only ten dollars in this world. Drake had told him to help himself. Drake wouldn't care if he emptied the box. He was just putting a generous handful of them into his pocket when the housemaid came in.

Naturally, she said nothing, neither did he. She withdrew at once; the whole scene didn't last half a minute. Yet it lingered in Hazeltine's mind for a good many years, the housemaid coming in and surprising him in the act of stuffing his pockets with Drake's cigarettes.

"Very well," he said to himself, "I'll do it. I'll go this morning."

Vacillation was not one of Hazeltine's faults. He tried to avoid such things as he found unpleasant. When he saw obstacles in his way, he turned aside down another path; he was never direct when he could help it. But when he could not help it, when he had to make a choice, he was resolute enough.

He fetched a time-table from his desk and looked up trains; then consulting his watch, found that the next one would get him into the city a little after one o'clock.

"No sense in that," he thought. "I'd only have to buy my lunch. I'll wait and take the two-forty."

This was prudent but not agreeable; he by no means enjoyed lunching with his aunt and his cousin Sylvia and possibly one or two of their friends, himself the only man, while all others of his sex were away attending to large affairs. And he was unusually sensitive to-day. It couldn't be helped, though.

He lit another of those cigarettes and began walking up and down his bedroom. It was a room not very familiar to him, for the Bradleys had moved twice since his first interminable visit, but there was in it a certain queer little desk which his grandfather Martinsburgh had given him on his tenth birthday. He had never had a place to keep it and Mrs. Bradley had taken charge of it; wherever she went that little oddity went also and was put into one of the guest rooms to wait for Basil. Sometimes the sight of the thing filled him with an unaccountable pain; it did this morning. He sat down before it; it was rather low for him now, but he could remember when it had been enormous, august, thrilling his soul because it had a real lock and a real key.

He had written so many letters at that desk, to his mother, his grandfather, to pretty girls, to creditors. There was not a paper in it now, trust him for that, but there were little ghosts of words singing faintly all through it.

He rested his head on his hand and thought seriously of Harold Coons. More than once Harold had said that he would find Basil a job; undoubtedly he would do so, he would enjoy it, and he would give Basil advice, too.

"If there was any other dam' thing I could do ..." thought Basil.

But there was not. He must go to Harold and he must accept the particular sort of job Harold would find for him. It would be something paltry and offensive. Harold liked people to begin at the bottom of the ladder.

"Licking stamps," thought Basil. "At twenty dollars a week. By Heaven, I'd rather lick boots, and be better paid for it. But there's no opportunity for me in the boot-licking line just now. No, I'll have to do this and it'll be my finish."

For he had no illusions about his position. If he were not decently dressed, if he were not available whenever he was needed, he would soon be forgotten, he would get no more invitations, no more little presents and in consequence must live upon the proceeds of his stamp-licking. And this prospect was exceedingly bitter to him. He did not object to work; he wasn't indolent, not fond of luxury, not extravagant. No, what dismayed his just and reasonable mind was this idea of a treadmill existence, working in order to eat and eating in order to work, working without adequate reward. He really wanted so little, only an unruffled, gentlemanly existence among his peers. Well, he had failed, had missed his chance at that, and he could see no way to retrieve his error. He was too moderate for despair, but he was close to it, very close.

Lunch-time came and he went downstairs. Two tennis-playing friends of Sylvia's were there, young married women; to one of them Hazeltine was well known and of no interest, but the other was a stranger and to her this cousin of Sylvia's was a gallant and engaging figure. She was kind to him, and he was very grateful to her.

He was in the hall taking leave of this kind little creature. The car was waiting outside to take him to the railway station. She went so far as to offer him a delicate small hand, burnt a rich tan. He took it, held it, looked down at her with that subtle smile of his....

"Telephone, Ba—sil," said Sylvia, in her sweet drawl.

He went into the library and picked up the receiver. He had an open mind; he hoped for good, yet was prepared for evil. A feminine voice he did not recognise addressed him.

"Mr. Hazeltine? Oh, Mr. Hazeltine! You don't deserve to be spoken to!"

"I know it," said he, with proper humility.

"I telephoned to you twice at your hotel and left word for you to call me up and you never did!" He knew her now; it was Mrs. Garvey.

"Awfully sorry," said Basil. "But I didn't get your messages. If I had—"

"I don't believe you," said Mrs. Garvey.

Basil made mighty civil protestations. When he had received those carelessly disregarded messages from Mrs. Garvey, matters had been very different with him. He did not disregard her now; on the contrary, he thought he would like very much to meet her husband. They were, of course, the wrong sort of people, the sort that in other days he would have thought it imprudent to encourage. But now it was otherwise.

"Very well," said Mrs. Garvey. "If you're really sorry, Mr. Hazeltine, then come to-morrow for the week-end. There's someone here who specially wants to see you."

"I say, Mrs. Garvey! I don't need extra inducements...."

"It's Mrs. Huested!" said she triumphantly. "And I promised I'd get you. You won't disappoint me, will you, Mr. Hazeltine? I'll send a car over for you to-morrow afternoon. Oh, no trouble! We're very near. About four o'clock? Splendid!"

When he turned away from the telephone, he dropped into a chair nearby and sat there for some time, staring blankly before him.

Anyhow, he would not go to see Harold this day.

CHAPTER TWELVE

SAFETY

Hazeltine was welcomed by a Japanese servant and shown to his room. Another Japanese appeared and unpacked his bag; he was served with a whiskey and soda, informed that eight o'clock was the dinner hour, and then abandoned.

He went downstairs, but there was no one about, for Mrs. Garvey had learned that the Smart Hostess leaves her guests alone to amuse themselves. She had read about house-parties of this sort, only it did not seem to be successful here. Her guests would not try to amuse themselves; they drifted about, languid and aloof, and the Smart Hostess knew not how to revivify them. Instead of the jolly informality she desired, the atmosphere was that of a good hotel where people came for a rest.

Basil knew nothing about his hosts, not even current gossip, but after all, his concern was not with them. They and their hospitality were but the background for his own little drama and he was so pre-occupied with this that he was glad to be left alone. He made himself comfortable in a corner of the screened veranda with a small table beside him holding a box of cigarettes, a bottle of whiskey, and a siphon of soda; and he meditated.

It was, he thought, characteristic of Mrs. Huested to want to see him at the Garveys'. She was an important figure here; she would be meeting him on her own ground with Basil at a slight disadvantage. A confession of weakness.... He smiled a little to himself. Very well; let it be her way; he could ...

His revery was interrupted by the appearance of an unknown young man who dropped into a chair beside him and helped himself to a large drink. He was an amusing fellow, with an arrogant, high-bred face, black as a gypsy's. He had been here before and knew the resources of the place, and he talked about the Garveys with a frankness quite without punctilio and without too much decency either. He suggested a ride.

"That's what I came down here for," he explained. "My people have given up horses, you know, and you can't hire a decent mount. So I told Garvey the proper thing for him to do was to start a stable. Bought most of the damned horses for him myself, so you can rely on 'em."

"I've no riding breeches along," said Hazeltine, regretfully.

But the obliging stranger went into the house and found a pair of breeches that fitted well enough and Hazeltine accepted them without question. They rode out to a country club where they had several drinks; then they went to visit a girl in whom the young fellow was interested, and at her house they had more drinks. It was late in the afternoon when they set off homeward, cantering along the beach under a sky still smiling wanly for memory of the sun. A tasteless, tepid shore breeze blew; they moved in an artificial and weary universe; and great languor fell upon Basil, and vague sorrow—he wished to ride forever along the shore of the quiet sea, the hoofs of the nervous little mare splashing in the water. He did not want to return to the Garveys'; he did not want to.... He was mortally tired of problems financial and ethical; he would have asked nothing better than to go out into the wide world with his present companion, a fellow of complete and arrogant carelessness. But his present road led away from the wide world toward a small and sharply defined corner of it, and, for all his discontent, he went forward.

It was dusk when they rode in at the gateway and the lights of the house gleamed bright. The stables half-timbered in an Elizabethan manner and nestling in a little grove of pines were lighted too, and looked for all the world like one of those inns seen on the stage. And Hazeltine's melancholy increased beyond all measure; he was homeless, friendless, a stranger here; where on this earth was he not a stranger?

He was sorry that he had come. He had talked too much, smoked too much, and his bad mood had grown worse. He stood in the deserted little card-room, looking through the doorway into the ballroom and he was disgusted with everything, with everyone.

There was Mrs. Garvey, dancing with feathery lightness; nothing more wearisome could be imagined than her mechanical smile, her airy banter. The other women were quite as bad, if not worse. He would admit that Mrs. Huested was superior to the others, a remarkable woman. She had met him with perfect unconstraint, brusque and off-hand with him as with everyone else; not even a glance of understanding had passed between them. But it was she who had summoned him here, and he had come and the time was not far distant when their affair must be discussed.

He had skilfully avoided her after dinner, and without any excuse had kept out of the dancing. But he was uneasy; he knew this wouldn't do; it was certainly not for him to be elusive and capricious. Neither was it for him to play a man's part, to pursue, to entreat. He must wait, with modesty and decorum, must answer only when addressed.

"I'm sick of it," he thought, rebelliously.

He watched her dancing. She was not a good dancer, but she loved it; her grim Red Indian face was impassive as always, but her eyes gleamed—she was indefatigable, she was terrible. He was seized with panic, hastily swallowing the glass of brandy on the table beside him; he fled, crossed the hall, went out of the door, and stepped out on the terrace. And into a new world. So very still out here; the wide lawn was black, black the trees against the pale sky. Hands in his pockets, he descended the shallow steps and set off across the turf.

He stopped half-way to look back at the house; the lighted windows of the long façade marked the terrace with bright bars, and dim and dainty little sounds echoes of voice and violin were wafted out. He hurried on to leave all that behind.

He turned aside along a gravel drive that led to a jetty belonging to the Casino. There was a bench here under a lamp-post and he sat down in the circle of light. Such a quiet night! The tide was on the turn and washing in a tiny tumult against the jetty, but out beyond there seemed to be no smallest movement of the waters, only dark silence.

He grew restless and getting up, strolled out to the jetty's end. He lit a cigarette, but it tasted acrid in his mouth and he flung it away, to savour instead the rank salt wind; he stood still, staring at nothing, shaken with longing—with longing for some impossible ecstasy, such as no man has ever known, for some fierce delight no heart could endure, for the sight of beauty that never has been.

For a moment he contemplated getting into one of the boats moored there and rowing out, but he knew there was nothing for him on that forlorn sea. Or anywhere else.

"No life," he muttered. "Somehow—I've missed it."

Yet he could not think what he had missed or what he meant by life—or what regret for what lost thing so hurt him.

"I'll go in and get another drink," he thought. "That's what I need."

But as he turned back, he saw a figure standing beneath the lamp on the driveway.

"Why the devil couldn't she let me alone?" he thought, savagely. He would have been willing to behave very uncivilly in order to escape her just then, but nothing would help him; he was neatly trapped out there on the jetty. He came forward slowly. Mrs. Huested did not stir. She had a remarkable capacity for stillness, the practical patience of a spider.

"Do you want to be alone, Hazeltine?" she asked, brusquely.

"Oh, no," he answered, with the falsest sort of politeness. "Alone with you...."

"You were almost ready to jump into the sea, weren't you?" said she. "You've been running away from me all evening. Now you're caught."

Her smile, rapacious and mirthless, exasperated him. In her shimmering dark dress, she had a barbaric, hateful charm, the charm not of beauty but of power. Caught he was and helpless.

"All right," he said. "Now that you've caught me, be merciful."

His tone was very nearly contemptuous. Here on the border of the dark sea, in the monstrous indifference of the bland summer night, he could not hold to prudence and to wisdom. This was his world too; he also had a birthright in it.

"Basil," said she. She seldom used that name for him and it came awkwardly. "What's the matter with you?"

"Nothing, thanks."

Her hand fell on his shoulder.

"There is," she insisted. "I saw it; why won't you tell me?"

"Why should I bother you with my little troubles?" he asked, suavely. He wanted so badly to be let alone, the touch of her hand was almost insufferable, and the sound of her voice. He knew he was behaving with incredible folly; no matter; for once he didn't care.

"You know," she went on, "I've been thinking a lot about you, Hazeltine. And I'm sorry for you."

"Thanks," said he.

"I mean"—she went on, almost gently, "that I think things are pretty hard for a fellow like you."

"Sometimes they are," he admitted.

"Well it's this way, Hazeltine ... You think I care such a lot about money and things like that. I don't. I've got all I want. And I don't judge a man by what he's got either.... I've sort of lived on money most of my life—and I'm damned sick of it. I'd like—I'd like to think I was doing some good to someone...."

He found an extraordinary relish in making no reply at all to this speech. Let her be as angry as she liked; he didn't care.

But she was not angry.

"Hazeltine," she went on, "if you're in trouble—well—you can count on me as your friend. I can see you're worried. Now, look here! Maybe I'm not putting it the right way, but—if it's money that's worrying you, Hazeltine, if you want a little loan ...”

“No thanks, I’ve more little loans already than I’m ever likely to repay.”

She was silent for a long time. Hazeltine listened to the gentle wash of water against stone, stared up at the ambitious swarm of insects flying about the light. He was curiously detached and happy; his heart was light, as if freed from the bitter oppression of deceit.

He was honest to-night; no matter what happened, no matter what she said, he would not pretend, he would not lie.

“Hazeltine,” she said, at last, “you lived in France a while, didn’t you? Huested used to go over every two or three years on business and he used to talk a lot about their ways. About their marriages ... *les mariages de convenance*, you know.... Well, I’ve thought a lot about this. I’m older than you, and I’m not ...” She stopped short; it was not her way to depreciate herself. “You and I—we ....” Again she stopped and Hazeltine was filled with a vehement desire to keep her silent, to prevent her harsh, troubled voice from disturbing the fair night.

“I guess you understand,” she began, when he interrupted her.

“Natalie,” he said, “you want me to be frank, don’t you? Very well, then. I can’t ask you to marry me. I can’t marry anyone. I’m not in a position to do so, and I never shall be.”

Her hand fell from his shoulder and she turned away.

“All right!” she said. “Then *I’ll* ask you, Hazeltine. I don’t care about your ‘position.’ Don’t say anything now. Think it over. No, don’t come with me. Think it over!”

Think it over he did, during a long, restless night, and was up early the next morning. Chiefly, he was astounded by his own rashness and the success which had attended it. For once he had been genuinely careless as to what effect he made, and see what had happened! The grim and formidable Natalie grown gentle, almost humble. Was it possible that he had been employing a wrong method all these years, that he might have got more by being bolder? He was inclined to believe so.

But instead of being pleased with this discovery, he was profoundly uneasy. All very well to be careless and indifferent once, when that strange mood was on him, but to play that part in cold blood when so much was at stake, to assume a new role during the critical third act of his own drama—that dismayed him. In sober daylight he regarded the Basil of the night before with astonishment and a pathetic admiration. After all, there was something rather magnificent in the risk he had taken with his one great chance, he with his lone ten dollar bill. He smiled as he went downstairs.

As is natural to those who rise earlier than the rest of the world, he was at first triumphant, scornfully superior to sluggards. He had breakfast from the buffet all alone and smoked two or three cigarettes on the terrace, and then he began to experience a vague sense of injury, because the silence and the solitude continued. He did not like to be left alone with his own thoughts; there was before him an extremely difficult and painful interview; he had made up his mind as to the general line he would take, but the details he refused to contemplate.

So that he was glad to be joined by another guest, a business-haunted fellow who carried with him a weight of anxiety regarding jute; he was pleased to see Hazeltine and to tell him some of his grave fears and together they swallowed as much of Garvey's Scotch as they thought best. And then, one by one, other people began to come down, and by the time Mrs. Huested appeared, there was a fair-sized group assembled in the fine old hall. She paused at the head of the stairs to look down upon that scene; it was impressive; she could not but admire Annabelle for having got this up. All these well-dressed people, the hall with antlers and other trophies hung about it, the general effect of manorial ease and luxury.... She herself couldn't have accomplished this; what is more, she wouldn't have tried; but she admired.

She looked about for Hazeltine, perhaps to catch him off his guard, and be fortified by seeing something in him which she could properly despise. There he was; she saw the crown of his fair head; he was standing among the assorted dogs which little Garvey had bought, because he knew dogs belonged in country-houses; bewildered and misunderstood dogs, they were, living in anarchy. Hazeltine was playing with a red setter. It was hard to be scornful; when he spoke, his cool, quiet voice was curiously distinct among all the others. He didn't look like anyone else; he was different, with his own peculiar distinction and charm. She stared and stared at his young head. No one like him in the world! She thought of Norris, who wanted to marry her and who in his overwhelming richness couldn't be suspected of the faintest interest in her very inferior fortune—Norris, bald, heavy and dull. She thought of the late Alvah Huested, irritable, preoccupied, harassed to death at forty-five by his passionate money-making; his friends so like him; the loutish youths she had known in her girlhood in a little Minnesota village.... Compare them with Hazeltine.

"I don't care!" she thought. "I don't care if I am a fool."

She descended leisurely, arrogant in her scorn of any attempt to please. Here she was, solidly before him in the light of day, aware that she was not pretty or seductive, that she looked every year of her age. All her cards were played and she was not sorry or abashed. She passed by him with a curt nod, intimating that she didn't intend to trouble him. But he followed her and stood patiently by until she had finished speaking to Garvey.

"Shall we go out on the terrace?" he suggested.

It was a sweet fresh morning, a Sunday tranquillity lay over the country; there were even church bells in the distance, clear and delicate. A good setting for the third act.... The dog had come after him, hoping for a walk. Hazeltine stopped to pat the creature's head, for an instant's reprieve; then he straightened himself.

"I've thought it over, Natalie," he said.

"Didn't take you long, Hazeltine."

"No. You see, it's not altogether a new idea. But ..."

"Well?" she demanded, after a long wait, but still he hesitated for the simple reason that the words stuck in his throat. He did not relish his role as hero.

"I don't believe you realize the position this puts me in," he said, at last. "Whatever I say, you won't believe me. You've already made up your mind that I'm ..." he paused ... "that I'm a fortune-hunter," he added, deliberately.

Her swarthy face grew red.

"Well, what of it?" she asked coolly. "I don't expect you to be madly in love with me. I know—"

"Natalie!" he protested, really shocked.

"I don't!" she went on. "I know you're not. It's what I said, Hazeltine, a *mariage de convenance* .... You can help me to get in with the people I want to know and I guess I can help you in other ways.... We needn't be so damned sentimental about it."

But Hazeltine was too clever to be caught that way; he was obliged to refuse the enormous relief of being honest, and had instead to take a lofty moral position. He said stiffly:

"I'm sorry, but I can't see it that way. If there's no affection or respect between us—"

"Oh, let it go at that!" she interrupted, roughly. "Do you want to marry me, or not?"

"No," said he. "I don't."

He waited to see the effect of this.

"You—" she said. "Well, all right. Then...."

"You'd make my life a hell for me," he continued sternly, "with your eternal distrust and suspicion. You won't believe there's anything decent in me. You think, in fact, you're candid enough to say to my face, that you think I'm the meanest sort of adventurer."

"I don't think like that, Hazeltine," said she, anxiously.

But the hero was adamant.

"That is what you think," he said. "And you'd think it again and say it, too, the first time you lost your temper."

"But don't you see," she said, "it was only because I didn't want to make a fool of myself, Hazeltine? You never said ... I didn't know you ..."

There were certainly tears in her shrewd little eyes; her face was no longer impassive, but wretched, filled with bitter and sorrowful distrust of him, though still more of herself and her own heart.

"O God!" he thought. "I can't do this; I can't!" He bent to pat the dog's head again.

"Natalie," he said. "I'm not much good, you know."

"You'd better let other people find that out for themselves," she answered, tartly. "There's no sense in running yourself down."

He was beginning to recover himself.

"You see," he said, "marriage can't be a 'business proposition.' And if it were, it would be a bad one for you. I've nothing to give."

"Well, I don't expect ..." she began and then she broke down. She walked briskly to the other end of the terrace and leaned her elbows on the balustrade. What could he do but follow her and lay his hand lightly on her shoulder? And she turned, with a look of mute and terrible enquiry, searching his face.

"Basil," she said, "you can't help knowing ..."

But he could not endure this. Something was due her; he would not utterly betray her.

"Natalie," he said, briefly, "I was in love once in my life. I can't be again. Not—like that."

For an instant the affair hung in the balance. For an instant this thing seemed monstrous and impossible to them both. It was Hazeltine who turned the scale.

"Only affection and loyalty, Natalie," he said. "If that's enough...."

It was not enough; he knew it and so did she. But she accepted it.

CHAPTER THIRTEEN

VAINGLORY

Charles Keyes enjoyed making his cousin Basil wait, not at all from malice, but because of his subtle sense of humour. He could have appeared directly his visitor was announced, but he made up his mind to smoke two cigarettes before coming out of his bedroom, and he did so, smiling subtly all the while. He was a dark and slender young man, quite strikingly handsome, with delicate features always illumined by that faint enigmatic smile. Violet Smith had described him as a perfect Madonna type, but that had not appealed to his sense of humour; he preferred what another and more discerning lady had said of him, and to him—that he was strange and inscrutable, smiling at life like a cruel stone god. He felt like that sometimes. He was rather lazy, and very squeamish, so that he had but a small store of worldly experience; he said, however, that he knew life by intuition, and that a man of true sensibility could learn more from reading the poems of Verlaine than the ordinary man would learn from ten years of direct contact with life.

Charles had a good deal of money and very little to do except to keep an eye on it, so that his Machiavellian brain was half-starved and he was glad to see Basil, because Basil always came to borrow money, and that made Charles feel that he held Basil's fate in the hollow of his hand. Also, he liked Basil. They had been a good deal together in their boyhood, and though the Keyes were superb and unblemished and the Hazeltines slightly questionable, and Charles was, so to speak, a sheep and Basil a goat, still they both had grazed in the same pastures. They understood each other.

Through the curtains Charles could observe the patient Basil and he felt sorry for the poor chap. But he did not mean to lend him any substantial amount, or to be very genial about it, for fear of encouraging him. Charles had that profound respect for money found in those who have always had plenty. He did not know, as poor people and shiftless people know, that you can exist passably well with very little of it.

The allotted time having passed, he drew aside the curtains and entered that sitting-room of his, furnished in black and mauve, with a flaming, glowing deep-blue stone lamp as a colour note.

It was a room of bachelor serenity, such as no woman could achieve;

you felt that nothing was going forward here, no hidden domestic processes; everything was completed, the details of existence all arranged once and for all; the establishment was in order and you could simply live about in it. A feminine establishment is always functioning; no matter how cleverly it is devised, the thing is a machine. A *ménage en garçon*, on the other hand, is static, is not a machine but an accomplished fact. In the case of Charles, this exotic background was a work of art.

He advanced and offered his hand with a smile.

"Ah!" said he, "I thought you'd forgotten me."

Basil did not miss the implication, but felt no resentment; he was well-disposed toward Charles, he had no objections to his being malicious, as long as he was malleable. And he was. That subtlety of which he was so proud was as nothing compared with Basil's, for Basil was practical and resolute and Charles was vague.

"Not likely," said Basil, in just the right tone, casual and friendly, neither presumptuous nor servile. Then like all competent borrowers, he came to the point at once; he considered delay in such matters a fatal blunder. If the other fellow knew or suspected what you were after, it was not only awkward but dangerous to waste time leading up to the request.

"Think you can help me out once more, Charles?" he asked. "I'm cleaned out. And I need rather a lot, just now."

"Who doesn't?" murmured Charles.

"It's a bit different this time," Basil went on, "because I can safely promise to pay you back. I've got a job."

"Poor devil!" said Charles. He meant it. He was sorry that Basil had a job; it spoiled him as a type.

"It's not a bad one," said Basil, modestly. "Five thousand a year."

"Five thousand," repeated Charles, repressing an un-subtle curiosity. "Very clever of you, my dear Basil."

The cleverness, however, was Mrs. Huested's. It was she who had suggested this, with a kindly attempt at tactfulness.

"There's a pretty good job out at the factory," she had said. "We've been considering one or two men to fit it, but if you'd like to try it, Hazeltine ... There's no reason why you shouldn't make good. You've got brains and education, you're quick, you'd soon get the hang of it. Ferris is coming out here tomorrow to see me, and I'll speak to him about you, if you want."

Basil had willingly consented, and had thanked her, but with moderation. He understood her intention and though he didn't blame her, though in fact he agreed with her that this was the best course; still, it rankled. She was trying to bolster up her straw man, giving him a job and a salary before she married him. Of course, this was very much to his advantage; he could now pay his debts; he could even buy a wedding present for his bride; he could hold up his head. And still it rankled. A very obnoxious and absurd comparison had suggested itself to his lively mind. He had lately been reading Dumas. He could not forget that conscientious custom of French monarchs in finding suitable positions about the court for those ladies whom they delighted to honour. The notion made him laugh, but without gusto.

And now he had to tell Charles about this, Charles who would not miss any of the fine points.

"I'm turning over a new leaf," he went on. "I'm going to get married this autumn."

"No?" said Charles, raising his fine dark brows.

"Truth," said Basil and was silent for a moment. It was hard for him, it was bitter to go on. He knew what Charles would think, for Charles had no mercy upon outsiders. He respected genealogies; he would be disgusted and shocked.

"Yes," he went on. "It's Mrs. Huested. You remember her, last summer in London?"

Charles lit another cigarette with much deliberation. "I was afraid you'd bungled that," he remarked. "Congratulations, my boy."

And he summoned his man to bring in some of his cherished brandy. He drank to the health of Basil and his bride; he was playfully malicious, he was offensively amused, but certainly he was not shocked. He made the suggested loan readily; he was extraordinarily lavish with the brandy, in the hope of being still further entertained by the spectacle of Basil with his cautious tongue loosened. That, however, was denied him. Basil was silent and moody as he had never before seen him.

For Basil had been obliged to learn something which was very nearly intolerable to him. Charles was not shocked; he didn't think Basil was making an unpardonable misalliance, or throwing himself away. On the contrary, he obviously considered this a rare piece of good luck for his cousin. He expected nothing better from him; nobody would. He might do far worse than this and still not shock anyone. No one expected anything better of him.

He went back to his hotel not very steady in his gait and not very clear in his thoughts. Everyone was against him, everyone despised and belittled him, he was the victim of a great conspiracy to destroy his soul. Nobody was going to be shocked.

Without apparent cause the image of that fellow Mac Donald arose in his mind.

"He'd be shocked right enough," thought Basil. "The idea of a man my age marrying a woman almost old enough to be his mother, just for her money.... He'd think it was a crime."

And the idea of Mac Donald's horrified amazement gave him the most remarkable solace.

He woke up late the next morning and found awaiting him a letter from his betrothed.

> DEAR BASIL [she wrote, in her intimidating hand], Saw F. yesterday and the matter is arranged. Call on him out at the works sometime before the end of this week, telephoning in advance for an appointment. Shall stay here with the G's for a few weeks longer and hope to see you next week-end. In the meantime, wish you would use the limousine. I do not want it here. Telephoned Ellman yesterday to keep it at your disposal and hope you will get some good out of it. Hope you are well.
>
> Affectionately,
> N. H.

"She thinks it wise to use no names," reflected Hazeltine. "As if I were a blackmailer."

But he could not be very much amused. With a serious expression, he replaced the letter in its envelope and the envelope in his breast-pocket. This thing was becoming very real; he really was going to be married, and to Natalie Huested. He was safe now—his adventures, his difficulties at an end; indeed, this marriage now seemed to him not only the end of his desperate anxieties, but a high wall barring the road of his life altogether.

Such melancholy notions as these, however, he attributed to Charles's brandy; they were unwholesome; he set himself resolutely to combat them, and as he ate a sturdy breakfast in the grill-room they began to disperse. He was able to look at the matter with his usual common sense. The future, after all, was no vague mystery; it was a wall that crumbled into dust as you drew near it. What concerned him was the present, and in the present there were undoubtedly compensations.

When he had finished breakfast, he telephoned to the garage, and with affability told Natalie's chauffeur—his chauffeur—that he would want the car at ten o'clock. Then he went to the desk, to that off-hand clerk.

"Let me know when my car comes, will you," he said, off-hand himself. And there was relish in that.

There was relish in life altogether. He went uptown in the superb car, stopped at his tailor's and paid his bill, a part of it, not all; he considered that a poor policy; and had himself measured for a new suit.

"A business suit," he said.

For was he not about to become a business man, assistant manager or something of the sort out in Natalie's factory?

"Yes, sir," said the tailor. "You've got thinner than when you was last 'ere, Mr. 'Azeltine, sir."

Hazeltine smiled, but he was not pleased. Thinner, was he? He remembered the last few weeks.... Suppose Natalie hadn't ...?

But she had, and his difficulties were ended; never again would he have to fill his pockets with Drake's cigarettes. He had money in his own pocket now, and the certainty of more; he had this car, he had a beautiful free day ahead of him. It occurred to him that his state of mind was sinfully ungrateful. He was wasting his blessings; after so many tribulations he had got these things, and he was not properly enjoying them.

The trouble was, that he was lonely. Without being unduly altruistic, he was aware, nevertheless, that he needed someone to share his pleasures, and to admire. It was the natural result of newly acquired wealth. And for him the normal methods of display were barred. He could not go among his peers; he knew only too well what any of the women he knew would think, or even say, if he appeared in this car. He had never yet made himself ridiculous, and he did not intend to do so now; the car was going to emerge quietly from the shadows, just as he himself would unostentatiously become a prosperous business man. People would see him driving about, they would talk, they would speculate, but he would keep out of the way for a little while, establishing a legend.

In the meantime, though, he must have someone. Someone who would not be amused by his condition. Naturally, it must be a woman. Like a homing pigeon, his thoughts flew to Agnes Brian. Never in life would that girl find him merely amusing.

He had certain qualms, which did him credit. But reason soon choked them to death; reason assured him he was doing a thing certainly harmless and possibly kind. He drove downtown to the house on West Tenth Street in a very cheerful mood; his only doubt was, whether he would find her at home. If she were out, he would leave a message for her, because he was determined now to see her again. No one else would do. He knew that in her eyes he was a different sort of Hazeltine, and the knowledge comforted him.

He rang the bell, the same woman opened the door, and according to formula he said:

"Miss Dennison?"

But this time he got another answer.

"She don't live here anymore."

He was immeasurably disappointed.

"Can you tell me where she's gone?"

"No," said the woman and she was undoubtedly hostile, "I can't, but you might ask the other one," she added. "She's up there still."

"Thanks," said he and was off up the stairs with youthful eagerness.

So he came knocking at her door, and Agnes, in tears, in despair, at the most bitter moment of her life, opened the door and found him there. He was like a knight, tall and fair and splendid, kind and strong. He held out his hand, and she took it, and clung to it. She could not speak at all. Her face was dirty and streaked with tears, her tawny hair was pinned up in a great untidy knot, she wore a faded blue linen smock covered with ink stains. And she was so lovely.

"What's the matter?" he demanded.

She shook her head mutely.

He took her other hand and the fingers were tied up in a clumsy bandage. He held it very gently.

"Look here," he said, "get ready and we'll go out somewhere to lunch. You're ..."

"No," she said. "I can't. I can't go out. She won't let me."

"Who won't?"

"The landlady," she answered, with a sort of fierceness.

She had turned her head aside and her face in profile had an austere and mystic beauty that stirred him profoundly.

"Then let me come in," he said.

For a moment she hesitated.

"I don't know," she said sombrely. "It's a bad time for you to come."

And it was, a very bad time for both of them. Yet he did go in.

CHAPTER FOURTEEN

CHIVALRY

The trouble with living in Bohemia is, that it is such a little and a helpless country, its frontiers so ill-guarded. So that no Bohemian can live out his life without some time wandering across the boundaries into the world of burghers and princes, or, still worse, without meeting at his own threshold some stranger from that world. And there is such pain in that. The glance of a stranger is black magic in Bohemia; the gay little room becomes squalid if a stranger sees it, laughing love turns maudlin or cruel, the bright things grow tawdry. No; Bohemia ought to be an island, very far from other lands, very hard to enter; the immigration laws should be drastic, for the climate suits only a few; so many sicken there and die.

That is what happened to Agnes's mother. She was trapped in there and she died of it, and her child, bewildered and terror-stricken, was spending all her young strength to escape.

"You don't know how I hate anything frowzy!" she cried. Hazeltine agreed with her, but he never quite understood. He was well enough acquainted with a sort of backstairs life; he had been in the trenches, he had seen violence and evil. But Bohemianism lay beyond his orbit; he could not even imagine the Bohemian point of view.

He found Agnes that day trying to clean and set in order the rooms she had shared with Miss Dennison; it was plain to him that she was trying to do the impossible, and at top speed. She was washing and scrubbing everything. The floors were wet, and all the chairs, the pictures were down, the books tied up in neat brown paper parcels.

"If I'm put out on the street to-morrow morning," she said, passionately, "no one's going to find one speck of dirt or dust here."

Agnes had not been born in Bohemia; she had drawn her first breath in a New York hospital.

"I love hospitals," she once told Hazeltine with fervour, and it was true. So had her mother. That ill-starred lady had found the ten days spent in the maternity ward the happiest in her married life; she and her baby had been quiet and clean, and upheld by the inhuman discipline. No visitors were allowed; and Mrs. Brian felt that Heaven could offer little better than utter cleanliness and no visitors.

Not that she was unsociable. On the contrary, she had always enjoyed people until she had become a debtor. But when Agnes grew old enough to know her, she had long ago ceased to be hospitable. A knock at the door probably meant a bill, and if it happened to be a friend, that was quite as bad, because of the things that friends must see in the various places she called home.

A gallant woman she was, with a cool and quiet sense of humour and a dignity never conquered. She had been a Miss Phillips of Vermont, of a scholarly and poverty-stricken family. She had wanted to go on the stage and she had done so with invincible dignity; she had attended a dramatic school in Boston and had at last got a very small engagement in a truly majestic company, touring with a Shakespearean repertory. She had no great talent or great beauty, but she was intelligent, she carried herself splendidly, her voice was pleasing, and in person, tall, dark, a little gaunt, with her deep-set glowing eyes, her firm lips, her humour, and her good-breeding, she had a charm of her own. She might have done well, but she had almost at once married Augustine Brian. *He* was charming enough in those days, but Agnes could remember him only when he had grown heavier, sadder, destroyed by a singularly ineffective remorse. He used to come home and sit hunched in a chair, brooding, tears in his eyes.

"Agnes," he would say, gloomily, "your mother is an angel." Even at a very early age Agnes had seen the incongruity of this. She could remember herself, certainly not more than ten years old, standing before him, a terrible little creature, her brow furrowed lion-like beneath the round comb which held back her tawny hair, her little ardent face quite pale, denouncing him. He never tried to defend himself. She would call him a beast, which was the worst word she knew for many years, and he would answer, sadly:

"And don't I know it myself? I'm not worthy of her. She's an angel." He was perfectly serious about this; he admired his wife and his child, and he thought it tragic that he could not feed and clothe and shelter them adequately. But he was unlucky; he had, he said, been born unlucky and what could he do? He was an actor at the time of his marriage and a fairly good one, but very soon after, he was visited by an attack of his incurable malady, a disease which he called 'getting discouraged.' He was helpless in the grip of this thing. He had to give up the stage and go back to newspaper work, which was another of his many trades. He used to get discouraged at that too, and announce that he could surely do better somewhere else. Then they would all go somewhere else, to find the same harassments and confusion. Dingy furnished rooms which they took just for a week, and lived in for months, third-rate boarding houses, debts and humiliations and anxiety—that was their life.

At last his wife and child used to stay in New York when he went somewhere else to do better. They were secretly glad when he had gone, glad to be alone together. They lived, Beth Brian and her daughter, like the two angels he called them, in a hidden corner of hell, shutting themselves in, reading to each other, sewing together, eating their meagre meals, living a finicking, impossible existence. They used to laugh and to be amused by the world outside, but they were frightened all the time, and secretly glad when Brian came back, because he opened the door to the world.

He always came back riotously happy, and even Agnes could not quite resist him when he was happy. He would bring friends with him, and great paper bags full of food which he cooked as no one else could cook; he would be so joyous and so noisy and funny with his songs and his jokes. And though his friends sometimes offended, he never did; there was a queer, touching sort of innocence about him, always, and an unfailing gentleness.

But this failed to soften his child's bitter resentment against him. Her love for her mother was the very breath of her life and she saw her mother slowly worn down by those miseries which she could endure but not conquer. She remembered her mother standing in the doorway of one of their miserable rooms, talking in her restrained, dignified voice to an insolent landlady; she remembered a day when her mother had a headache and admitted that she would like a cup of tea and there was no tea at all, and no money to get any.

And she remembered her mother going away to the hospital. She packed a battered little bag, putting into it three cotton night-dresses, a very clean hair-brush, with the bristles worn down to a sort of stubble, a comb, an old flannel dressing-gown, and a toothbrush.

"She hadn't any slippers," Agnes told Hazeltine.

Five years had not effaced the agony of that. Her mother had gone with no slippers, back to the hospital where she had been so comfortable before. And the monstrous thing, the thing her poor passionate, abandoned child of fifteen could not bear, was the mother's strange resignation; she had been quite peaceful and happy.

"It's better like this," she said. "I've been wrong. I've been a coward about you, my darling. You're very strong ... and so good, so good, my baby. Nothing can hurt you. God will keep you, my baby. You'll be happy."

Agnes told Hazeltine that her mother had said she would be

happy.

"I hope she doesn't know," she said. "Happy ...!"

This was on the occasion of his third visit and their friendship was so far established that he could put his arm about her and her head rested on his shoulder. On his first visit when he had found her getting ready to be put out on the street, she had told him very little. Once he crossed the threshold, she had become curt, almost rude; she said she had to get on with her work, and that if he stayed he would have to come into the kitchen. So he followed her to the kitchen, a lugubrious little cell, and without another word Agnes got down on her knees to finish scrubbing the floor. There was bravado in this, there was defiance; she wished to efface the memory of her glance and her handclasp; she wished to demonstrate that Hazeltine's presence was unimportant.

It was a transparent enough device, and it touched him. Obliging he had been all his life and often from good-humour as well as from policy. Often he had done little things for people without expecting any reward. But the impulse he felt now was entirely new. This was pure benevolence; this was chivalry. It made him very happy. He wanted to offer financial assistance to the absurd and endearing girl, to pay the rent and set her free. He could not, because he had no cash to spare; what he had borrowed from Charles Keyes would have to last him indefinitely, but he really did want to offer.

"I'll start that job at the factory to-morrow," he thought. "By Jove, I will!"

Thus was Hazeltine, like many another man, inspired to great effort by a woman.

"Look here," he said presently, "you'll have to go out, you know, to get your lunch."

"I don't have to," said Agnes. "Missing one meal isn't likely to be fatal to me."

He was silent for a time, watching her. There was no aura of domesticity about Agnes scrubbing a floor; she worked with a sort of fierceness, as a captive sailor might scrub the deck of an enemy ship. She had a fine, free vigour which he thought admirable. But the spectacle was distressing.

"Look here," he said, "let me do that for you."

"You!" she said, and stopped work to stare at him.

"Even I," he said with a smile. He fancied there was a tone of scornful incredulity in her voice, but it was not so. "I'm a bright lad," he went on, "honest, willing, and strictly sober. If you'll give me a chance—"

She got up and faced him, drying her hands on the smock.

"I'll stop," she said. "Let's go into the other room. Have a smoke?"

From the pocket of that smock she brought out a packet of cigarettes.

"I'm afraid they've got wet," she said. "I'm afraid—I've been kneeling on them."

"Thank you," said Hazeltine, taking one.

Their eyes met; she essayed a doubtful smile, but Hazeltine did not even try.

"Oh, don't smoke it," she cried. "It's horrible. I've got some more." She wanted to go past him, but he was planted in the doorway.

"It's not horrible," he said. His steady blue eyes were fixed on her face for a moment. She returned his glance resolutely; then she turned away.

"Won't you come out to lunch with me?" he asked.

"I can't. She'd be in here like a shot, the moment I'd gone, and she wouldn't let me in again."

Hazeltine had grown quite pale.

"By Heaven, I've got to do it!" he thought. "I can borrow a bit more from—let me see ..."

He was thinking intently when Agnes spoke again.

"I could pay that rent if I wanted to," she said. "I've got the money. But I don't think it's fair, and I won't."

How pleased was Hazeltine to hear this!

"Do you think the landlady's swindled you?" he asked.

"Oh, not Mrs. Johnson. She's got nothing to do with it. It's just—" She stopped, "Anyhow it doesn't matter," she said.

Not until considerably later did she explain anything of this to Hazeltine, and she told him very little then, only that she and Coralie had had a row, and that their financial affairs had got pretty badly mixed up. And even this she tempered by telling him how good Coralie had been to her.

By patience and by putting two and two together he discovered, weeks afterward, that Agnes had scrupulously paid to Coralie her half of the rent and all other bills and that after the row Coralie had gone away, taken all the money available, and leaving the bills in their original condition. He believed he could understand how such treachery would affect a girl like Agnes, but he never did understand. He thought it a necessary though painful step in her education, and it wasn't; she learned nothing by it; she was only dazed and appalled. She was not a fool; she had not needed to be taught that there were bad people walking this earth; she had known that, and expected to meet them. But what she did not comprehend, then or at any other time, was that bad people could do good, that cruel people could be kind.

Coralie had been kind to her.

"You don't know how kind she was," she told Hazeltine. "When Father said he was going to marry again—I was younger then, you see—I—made an awful row about it. Because for him to put someone in—in Mother's place.... I said I'd never speak to him again, and I never have. He's out in California now, with that woman.... He writes sometimes, but I never answer.... And Coralie was so wonderful then."

These words gave Hazeltine no adequate idea of the situation. After her mother's death Agnes had spent two miserable years in a convent school; then she came home, to the usual sort of place—two little furnished rooms, and to the usual confused and anxious life. She had decided to reform her father. She had learned typing and shorthand and got a job, and once in possession of a salary, she had become frightfully dictatorial. She had tried to bully her father into some sort of order; she made gallant efforts to pay their debts, and to economize; she hurried home after office hours to prepare vegetarian meals, cold, austere, and frugal; she looked after her father's clothes and his health and his general welfare; every pay-day she put two dollars into the savings bank and she showed him, by means of pages and pages of figures, that in a few years time they could take a trip to Europe.

Augustine Brian appreciated all this; he admired his child and desired to please her, and he sometimes thought he could have endured this existence if she had known how to laugh. She never did, and never cried either; not in his sight, anyhow. When he felt it necessary to talk in a melancholy and remorseful way about his wife whom he really missed, Agnes was very curt and unkind. And for gaiety, she offered him Coralie and her circle.

Coralie was at that time known as Mrs. Greville and had a husband whom she later divorced. He was a literary man, not exactly a writer, you understand, although he did write. Coralie was also literary; she was a reader in the publisher's office where Agnes worked, and she had literary people always coming to her flat. Agnes used to go among them, awed and delighted, and several times she brought her father.

Augustine Brian did not like Coralie or her circle, or the dainty, informal snacks they served. He had been brought up in another tradition; he was a robust man, he would swallow Ovid with gusto, but he did not like divorce. And when they talked of modern poetry, he meant only Francis Thompson and neglected any poet who might be present.

His life with his dutiful and severe child was not a comfortable one. He endured it for nearly a year, and then he found a new wife. And Coralie got Agnes. They took a small flat together; they began in a high-minded way with Coralie as a mentor, they read and they went to concerts.

That did not last long. Coralie grew tired of being a mentor. She had the temperament of an actress and she wished to rule not through superior wisdom, but by the spell of her personality; she had done that all her life and the management of young Agnes was child's play. She was, to Agnes, a woman embittered by terrible experience; she was cynical; and when she was for a moment gay and tender, that was the woman she might have been. Agnes used to argue with her about being cynical and Coralie would say that the friendship of Agnes almost restored her faith in life. And through all these vicissitudes Agnes felt that she was the hardy, practical, coarser-fibred one, shielding and protecting the wounded Coralie.

The row had come out of a blue sky, senseless and horrible as a nightmare. Coralie had suddenly accused her of 'caring for' Richard.

"But I don't!" cried Agnes. "Not one bit! I've been telling him so for weeks and weeks."

"You mean to say he's been making love to you for weeks and weeks?"

Agnes had tried to explain that it wasn't lovemaking; it was only a long and serious argument in which Richard had endeavoured to convince her of the advantages of marrying him, and she had explained why she would not do so. But Coralie did not believe her; she had said things—monstrous things—that changed the world.

The trouble was, of course, that it was Coralie's show and that while she had been acting with all her skill in the centre of the stage, Agnes, the audience, who should have been engrossed in the spectacle, was acting a little drama of her own in the outer darkness. So Coralie, in a very genuine rage, had quitted the scene.

The only substantial part of this nightmare for Agnes was the bills. Coralie's fury and her words were incomprehensible, but the bills were a tangible insult which she could resent. Every week she had paid to Coralie her half of all their expenses and now the landlady told her that no rent had been paid for three months.

Agnes was entirely determined not to pay this. As she told Hazeltine, she had money enough, because for three years she had been saving laboriously, dollar by dollar, but she would not touch those savings. Augustine Brian's child had learned the value of money.

Frank to bluntness in other matters, she had a New England shamefacedness in regard to money. She was reluctant to mention it; it seemed indecent. And to Hazeltine, who would blithely confess to anyone that he was 'cleaned out,' this was incredible. It was another of these things he never understood. He had no idea how hard it was for her to tell him even the little she did tell, no idea how touched she was by his concern.

He had appeared to great advantage that first day. "Then if you won't come out," he said, "let me bring something in for lunch?"

Rather grudgingly she consented to that, and while he was gone she cleared off the kitchen table, because in spite of all her efforts to escape from Bohemia, she was still hampered by paper-bag ideas; she took it for granted that Hazeltine would bring something in a paper bag.

He returned carrying a neatly wrapped cardboard box; he was followed by the chauffeur, carrying two larger boxes, and in these boxes was everything necessary to a proper lunch, even a table-cloth. It was by no means an ostentatious meal. Hazeltine had gone to a second-rate restaurant for it and he had not failed to consider the cost of each item; he was not proud of the result. He thought, indeed, that this was the least he could do, for he knew nothing whatever about paper bags and kitchen tables.

And Agnes saw that. She realized that here was a creature of finer clay.

He said he wanted to see her again and Agnes appointed to meet him at noon the next day in the Library at Forty-Second Street, to give him her new address. He was there, waiting for her; he was really there, tall and splendid, with his steady glance, and his wonderful smile.

"I've made arrangements with Mrs. Johnson," she said. "I'm going to stop on there for a while."

The arrangement was that Agnes had parted with her precious savings so that she could keep those rooms that had overnight become dear beyond measure to her.

"Good!" said he. "Now let's have lunch."

"I've had mine," said Agnes. "But I'm not going to the office to-day. It's no use. I can't type until my hand's better. So I thought perhaps you'd come to tea this afternoon."

"What's the matter with your hand?" asked Hazeltine.

"Oh, I whacked it with a hammer," said she.

He held it in his own, a sturdy little hand, a pretty hand; he looked down into her face with that smile that came readily.

"Of course, I'll come," he said.

He knew very well how foolish this was; someone might see him and tell Natalie and there would be the devil to pay. Yet there was such a charm about this little affair, such a sweet and innocent glamour. He had never before met a girl like Agnes and he felt pretty sure he would not meet another. Why not see her just once more? His days of freedom were nearly over, and this little interlude would be a thing good to remember. He went that afternoon.

And regretted it. She had made preparations for him; all trace of yesterday's packing was gone and the room was in immaculate order; she herself was severely neat and sleek. And the tea.... Such a finicking little-old-maid tea! A lace cloth on a round willow table, and set out on it an array of dainties, two kinds of sandwiches, three kinds of sickly cakes and, most intolerable, a silver cake-basket in which she had laid a small doily and on top of it a row of cigarettes. No, never had he seen anything so pathetic. Compassion destroyed him.

He knew, none better, how to make love with perfect discretion, but for this he needed a partner who was also discreet and able to appreciate finesse. Agnes did not know this game. She had no skill at all; only her stiff-necked pride.

He consoled himself as he went away, by remembering that he had really said nothing at all, absolutely nothing. Neither had she. But he was also obliged to remember the look on her downcast face, that sorrowful and bewildered look. He had asked her to come out in the car on Sunday. That, of course, was impossible; Sunday belonged to Natalie. He would telephone and postpone the ride forever.

But in the end, he decided that he couldn't do that. The cigarettes in the cake-basket.... Agnes with her little bandaged hand....

She had just finished a supper composed of the remains of the tea when he came back. She could scarcely believe that he had returned.

"Oh," she cried. "But I didn't ... Come in, won't you?"

The room seemed so very quiet in the lamplight, and she herself so terribly alone.

"Look here," he said. "About Sunday ... I had no business to ask you...."

She would have scorned herself if her glance had wavered, if there had been the least unsteadiness in her voice.

"Well," she said quietly. "There's no harm done. I'll ..."

"You see," he went on, "I'm engaged to be married."

Not his fault, was it, that she should read into his tone so lofty a meaning? He indicated in no way that he was martyr to honour; that was her own notion. He didn't even imagine the preposterous ideas she had—that he was forced by honour into a loveless marriage, that he was marrying to save his family or his best friend or the good name of some unhappy woman. Naturally, he could not suspect such romantical ideas, but there were other things he did suspect. He knew very well that the tone of this interview was cruelly wrong.

"So you see," he said, "I'd better not come again." That dear smile of his, that strong and tender voice....

"You can always come if you want," she said, in the same quiet way. "I'll always be your friend."

It was *her* suggestion. It was she who established that unique friendship. Not his fault, was it? He did come again. He knew he could trust her, and trust himself; good friends they were; he called her his little pal. There was not a hint of love-making again. When he had time to spare, he came to see her; he brought her flowers or a box of chocolates, and they sat in the lamp-lit room, talking in a quiet, friendly fashion.

Yet in spite of his scrupulously honourable behaviour, Hazeltine sometimes entertained the strange fancy that he was doing very ill indeed.

CHAPTER FIFTEEN

HAZELTINE EMERGES FROM THE SHADOWS

This friendship was a solace to Hazeltine in a period of considerable difficulty and embarrassment. Agnes would, no doubt, have been glad to know it, but he felt it impossible to explain. There was no one in whom he could confide; he had to endure his anxieties alone, and though he was accustomed to this, they weighed heavily upon him.

Squeamishness, that was his trouble. He could not make up his mind to explain Mrs. Huested to his world. The car and the chauffeur did him no good at all, because he could not bring himself to use them with candour. He thought he would tell Mrs. Coons first; he went there to dinner and Dot gave him an excellent opening.

"Saw you going down Madison Avenue yesterday in the most gorgeous car, Basilisk," she said.

And instead of taking the advantage of this he said, "Yes.... Belongs to a friend of mine"—with the sigh of one debarred from any authentic gorgeousness.

He went out to see Natalie, but he went by train, for he did not wish even the Garveys to see him in his splendour, and he was too discreet after he got there.

"What's the matter with you, Basil?" Natalie asked. "Don't you want to see me alone?"

"I'm thinking of *you*," he answered sternly. "D'you want all this pack gossiping about you?"

This awed her for the moment, but did not satisfy her, and he knew it. He got back to the City and he provided a sound reason for not coming out the next week-end; it was only a breathing space, though. He received a letter.

> DEAR B.
>
> Am sending you a fountain-pen. It is the best I could buy. Hope you will like it. Advise you to go out to the factory and see Ferris without delay. He has been expecting you for some time.
>
> Have not yet told the G's about us, but I guess they suspect. What do you suggest? A girl I knew back home gave a lunch and had a pie with ribbons. Each guest pulled a ribbon and on the end was a card with her name and the man's and a line saying. 'Now the secret is out.' It is damned silly, but it seems better than just standing up side by side and announcing it. Let me know what you think.
>
> N. H.

This was unmistakable. He was obliged to face the situation now, to take matters in his own hands, or very dreadful things would happen. He could not even smile at the thought of the pie; it was a symbol of a greater thing; it appalled him.

The chief thing, of course, was to save his face, to appear as little ridiculous as he could. He must never smile himself or give anyone else occasion to smile; he must be earnest, quiet, but not heavy; obviously, there was no use even pretending that this was a romance, but if he managed properly, it need not be a farce.

"She'll want a church wedding," he thought. "She'll very likely make a point of that, and want my friends there, with hers. I'll have to put her off that somehow."

He reflected and at last he decided to go out to the Bradleys' and with all possible tact make his aunt aware of the existence of Natalie Huested. Mrs. Bradley had always been indulgent to him, for the sake of old times, for the sake of his mother, and perhaps because she liked him a little. She might accept Mrs. Huested; if she did, life would be pleasant for Basil; if as the husband of Natalie, he could still exist among his own people. He felt pretty certain that it could not be so, that Mrs. Bradley could not swallow Natalie, but he hoped. And if the worst happened and he had to spend his life among Garveys, still there were compensations.

His interview with Charles had taught him a lesson. He did not expect the Bradleys to be shocked. They, like Charles, would take it for granted that he was fulfilling his natural destiny; no doubt, it would seem to them entirely characteristic for Basil to marry a middle-aged and barbaric widow with money. But for all his cynical resignation, the thought caused him a certain pain. The Bradleys belonged so intimately to his past, to a time which he fancied had been somehow better than the present. They had known him as a boy, and if this marriage seemed to them the natural end of his career, then there could never have been any promise in him. Then he was not even a sinner; he was merely a victim of destiny.

He let the chauffeur go for the afternoon, because he did not relish the idea of the man's conversing with the servants in his aunt's kitchen, and he drove the car himself, very carefully, for he had neither an owner's nor a driver's license. It was the fairest, brightest day, the august benevolence of the harvest season lay over the country, the grain stood high, the apples were ripe in the orchards, the car sped along smooth highways, and the wind with all those sun-warmed perfumes blew against his face, and he became happy, in his own way. He lived just in this minute, in the sun, under the blue sky, on the open road; he was happy because he was young and healthy and alive in the summer world; he was very innocent in his happiness as a child is, or a tiger, because he did not think, did not remember, did not hope.

His face was still bright with that careless joy when he turned in at the gate. Sylvia was sitting alone on the veranda, pleasantly doing nothing. The sound of a motor made her look up; the car came along the drive, stopped, and Basil got out. Basil had been driving that superb car!

Sylvia politely concealed her surprise.

"Hello, Basil!" said she.

"Hello, Sylvia!" he answered. He was glad that the first one to greet him in his new splendour should be this kind and uncritical girl. One of his own people....

"Just in time for tea," said she. "But what a simply marvellous car, Basil!"

"Not so bad, is it," said Basil cheerfully. "I'll have a wash and brush-up first, if you'll wait."

So he ran up the stairs, two at a time, still in that joyous humour; even the sight of the room where he had suffered such grievous anxiety cast no shadow over him; he whistled as he moved about. The sun was shining in at the west window; it seemed to him that he asked and needed no more in the world than that.

Then, his usual neat and immaculate self, he descended. The narrow hall had once run directly through the house, but after a new dining-room had been added in the back, the hall stopped there, and if the door was closed, it was dark. It was dark now; he could dimly perceive two figures there, and heard his aunt's voice, so he greeted her.

"Oh, Basil," said she affably. "How nice.... And here's an old friend of yours.... You'd still recognise Basil, wouldn't you Jocelyn?"

"Even in the dark," came her clear light voice. She had moved toward him; he saw her white-gloved hand extended, but he couldn't, he dared not touch it. He could not speak.

"No," he thought. "No.... God in Heaven! I can't bear this.... I've got to get away. I can't see her. O God! I've got to get away."

Because Jocelyn had gone. There was no Jocelyn. If she came to life.... It was a thing so intolerable that he had not even feared it. She must be forgotten, or he could not live. He could not believe that she stood before him, that he heard her voice, that the anguish was not in the forgotten past but in the present still to be endured.

"Let's go into the library," suggested Mrs. Bradley, a little amused by these two silent figures. "And tea at once, please, Sillinger. Isn't it wonderful to have Jocelyn back again, Basil?"

He was obliged to enter the room with them; he must speak presently, must look at her. But not yet. He was aware of Sylvia passing him a box of cigarettes; he took one, and lit it; a deep inhalation steadied him a little. He turned toward Jocelyn, with a smile.

"It's been ..." he began, but the smile turned to a ghastly grimace, his throat contracted. For she had not changed, not in these five years. And nothing of what he had felt for her had changed either.

Mrs. Bradley found this one of the most fatiguing half-hours she had yet endured in the course of a very conscientious existence.

Jocelyn was always a little exhausting; she was so quick, so fervent; her slight physical endurance seemed strained to breaking-point. There was something tragic in her eagerness, as if she were hurrying to live ten years in one, trying to compensate herself for some dreadful loss of time. One could never feel at ease with her, poor, lovely creature.

But Basil should have done better. It wasn't like him to be so trying, sitting there without a word, starting nervously if you spoke to him, his face so pale, so strained. After all, thought Mrs. Bradley, he couldn't have cared so very much; he certainly hadn't appeared heart-broken when Jocelyn got married.... Oh, this was too much! Before poor Jocelyn had half-finished her first cup of tea, there he was, asking her to come out and look at the sunset, looking at her, oblivious of everyone else. Of course, Jocelyn agreed; she always agreed.

Side by side they descended the veranda steps. The sun had gone, but as if only for a moment, the sky had an expectant brightness; it was still day, with the day's fresh colours all about them.

"Let's go down to the Point," she said. "Unless you'd rather go somewhere else ...?"

"I don't care, Jocelyn, I'm never bound anywhere, or getting anywhere. You see, I'm just the same."

"Oh, but you're not! When I first looked at you, you seemed so different. I thought I'd cry over it."

"Not worth the trouble, dear girl.... You haven't changed, not in any way."

There was not, as he looked at her, the faintest shadow of five lost years upon her; the same glamour was there, all the old enchantment.

"If things happen to you, then I think you don't change," she said. "Because every sad or terrible thing makes you more and more your own self.... But if nothing happens, I suppose you can quietly develop your—soul, and grow."

The long string of beads she wore clinked faintly against her metal belt, making a tiny music, like an echo from an Indian bazaar. She was dressed in dark, delicate clothes, a wide hat, with her own grave elegance; she was patient, she was quiet, there was in her no coquetry; yet what other woman had such power to stir the heart?

They went on silently, down a road which they had walked many times together, and whether he was in torment or in ecstasy, he did not know. Of one accord they turned aside across a stony field, and came out upon a little spit where the wind blew gaily. The waves broke farther out, against a sand-bar, and reached their feet subdued; the water was dull under the pallid sky.

"I'd like to hear something about you," he said.

"But haven't you heard? Didn't anyone tell you, Basil?"

He flushed a little. He had heard a good deal about her separation from Lewis.

"Yes," he said. "I think I understand."

"Oh, I knew you would," she said.

He was silent for a minute, struggling against speaking these shameful words. But he could not help it.

"And yet," he said half-aloud, "you've come back to him."

"That? You mean that?" she said, in a voice that startled him. "You mean Lewis?"

He tried to look at her, but her face was averted. "What else could I mean?" he demanded. "What else was there to hear? Some other ...?"

"My children ..." she said. "I had two children and they both died." Said it without emphasis, a simple statement and it made no particular impression upon Basil. He began some expression of sympathy, but she was not listening.

"My two children," she went on. "Jackie ... he was so little, only a baby.... I thought he was getting better. I knelt down beside him and he moved his tiny hands in such a sweet, funny little way. I thought he smiled at me.... I thought he'd just gone to sleep, until they told me. I had him only one year, one year...."

"Jocelyn, dear girl, don't talk about it, you'll—"

"Let me talk," she cried, "or I can't live anymore. The other one, my little Lew.... I had him with me four years, every minute of the four years. He slept beside me in a little crib, and I could hear him breathing in the night. He never moved if I turned on the light to look at him.... Oh, he was such a silly little baby! He wouldn't stir away from me. If anyone else looked at him, he'd run to me and hide his face in my skirt, with such a scowl! And he was always clinging to my hand. I thought—I thought I loved him so much that he *couldn't* die...."

Suddenly her fingers closed on Basil's in a fierce grip.

"Oh, Basil, Basil! He's gone! Both gone, both my little babies.... I'll never see them again, or hear them. Basil, how can I bear that? I've tried. Tell me something to think of, to say to myself, so that I can bear it...."

But Basil was silent. And it was not pity that kept him silent; it was a monstrous and terrible anger. She was cheating him; this agony of hers was treachery toward him, something she had endured alone, which he could never share.

"I'm sorry," he muttered.

Her grasp on his hand relaxed, as if she were reluctantly abandoning him. He knew well enough how cruelly he had failed her; he had given not even an imitation of what she sought. Yet still he was concerned in a violent mental effort to find the right words, not to comfort her, but to bring her back to him.

"Did you have friends with you?" he asked.

"Oh, yes," she answered, with polite readiness. "Everyone was very kind. I liked being in England. I had wonderful friends."

He let her go on talking at random, because she could not endure silence; he listened with jealous interest; now and then the name of some unknown man, casually mentioned, gave him a pang of fear; he asked artful questions, traps for her to walk into and betray herself. But he learned nothing.

They walked back to the house. She asked him about himself now, in her old way, with the immeasurable good-will and sympathy she had for everyone, and above all for him. She had quite recovered herself; there was not a trace left of that sudden passion. But he remembered it, and it filled him with a great fear. He could not understand; only he knew that some terrible thing had happened, some irreparable loss had befallen him.

CHAPTER SIXTEEN

NO USE BEING A FOOL

The worst thing he had ever done was to forget Jocelyn. Deliberately, for his own comfort he had denied her; he would not remember her, because the memory brought pain, and he would not suffer.

He remembered telling Natalie that he had been in love once. Had been? What had put an end to it? Nothing. Rejected, buried under lies and lies it had always lived, the one true thing. He had had no capacity for friendships, no understanding of family loyalties and affections; there was but one human creature he was able to love. And he had chosen to forget her.

And in punishment, that love, once so innocent, tender, and homely, born to give him incentive for daily life, had become now a thing ignoble and terrible. He could not love Jocelyn with tenderness now; only with a passion which he knew to be impious. He wanted to escape from her, to forget her again; yet any place where she was not was barren as death to him; he could endure the sound of no other voice than hers, the sight of no other face.

"You'll stop for dinner, won't you, Basil?" asked his aunt.

He answered, "Thanks, yes," and fancied he spoke as usual, but it was not so. Mrs. Bradley was uneasy.

"I hope Jocelyn won't be silly," she thought. "It would really be much kinder not to encourage him."

Basil had not the air of a man greatly encouraged, though; on the contrary, in spite of the anxiety and annoyance which his singular behaviour caused her, she could not help feeling sorry for him. She had never liked him so well, either, because he had never before seemed so humanly unreasonable.

He was watching Jocelyn, who sat across the table from him. Why was she so bright and lively? Not for him. That look she gave him, warm and eager, was for everyone else too; no matter who spoke to her, she listened with the same thirsty air, as if expecting a sublime revelation in the next words.

"I'm included," he thought. "Simply another fellow creature, that's all."

She turned toward Leavitt, a neighbour who was there for dinner.

"No," thought Basil. "That smile was different. She knew she was going to find Leavitt here. O God! I can't bear this!"

But he had to bear it, had to sit through that dinner, to answer when he was spoken to, and to behave as he had been trained to behave.

After dinner they went out on the softly-lit veranda for coffee, and presently Sylvia and her brother went on to a dance; there were only his aunt and Leavitt and himself, and Jocelyn. He saw Leavitt looking at her; he saw her with Leavitt's eyes, a beautiful woman with something exotic and maddening in her passive grace. She was all in black, with no jewels; her soft hair was black; her long, shadowed eyes, her mouth sensitive and wide had, he thought, a curious smile hovering over it. Five years? What had she done, what had she felt in five years? She was changed, he saw it now. He could not understand her now.

"Suppose we run over to the club," suggested Leavitt. "There's some sort of show on, I think."

"How nice!" said Mrs. Bradley. "Unless you're too tired, Jocelyn dear?"

"I'm afraid I am. But please go without me."

"Oh, no, Mrs. Martinsburgh," said Leavitt. "I'm sure we—er.... But suppose we take a little drive?"

"I was going to suggest that myself," said Hazeltine.

Leavitt's mild, bespectacled face turned toward him, a little affronted.

"I have my car here," Hazeltine went on. "You can take Mrs. Bradley over to the Club, Leavitt."

"Your car?" said Leavitt, genuinely surprised. He had no intention of being offensive; it was no great matter to him whether he took Mrs. Martinsburgh for a drive or not, but he had known Hazeltine for a great many years and he was interested in this idea of his having a car. But Hazeltine chose to see a deliberate affront. It seemed to him a thing of odious significance that Leavitt should be surprised. The role assigned to him was that of beneficiary, never that of owner or giver. But he would not have it so; this time Jocelyn should see him as any man's equal.

"Yes, my car," he said truculently. "Any objection?"

"Simply that I was the first—" Leavitt began, when Mrs. Bradley intervened.

"Come, Paul," she said briskly, "you may take me over to the Club."

Her authoritative, almost severe manner put an end to further discussion; indeed, she was not pleased with this diversion.

"I'm surprised at Basil," she thought. "As for Jocelyn, she'd let them tear each other to pieces and never say a word.... Poor soul! I suppose she's constitutionally unable to, but, at her age ..." She sighed. "I know there are going to be all sorts of complications," she thought.

Basil drove the car up a lane, and stopped. "So we can talk," he said.

But neither of them had a word to say. It was a still, cool night, very dark; the stars gave no light to the black sky; the breeze that blew stirred the thick dust in the lane, sending it in a patter like rain upon the broad-leaved bushes by the roadside. A night without perfume, without heart.

"Jocelyn," he said at last, "what are you going to do now?"

"I don't know, Basil," she answered, simply.

"But you—you're going to see Lewis?"

"Yes," she said, with the same readiness. "He wrote to me. He asked me to come back."

"And, of course, you came," he said bitterly.

"You'd always come back—to anyone—wouldn't you?"

"If I could."

"What do you mean by that? If you could? Do you mean that ...?"

He stopped, well aware of the gross impropriety of his questions. No matter, he had to know ... "that you couldn't be reconciled to Lewis?"

"I haven't seen Lewis yet," she answered, faintly.

"But, good God! You must know," he cried angrily. "What do you mean to say to him when you do see him?"

"Please, Basil ...!"

"Oh, I know it's outrageous and all that sort of thing, but ... you've always been honest with me. And merciful. You must see now.... You used to understand."

"Won't you please try to understand a little, too, Basil?" she asked.

"No, not any longer. I can't. I want to know. *Can't you see?*"

She was silent for a time.

"What is it you want me to tell you, Basil?" she asked at last.

"Why you came back."

"That?" she said, as if in sorrowful surprise. "I thought I had told you.... I came because ..."

"Oh, don't say because Lewis wrote you a letter, again," he interrupted.

"No.... But it was Lewis's child, too. He'd remember—all those little things. He'd feel ..."

Her voice broke, but Hazeltine remained unmoved. He could not believe her now, this woman whom he had once trusted with all his soul. She was wilfully evading him. Did she love Lewis still? Had she ever loved him? She was not the same. What had changed her?

"If there's someone else," he thought; "if she'd only tell me, I could bear it."

For the one possibility he could not face was, that she loved no one. Let it be any living rival, and he could still hope.

"Basil," she said, "do you know you haven't told me anything about yourself yet? Or what you've been doing. I've thought of you so much—"

"I wonder if there's one thing you've thought of," he said. "What I said to you the last time we met ...? I dedicated my life to you, didn't I? I said if ever I did anything worth doing it would be done for your sake."

"Oh, but, Basil my dear!"

"No, wait until you hear. Do you know all I've been doing these five years? Nothing. Absolutely nothing, my dear girl. I might as well have been dead. And now ..."

"Oh, please," she entreated.

"And now," he went on, "I'm going to get married. A woman much older than myself, for her money, of course. Just what you'd expect, isn't it? She gave me this car. She wants me to 'have everything.'"

"Dear Basil, don't!"

"I want you to know. Somehow it never entered my mind that I'd have the pleasure of telling you, face to face, what a damned fine fellow I am."

"Basil, what does it matter? I'm not God, I'm not your judge. Only your friend."

"The best thing I could do," he went on, "would be to cut my throat. Only, you see, I haven't any dangerous weapon. Nothing but a safety-razor. Everything in my life's so very safe. No risks for me."

"Basil," she said, in a voice so low he bent to hear her better, "is it my fault?"

"Your fault?" he said. "Jocelyn.... Your fault?"

He turned away his head; he thought that pitiful enquiry terrible beyond endurance. His anger, his base suspicions, all his injustice toward her came to crush him now. His worthlessness her fault?

"Basil!" she said.

He did not move or answer, and in her anxiety, she reached out in the dark and took his head in her hands, turning it toward her.

"Won't you tell me?" she began.

He seized her in his arms and held her close to him—only for one instant; then with a sigh that was like a sob he let her go.

"It's ... I can't talk," he said.

He started the engine, and backed out of the narrow lane, drove back to the Bradleys'.

"Good-bye, Jocelyn," he said.

"But you'll come back, Basil?"

"I've never gone away," he answered. "I've always been here, just where you left me."

For the first time in his life he knew the anguish of confusion. Not one thought, not one emotion was clear to him. He didn't know what he wanted or what he feared. He drove home along the dark road, and his own thoughts seemed streaming off into the air behind him, born and dying in the dark.

He left the car in the garage and walked to his hotel and with the cessation of swift motion, the tumult in his brain began to clear.

"There's nothing but Jocelyn," he thought. "The other things don't matter. Jocelyn's come back.... I lost her before, and now she's come back. And now —but is this another chance? If it is ... God, let it be another chance! Let me try once more, God! I'll make a clean sweep of all this mess; I'll start all over again. Only let this be another chance!"

But it seemed to him that God would despise such unreason; he felt that he must convince God of his own desperate need and of his good faith.

"I haven't had anyone who cared what I did," he explained, "but if I can have Jocelyn ... I'll be different. I'll start all over again. She's so good, so innocent and kind and good—"

He entered the hotel and as he went to the desk for his key, the night clerk gave him some letters and a package. He put them into his pocket and went upstairs in the lift.

"I'll write to her," he thought. "I'll ask her to come away with me. I don't care where, and she won't either. I'll work for her—"

He unlocked the door, entered his small, close room, and turned on the light.

"She loves me," he thought. "She always has. If I'd ..."

He had a bottle of whiskey hidden in a travelling bag, and he brought it out now, feeling quite sure he was never likely to need it more than at this minute. He swallowed a drink and poured out another which he set on the table. It was very hot in the room; he took off his coat, but felt none the better.

Something was wrong; his hand shook so; he was so strangely obsessed with the idea of haste. Everything must be done now, at once; he must begin now, abolish the past, face a new future.

He took the letters and the package from his coat pocket and sat down by the table. Naturally he opened the package first, and found in it an appalling gold fountain-pen with his initials engraved on it. A costly gift, and she had made no foolish attempt to depreciate it; hadn't she said it was the best she could buy?

He sat down on the edge of the bed, staring at the pen. He was not yet incapable of being hurt. This hurt.

"I'll have to write to her," he thought. "At once."

He swallowed the second whiskey and poured out a third. His shoulders began to shake with laughter not at all mirthful.

"There'll be no pie," he thought. "No pie with ribbons. What am I to tell her? Just that Jocelyn's come back?"

Even the thought of her name sobered him. He stared before him, with a faint smile.

Jocelyn come back, the gentle fervent Jocelyn, who moved in a little clinking music, like a strayed idol, dismayed in this world, but so valiant, so eager.

"I'll make her happy," he thought, "I'd give my life to make her happy."

He meant that. It is the impulse of the soul to offer sacrifice, to cry, in the black hours—let it be me, Lord, and spare this beloved one! My life for this life. Mother for child, lover for lover, friend for friend, with every one of these comes the passionate moment of dedication; my life for this other's happiness. And Heaven will have none of this. Heaven rains down a hundred petty joys, a hundred hundred compensations, until the austere sacrifice is left in the willing hands, a sweet perfume to the nostrils, not of God, but of the frustrated donor. Do they not tell how God gave to his one son the perfection of sacrifice? It is the great gift, the great privilege, only for the elect. For the humble multitude there can be no sacrifice. It is not accepted.

Hazeltine was then ready, more than ready, to give all he had, to forget what had been always sweet to him, to face all that he had dreaded for Jocelyn.

"I'll write to Natalie first," he thought. Because he could not think as he wished to think of Jocelyn until that was done. He fetched pen and ink and sat down to the table.... He could not help remembering so many painful things; he could not help realising that this course was suicidal. All those debts, the loan made by Charles, the solid obligations toward Natalie ... it was flagrant dishonour. No matter, let his honour be thrown upon the sacrificial pyre with everything else he had.

He picked up the pen and after very little hesitation began to write. It was a beautiful letter; indeed, when he read it over, he felt that it was very much too beautiful and tore it up in disgust.

"The least I can do is to be honest with her," he thought.

He tried again. Boldly and briefly he told her that the only woman he had ever really cared for had come back and that he could think of no one else. He could not insult her by asking her pardon, only he hoped that she would know it was because he held her in such high esteem that he was so candid.

He read this letter over, twice. And the thought that had been in his mind, in ambush, sprang out and confronted him.

He had left a loophole in that letter. He had suggested that if she did not object to a badly damaged heart.... He grew a little pale, he did not like the thing's aspect.

What was the sense in giving up Natalie unless he were sure of Jocelyn?

He put on his coat, caught up his hat, and went out in a sort of panic. Not much swagger about young Hazeltine now.

He walked for a long time, and when he went back to his room, he had made up his mind as to what he should do. He wanted Jocelyn. He would give up everything in the world for her, gladly, and think it well lost. There was nothing too painful or difficult to attempt for her sake, nothing he would not endure. All his love was for her; he had given none of it to any other living creature; he could not.

She was the first to whom his self-sufficing spirit had turned, years ago; from her he had learned what little he knew of companionship. His love for her was an old and deeply rooted thing, indestructible.

But if he could not have her, if he must be bereft of the one great thing, then he would cling tenaciously to the little things. That was the best he could do.

> Jocelyn [he wrote], I love you, Jocelyn. Nobody but you, ever. Only tell me what you want. Whatever you say, I'll do. If you will come away with me, I'll leave all this sorry mess I've made of my life and begin again your way. If you want me to wait, I'll wait. If you want me to go away alone, I'll go. Only tell me, Jocelyn. I love you so.

And when he had posted that, he knew a little peace.

CHAPTER SEVENTEEN

APOTHEOSIS OF LEWIS

Mrs. Bradley and Jocelyn were dining alone in a tranquillity they both enjoyed. They might be as inconsequent, as aimless as they liked; there was no one to be amused or annoyed.

All the light in the room came from four shaded candles on the table. Sillinger stood quietly breathing, thinking, and living his own life at the buffet. He made no noise about it; had he made the discovery of Archimedes, he would have uttered his eureka only to himself. It was a hot night with a fitful wind; the wide low windows framed a picture of clouds streaming past; the sea at the foot of the garden ran high.

The two women spoke in low voices.

"But it was very odd of Lewis," said Mrs. Bradley. "After writing you a really beautiful letter like that, not to be home when you came all the way from England."

"Mrs. Welley said he'd been wretchedly ill and out of sorts, and really needed a little rest...."

"He might have left some word for you, my dear."

"I know ..." murmured Jocelyn. "But sometimes it's so hard for Lewis to do some simple little thing like writing a note...."

"Sometimes it's so hard for Lewis to think of anyone but himself," Mrs. Bradley remarked, tartly. "He's like his great-great-grandfather Martinsburgh. My father often used to tell us about him. He was a young man at the time of the Revolution. A very handsome and brilliant man. He took the side of the Colonists, but in the middle of some campaign—I really don't remember which—it came into his head that he wasn't appreciated, so he went over to the British. And they didn't appreciate him, so he shot himself."

"But Lewis—"

"My dear, I knew Lewis before you were born. He had that diabolical Martinsburgh clever selfishness, just as Julia had, and Basil and Lewis have. They're all alike."

"But I don't think Basil and Lewis are alike."

"Well, they are," said Mrs. Bradley.

You could say things to Jocelyn, because it was impossible to prejudice her against anyone; it was like reciting things from the prayer-book about smiting your enemies; it was rather agreeable and not at all malicious.

"They *are* alike," she went on. "Both perfect egoists. Of course, Basil's younger, but he's travelling the same road. He's going.... Mercy! Sillinger.... What ...!"

The long curtains had blown out suddenly into the room, brushing a vase of flowers from a small table with a disconcerting crash. Sillinger briskly repaired the mischief and looped back the curtains, but Mrs. Bradley could not regain her former calm.

"Sometimes I have such a queer feeling about this house," she said. "As if I'd lived in it before."

This was not the first time she had made this remark; her husband had said in reply that it was too bad her ghost hadn't retained possession of it, because it had risen so enormously in value. It had in former days been an unpretentious little farmhouse and only very recently a gentleman's highly desirable country residence. The house had been entirely remodelled and the grounds laid out and a breakwater built, all frightfully expensive in spite of Mrs. Bradley and the architect combining to obtain an effect of simplicity. They still called it a farm, and to be sure there were chickens and two cows and a fruit orchard and a vegetable garden somewhere about the place, maintained chiefly for the benefit of the disgruntled Swiss who had them in charge. Mrs. Bradley sometimes went to inspect all this, but she was perhaps not so rustic as she imagined. Country nights made her uneasy.

And it was so strangely quiet to-night. Sylvia was in town, with a friend; Drake had gone out; her other son was off at college, and her husband was at least three thousand miles distant. She loved Jocelyn, but somehow Jocelyn wasn't comfortable. When you looked at Jocelyn, you were obliged to believe that sometimes unpleasant things really did happen, to some people.

"I'm afraid it's going to rain," she observed. "And Drake's out in that open car.... Jocelyn ...what was that?"

"I didn't hear anything, dear."

"I do! What a horrible, ghastly sort of night! I wish somebody would drop in.... Sillinger, I think we'll have coffee in here. And can't you give us more light?"

As if by magic, the room was dazzlingly bright, too bright. Mrs. Bradley appeared pale and as if startled by the effect of her words.

"And please close the windows," she added.

But that did not keep out the sound of the sea tumbling against the breakwater, and the desperate struggle of the neatly rolled awnings outside in the rising wind. Sillinger brought in the coffee and withdrew.

"I've never known the house so ..." Mrs. Bradley began. "There! Listen, Jocelyn! Isn't that just like that old spinning wheel up in the attic whirring?"

"It's an insect," said Jocelyn. "One of those cricket things."

"But listen! No, don't listen! Try to talk, dear. I'm hideously nervous.... Oh, mercy! What was that? Someone running?"

"Only the rain beginning, dear Mrs. Bradley."

"It does sound like someone running, doesn't it?"

Jocelyn rose and drew her chair close to Mrs. Bradley.

"Do drink your coffee, dear," she said. "I think it will do you good."

"As a rule— Jocelyn, there is someone on the veranda!"

"Someone come to call," said Jocelyn.

The bell rang sharply and Sillinger went down the hall, fleet and quiet. Mrs. Bradley laid her hand on Jocelyn's arm.

"I know it's a telegram," she whispered. "Or a cable. Sillinger, is it a telegram?"

"No, madam," said Sillinger, firmly. "It is Mr. Martinsburgh."

Lewis followed at his heels and as Sillinger drew aside, he stepped into the doorway. And his appearance seemed to the perturbed Mrs. Bradley as strange as anything she had ever imagined.

"Lewis!" she cried.

"Did I startle you, Aunt Evelyn?" said he, startled himself by her odd expression. "I'm sorry."

"Yes, you did, rather," she answered.

She spoke with something less than her usual affability, for, to tell the truth, she was not glad to see Lewis. Such a very awkward situation, this sudden meeting between a husband and a wife who had not seen each other for three years, and then had parted for reasons never explained.... Suppose Lewis should make one of his scenes?

"And Jocelyn couldn't stop him," she thought. "She wouldn't even try. If someone were murdering her, she'd wonder if it wasn't her own fault."

But Lewis had begun to speak in a gentle, ordinary voice.

"I'm very sorry, Jocelyn," he said. "Naturally, I'd meant to be at home when you got there. But I was up in Canada, on a little fishing-trip, and my guide broke his leg, so I couldn't make it. Mrs. Welley told me you'd come out here...." He turned to Mrs. Bradley, "It's been a very long time," he said.

She was seized with compunction, because he looked so weary, and because he was behaving so well.

"Don't let it be so long again, Lewis," she said. "Sit down and have coffee with us."

He pulled up a chair next to Jocelyn, and she smiled at him in exactly her usual way. There was not a trace of constraint or awkwardness in either of them.

"You're looking very tired, Lewis," said his aunt.

"It's age," he answered. "I was like a prehistoric animal in a glacier. I was beginning to think I was indestructible. But now—I'm beginning to thaw. Now I'm growing older."

She discerned that this preposterous statement was intended for Jocelyn, and she waited in vain for Jocelyn to reply to it. Only silence followed.

"Mr. Quillen must have missed you," she went on, brightly.

"He'll have to get used to it," said Lewis, with a smile. "I've finished with the making of money. I'm going to use what's left of my life for living."

Mrs. Bradley was always sorry to hear anyone talk in that way about living; invariably, it meant something a little immoral. People who said they were really going to live, women who wished to live their own lives, men who boasted bitterly that they had lived.... Too bad Lewis was contemplating that.

He looked capable of alarming things. His fair head rested against the back of the chair; with his thin face, his luminous eyes, he had an appearance of fierce austerity, so that the cigarette between his lips seemed shockingly incongruous, like a saint smoking. His preposterous words recurred to her—a prehistoric monster in a glacier, beginning to thaw.... With some sort of apology, she left the room, and was very glad to go.

He had written that beautiful letter and here she was. He was not sorry; simply, he had lost interest in the affair; he was thinking of the plan he had made of buying a little camp in the Adirondacks and living there, summer and winter, like a hermit. That was the life which suited him; up there in the woods he had been calm, strong, and happy. He was calm, strong, and happy now, but he did not want that strength assailed. He wanted so badly to be let alone and nobody ever did let him alone.

"Jocelyn, dear girl," he said, gravely.

She raised her head; her eyes were brimming with tears, but she smiled at him.

"Dear Lewis ..." she said. "Oh, I'm so sorry ...!"

Something came back to him, then, some memory of her old kindness and loyalty, and of the happiness he had known with her before she left him. Her dear face, when he came home in the evening, her happy pride in him when he had talked unusually well at the dinner table, her great anxiety to understand what he wanted, her innocent bewilderment when she could not understand.... Always kind, always.... She had never blamed him, only wondered, in dismay and sorrow, why she had so utterly failed. Before she left him—better to say, before he had driven her away, for he had done that. When their child was ill, he had ceased to love her—when he had seen that awful, blank look on her face, that look which ignored himself. He had told her it would be better for both of them if she went away. And, of course, she had gone, with that other child that she loved more than she loved him.

"They've both gone now," he thought. "She has no one now." And now he could pity her in her desolation. She had come to him for assuagement, poor lovely Jocelyn. She had no one but him.

No one but him. The idea filled his heart with a strange and violent tenderness. Very well; he would be everything to her; he would be wise and loving as God. He would dry her tears and comfort her heart; she had only him, but that should be enough.

"Jocelyn," he said, slowly, "haven't you suffered enough?"

"Enough?" she repeated, startled. "Are there any bounds or limits to that? My children ... Lewis.... No. I don't want to speak of it. I can't...."

"The only suffering *is* in the bounds and limits," he said. "All the pain is in struggling. Don't you know that?"

Her dark brows drew together, in her effort to understand.

"No," she said. "I don't know anything. That's what I've always longed for—a great loud tremendous voice, shouting out the truth.... There's no still small voice inside of me, telling me what to do. When I was little, I used to cry with envy of these men in the Old Testament who heard God speaking. I wanted that so dreadfully! I'd have obeyed any commands—only I couldn't make them up for myself. I wanted to be told, and I never was. I've prayed, Lewis.... If I knew, if I were sure—that they were just gone, ended, forever and ever. I'd try to bear it—waiting to end myself. But I don't know.... I'm waiting and waiting ... because I think—there's some word ..."

She bent her head, very low; her slender, bare arms were stretched out across the polished table; she was motionless, supine, without hope or spirit.

Then Lewis began to speak. She lifted her sorrowful head; her eyes widened. Here was the voice for which she had longed in her agony, here was the accent of truth. On his emaciated face was the look she had sought in vain, the serene and lofty expression of spiritual grace.

Suddenly it vanished. He fancied that his soul collapsed inside him, like a pricked balloon, and he could not speak another word. He was not especially disconcerted; for, after all, he had said enough; but he was anxious that Jocelyn should not discover his disintegration. He looked at her and he marvelled at the effect of his words.... But he had meant it all; he had explained to her the very meaning of life. It eluded him now, though, because he was so tired, he had talked so long.... A yawn rose in his throat, which he stifled.

"No," he thought. "No. I mustn't spoil it. I've helped her.... How did I do it? I can't remember just now.... No matter."

He rose, impatient to be gone. He stooped to kiss her forehead, and crossed the room hastily; in the doorway he turned for a moment, and saw her still sitting there, lost in thought—of his words.

He went up the stairs, it was very late; everyone else was in bed. The sleeping house was filled by the great drumming of the rain and the rush of the wind. It was not like a storm at sea, he thought, for there you were moving, going forward under the care of those competent fellows who never slept. No one in charge here, the house stood helpless in the tempest.

He turned on the light and shut the door, and alone in the bright room he tried to recapture the mood of serene strength. He tried to feel again that compassion and tenderness he had felt for Jocelyn. Desolate, beautiful Jocelyn.... He had given comfort to her sorrowful heart by his words—no, not his words; it was what he himself had felt that had comforted her.... He loved her, with a sublime, unselfish love....

"But that can't have gone!" he cried to himself, in anguish. "That was real.... When I see her again, it will come back."

He looked in the mirror, to see what manner of man was this. And the image was horrible to him.

"Not older ...!" he thought. "My God, I can't grow older! I'm immortal, I can't die. I can't change! All that.... It did no good. I'm just the same.... If I were blown to pieces by dynamite, every little molecule would go on with the same devil's dance. No ... No ...! Mac Donald said once that if I'd find something to take me out of myself ... But, merciful God! ... if I take *me* out of myself, there's nothing left ...!"

He flung his arms up in a wild gesture, and the flashing of his hands across the mirror startled him.

"This won't do," he said, aloud. "I thought ... I'm afraid I came back too soon.... But I felt ... I was sure—up there in the woods.... No! It was so! I'm tired to-night, that's all. In the morning when I see Jocelyn again ..."

He knew that he did not want to see Jocelyn again.

"But I do!" he insisted to himself, in terror. "As soon as I saw her— I loved her. Why shouldn't I love as well as anyone else? I do. I'm very sorry for her.... I'm thinking of her, I tell you; not of myself! Not of myself.... Have I any self to think of? After all, is there any sort of integrity? Any one thing that's always there—a soul? The cells of my body change.... But if there is a soul, it can't be very variable; it would be something you were born with and died with.... This body isn't the body that used to be me; it has died and been reborn time after time.... If you change, what happens to your soul? What is it that changes? Here is an animal which is now not what it was five minutes ago. Something else but the body changes.... That's what tortures so.... A fellow like that damned Basil ... he's amorphous, shaped by his circumstances.... There's Mac Donald—one solid piece—immutable...."

He lay down on the bed fully dressed with the lights still burning. And the most curious fancies came to him. He thought that God was going about the world with a hammer, testing people. He picked up Mac Donald between His thumb and forefinger, and chipped pieces off him, but when he was set down, Mac Donald went off, none the worse, at his brisk, sober gait. Then He took up Basil, but Basil was made of gutta-percha; his bland, handsome face lengthened out into the most comic grimace; he didn't care, he couldn't be hurt.... When it came to be Jocelyn's turn, she dwindled at the first tap of the hammer into the tiniest little figure, and ran off, her hand over her eyes....

Then he himself was picked up; he looked up into God's face, but could not catch His eye ... he wanted to explain, but could not speak.... The hammer descended and struck him very lightly on the crown of the head, and at once he flew into a million sparks, whirling off into the darkness. He certainly had no head now, yet it ached so terribly that he cried. And the tears fell steadily, in long, straight lines, while the fiery sparks that were himself whirled among them. It was very beautiful; someone was watching it with calm delight. Once you get outside of yourself....

He heard Jocelyn's voice, very far away, speaking so faintly and sadly.

"But now, you see, you can't help me; oh, why didn't you stay together? Oh, why didn't you stay together, so that you could help me?"

Her voice troubled him.

"I will!" he said, from the middle of the superb display. "Wait a minute ...!"

He commanded the rain of tears and the whirling sparks to stop, and suddenly they all rushed together with a frightful impact....

He opened his weary eyes. The night was gone and the rain and the wind; the dawn was breaking. Another day had come, to be piled on top of the great load of other days weighing on him.

CHAPTER EIGHTEEN

HAZELTINE GETS AN ANSWER

It seemed good to Hazeltine to walk from the railway-station to the Bradleys' this afternoon, in order to prepare himself for what he was about to receive. The humble lover, who had asked only to know the will of his beloved, was, nevertheless, unable to wait until she made it known, and had come to demand an answer from her. He had waited three days in a blank and reckless idleness; he had not gone to see Ferris at the factory, he had not answered Mrs. Huested's letter, he had seen no one, gone nowhere, had tried to stop the current of his life until he should hear from Jocelyn.

And never once had he been able to imagine a satisfactory reply. What could she say? That she, the compassionate, the merciful, would betray and abandon her husband? Yet neither would she betray and abandon Hazeltine. She had never yet been deaf to anything he asked, never yet sent him away uncomforted; she would not now. She loved him, with a love he had never understood but had always counted upon as one counts upon the rising of the sun. Once, only a little time before her wedding, she had offered to give up Lewis and to marry him; he had refused then, for her sake; but he would refuse nothing now, because his love had changed. Honour or dishonour, ecstasy or wretchedness, he did not care now, so that she shared it with him. He had learned to live without her, and then she had come back; he had forgotten her, and she had made him remember; and now he could not and would not forget ever again, or live without her.

And he could not live with her. The thought of it was a fantastic impossibility and he knew it. He had no hope, yet he clung to his blind faith in her. With careless cruelty, he had tossed his fate into her hands, leaving to her gentle spirit the monstrous responsibility for his life. He was, and he knew he was, taking a shameless advantage of her love, but he did not care. She was all he had, or had ever had. She would not forget that; she would not abandon him, now that he had given his life to her. God knew what she could do, but she would surely do something for him; she would not send him away to live without her forever and ever. Not his fault that his love had changed, had become a passion without tenderness and without hope; it was his great misfortune and hers.

It was a three-mile walk, but he covered it rapidly with that gait of his which was so deceptively nonchalant and desultory. Autumn was on the way, but not yet come; the countryside was still in undimmed green, fresh and tranquil, but the grain stood almost ready for its life-giving death; many of the birds had gone; it was that rare hour when the summer stood still in full perfection before the great winds came. The butterflies were out in full force to-day, all white ones, flitting before him like torn scraps of paper, he thought. He wanted to think, but he could not; his mind seemed curiously blank, his life in abeyance, waiting for Jocelyn's decision. He had no hope but his hope in her blessed mercy.

At last he saw the roof of the house that sheltered her, and presently came to the artless fence of white palings which enclosed the Bradleys' farm. He entered the garden through a low wooden gate of rustic simplicity, and went up the flagged walk, passing a perfectly genuine well with a real well-sweep, mocked at by an automatic sprinkler whirling on the lawn, sending its glittering rainbow spray to the very edge of the outmoded well. It was all very agreeable and serene, if not pastoral.

He pushed open the screen door and entered the house; there was no one about on the lower floor and he was about to ring for Sillinger when his aunt came downstairs, with an unusual air of haste.

"Basil! How nice of you!" said she, with that unfailing courtesy which endeared her to her family more than far greater and sterner virtues. "Annie saw you from the window.... I was resting," she explained, for like many other persons, she never really slept by night or by day. If anything happened which she did not hear, it was only because her door was closed, or the wind made such a noise. "We'll have a nice cosy little tea all by ourselves."

She had always been kind to him, but never quite in this way, and he took alarm. She had come down so hurriedly, her swarthy face a little floury from a hasty application of powder, the ribbon bows on her black lace negligee all awry. And she laid her hand on his shoulder, smiling at him as if she were sorry for him.

Indeed, she was sorry for him. He did not know how he looked, how strained, how desperate. She remembered that day, long ago, when she had had to tell him of his mother's second marriage. He had grown white as a ghost; he hadn't said a word, only shrugged his shoulders in a rather irritating way; but he had let his hand lie in hers a long time, had sat beside her on the sofa, his head turned a little aside, his blunt boyish profile without expression, and yet, she had thought, very eloquent.

"Oh, poor Basil!" she thought now. Perhaps he might have been different.... But she had no hope that he would ever be different now.

She began to talk brightly.

"Isn't it a wonderful day?" she said. "I don't see why it's the established convention that the summer ends on Labour Day. September's really the loveliest month in the country. We shan't be going into town before the middle of October.... Cake, Basil? Only bread and butter? There's some really delicious homemade gooseberry jam...."

She was grateful to him for playing up to her, for talking lightly and easily, telling her little bits of gossip. So that after a few minutes she could say, quite casually:

"You'll stop for dinner, of course, and see Jocelyn.... She's gone to the Evans' this afternoon, but she'll be home soon. And—Lewis is here over the week-end...."

He set down his cup blindly, and it struck the edge of the saucer and overturned.

"Lewis!" he said. "Lewis is here?"

She leaned across the small table and laid her hand on his arm.

"Basil, my dear boy," she said. "You won't be foolish, will you?"

"Then they're ..." he began, but could not go on for a moment. "They're completely reconciled, eh?" he asked, with a smile.

"I don't believe there ever was a quarrel," said she, frankly. "I never quite understood.... But you can see for yourself, my dear boy, that it's the best thing for Jocelyn—if they can manage to get on together...."

"Yes," he answered, politely. "Of course."

He showed that he wished to talk of something else now, and Mrs. Bradley was more than willing to oblige him. And if in the past she had thought her nephew too diplomatic, too adroit, she had only appreciation for those qualities now. Even when Jocelyn came in, alone, he showed no signs of awkward emotion; he was simply friendly toward her; evidently he was not going to be difficult.

"Shall I play for you, Basil?" she asked.

No one could blame him for agreeing readily to that and Mrs. Bradley, vexed and alarmed, was obliged to see them go off alone together into the music-room.

"I can't go and sit there with them," she thought. "That would be too ridiculous.... But Jocelyn ought to have more sense...."

Hazeltine thought that himself. She had gone back to Lewis, she had not even answered his letter; why not let him alone? He wasn't so infatuated that he could not understand a hint.

"And now," he thought, "she'll try to explain—all that nebulous moonshine that she calls her love for me. All superfluous. Lewis is explanation enough. If I see Lewis ..." His hands clenched. "By God! I'll ... No. I'll do nothing. I'll have to see Lewis any number of times, unless I vanish off the face of the earth, or he does. I've got to bear this."

He stood behind Jocelyn, looking down at her dark head; a faint smile came to his lips for the odd little mistake she always made, just here, in the *Lieder* she was playing; it began Mendelssohn, but it ended pure Jocelyn. She never played anything quite right, she made the oddest changes and improvisations, not wilfully but as if she were asking wistful little questions of the masters she could not follow.

A fallible creature after all, not unattainable, not incomprehensible. He had been thinking of her as if she were a supernatural creature, to decide his destiny, and she was not; she was only Jocelyn; she was only a woman and he only a man.

So dear to him in her familiar beauty.... He remembered her playing like this years ago, when her shining dark hair fell about her shoulders and her little hands were sunburnt and scratched....

He used to sit and listen to her then, and feel happy, contented just to be near her. Even later, during that poor, futile little engagement ... when he had so often held her in his arms and kissed her, there had been a sweet solace just in being with her. All gone now, every trace of it—that tenderness, that comradeship. He glanced quickly behind him, no one was in the hall, then he stooped and kissed her cheek.

Her hands fell silent on the keys, her head bent lower; she did not speak, did not stir. What was this? Humility ...? Submission? Was she confused ...? He grew impatient with her silence.

"Jocelyn, you got that letter?" he asked.

She answered, "Yes," in a voice like a sigh.

Again he waited, until anger rose in him.

"Well?" he demanded. "I suppose you read it?"

She glanced up and her expression dismayed and exasperated him; a little anxious smile was on her lips.

"Yes, Basil, I did," she answered him.

"Well?" he said, again. "What's the matter? Won't you speak? I'm— can't you see? I'm waiting...."

"Oh, Basil, my dear," she began, and stopped, and reaching for his hand pressed it against her cheek, "I don't know what to say," she went on. "I can't decide, Basil. Not anything. All I can do is—to under-stand—a little. And to be your friend."

"No," said he. "That won't do. You've got to tell me what you want."

"As if I knew!"

"Well," he said, "I do know what I want. I want you. I love you. And when I say I love you, I don't mean anything beautifully mystic either."

"Don't, please ...!"

"If you don't want to hear me, you've only to say so. If you want me to go, I'll go. I told you that. All I ask you is to speak plainly—if you can. You told me once that you loved me. Is that finished?"

She rose and stood facing him.

"Basil!" she said, "you're cruel and unjust. How can you ask me that—now?"

He seized both her hands and drew her a little aside so that no one passing by the hall could see them.

"I do ask you," he said. "It's all you can do for me now. I've been such a fool—such a pitiful fool.... I wanted to be. But I knew all the time that it was too late. I've got to lose you whatever you say. Only, I want to *know*."

He had never seen her face like this, not gentle now; her dark eyes were fixed on him with a look bitter and resentful.

"It *is* too late," she said.

"I know it," said he. "I'm going. But not until you've told me—point blank—without any merciful evasion—if you love me."

"You want me to say—what will hurt us both, all the rest of our lives?" she asked, scornfully. "You want me to say what we can't forget? If you do love me—if you ever did—go away now—so that we can keep all the dear lovely things to remember ..."

"No," he said. "I don't care—whether it hurts me, and you too, I want to know. All my life I've given you all the love I'm capable of. I want to know if it's been—if you've ever once, for one minute, felt anything like that for me. Or if it's all been—the most damnable farce."

"And you come now, five years too late ... to torment and hurt me so!"

"I will know!" he said.

Their eyes met in a long, unwavering look. His heart beat so that he could scarcely breathe.

"Very well," she said. "If you will know. I'll tell you. I do love you. Only you. Always you. And I never knew it—until it was too late."

"Jocelyn!" he said. "Oh, God ... Jocelyn...."

"And you think I don't know what love is?" she said. "You think ... you ask me to tell you what to do. Do you imagine—my own life's so easy to ...?"

She pulled her hands away and covered her face with them.

"You see now—what you've done," she said, almost inaudibly. "Now go away, for God's sake. You've ruined everything. Now it is finished—all our friendship—all the things that were dear and sweet to remember, all ruined now...."

He knew it. He had his answer now, plain enough.

He turned away from her, went out of the room into the hall and almost ran into Lewis, who was standing there, talking with Mac Donald. He made no attempt to speak; he took up his stick, pulled his hat down over his eyes, opened the door, and went out of the house.

There was a strange, pallid dusk outside, deathly still. He was half-way down the flagged walk when the house door closed again and he heard someone coming after him. He quickened his pace; there was no word any human creature could speak which he could bear hearing now. He strode out of the little gate and it clicked behind him, and almost immediately it clicked again, behind his pursuer.

An insensate determination not to be caught filled him. It seemed to him a matter of vital importance not to be caught. He heard the footsteps gaining upon him along the asphalt road; he swore under his breath, and went faster and faster, and the other came on faster. He swerved aside, and leaped over a barbed wire fence into an orchard.

He had no idea where he was going. The most preposterous ideas came into his head; for a moment he wondered if he could hide behind a tree, if he should double back, if he should begin to run.

"If it's agreeable to you," said an equable voice from behind him, "I'll keep you company to the railway station."

Hazeltine stopped where he was and began to laugh.

"So you're the Hound of Heaven!" he said.

"I doubt I've the patience for that," said Mac Donald. "However.... Will you not smoke as we go along?"

He was proffering a respectable cigar-case, but Hazeltine took no notice of it.

"Look here!" he said. "Did Martinsburgh send you after me?"

"He did not."

"Did anyone send you?"

"No one. I came—out of friendship, as you might say," replied Mac Donald, seriously.

This made Hazeltine laugh again, for the idea of Mac Donald pursuing him through an orchard in the violet dusk, out of friendship, was a curious phantasy.

"Well," he said. "I'm sorry, but I'm not going to the railway station, just now. I think ..." He paused, leaning back against a tree and looking up at the veiled sky—"I think I'm going to the devil," he said. "That's the tradition, in the circumstances."

"Ah, well!" said Mac Donald, "tradition is a wide field. There is a precedent for any course of action you might be inclined to follow."

"No," said Hazeltine, firmly. "When you can't get what you want, you're morally bound to go to the devil."

"On the contrary." Mac Donald struck a match to light his pipe and the glare illumined for an instant his lean, serious face. "To my thinking, the man who's able to say that is incapable of folly. It's the supreme wisdom."

"What is?"

"To know that you cannot get what you want on this earth. Most men live in the childish delusion that they can, or they fall into the slothful weakness of wanting what they can easily get. But to see clearly that a desire is impossible."

Hazeltine stirred restlessly.

"But even at that," he said, "I feel obliged to go to the devil."

"Ah, well!" said Mac Donald. "I'll just go with you, a part of the way."

CHAPTER NINETEEN

THE INCREDIBLE HOUR

Easy is the descent to Avernus. So Hazeltine believed; all the way into the City he sat silent beside the silent Mac Donald, and his mind was intent upon some flaming sin that would bring him peace. In the lofty hall of the Pennsylvania Station he parted from Mac Donald, very brusquely, and set off across Thirty-Fourth Street, sombrely looking out for temptation.

But he could not find the way to hell. He remembered from childhood the Doré illustrations to Dante's *Inferno*. "Abandon hope, all ye who enter here"—that was the inscription over the portals. And that was exactly what he wanted—to abandon hope, to enter that region of crude and violent physical sensation where the soul would know the quiet of despair.

For it was hope that was his agony. He wanted an end; he wanted life to stop, even for a moment; and there was no end and no stopping. He had to go on. For what? Jocelyn was all he had and he could no longer want her, because, if she came to him, she would not be Jocelyn. He could not want her, or anything else. There was nothing now. Yet, though he knew there was nothing left for him, something in his heart cried out in terrible hunger, something that wished to live and would live, and was not to be beaten into despair and silence.

"I hurt her," he thought. "She was all I had—and I hurt her. She said I'd ruined everything—all the things that were dear and sweet to remember.... It's true.... That's all gone now. But I can't forget again. I can't—go back.... Natalie ... I can't go back to Natalie, now.

I can't go on, either. Nothing ahead of me...."

Suddenly he missed Mac Donald. He was sorry he had got rid of him; the man obviously had wanted to stop with him.

"To save my soul," he thought, with a grin. "He'd be interested to hear about the state of my soul. He'd like to talk about it. He'd have any number of moral and philosophical observations to make."

And in all the wide world nobody else was interested in the state of his soul. Jocelyn could only love; she was as indifferent to moral values as a poor sorrowing Dryad. He had no friend.

"That fellow ..." he thought. "It's damned queer.... Every time I've seen him ... he upsets me."

Then the strange notion occurred to him that Mac Donald was somehow responsible for all this; the old incomprehensible antagonism he had felt for the man stirred in him again.

"I'd never have had that row with Lewis if he hadn't ..."

He would not complete the thought, could not quite understand what Mac Donald had done. And it was not worth troubling about; there was some other thought, terribly important, that he must discover and examine.

He gave up looking for Hell. It was not for him. Perhaps no one can find it who has not had some glimpse of Heaven, and he had never had that, never one moment of pure ecstasy. Such a meagre life, so grey and sad to look back upon, so unmeaning....

Mechanically he turned toward his hotel, entered it, and went up to his room. He turned on the light and locked the door, leaning against it, with an anxious frown on his face. It seemed to him that he had forgotten something, and it worried him. He was curiously uneasy; he stared before him at the very bright, bleak little room....

"I've got to think this out," he muttered.

So, standing there, he did think, and he saw his road plain before him.

No great light broke upon him, no revelation came, nothing from outside. It was his own mind, using the same stock of ideas, working according to its own law; he was not inspired, he simply thought. And he saw clearly that his life was a shameful confusion to him and a burden; he saw that he had taken a wrong way, which led to no peace or honour, and that he wished now to follow another way.

He had heard often enough that love transforms a man. It had not done him this service. He loved Jocelyn, but his love had taught him nothing; he suffered, but his suffering seemed to him without meaning. Some other leaven was working in him.

The story of a man's downfall is always convincing; it is an old story which everyone believes. But any account of a human creature's victory is suspect, is called romantic and a nice sort of lie. Almost any man will assert that a thing is too good to be true, but scarcely a saint will hold anything too bad to be true. And yet, though a thousand will accept the fall of man, and only one will credit a resurrection, it is plain that falling man does not reach the pit. Something keeps him erect on earth. He is forever falling, destroyed by his own vileness; his civilization is crumbling. Yet it forever springs up again, and he himself still stands. Something gives him balance, some hard indestructible core within him which keeps him from flying up, light as an angel, or from toppling over into whatever abyss there may be. Some do go, some perish; but always enough are left.

Whatever this balance is, Hazeltine had it. He had been useless enough and at no time admirable; he had been consciously and deliberately a time-server, a parasite, not honest, not loyal. But just because he had been so, consciously and deliberately, through his own choice, and not because of any inherent weakness, he was able now to choose another course and to follow it.

He made a strange enough beginning, but one which seemed to him not unworthy. He bribed a certain complaisant bell-boy to go out and fetch him a bottle of whiskey. He had to pay very dear for this contraband, but he was willing to do so. He took a drink and then, as he had hoped, his fatigue turned to a delightful drowsiness, and he looked forward to a refreshing sleep, forgetting everything.

He undressed and lay down in the dark, quiet room; his weariness was exquisite, his mind felt blank and innocent. But sleep did not come. He began to think again, calmly and lucidly; then his thoughts came faster and faster—sharp anxieties, doubts; to his dismay he could not lie still. Hadn't he forgotten to lock the door ...? Had he left a cigarette smouldering ...? Was it really sixty-three dollars he had in his pockets? Only that much left of what Charles had lent him? Charles ... he must write to Charles.... His brain was racing like an engine; he imagined that his body shook from the violent vibration of it....

He sat up in bed in a cold sweat, with clenched hands. A clock struck the hour, and, almost upon its heels, the half-hour; the night was galloping past, and his need for sleep and oblivion was a matter of desperate urgency. Four o'clock struck; he thought, in terror, that the night was gone and he had not slept.

"I will!" he thought. "I must! I'll close my eyes and count...."

But his eyes would not stay closed. He tried to address himself calmly and reasonably.

"It doesn't matter if I can't sleep, for one night, you know. I'm young and healthy. I'll make up for it to-morrow. It can't hurt me, you know.... I've missed a night's sleep often enough before and it didn't hurt me."

But he had never before so craved for sleep. He turned his back to the window, in order not to see the dawn; he stretched and yawned, told himself that he was comfortable. And then, with an uncontrollable impulse, sprang out of bed.

"A drink will do me good," he said.

He wanted a drink more than sleep, more than he had ever wanted anything. Barefooted he crossed the room to the wardrobe, pulled out the travelling-bag in which he kept such precious stuff, unlocked it and brought out the bottle.

"This is bad, you know," he said. "I've never felt like this before. Shouldn't take a drink when I want it so much.... And I haven't eaten since—I don't remember—a long time."

He poured out a moderate glassful and swallowed it, neat. Anxiously he waited for the result. Nothing! He poured out a much larger drink and gulped it down, and then, very slowly, there came a blessed sensation of peace. His tense nerves relaxed, the fierce activity of his brain slowed down, became tranquil and orderly; he sat down near the table, stretched out his long legs and smiled.

"That's what I needed," he reflected. "I could do with another." So he had another, two more. He was now perfectly comfortable, clear-headed, serene. There was trouble ahead of him, which he would tackle at the proper time. Just now it didn't matter. He thought with friendly regret of Jocelyn, whom he had left years and years ago.... There were other people too, but they were rather vague.... A little water this time. Too bad there was no soda.

"I'd smoke," he thought, "if I could reach the cigarettes."

But he knew he could not, and that made him laugh. He became aware then that somebody disapproved of his laughter. He knew perfectly well there was no one in the room with him, but he was indignant with this person who was not there.

"I'll have all I want!" he said. "D'you hear? All—I want!"

He lifted the bottle with a shaking hand, and filled the glass. He knew it was full, but he could not stop pouring at the right moment; the glass brimmed over and the liquor ran down his sleeve. He laughed until tears came.

The person who was not there remonstrated with him. He shook his head, and that made the room turn slowly upside down and round and round, and he laughed still more.

"You'll never—get rid of me," he cried, weak and shaken with laughter. "I'm going to sit here—for the rest of my life!"

He closed his eyes, the lids fluttered and closed again, and he fell asleep.

At noon the chambermaid knocked and getting no answer, opened the door. There he was in the chair, his head thrown back, arms hanging limply at his side, his slender bare feet crossed, a gentle smile on his lips. She observed, and she understood, the whiskey bottle, but she was touched to a profound compassion.

Moving quietly, she set the room in order, and then drew down the shade.

"Poor feller!" she said to herself.

It was a benediction upon his new life.

CHAPTER TWENTY

THE FIRST STEP

It was raining steadily; it had been raining all the day, a day without light or colour, dull and long. And this was the weariest time of it, the blank half-hour before dinner. Mrs. Huested was shut up in her softly lighted room with nothing to do, nothing to divert her restless thoughts.

She was in full toilette, in black, with diamonds; when she moved, floating draperies stirred about her solid figure; her swarthy face covered with powder of a golden tinge and touched with rouge on the high cheek-bones had a fierce, bold brightness. She looked her best, yet this gave her no satisfaction; it was bitter to her masterful spirit that, in order to conquer, she was obliged to make use of such contemptible devices—paint, powder, perfume, even little gauze wings on her shoulders. If only she did not have to conquer at all! If only some gentle blessing would come to her unsought, unasked!

And nothing ever had so come. She had had to bargain or to fight for everything she had, and she was tired of this; she wanted, not to buy, not to triumph, but to be given something—even the most trivial, most ephemeral happiness. If Hazeltine would only come to see her gladly and freely.... She did not expect him to love her, or to admire her, but if he would just be glad to see her, that would be enough.

"But he'll apologise," she thought, and the idea of these apologies was intolerable. He had not answered her letters, had not gone out to the factory, hadn't even thanked her for the car and the cigarette-case; she had telephoned twice to his hotel and left word for him to ring her up, and he had not. Something else had interested him so greatly that he had forgotten or ignored her. She felt sure it was another woman, and the conviction caused her surprisingly little pain; she thought that if Hazeltine would come to her and tell her about this other woman, would sit beside her and talk frankly, she could so easily forgive him. More than that.... In her heart she felt for him an indulgence beyond all measure, and she was ashamed of it, ashamed of asking so little.

"He'll apologise ..." she said again to herself. "He'll come with some sort of lie.... He'll pretend to be sorry ... he'll say he's not much good, anyhow.... He always says that—and it's damned clever too, because then I've either got to argue that he is some good, or let him see that I don't care how worthless he is."

And she didn't really care; it made no difference whatever. If he would come to her, she thought, with a tale of his follies, no matter how disgraceful, it would be sweet not to forgive but to encourage him, to pay his debts, to relieve his anxiety, to save him from his just deserts; if she could just draw his head down on her shoulder....

"Bah! I'm an old fool," she said, half-aloud.... "Too bad I'm not ten years older...."

She went to the window and drew aside the curtain; nothing to see out there but the rain that fell steadily. She looked forward with impatience to dinner-time, when she could go downstairs in this new Paris gown, and, without beauty, without wit, harsh, and scornful, she could dominate the group at the table. Little Garvey and that friend of his would talk to her about financial matters, respectful of her opinion; Annabelle would treat her with deference; that flippant young divorcée who was a guest for the week-end would be mighty civil; there would be good food, good wine, satisfactory talk. She liked all that; she would be stimulated and refreshed and would forget her lamentable weakness....

There was a little tap at the door. She opened it instantly and there was one of the Japanese servants.

"Missa Hazetine downstairs to see you, madam," he said, with a gleaming smile.

She came out so abruptly that the little man had scarcely time to draw aside, and went down the stairs, not in haste, but with a sort of relentless energy. As she was half-way down the flight the dinner-gong sounded. She frowned. It was exasperating of Hazeltine to come just at this instant; no doubt he did it on purpose, to avoid having to make explanations until he had seduced her into a good-humour. She would have to sit at the table with him, hear his voice, see his smile, meet his eyes....

He was standing at the foot of the stairs, waiting for her, and at the first sight of him, all her annoyance vanished.

"Hazeltine!" she said. "What's the matter with you?"

"Nothing," he said. "Can you spare me just a few minutes, alone?"

"Come into the conservatory," said she, and he followed her across the hall and through a door at the rear, into a fantastic world, where palms grew, and orchids, sheltered from the cold rain of the North Atlantic coast only by glass. The air was hot and moist, with an earthy smell; there were no lights visible and yet every corner was mercilessly bright. She closed the door behind them.

"Hazeltine!" she said. "My dear boy.... You've been ill!"

"No," he said. "Only drunk."

Her face grew scarlet; she turned away, as if to leave him, but after all, she could not. He looked so miserable, so sick, so young.

"That's a nice thing to tell me," she said, sternly. "I wonder you're not ashamed of yourself, Hazeltine!"

"No," he said. "No.... Look here! I want to be honest...."

Something in his voice arrested her; she turned toward him again. He was standing, hat in hand, under a palm tree, and somehow she was reminded of that popular figure of romance, the beach-comber, the fallen gentleman exiled in the tropics. He looked shabby. He was not; he was neat and immaculate as ever, but he looked shabby. She felt morally certain that his pockets were empty, that he had come to her after some shameful experience, penniless and downcast. And he wanted to be honest ...?

"Sit down," she commanded, in a kindlier tone. "And if there's anything you want to tell me, Hazeltine ... you needn't be afraid.... I'll understand...."

"I don't know how to tell you," he said, simply.

A great tenderness came over her; she drew nearer to him and laid her hand on his shoulder.

"Never mind, Hazeltine," she said; "don't try to tell me, then. Maybe I understand."

"I'm glad you don't," he answered.

She pulled her hand away, looking into his face with a dawning disquiet. He returned her look steadily.

"I want to be honest with you," he said.

"What do you mean, Hazeltine?"

"I'll try to tell you," he said. "But ... It's this...." He stopped for a moment. "My life's been nothing but a beastly confusion.... I've gone the wrong way, and now I want ..." He stopped again. "I want to try a different way."

"I don't know what you're talking about," she cried. "Unless ... D'you mean you've come here to tell me—you don't want to marry me? You want to back out of it?"

"I've got to," he said.

"Now, see here, Hazeltine, I'm not one to make a scene.... You said you wanted to be honest with me. That's all I want. You needn't drag in any high-minded moral excuses.... I can stand the truth.... What you mean is—you're in love with some other woman."

"No," he said, "It's not that."

"That's a damned lie."

He answered without a trace of resentment.

"It is the truth, Natalie. I've been in love, and it didn't make any difference in me. It's exactly what I told you. I want to be honest.... I'm sick to the bottom of my soul of all this chicane—all this smiling.... I never want to smile again as long as I live."

"I don't know what you're talking about," she said, again, scornfully. "It's plain enough that what you want is to be released from your engagement to me. All right! You're free! You can go to your other woman."

"There isn't any other woman—for me to go to," he said, patiently.

"And I tell you again, Hazeltine, that's a lie. You wouldn't have come here to me like this—after all I've done for you—if you hadn't been so much in love with someone that—"

"Love ...!" he interrupted, with a sort of despair. "Do you think that's all there is? No.... I can't explain.... Only, I couldn't go on. It's impossible."

"All right!" said she. "I'd like to know what made it impossible, so suddenly."

"It wasn't sudden," said he. For he knew he had had a premonition of this hour long ago, long before that last interview with Jocelyn. It was inevitable.

"I'm sorry," he said, and he wished it were true. Someday he would really be sorry—for her—but now he felt infinitely detached and aloof.

"Hazeltine," said Mrs. Huested, in a low, unsteady voice, "I hope to God you'll pay for this someday."

"I'd be glad to," he said.

She opened the door and went out; he stood where he was for a moment; then looking about him, he saw another door opening on the garden. He drew the bolts and went out; the door would not close behind him but banged to and fro in the wind, and the chill rain drove in among those shivering alien plants. Hazeltine, however, was a native and a hardy growth; he was not perturbed by such weather. He went across the lawn, sodden and spongy underfoot; he came out on the highway, and in ten minutes' time had arrived at the railway station.

He had lost everything. He had lost Jocelyn; he had lost all hope of a comfortable future; he was in debt and dishonourably so, to Mrs. Huested, to Charles Keyes, to many others. Yet all this was not a burden to him; on the contrary, it seemed to him that the burden which had weighed upon him all his life was now lifted, and that for the first time he was free.

He did not know what he was going to do; he did not care. He did not even know why he had turned his back upon the few things he cherished in the world and set out upon a new road. He started alone, unenlightened, unbefriended, with only that one conviction— that he wanted to be honest.

The lounge of his hotel was one of the advertised attractions of the place; it was described as homelike. Here, among great pillars of polished stone, and artificial palms, were armchairs and sofas, fatly upholstered; here sat women, reading, embroidering, or chatting; here was actually a child, a pale tiny thing in a wisp of a pink dress that left bare her frail little arms and neck, a creature incredibly airy and fragile, horrible in its baby coquetry. And an old lady, knitting.... They were, Hazeltine thought, like refugees being made as comfortable as possible in a railway station; before long they and their effects would be moved out and the great pillared hall left bare and clean, ready for business.

The child in the pink frock knew him and always spoke to him, and he was always kind to her, though careful to evade her flamboyant mother, who, he knew very well, was perpetually waiting to catch his eye and to smile. The child ran up to him to-night with her mechanical, knowing little grin, and caught hold of the sleeve of his rain-coat.

"Why, Mr. Hazeltine!" she exclaimed, archly, "you're all soaking wet!"

"I've been out in the rain," he explained, politely. He had always felt sorry for the poor little devil, and though he wanted very badly to get away now, he could not dismiss her abruptly.

While she spoke, her appraising glance travelled over him; he felt that she knew exactly how much his clothes had cost, and could thoroughly appreciate their correctness.

"Don't you catch cold, now!" she said.

"I shan't," he assured her, moving a little, but she still clung to his sleeve.

"If I'm not intruding—" said another voice behind him, and turning, he saw Mac Donald. The child saw him, too, and, not pleased by that lean and serious face, or perhaps scornful of his necktie and his boots, flitted off.

"Come upstairs and have a drink?" asked Hazeltine.

"I'll not refuse," Mac Donald answered, gravely.

So they went up in the lift together, and Hazeltine unlocked the door of his room. And as he did so, an unusual feeling of awkwardness and constraint came over him. This was the first guest he had entertained here; neither his means nor his temperament had inclined him to hospitality, and he regretted his invitation. He had nothing to offer but half a flask of whiskey, not even any soda-water, and for excellent reasons he did not care to order any from downstairs. It was humiliating.

"Sit down," he said, briefly. "You'll have to put your overcoat on the back of the chair. Sorry, but there's no other place."

He disdained any pretence of hospitable bustle; he set out on the table two cloudy glasses and the flask, and from his pocket drew out a box of cigarettes.

"Here's the night's debauch," he said. "Water?"

"Thank you, I'll have just a drop neat," said Mac Donald. He swallowed a little. "It is very good whiskey," he observed, politely.

Hazeltine made no attempt at answering; his jacket felt damp, and he took it off, and sat at the table in his shirt-sleeves, smoking, staring thoughtfully before him.

"I was here this afternoon enquiring for you," said Mac Donald, "but I was informed you were out."

"Yes, I was," said Hazeltine absently. "But—look here!" he added, with a faint frown, "what did you come for, anyhow? Anything in particular?"

"Just a friendly visit, as you might say," replied his guest, sedately. He took out his pipe, filled it, and lit it. "The last time I saw you—" he said, with a glimmer of a smile.

Hazeltine smiled too.

"I said I was going to the devil, didn't I? Well, I've come back," he said.

"I doubted you'd find the journey agreeable. And I just called to enquire where you might be going next."

There was something singularly agreeable to Basil in the man's cool and sober friendliness; it was exactly the tone he wanted at this moment.

"I don't know," he said. "Perhaps you can give me some advice."

"I'm no great hand at advice, and I've not the qualifications, considering the way I've mismanaged my own affairs," said Mac Donald, firmly.

This somewhat discouraged Hazeltine and he fell silent.

"If you'd care to state the facts of the case," said Mac Donald, "we might discuss it."

"I've made a pretty bad mess of things," said Hazeltine, slowly, "and I'd like to clear out. But—it is not so simple as it sounds."

"It is not," Mac Donald agreed.

This, too, was not encouraging, yet it suited Hazeltine.

"I can't even walk out of this room," he went on, "without leaving my trunks behind. And it's going to be hard—damned hard for me to get a job."

"Ah," said Mac Donald and nothing further for a long time. Hazeltine had no objection to this silence; he did not expect assistance from anyone; he was very well used to living in isolation; whatever he had got, he had got by preying upon his fellows, and he did not look for manna from Heaven. Simply, he liked to talk to this fellow.

Mac Donald reached in his pocket and brought out a small book which he laid on the table.

"If you'll look at that—" he said.

Hazeltine picked it up, but hastily put it down again, amazed. It was a savings-bank book.

"If you'll examine it," said Mac Donald severely, "you'll see I've a bit put by for a rainy day."

Hazeltine flushed.

"I see," he said. "The grasshopper and the ant, eh? Well, I wasn't driving at that, Mac Donald. I wasn't going to ask you to lend me money. And I don't need any comments upon my misspent youth. I've not ..."

"Man! You're unduly suspicious," cried Mac Donald. "I've noticed it in you before. You're over-ready to take offence. I've tried to make it plain to you, but you will not understand." He was obviously very much affronted; he rose, put the bank-book into his pocket, and took up his overcoat. "I'll just be stepping along," he said, stiffly.

"No! Look here! Wait a minute," said Hazeltine, anxiously. "I dare say I didn't understand you. But ..."

"I had it in mind to suggest that you settle up your affairs here and come home with me for a while, to the little house I have," said Mac Donald, still more stiffly. "It was what appeared to me a very practical suggestion. But as you choose to see in me the offensive self-righteousness of the ant—"

"But, look here, Mac Donald," interrupted Hazeltine, ready to laugh, "you don't know me or anything about me.... It's so damned unreasonable ..."

"No doubt, it's as you say," said Mac Donald.

Hazeltine rose too.

"If the offer's not withdrawn," he said, "I'd like to accept it."

"It is still open to you."

There was a moment's silence.... Then Mac Donald turned toward his host.

"Man!" he said, "the truth of it is—I like you!"

CHAPTER TWENTY-ONE

MANORGRANGE PARK

Hazeltine's entrance into a new life was markedly lacking in dramatic interest. The next day was Saturday, and Mac Donald had said that he would call for him at half-past one; he did call precisely at that hour, and Hazeltine walked out of the hotel with him. Simply walked out of that existence, and felt neither regret nor elation. He was, indeed, in that sort of vacuum which sometimes lies between a decision and its consequences; he had spoken, but his words had not yet become flesh; he had acted, but his action had not yet taken effect; he was like one who has flung a vase over the edge of the cliff—the thing still glittered in mid-air; it scarcely seemed gone; the final, definite crash had not yet come.

They took a train at the Grand Central Station. And when they were settled in the smoking car, it occurred to Hazeltine for the first time that Mac Donald could not be an isolated phenomenon.

"See here!" he began, rather anxiously, "I should have asked you before ... are you married, Mac Donald?"

"I am not," answered the other, with something like complacency. Hazeltine was relieved.

"A house of your own made me think—" he explained.

"The house was bought for my mother. But unfortunately she died last year."

"Hard luck!" said Hazeltine, sympathetically.

"It was. The house was such as I thought suited to a woman of her years and tastes, and I cannot say it is what I should have chosen for my own occupation.... Ah, well." He sighed. "A remarkable woman, my mother was," he continued. "She'd not had what you might call advantages, but she'd a remarkable mind. A great reader—she'd quote you pages from Milton and Shakespeare. Her letters were better than many I've seen printed in books. What you might call a commentary upon life." He paused a moment. "I'd not been home for six years and during that time I had exactly three hundred and eight letters from her, never less than five pages in length, one every week, and two extra every year, one for Christmas and one for my birthday. When she died, they sent me back my letters as she'd requested; there were three hundred and ten of them, two more, you'll observe, because I'd written twice before I'd news of her death."

Hazeltine suppressed a smile.

"That's hard luck," he said again. "So you're living alone?"

"I've my sister Helen there, and her child—"

"But—see here! Your sister may not like this, you know. Perhaps I'd better—"

"She'll like it," Mac Donald assured him, briefly. "And it's to be remembered that it is *my* house."

So Hazeltine made no further objections.

"It is not a large house," Mac Donald remarked, "nor what I'd expected it to be. In a manner of speaking I might say very truthfully—'tis a poor thing, but mine own.... However, you'll soon see for yourself."

They descended from the train at a brand-new station, amid a crowd of home-going husbands and fathers, and a few women.

"The house is ten minutes' walk from the station, I'm told," said Mac Donald, "but I've not found that road yet.... We'd best take the tram, as you've your bag."

So they got into a trolley car, passed through a neat little town and out into the country, and presently descended before an iron archway, over which was a sign proclaiming this to be "Manorgrange Park. The Garden of Homes."

"It is a queer crop they've sown in this garden," said Mac Donald. "Ah, well! We'll just see what comes of it...."

They passed through the gateway and set foot upon a long, straight cinder walk bordered by famishing saplings; here and there foundations had been dug, but no workmen were about; nothing stirred under the blazing sun. There were only four houses standing in this large desolation, yet so strong is the sense of property in man that no one had dreamed of watering or tending any but his own thirty-foot front. It was a hideous and a melancholy spot.

When they were half-way down the street, the door of one of the houses opened, and out rushed a being who might have been the spirit of Manorgrange Park incarnate, a squat, white-haired child, with an expression of witless impertinence on its dirty face; it sprang aboard a vehicle awaiting it and by means of a lever violently worked back and forth, it bore down upon them at a pretty good speed, shouting "Ki-yi ki-yi." So very resolute was this child that they were both obliged to step off the walk into the road, for the passing of triumphant infancy.

"As you'll see in the prospectus," said Mac Donald, "Manorgrange Park is a Paradise for Children. And that makes it somewhat like the other place for adults. ... Here we are!"

It was a little two-storied house of unstained shingles, with a veranda in front. Hazeltine sought in vain for some good thing to say of it.

"A cozy little place," he murmured.

Mac Donald took no notice of this. He did not use a key, but rang the bell and the door was opened promptly by a very little girl of remarkable composure. Mac Donald patted her head; neither of them smiled.

"Ask your mother if she'll step here," he said, and off the child went. "Step into the parlour," he added to Hazeltine.

It was instinctive with Hazeltine to make a quick and accurate survey of any new place; he had to know where he was, to understand his environment; he looked about like a cat, seeking for all the good hiding-places and exits. But this parlour was an un-compromising room, quite square, furnished with cheap and respectable comfort, as ugly as so clean and orderly a room could be.

"My sister," said Mac Donald, more in explanation than in introduction of the young woman who entered. "Helen, here's a friend, I've brought home, who'll be stopping here a while."

She looked up with the bluest eyes that ever were, and gave him a fugitive smile which left her face very grave.

"I'll just take these upstairs," she said, and would have picked up Hazeltine's bags if he had not forestalled her. Again she smiled, and led the way up the narrow staircase, and opened a door. Such a queer little room! The walls were painted a girlish pink; the white iron bed, the chest of drawers with a ruffled cover on it, the chintz window-curtains, the small rocking-chair all combined toward an effect of *jeune fille* primness. So that Hazeltine felt enormous and somewhat gross for a moment.

"It's very good of you," he said to the sister. "I hope I shan't be in the way."

"Oh, no!" said she, startled; and at once disappeared. But she was back again before he had closed the door; with an apologetic murmur she flew past him and set to work putting fresh white covers upon the chest of drawers, the table, the back of the rocking-chair, the top of the desk; then vanished again.

There was a sweet, clean smell in the room. There was a tree outside the window, with leaves still green, through which the sun came mildly. There was an air of peace and decency here.... Hazeltine sat down in the rocking-chair and stared at his bags. He had a great disinclination to unpack them, to bring out his elegant personal effects....

A knock at the door, and when he opened it, there was the tiny girl, with clean towels over her arm. "Mummy's bringing tea," she said.

Hazeltine was rather disconcerted by this assiduity. In came the sister with a tray; she set it on the table, and started to pull forward a chair for him, but he stopped that.

"I wish you wouldn't give yourself so much trouble," he said, but she only smiled, and went away, with the tiny girl holding to her skirt.

But he was determined to end this. He gulped down a cup of tea, scalding hot, and taking the tray, went downstairs with it. At the foot he paused, not knowing where to go in that quiet house; the parlour, he could see was empty.... Then he heard a small voice, saying:

"But there's two cents back for the bottle, Mummy! So, it's only eight cents, like."

He went toward that voice, and through the open doorway of the kitchen he saw the sister and the tiny girl standing side by side at a table, rolling sultanas and currants in flour.

"Ah! But it's just eight cents here and eight cents there that mounts up so!" said Mac Donald's sister gravely. She turned, and with her hands still in the flour, bent her head; the little girl raised her rosy face and they kissed each other, and went on with their work.

Hazeltine was always interested in women, and above all was he interested in a sister of the unique Mac Donald. He stood where he was for a moment, looking at her.... She was a slightly built little thing of perhaps twenty-five; her features were regular and a little sharp, her face colourless; she was not pretty, but her blue eyes were kind and her dark hair curled sweetly about her temples. And in her starched dress and clean apron, busy at her homely task, with the child at her side, there was an ancient magic about her; she was not the eternal feminine, not the victorious and heart-stirring woman who incites to any folly, any splendour. She was something far older than that: she was the mute and patient figure forever in the background of all glorious pageants; not the goddess, but the handmaiden.

She wheeled briskly about just then to dust off her hands, and caught sight of Hazeltine. With a shocked expression she flew toward him and took the tray.

"I thought you'd be resting," she said. "Jack's gone down to the town for tobacco.... But there's a fine lot of books in the parlour, Mr. Hazeltine; I don't doubt you'll find one that'll suit you, and you could read out on the veranda where it is cool."

"No, thanks," said Hazeltine. "What are you doing?"

"I'm just baking a cake," she told him, seriously. "But I'll show you where the books are and—"

"I'd rather stay and watch, if I don't bother you," he said. "Can't I help you?"

"Eh? Oh, no! If you'll take a chair ...?"

But he did not want to take a chair; he leaned against the doorway, and he tried to talk to her. She was very civil to him; she explained each step. "Now that's the flour I'm sifting—three times, you'll notice, to make it light." But there was an appalling sort of innocence about her, as if she did not know she was a woman. Hazeltine had never encountered this before. All the women he knew, even Dot, had a certain feminine self-consciousness, had been trained to please. And this little thing knew only to serve. They could not talk to each other; he tried, and at last he gave up and fell silent.

Suddenly that silence was intolerable to him. He had come out on the veranda with Mac Donald; Helen had come out too, to wait for the moment when the roast must be taken from the oven. The sun had gone down; it was growing dark. There they were, three persons, sitting in the dusk, and all of them silent.... These were not his people and these were not his ways; they were strange to him and he to them, and he was terribly lonely. His own sort of people were never silent like this; there was among them a tradition that words must be exchanged, however facile and meaningless. And it was a good, a wise tradition—he saw that now—a seemly and pleasant thing, a clothing for the stark soul. His own people, his own sort ... the clear light laughter of women, the easy camaraderie of men, the fine illusion of solidarity ... other twilights on other verandas, with drinks and always the sound of voices.... It was good even to be at the Garveys'; there was a vista there of lawn and trees, and the sea was near; there was a fine old house with servants moving about, with flowers, exquisite china, silver, a sort of beauty. And this ... the meanness of this, the jerry-built house, the cheap, ugly life—the meanness of this, the isolation....

He got up and walked to the railing, looking up at the cloudy sky. But he did not see it; he was facing something else.

"It was bound to be like this," he thought. "There'll be more bad moments—sure to be. The only way to take it is to see it as a *fait accompli*. No harm in looking back—even in regretting. But if I look forward—and long ..."

There was nothing he dared long for now. He intended to do his best, but he had no flattering opinion of his own ability; he expected no more of himself than he did of others.

In nearly thirty years he had accomplished nothing; he had nothing left, not one sincere friendship, not one untarnished memory. And he thought it very unlikely that, at the end of another thirty years, he would have much more. He did not care particularly what happened to him now; in fact, he didn't see what could happen to him of any significance. Love, honour, youth—and every penny he had—all lost. What remained was that life of decent and honest obscurity; it was what he wanted, what he had chosen, but it aroused in him no excessive enthusiasm.

"It's better, though," he said to himself, and he meant that. It was better; even Manorgrange Park was better than what he had left, than to stand hat in hand, to lie, to smile.... For Lewis, for Mrs. Huested, for Harold Coons, for so many, many others, even for Jocelyn he had choked down such shame, such bitterness and hot resentment, and smiled....

A chair scraped faintly as Helen arose and went into the house, and presently Mac Donald spoke.

"You'll be finding it quiet here," he observed.

It came into Hazeltine's mind to give a surly grunt, such as he had often heard but never before imitated. It pleased him to do this; it was his reward for being here. He was much gratified to find that Mac Donald did not take it amiss.

"Well," he said, "it's a good place for Helen and little Janet."

"Is your sister a widow?"

"She is not. Her husband is at sea."

"A sailor, eh?"

"No," said Mac Donald, "a ship's engineer." He paused a moment. "My second brother's a ship's engineer," he went on, "and it is his vain contention that he's a sailor-man. But as I've often told him, an engineer is no more a sailor than was Jonah in the whale's belly. He goes crawling over the seven seas, shut away from the light of day in his engine-room.... Eh! It is past understanding...."

Hazeltine smiled to himself in the dark.

"Good deal of responsibility for you, isn't it?" he asked.

"I'm used to responsibility," said Mac Donald, blandly. "But it's hard for Helen, maybe," he added.

Hazeltine was curious about Helen.

"Your brother-in-law?" he asked, tentatively.

"Well! He's unfortunate as you might say.... But Helen is very fond of him."

"Then he's not altogether unfortunate," observed Hazeltine.

"Eh? You mean because he's involved someone else in his difficulties? That's one way of looking at it," said Mac Donald, good-humouredly. "Well, my lad, with your personal attractions you should have no trouble in finding a woman to pity you, if that's what you want."

Hazeltine was about to make an amused denial, but he did not. He wasn't so sure that that was not what he wanted, after all.

"Pity's a poor diet," Mac Donald went on, equably. "It is not strengthening."

"Sympathy's another thing, though."

"Not from a woman. All the sympathy they have for a man is pity, and they will pity you for anything whatever!" said Mac Donald, with a certain vehemence. "They will pity you because you cannot sew on a button or because you've a cold in the head. And they will pity you in just the same way if you commit a crime. It is very demoralizing."

Hazeltine smiled to himself again. It would be difficult, he thought, to pity Mac Donald, whatever his tribulations; yet he imagined that someone had attempted it.

Helen came out then to call them in to dinner. They went into the little dining-room, somewhat too brilliantly lighted by an electrolier with a red silk shade; the round table was covered with a spotless cotton cloth and set out with humble blue-and-white china of the Willow pattern; the little girl sat meekly in her high-chair, a bowl of bread and milk untouched before her. Helen stood near the pantry door. And it was so unquestionably Mac Donald's house and Mac Donald's dinner.... He was very gentle to the little girl when he noticed her at all; he was plainly very fond of his sister and she of him; they almost smiled when their eyes met, and he spoke to her with a friendly sort of deference. But it was so overwhelmingly his dinner, cooked for him, served for him, offered by him to his guest. The little blue-eyed handmaiden, flushed and a little anxious about the meal in the presence of the magnificent Hazeltine, got up from her place a dozen times to hurry into the kitchen and back again. At first Hazeltine rose when she did, but that obviously disconcerted her, so he kept seated; he tried to behave easily and naturally, and he failed. Mac Donald had a way of talking to him as if they were alone, and Hazeltine could not for a moment forget that there was a woman, and a young and almost pretty one, present. He did not even like to ignore the solemn little girl, yet he could not find a word to say to her. And for Helen to be waiting on him, standing beside him to fill his glass with water ...

A great depression and weariness came over him. He had never had a home, but he felt all the bitterness of homesickness now. These were not his people, and their ways were not his ways; he was strange to them as they were to him. He was in exile and longing for his home.

CHAPTER TWENTY-TWO

MARKET VALUE

Mr. Lucas Horlick had come down to his office somewhat earlier than usual that morning, and found none of his staff there. This enraged him, and at the same time caused in him a grim sort of joy; he unlocked the door with his own key and entered the showroom, very dark and cool after the hot street. He passed along an aisle made by long counters upon which were samples of imported china and bric-a-brac, shrouded now in white covers. Here, before his very eyes, was his business being neglected.

Of course, Mr. Horlick had always known that they all came late, that nobody in the place did anything in his absence; nevertheless, the positive proof was a satisfaction. It showed him how right and how just he was and had always been. And he did not have many satisfactions in his life. He was a solitary and gloomy man; he was cursed with the romantic temperament. He had cherished the romantic illusion that with money he could buy romantic delights; he had expected to travel and see a sun-bathed and exotic world; he had expected to be greatly loved. He had now made the money, but discovered that in the process he had cruelly and horribly become fifty years old, a grizzled, morose, and rather untidy man, completely unloved and, by having made a trip abroad every year on business, completely undeceived about travelling.

He entered his private office and sat down there, to wait like a spider in a web. He took pleasure in imagining the dismay of the office-boy when he should arrive and find the door already unlocked; the thought of the stenographer coming in a silly feminine flurry. Above all, he liked to think of that young fellow who had asked him for a raise. Asking for a raise, and coming in at this hour of the morning! He lit a cigar and leaned back in his chair; his wrath burned slowly and beautifully, like the cigar, and it was grateful in his nostrils. A knock at the door...."Come in!" said he, and hoped it was that clerk. The handle turned and there entered—the very image of himself! The image, that is, of the self he had intended to be, of the man who was to have been greatly and exotically loved; the likeness at this moment of time was not visible. A tall, good-looking young man, nonchalant, supremely elegant; it was a sweltering morning, but this apparition was perfectly cool; he took off his hat and smiled faintly.

"Good morning!" he said. "You advertised for a correspondent—"

This was an outrage! This embodiment of his frustrations was not going to bully him.

"See here!" he cried, "I said apply in writing—"

"Yes, I know," said the other. "But I don't have much luck with letters." His smile was a little wistful. "I thought if I could see you—"

"Well you can't," said Mr. Horlick. This fellow had a disgusting foreign intonation—what Mr. Horlick called an English accent—surely a strange thing in an English-speaking person. And he had an easy air of self-assurance.... "When I say 'apply in writing,' I mean 'apply in writing,'" said Mr. Horlick.

"Yes, but look here!" said the other, "I *know* I could do the work. I have a thorough knowledge of French—I went to school in France, you know—"

"Go home and write me a letter about it."

"Look here!" said the other, "just give me a chance to show you! Give me some letters to answer—give me something to translate."

"I said 'apply in writing.'"

"But look here! I'll come for a week for nothing, just for the chance—"

"Not here, you won't," said Mr. Horlick, with rapidly mounting anger. "I wouldn't have you in my office on a bet."

The young man seemed startled by the positive malignancy of the other's tone.

"If you'd—" he began, but Mr. Horlick cut him short.

"You'd better go on the stage," he said. "That's the place for you, my lord duke!"

"You'd better go to hell!" said the young man, turning on his heel.

This not very clever retort served the double purpose of infuriating Mr. Horlick and of satisfying Hazeltine. For this applicant was Hazeltine, and this manner, which had so enraged and disgusted Mr. Horlick, was Hazeltine's new and improved manner which he fondly believed to be crisp, trust-inspiring, and business-like. He had learned some time ago that there was something about him which aroused a violent hostility in certain persons; he had earnestly studied the matter, and believed that he had now corrected his errors in deportment. He no longer carried a walking-stick; he remembered never to light a cigarette during one of these painful interviews; he was no longer ingratiating, but attempted to appear self-confident.

He was, indeed, growing almost truculent, his hope turning into defiance. Twelve days had he lived in Manorgrange Park, and eleven of them had been spent in hunting a job. Sunday he had occupied in writing answers to advertisements in the newspapers with no more result—except for the cost of postage—than if he had thrown his letters into the wastepaper-basket. Almost all the money he had borrowed from Mac Donald had gone for carfare and lunches, and he had found no job. Nobody wanted him; certainly nobody needed him.

And this made its mark upon him—this thought that nobody needed him, that what he did or did not do made no possible difference. He seemed to himself the one living creature with no stake in life, with no one to be injured or to be helped by his actions, with nothing to lose and precious little to gain. He was not discouraged; all his life he had conquered adverse circumstances by his patience and adroitness; time after time he had had to learn to adapt himself to new environments; he saw the majority of his brothers earning their bread and he was not disposed to think himself below the average. But every rebuff, every failure told on him. He was the lone hunter against a hostile world; he was not discouraged but he was, in his own cool and lucid fashion, entirely reckless. He had taken it into his head to lead an honest life, to work for his bread; he would do that and he could do that, but he recognized the unimportance of the affair. He did not think that God was particularly interested and he was quite sure that none of his fellow-creatures were. Nobody cared much what happened to him and neither did he himself.

And still, with his own sort of courage, he kept to his appointed course. He went out of Mr. Horlick's office, passed through the long, dark room, opened the door, and came out into the dazzlingly bright, hot street. The copper sun was mounting a brilliant and unclouded sky; there was no breeze, no mercy of any sort from Heaven. He was in a section of Broadway hitherto unknown to him, a region of wholesale shops with windows displaying sample hats, sample porcelain, sample fancy goods, and notions. The surface-cars went dollopping by, and rattling drays, and motor-trucks and nimble taxis, and hundreds of unknown, completely indifferent persons. He saw men with straw hats pushed back from sweating brows, and handkerchiefs tucked into their collars and strained, preoccupied faces. He envied them; he wished he could be as they, strained, preoccupied, and sweating. He felt a hopeless amateur, aloof and lonely. He wanted to go home, to Helen....

This idea startled him. It was the first time he had definitely recognized the house in Manorgrange Park as a refuge, and the first time he had anxiously longed for the solace of Helen's company. He had some time ago learned to appreciate her kind and uncritical welcome at the end of a bitter day; he had, since his first hour in the house, taken a benevolent interest in Helen. But now he thirsted for an hour with her. He imagined how it would be if he went home now, and let her see the weariness and disgust he endured. She would come to the door, in her starched dress and her apron; she would say, "Oh, Mr. Hazeltine!" and she would instantly set about doing something for his comfort, cooking a lunch, making a cup of tea. She would ask no questions, she would think no questions, she would see only that he was unhappy. And she would think his failure due to someone else's fault. He knew she thought that. He knew she admired him. And he wished to be admired; standing there on the corner of Broadway, under the fierce sun, he felt desperately in need of admiration.

All this was new to him, and disconcerting; it was weakness. From his pocket he took out a paper on which he had pasted advertisements culled from the morning newspaper; he pushed his own hat a little to the back of his head; he unbuttoned his jacket, and, with a hasty stride and a strained, preoccupied face, started off about his lamentable business.

The next place was a downtown insurance office which had advertised for a junior clerk. Several applicants were already there, most of them boys, years younger than himself, and he felt ashamed, sitting there among these smart lads. But he stayed; he waited for his turn, and for his defeat, and then went off to his next ordeal.

He went uptown to an office on Forty-Second Street. The advertisement asked for a young man of good education and appearance; experience unnecessary; and Hazeltine had already learned that, as a rule, where no experience was required, a pathetic innocence and trustfulness was desirable. However, he applied, and he was offered a Unique Opportunity—selling sets of books from door to door. There was no salary, but he ought, the sales manager said, to be able to make fifty dollars a week from commissions.

"Or sixty," said the sales manager. "Easy."

But Hazeltine declined. It seemed to him necessary that weak and erring man should be rewarded for his efforts as well as for some supreme accomplishment; he wished to be paid for trying to sell books, and that was out of the question.

Next he went to an art gallery on Fifth Avenue. The dealer wanted an assistant with a 'knowledge of art'; Hazeltine knew nothing about Art and cared less, but he had to try everything. And he had a secret conviction, common to his class, that he had an instinctive knowledge of such matters. He was sure he knew good pictures from bad; he knew he had good taste.

The dealer recognized him at once, not as an individual, but as a representative. He made his living by selling pictures to persons like Hazeltine, who had that instinctive knowledge of Art. He himself had a great deal of intuition and he was sorry for the fellow.

"No," he said. "You'd never do for this job. Why don't you try the booksellers?"

Hazeltine thanked him, and on his way out politely lingered to look at the pictures hanging in the gallery. He liked some of them.

It was noon now, and he was hungry. He went into Childs and had an insufficient meal, the last meal his pocket would afford. He would have to borrow from Mac Donald again to-night. He drank his coffee too slowly to suit the harassed little waitress; in her crisp white uniform she went flying back and forth along the tiled floor, shouting her orders in the kitchen, carrying her heavily loaded tray, clattering the dishes on the white, uncovered table. She was earning her living. All the men and women who hurried in and out were earning their livings, he thought; everyone but himself.

There were still three places left on his list, and he went to them in a listless, indifferent mood. He knew he would not get a job this day. At three o'clock he had finished, and he went home.

"There's Mr. Hazeltine," said little Janet.

Helen came to the window and, to be sure, there he was, coming down the long, long street with his customary nonchalant stride.

"Oh, dear!" said she with a little frown. For this nonchalance did not deceive her in the least, any more than her brother's reticence could ever mislead her. That pity, so offensive to Mac Donald, was rampant in the woman, and she had even infected the small girl with it; together they laid artful plans for the assuagement of the two pathetic men, flattered them, cajoled them, most subtly and wickedly attempted to demoralize them.

"Now, mind you don't worry him, sweetheart!" said Helen. "He'll be wanting to be let alone, with all he's got on his mind. Just run and see if the kettle's on the boil."

It was, and by the time Hazeltine reached the house, Helen was able to tell him that she had just made a pot of tea for herself—a lie which she uttered without flinching in the presence of the child.

"Will you have your tea upstairs in your own room, Mr. Hazeltine?" she asked. "You'd rest better—"

"No, thanks. Here, with you," said Hazeltine. "And look here! No toast this hot day!"

"But I was just thinking I'd like a slice of toast!" she cried.

"You never thought of it until you saw me," said Hazeltine, sternly. "No. We'll have bread, and I'll cut it."

She had never got used to this singular fancy of Mr. Hazeltine's for helping her; it confused and troubled her, but she knew no way of stopping it.

"I wish you would not," she said, plaintively.

He looked down at her, but she did not meet his glance; she stood in the doorway of the kitchen, in her clean, stiff dress and apron, her head bent, the dutiful little handmaiden, so gentle, yet unassailable in her innocent decorum.... Hazeltine was by no means indifferent to Helen.

"Why shouldn't I cut bread?" he asked. "It's about all I'm fit for...." He said this for the sole purpose of arousing her generous indignation, and it succeeded.

"Mr. Hazeltine!" she said severely. "However can you say such a thing?"

"I haven't got a job yet," he said, with a sigh. "I'm beginning to think

I'm not much good...."

"It's just a shame!" she began. "To hear a man of your abilities say—" But she caught sight of Hazeltine's face then and stopped hastily, her cheeks growing scarlet. He had not the expression of a truly dejected man; he was watching her with a half-smile.

"What abilities?" he enquired.

She moved out of the doorway.

"My brother has a fine opinion of you," she observed.

She made no further objection to his cutting the bread then, but he knew that all the time he was in the kitchen she was confused and uncomfortable. And he liked it to be so. It was flattering to him that his presence should so disconcert the nice little thing, and any sort of flattery was peculiarly welcome to him at this time.

He helped her to carry the tea out on the veranda, and when he asked her to stay with him, she consented, reluctant, but acknowledging his claim to be entertained. He was her brother's friend; he was a guest; nothing should make her forget this. She was unusually stiff and silent this afternoon, though; he could win from her only the most grudging smile, the most cautious replies. So, after a little, he too fell silent, and was content to watch her, sitting there in unwilling idleness, the breeze stirring her dark hair. Let her be as aloof, as taciturn as she pleased; she gave solace and peace to Hazeltine, all the same.

Mac Donald was a thrifty and cautious man, for the most part, but there was an odd streak of prodigality in him; he was capable of amazing follies for those he liked. And Hazeltine was one of these. He had offered Hazeltine his hospitality. Hazeltine had come into his house, and he was welcome there forever. Whether he got a job or not was his own affair. Mac Donald's friendship was uncomplicated by any notion of moral responsibility; he did not feel called upon to examine Hazeltine about his soul, or to give him good advice. He just liked him.

This led to misunderstanding. Hazeltine knew that Mac Donald liked him, but he could not estimate the strength of that liking. He knew he could rely absolutely upon the man's loyalty and discretion; it was his justice he feared. He believed Mac Donald to be the sort of man who can't sleep if he has not paid a bill; the sort of man who always did pay his debts, and who, in strict justice, exacted payment from others. He imagined that Mac Donald had helped him from some lofty motive, had wished to give him a chance to rehabilitate himself. And, in consequence, he felt obliged to justify his lack of success. That evening, when they were alone; he began the tale of his futile search for work, and gave a pretty detailed account of the money he had spent.

This affronted Mac Donald, and hurt him. He did not admire Hazeltine's self-justification. He was willing to take it for granted that the fellow was doing the best he could, and anyhow it was none of his business. He found the narrative unendurable.

"Man, you're not accountable to me!" he interrupted.

"I'm in your debt," said Hazeltine, stiffly.

"I am sorry, if it weighs heavy on you," said Mac Donald, even more stiffly.

He opened his book and began to read, his pipe between his teeth. Hazeltine took up the newspaper. But while Mac Donald was able to lose himself in the pages of Bergson, Hazeltine found no solace in the account of other people's affairs. He was restless and lonely and dissatisfied. He wanted to talk to someone.

Helen was in the kitchen; he heard her quick, light step. Setting bread, he thought; he liked to watch her at that. If he went now and stood in the doorway, she would be glad to see him and talk to him. Very glad.... Mac Donald didn't care how much his guest talked to his sister. Because Mac Donald thought ...

"Well, he's right," said Hazeltine to himself. "Naturally, I'm—"

Naturally, or by strength of will, he was the man of honour Mac Donald thought him.

"No harm in talking to her, is there?" he asked himself, exasperated. Certainly there was no harm, yet, all the same, he thought he wouldn't. He sighed. He was willing, he was glad, to be this man of honour, but he could wish that his virtues were not so coolly taken for granted. If there were only someone....

There was someone. Again like homing birds his thoughts flew to her who was, apparently, selected by destiny to appreciate him. He thought of Agnes.

CHAPTER TWENTY-THREE

ALLURE

Hazeltine awoke the next morning with a rather dangerous sense of virtue. He rose earlier than usual, and there was something noble in that; there was nobility in not having enough hot water for a proper shave, and in dressing in the artless little room. An artless, high-minded sort of life, altogether.... It seemed to him that he really deserved to see Agnes.

The sky was wonderfully blue; the tree outside the window swung like a nodding plume; it was a cheerful day. And from the garden he heard the voice of little Janet, a high, clear, brave little voice, riding light on the wind. He went to the window; Helen was down there, hanging out washing to dry; great sheets were flapping about her, and decorous under-garments, snowy white; and, off by themselves, a row of her brother's black socks rocked in a stately dance. The tiny girl was handing clothes-pins to her out of a bag; she attended to this work seriously, but was able at the same time to hop on one foot and to talk and talk. Hazeltine watched her; it was the first time he had ever consciously observed a child, and he was curiously touched. Such a tiny, helpless creature and the companionable air it had! The friendliness of it, the unwavering faith.... He could perceive now that a child might be more than the promise of a human being; it was a human being itself, complete in its way, dear not for what it might become, but for what it was. A little friend, a comrade more loyal, more responsive than any mature creature could be....

"Poor Jocelyn!" he thought, suddenly. "I suppose that's what she meant."

Still his masculine mind turned with instinctive distaste from that subversive idea—that children could have as important a place as men in the life of a young and lovely woman. No; he preferred to think of her as inordinately concerned with Lewis, because Lewis could be thought of as a rival, and the jealousy one feels for a rival is an endurable thing. It is that wicked, obstinate love that women have for their babies, for their parents, for their brothers and sisters, that really estranges a man. Hazeltine could, at his best, hope that Jocelyn might find some measure of happiness with Lewis; he meant to be generous, and he was so. But what he really wanted was, to see her attention turned from her lost children to a man; if not himself, then someone like him.

He had sworn that he would not forget Jocelyn again, would not thrust aside that pain, which was life, for the sterility of oblivion. She was the beauty and illusion of his existence, and he did not care to exist, lacking that. Yet the thought of her caused him a chilly discomfort, like the thought of death; very tenderly he sent her back to the lonely heaven of beauty and illusion where she belonged, and turned his mind to the little and the pleasant things of daily life.

Mac Donald was already downstairs; he nodded his head, but he was speechless. Because it was washing day, breakfast was a few minutes late. It was Mac Donald's rule not to smoke before breakfast; his pipe was lying on top of the tobacco canister and as he walked up and down the room he could see it, and did see it, and it was hard to wait. In anxious haste, his sister brought in the meal, but except for a smiling 'good morning,' she did not speak either. And this faint flavour of disagreeableness and worry made Hazeltine feel a little superior, being himself so serenely good-tempered.

He looked at the newspaper. There were the usual things, which he read now with a critical eye. He marked three or four, without extravagant hopes, and ate steadily and well.

"We'll go in together," muttered Mac Donald. He was standing before a large framed engraving of Loch Lomond, straightening his tie; his pipe was between his teeth now, and he was once more a philosopher. He looked down at the tiny girl who had come up beside him.

"If you are a good girl to-day," he said, removing the pipe, "I'm not saying there might not be something in my pocket when I come home."

"I *was* a good girl yesterday, the whole, whole day!" said she.

"Oh! Were you, now?" he said. "That'll have to be taken into consideration, then."

He kissed her, and as he set off with Hazeltine, he was as near to smiling as he cared to be. But before they reached the station, that look had gone.

"D'you know where I'm going?" he asked. "I've a quarter of an hour to spare, and I'll just go down to the docks and look at the shipping."

Very well; Hazeltine pitied him; Hazeltine sat beside him on the train and pitied him for miles and miles in silence. And if his sympathy was a little too bland, if he was a trifle over-confident in his own regeneration, one would not begrudge him that. It didn't last long.

WANTED. Young man of refined appearance as assistant editor. No experience required but must have good education and some literary ability. Apply between 10 and 12.

S. BENG.

He had marked that advertisement, and he thought he would begin the day with S. Beng, whose office had the merit of being near the Grand Central. He went there, and on the upper floor of a large building found a door with the inscription—S. Beng—Publisher. He pushed it open and found himself in a forlorn and dirty office where a number of men sat in a row against the wall. A disdainful girl arose from her seat before a typewriter.

"About the ad?" she asked. "All right! Sit down over there." And he joined the row.

He had grave doubts as to whether his appearance was truly refined; he was pretty sure that his education had not been good, and his literary ability was totally unproved. Yet, when he looked at the other applicants ... There they were, all hat in hand, with their refined appearances offered for sale in a critical market, all waiting to face a cruel scrutiny.... Poor devils! Poor devil himself!

"And this," he reflected, "is independence. If my necktie or my accent aren't refined enough, out I go. A free man."

His turn was drawing near; one by one the others had been shown into an office opening out of the large room, never to reappear. You might fancy they were knocked on the head as they entered that small room. At last the fellow next to Hazeltine was summoned by the typist; he rose and vanished, but almost at once he appeared again in the doorway.

"Not that way! The other door! This way!" cried three female voices.

But the poor little man was flustered; he grinned spasmodically, put on his hat, took it off; his face was scarlet. A dapper little man, he was, with a sandy moustache.

"This way!" cried a most imperious voice behind him.

He had no courage, though, to face whatever it was he had left in that small room; he dashed past Hazeltine, out of the wrong door, and escaped into the corridor.

"Next!" said the typist, and that was for Hazeltine.

He found himself in the presence of a woman.

"Sit down!" said she, but as she remained standing, so did he, and merely bowed. It was the first time he had come before a woman as applicant for a job, and he liked it very little.

"Ever done any writing?" she asked.

"I never have," said he, suavely.

"College graduate?"

"No."

"High School?"

"No."

He was polite and mild in manner, but resentful at heart; he wanted to get away, and he fancied that after these answers it would not be difficult. The woman was silent for a moment, staring at him, and he returned a blank but observant glance. She was a tall, stout woman with a double chin, and she wore eye-glasses. Nature had not been very kind to her, yet she was not discouraged. There was a valiant show of rouge and powder on her face, her hair was richly touched with henna, and though her dark dress was severely plain, it was short and revealed a pair of coquettish satin slippers and sturdy limbs in that shade of silk stockings known as 'nude.' She tapped a silver pencil against her rosy finger nails, and stared at Hazeltine.

"Well ..." she said, "you speak like an educated man."

"I'm sorry," said Hazeltine, with affability, "but the only qualification I have is my refined appearance."

He thought that would end it, but to his surprise, the woman took him seriously.

"That counts for a lot in this work," she said, "if you can write."

"I've never tried."

"Well if you know grammar and all that—"

"I'm afraid I don't."

Still she hesitated, and it occurred to Hazeltine that this time he was being given a chance.

"No use being too squeamish," he thought, with a sigh. He was lamentably aware of the effect he was producing and of the still more favourable effect he could produce, if he wished. Business woman this might be, and the first he had met, yet she was no mystery to him.

"It used to be the pretty girl and the boss with the roving eye," he reflected. "And now—it's the young man of refined appearance and this lady. My God! I'm in peril!"

"You've got to have more self-confidence," she was saying. "Suppose you tell me something about yourself. What experience you've had and so on."

He knew very well what to say. In a modest tone, he explained that he had had no business experience at all; he had been educated in French, English, and American schools and—circumstances made it necessary for him to find something to do now. He saw how pleased she was with this.

"Now, I'll tell you," she said, when he had done, "I'm starting a new magazine. The pattern service—I'll take care of that. I know that end of the business from A to Z. But I want to get out a nice, bright little magazine, good stories and articles and all. I want somebody to get interviews with movie stars and all, and to look over the manuscripts when they come in, and to keep an eye on the departments I'm going to have. I want—" she paused. "What I want is a high-class man," she said. "Now, can you do that work? Think it over a minute!"

Again he looked at her, but his glance wavered, abashed, before those terrible eyes behind her glasses, the most piercing, the coldest eyes he had ever seen.

"That's for you to say, isn't it?" he answered. "I'd be glad to try—"

"All right! Try it for a week, then. Start tomorrow morning at nine. The salary's thirty dollars a week. Nine to five, Saturdays till one."

Then she sat down and wrote upon a card his name and address, and certain comments of her own.

"Now, Mr. Hazeltine," she said, with a bloodcurdling sort of pleasantness, "you treat me fair and I'll treat you fair. That's the way I do business. Good morning!" He went out of the office with a card she had given him.

S. BENG. Publisher
"ALLURE"

Alone and unaided he had got a job. Now was he more than ever justified in going to Agnes. He telephoned, to find out if she could see him then, and was rather taken aback to learn that she was not at home.

"She's out at her work," the landlady told him. "Gets back about half-past five, as a rule."

She ought, of course, to have been there, always to be there. Now, instead of Hazeltine's going eagerly to her and finding her waiting, it was he who had to wait for her, all through a long day.

He had nowhere to go, nothing to do, no money to spend. He knew very well that Agnes was not to blame for this, yet it affected his attitude toward her. It added another virtue to his score, and subtracted something from hers. He strolled about until it should be time for lunch, and he meditated upon women in business. There was Helen, at home; he appreciated, as never before, the beauty there is in a woman's being at home. You could always find her there and tell her things. He thought of S. Beng. There was a business woman! Agnes was not at all like S. Beng, but neither was she like Helen.

"She's harder," he thought; "more self-sufficing."

He ate a very frugal meal and then went to a fifteen-cent cinema. He was bored in there in the dark; he endured it as long as he could, but he left too early. So that when Agnes came home, he was waiting for her, outside the house.

The light of the setting sun was in her eyes, dazzling her, and she did not see him; a strange light it was, as if a gate had opened into space, and the pure, colourless radiance of heaven were streaming out. He watched her coming, swift and dark against that brightness. Self-sufficing, was she, that lonely young thing? Hard—that worn and sorrowful face? A good thing for her if she could have been sufficient to herself, for she had no one else; a fine thing if she could have been hard, to endure what came to her.

Pity and tenderness rose in him; he stepped before her and held out his hand, smiling down at her. "Back again, little pal!" he said.

In that light he was like a knight in shining armour, standing bareheaded before her with the sun on his fair hair. He didn't know what he was like to her; he never knew the splendour he had in her eyes, but he did see the look on her face.... She could not speak at all.

And for perhaps the first time in his life he felt an honest remorse. That friendship, which he had chosen to call honourable, was the cruellest, falsest sort of thing. He had been so careful to make her understand that he would give nothing, and that from her unmeasured generosity he would take nothing.

"I didn't think you'd ever come anymore," she said at last, very low.

How was he to answer his little pal? Go on smiling, pretending not to know? He had known so well, for a long time. He had come to-day, in a spirit of smug benevolence, to allow her to give him a little crumb of comfort—and she herself was famishing.

"Won't you come in?" she said.

It was the quiet, well-bred voice of a Phillips of Vermont that spoke to him, for it was to those lares that she turned for help. She went before him up the dark stairs, her thin shoulders so straight, her head so high. Augustine Brian might find beauty in the fate of maidens who waited in mute patience for their knights, but not she. She was still here, where he had left her, but it was because there was nowhere else for her to go. She had not waited for him; she would not have it so.

She put the key in the lock, to open the door of the flat. It would not turn. She bent over it, tried again, but it would not turn. A great anger and despair came over her; she rattled the key violently, kicked the door, and suddenly, to her horror, a sob broke from her.

"I just can't ..." she faltered.

"Agnes!" he said.

His arm was about her shoulders. He felt a little shudder run through her; she stood rigid and still.

"Don't!" she said.

But she was so dear to him. He had nobody else in the world. Honest and kind and dear she was, young, and lonely like himself. He couldn't live any longer without human solace.

"I do need you so!" he cried.

"You ought—to be ashamed of yourself!" she said, in a trembling, angry voice. "You told me—you said—you were engaged—"

"That's finished. Everything's finished.... I'm starting all over again.... Agnes, don't send me away!"

She did not answer for a long time.

"I never did," she said at last, so low he could scarcely hear.

He drew her close to him; he bent and kissed her averted cheek. She was still rigid and unyielding, but that did not chill him. It was a blessed comfort for him to hold her so; he was happy; he knew the words that would bring her wholly to him.

Only, he could not speak these words just now. He could not say "I love you!" She was too dear to him; he could not hurt her like that. He had to go away again now, and to think this out. He wanted to be honest with her. If he came back, he would say that to her, honestly; if he could not say it, then he would never come.

He raised her hand to his lips and kissed it; then without another word he turned and went down the stairs. She stood there in the dark until she heard the front door close behind him.

CHAPTER TWENTY-FOUR

HAZELTINE IS ONE OF THE HERD

Hazeltine stood in the doorway and Selma Beng sat behind her desk, and they looked steadily at each other. A terrible glance, epitome of their four weeks' struggle, an epic, a thing of profound moral significance. For every moment of every working day the battle had gone on, without truce, yet neither showed the slightest sign of weakening.

"If you want to succeed," said Mrs. Beng, in a reasonable tone, "you've got to forget yourself a little and work for the success of The Business. Throw yourself into it, heart and soul."

"That's not my point of view," said Hazeltine, quite as reasonably and more mildly. "What sort of success would my life be if I'd left my heart and soul in someone else's business?"

Because this warfare was one of opposing principles. Hazeltine in his day had been a notable exploiter of persons; he had known how to get what he wanted with the least possible expenditure of effort, and though he had renounced that course, and was now willing to pay an honest price, he was unwaveringly opposed to extortion. He was too accustomed to making bargains, with tailors and other tradespeople, with hotels, even, unfortunately, with his friends; he had never in his earlier years been trustful or lavish and he never would be to the end of his existence. It was to his credit that he was now prepared to make only fair bargains, that he now preferred a receipt in full from life to the loot he had formerly collected. But he was not capable of enthusiasm; he stood very firm on his feet, and it was his great principle Not To Pay Too Much.

Now, it was the especial concern of Mrs. Beng to inspire those about her with the most turbulent enthusiasm; that was her way, her method, the secret of her success. She had a remarkable talent for this; her business was a treadmill upon which Heaven knows how many willing horses had expired, and the thing was more horrible for being utterly senseless. Whatever she did, she made money, and then she used the money to begin something a little more expensive, and for each new enterprise she had the same fanatic passion, and was able to inspire her wretched employees with the same mania. She used to give them little talks that drove them into emulative frenzy.

"We must all pull together—all forget ourselves in the success of the business."

Then they all did pull together and did forget themselves, and before long Mrs. Beng forgot them also, in some new enterprise. And her great principle was—To Get Her Work Done, at any cost to anyone.

Hazeltine had come at a favourable season for observing her at her greatest. Here was the beginning of something new, the birth of "Allure," and all her staff lived in fevered hope and excitement. Even the office-boy knew how many subscriptions came in every day. Mrs. Beng would come out of her private room, followed by her two subscription salesmen and her two advertising salesmen, and she would say:—

"Now, people! We've passed the fifteen-thousand mark! Now, altogether for twenty thousand!"

And they would be filled with rapture, every one of those young women, and it was as if a cubit were added to the stature of each, and they were ready to work like demons for the twenty thousand subscriptions, though not an extra penny came their way. She was Napoleonic, only that she had no object: she led her armies nowhere.

Hazeltine was quite able to appreciate her remarkable qualities; in fact, he had never met a human being he so nearly feared. No man he had yet encountered could match her for energy and force, yet the worst thing about the creature was, that she wasn't in the least masculine. She had feminine traits and instincts that froze the blood. She had vanities: he had seen her powdering her nose; she ate chocolates; she was very proud of her small round feet. She actually had a husband. She told Hazeltine once that Mr. Beng didn't like her to wear earrings; and for a time he had been dazed, for thinking of that Mr. Beng. No; it was better not to think of him.

From the very beginning Mrs. Beng and Hazeltine had been in opposition. Her penetrating eye had seen how useful a well-trained gentleman could be to her, and she had set to work to arouse in him what she called a spirit of loyalty. She met with determined resistance. He, too, had seen his usefulness and he intended that it should, in some measure, benefit himself. He alone refused to become excited about the subscriptions or about new advertising, or about anything else. He arrived promptly in the morning, ready and willing to do a good day's work—and no more.

In the middle of his second week she had made appointments for him to interview people continuously from half-past eleven until three, and when he came back to the office to report, she saw that he had omitted one of these interviews.

"Because I wanted my lunch," he explained, artlessly.

Mrs. Beng leaned back in her chair and looked at him with that tight-lipped smile of hers.

"See here, Mr. Hazeltine!" she said, "don't you think this thing is big enough for you to forget your lunch for one day?"

"Lunch," said Hazeltine, "is a persistent sort of thing. You can't forget it."

"Frankly, I'm disappointed," said she. "I thought you had more interest in this thing. I thought you were capable of seeing that *your* success depends upon the success of the business."

There was no personal antagonism between them; they argued without rancour, even with a certain relish. Mrs. Beng liked Hazeltine; she told him that she was always willing to hear his point of view because she was fair-minded; that was her way. He had, however, seen the manner in which she annihilated the points of view of other people, consuming them in a blaze of enthusiasm, and he knew very well that nothing he could say would impress her. She listened to him for the sole reason that she liked to hear him talk and to look at him.

He was very obliging. From nine till five he would do anything she wanted, interview people, dictate letters, read proof, revise manuscripts, and he was remarkably neat and quick and clever at all this; he abhorred slovenliness. He worked with a will, too, was beautifully good-tempered, and he had the great advantage of being a healthy, well-fed, well-cared-for creature who did not tire or fall ill. Altogether he was worth more than she paid him, and it was a pity Mrs. Beng could not be satisfied with that.

She was not, though; he was doing quite as much as he ought to do, but nothing like what he could do, and it was intolerable. She tried scheme after scheme to make him stop after hours or to miss his lunch; in vain; he was like one of those maidens in a fairy-tale who are shut up to spin straw into gold, or some such task, and do it, aided by fairies. Whatever she gave him to do, he did—in office hours.

At last she hit upon a new plan. She wanted him to write an article upon the history of cosmetics, and she said he had better do it at home. To her delight, he had agreed; he had consulted with Mac Donald about it, visited the public library, and now, on this Saturday morning, he had brought in the manuscript. It was exactly as she wanted it.

The title was 'Roses of Yesterday,' and it was all about Milady, which was the conventional name for all readers of 'Allure.' Du Barry and Cleopatra were brought into it, roguishly yet with delicacy; there was a light touch throughout, and plenty of hints directed toward such cosmetics as were advertised in that issue. Of its sort it was a masterpiece. And Hazeltine had not written it with his tongue in his cheek; on the contrary, he had calmly and thoughtfully laboured to produce a masterpiece.

"Now suppose you see what you can do with 'The Story of Lace,'" said Mrs. Beng. "You can easily get up a three-thousand word story by—say—Tuesday."

"I think so," said he. "But do you mind telling me what I'm to get for this extra work?"

"*Extra* work!" cried Selma Beng. "It's not extra; it's part of your regular work."

"I see! Then I'll take a day or two off, to do it in."

"Now, Mr. Hazeltine, you know as well as. I do all there is to be done in this office."

"Mrs. Beng," said he, with great politeness, "there are also things to be done outside the office. For me, that is."

"What I expect from my staff is co-operation," she said. "It's a new thing, and we've all got to pull together—" And so she went on.

She had the black magic of oratory; no matter what her words, she held her listeners; the inflections of her voice, the glitter of her eyes behind the glasses, the effortless flow of speech destroyed reason. She was a woman working to get her own way—always a formidable thing—and, what is more, she was a superwoman of incalculable force, and actuated by fanaticism. Hers was the unholy eloquence which sways a mob; she could have stood upon a street corner and inspired a new crusade, if she had wished.

And all this was directed against Hazeltine. For more than an hour the battle endured; the rest of the staff had gone, and the adversaries were alone. Hazeltine was exhausted, no longer able to refute her arguments, no longer able to express himself with any vigour. All that remained was his inflexible resolve not to be imposed upon, and his admirable patience. He did not look for victory, but he would not be conquered.

It was not through reason but by chance, or instinctively, that at last he discovered the one effective weapon of the worker.

"Very well!" he said, "I'm sorry, but I can't do extra work without extra pay. My week's up on Wednesday—"

By this simple method he won! By refusing to work, by passive resistance, by non-co-operation, the one defense against all Mrs. Bengs. She did not want him to go; he was rare; it would be almost impossible to find his equal. She would not, however, admit that there existed such a thing as 'extra' work, but she said that if he would agree to do an article every month, his salary would be increased.

The weary Hazeltine was greatly tempted to let it go at that, but he did not. With courteous threats and persistence he wrung from Mrs. Beng a promise to pay him for the 'Roses of Yesterday,' and he held out for a more substantial increase in salary than she offered.

It was not his potential value as a worker which gave him so complete a triumph, either. This was not a battle between Capital and Labour; what gave to this struggle its profound moral significance was the fact that under a sort of matriarchy a solitary man held his own. Here was Mrs. Beng, a woman, possessed of all a woman's mystic prestige in addition to vast temporal powers and her own peculiar talents. Confronting her was this penniless young man, with no other weapon than his masculine patience and sub-tlety, and his masculine charm. Yet he conquered. Steadily their eyes met.... He was such an engaging young fellow, so handsome, so well-bred, so appealing with his mild manner, and his smile.

"Very well!" said she. "I agree!"

He nearly sighed, but managed to smile instead. And rising, Mrs. Beng offered her hand with a somewhat alarming geniality.

"Now, remember!" she said, "we'll expect a whole lot from you, Mr. Hazeltine!"

While he waited for the train, Hazeltine reflected upon the amazing air of solidity this life had now assumed. He rose every morning at a virtuously early hour and went off to work, and it was no longer a strange adventure, but quite natural. Quite natural and credible that he should live in Manorgrange Park and go to work every day and return every evening to a sedate dinner with Mac Donald and Helen, to read a little, to smoke a few cheap cigarettes, and go early to bed. He had not a single one of those things he had once believed all that were worth having in this world, yet he was not unhappy.

That was the strangest thing, that he was not unhappy. Without rebellion he could look forward to a life of this sort forever and ever. He wanted to understand this; he thought about it earnestly. Why wasn't he miserable?

And as he stood there among the crowd of homeward-bound commuters, the answer came to him like an inspiration. This life was the common fate of mankind, and he was satisfied because he shared in it.

He was better dressed than the men about him, but that distinction wouldn't last; his next suit would have to be a ready-made one, and then he would be quite like the rest. And this pleased him. He thought what a sublime and heroic thing is the life of an average man, the fidelity, the decency, the immense restraint which the patient animal exercises, fighting down the hot instincts of greed, lust, and aggression, so marvellously training and disciplining itself, with no master visible to threaten or to reward. The consequences of knavery were not appalling, yet how few knaves there were! There was so little to be gained by keeping faith, yet how few failed! They worked, they took wives, brought up children, they were knocked flat by illness, by financial disaster, by griefs and losses, and they struggled up again, and went on, so pitifully alone, for the face of their God was veiled.

And all these average men had built up on earth a sublime order. A witless thing, it seemed to Hazeltine, to make horrified protests against the wars, the crimes, the injustices that happened in the course of this tremendous experiment; the marvel was that this creature Man had, of his own will, made some sort of order from chaos, had built for ages and ages, not repetitiously, like the coral, but divinely, with changes, with improvements.

Even that these men beside him who were so tired, who so badly wanted to get home, did not strike and snarl, was a marvel. A great pride came over him, for them and for himself, too. Admirable, all of them.... There was the ticket-seller, who so neatly fitted into the scheme of things that he was capable of walking voluntarily into a cage and remaining there for hours, and could be trusted always to do so, and to handle money and to answer questions accurately. What illimitable trust everyone had in everyone else! The bitterest cynic, who saw civilization coming down, about his ears, nevertheless waited with childlike faith for a train to arrive when it was promised him; when he went into a restaurant and ordered a cup of coffee, he felt certain of getting it and of receiving change for the bill he so trustingly proffered. All life was founded upon the assumption that people would do what was expected of them, and, by Heaven, they did! There was not one human being in five hundred who refused the responsibilities sent by fate, by chance, by inscrutable God.

And those who bore the yoke were always in some way noble, and those who refused, with fine gestures, insisting upon freedom, were free, as chaff is free to fly upon the wind.

As his brothers, so would he do.

"I've got a rise in salary," he said to himself. "Tomorrow I'm going to ask Agnes to marry me."

CHAPTER TWENTY-FIVE

LEWIS GROWS IMPATIENT

The lamp-lit room had never had the quality of a home for Agnes. She had lived in it for two years; some of the things were her own, had belonged to her mother, and were dear to her, but the room, to her, was always Coralie's room, not hers; she had no home even to remember.

Yet, if she lived so unencumbered, it was not lightly, in the Bohemian tradition, but with a sad wonder, to find herself so lost and desolate. It was not ease and comfort she wanted; she was austere, scornful, in her vigorous youth, of the things of the body. It was her spirit that longed for a home.

She was reading this evening. She loved books, but got very little out of them, because she was afraid to trust them. "It's only in a book!" she would say to herself, sternly, if any delight sprang up from the printed page. An author was by no means a seer to her, but a rather weak sort of creature who imagined things, and it was wrong and very perilous to imagine things. She would accept only what was real, and unfortunately the real things which she could grasp affronted her. She refused the 'good times' the other girls in the office enjoyed; even the faithful Richard had become distasteful to her.

"If I can't have what I want," she told herself, "I'll have nothing."

But she never permitted herself to discover what she did want; she knew only that she hadn't got it.

It was a windy night; in the country the leaves would be torn from the trees and go skimming off along the roads, but here in the city autumn had not come; the dust and weariness of the summer lingered. The window beside her was open and the curtains— artistic green curtains bought by Coralie—streamed out into the room, and fell back, limp and disheartened. The taste of dust was in her mouth; she was tired from her day's work and yet restive, wait- ing for what never, never came.

She thought she heard that step on the stairs, but she had thought that before, and it was never true. No, it was only somebody else, going somewhere else. He wouldn't come again; she would not expect him.

But there was someone on the landing, outside the door. She kept her eyes resolutely on her book, and would not be waiting ... until there was a knock.

She got up then. She could not stop the beating of her heart or bring the blood to her pale cheek, but she could go quietly and deliberately across the room to open the door. And he was there. She waited for him to speak first, but he said nothing. The shaded lamp in the room gave little illumination out there, and his hat was pulled down over his forehead; she fancied, though, that she could see the shadow of a smile on his lips, and somehow it frightened her.

"Won't you come in?" she said, uneasily.

Still he did not answer or move. And he seemed to have grown so tall, too tall, almost monstrous.

"What's the matter?" she cried.

"Oh, nothing!" he answered, gaily.

She came closer to him.

"It's not ...!" she said. "It's Mr. Martinsburgh!"

"Who did you think it was?" he asked. "Let me in!"

She stood aside and he entered; he stared about him as if dazzled, and she saw, with dismay, the dreadful brilliancy of his eyes. He took off his hat and overcoat, and tossed them into a chair.

"Where's Coralie?" he asked.

"She's not here. She's—"

"I wanted to see her. I wanted to tell her—" He stared at Agnes vaguely. "I meant to tell her she'd ruined my life. I thought, you know, that she was responsible for all of this. But after all, I don't believe she is. No.... It was coming, anyhow."

He threw himself into a chair, and stared up at the ceiling.

"I feel very well to-night," he said, with a dreamy smile. "Strong, you know, and confident. I've made a clean sweep of everything. Such a burden off my heart.... I'm comfortable now. I never was so comfortable. Even the hair's lying so light on my head."

He smiled directly at her then and Agnes, distruster of beauty, trembled to see him.

"You shouldn't have written me those letters," he said, gently.

"I? But I didn't...."

"No ..." he said. "That's right. It was Coralie. But it doesn't matter. She's been writing. She says I ought to be made to suffer for what I've done! Who is she, to know who ought to suffer? And for what I've done.... She doesn't know what I've done. Nobody knows. Except myself. And I'm going to forget now."

He looked up at her with a sort of anxiety. She was standing squarely before him, grave and aloof as a young goddess; and, indeed, there was something almost divine in the effort of her frightened and bewildered heart to understand. She thought that it was her duty to understand, to listen without flinching.

"You see," he went on, "I want to forget myself. I'm so tired of thinking about myself—more tired than you realize. That's why I'm afraid.... If Jocelyn knew how much I have to think about myself.... You see, when I try to think about her, I only think about myself thinking about her. It's ... If I could get one plain, direct thought from outside—something I didn't make. But I have to make the whole world. Nothing's there until I can think what I think about it.... That's more reasonable than it sounds. It's a subtle sort of thing, but perfectly reasonable. I'm perfectly reasonable. Too much so."

He sighed and frowned.

"I'm not talking to you," he said, as if rebuking an interruption. "I'm talking to—well, to God, perhaps. God doesn't answer. He doesn't listen to me anymore. He is sitting up there in Heaven, thinking about Himself, and all his thoughts come alive. Not mine, though. My thoughts run round inside me like rats in a cage. They never get out." He drew a shuddering breath. "I'd have to put a bullet through my brain to let them out—"

"No!" cried Agnes, sharply.

"No!" he cried, like an echo.

They faced each other in silence for a moment. "God is not like that," said Agnes.

"You don't know what I've done," said Lewis, with a sigh. "'Know thyself'—that's a rule people give you. Of course, if you really knew yourself, you'd know God, too—everything. It's what I tried to do. I was always watching my own soul, studying it. Always looking inside. And now I'm shut up in there. Nothing from outside can reach me anymore.... Know thyself, that's the way to go mad." He rose. "I am mad, my dear," he said wearily. "Of course, I wanted to be, and, in a way, I'm glad but—"Tears came to his eyes and he brushed them aside with his transparent fingers. "It's sad," he said. "Very! Don't let people tell you to know yourself! Psychoanalysis—introspection—things like that—it's all simply picking your soul into pieces.... No, forget yourself. Then you'll stay real. I—you see—I'm gone."

He walked past her over to the mantlepiece and began lifting the objects there and setting them down again, one by one. Agnes was praying in her heart.

"Please tell me what to say to him! Please, God, help me to help this man!"

For she felt, not so much pity for him, as a terrible, crushing obligation. He had come here in his mortal anguish, and she who so loved God must help him.

"Mr. Martinsburgh!" she said. "Lewis!"

He shook his head without turning toward her.

"I'm gone," he said. "I can't hear you."

"You must hear me!" she said. "Oh, please!"

She came beside him and laid her hand on his sleeve; then he looked at her, and his smile almost broke her heart, because it was so like Basil's.

"You can get well!" she cried. "I know you can! Let me take you home! If there's no one there to—to look after you, I'll stay. I know—I know you can get well!"

"Yes, but I don't want to," he answered, casually. "I've got to see God. I can't wait any longer."

He moved away from her, across the room, and stepped into the dark little bedroom. As she followed, the door crashed behind him and the key turned in the lock.

"Please come out!" she entreated, rattling the handle. "Please open the door!"

There was not a sound in answer; she waited, fighting down a panic terror; suddenly it overwhelmed her; she beat on the door, calling:

"Oh, please, please come out! Answer me! Oh, please speak!"

This clamour added to her fear tenfold; she stopped, panting, and waited again.

"Oh, please!" she began, in a little wailing voice, when something came hurling against the locked door. She staggered back; it seemed to her that the whole world reeled and shivered from that blow. Some horror unimaginable would come out of that door now.... Nothing came. Only she heard in the stillness a strange, pleasant little sound, like water running from a bottle overturned.

CHAPTER TWENTY-SIX

NO CHOICE

Mac Donald was reading *Thus Spake Zarathustra*. The ideas presented were not congenial to him, but he was at all times ready to give respectful attention to a philosopher. He read, with impartiality, Marcus Aurelius, Schopenhauer, Epictetus and Rousseau; he liked to smoke, and to reflect upon all this wisdom which he greatly admired. Yet he was not influenced by it. His admiration was purely aesthetic; he contemplated a philosophic system as he might have looked upon some superb building, finding a grave pleasure in the design of the thing without considering it possible—or desirable—to model his own dwelling upon it.

A smile appeared on his lips; a tribute, that was, to Nietzsche, who, so to speak, challenged him to a duel. Some pages he found very difficult to understand; now and then Nietzsche conquered him, and it was this cleverness that made Mac Donald smile, congratulating his adversary.

The house was very quiet; Helen and little Janet had gone to bed, and Hazeltine never stirred. He was not reading; he was thinking, stretched out comfortably in that chair which was now regarded as especially his.

He would marry Agnes, and they would have a house like this. Exactly like this; furnished with just this endearing ugliness. Cheap little houses were heart-breaking if they were furnished brightly, with taste; they ought to be shabby and somewhat stupid, for then you could love them. A hearth-rug with the picture of a dog on it, a green velvet table cover with tasselled fringe, a framed engraving of Loch Lomond, a square, squat rocking-chair like a three-sided coop on runners—such things were truly household goods, things a man could go into battle for and die defending. Willow chairs and chintz and hammered brass—these were only decoration.

He believed that Agnes would understand this. And still more did he believe, without admitting it, that she would not need to understand in order to agree with him. He remembered how pleased she had always been with anything he brought her, flowers, or a box of sweets. He remembered her in the days of that well-managed little friendship of theirs; she had expected nothing of him, and, what was still finer, she had offered nothing. She had her own invincible dignity; if that look on her face betrayed her, it was not her fault. She didn't even know. She was so young, and so honest, and so dear to him.

He glanced at Mac Donald, the just man. Mac Donald admired Agnes; he had said so, long ago. No doubt this marriage would please him.

"He might think I ought to pay my debts first," Hazeltine reflected. "Only, the largest debts never can be paid. Not with all the money in the world. And the others—all in good time. I rather think I'll get on in business. I was a match for Selma Beng that could be put on any man's tombstone.... 'Allure' won't hold me long. I'll go ever on and up. I'll be able to look after Agnes."

Curious delight there was in the thought of looking after somebody! It made him aware, for the first time, of all the strength that there was in his stalwart body and his cool and deliberate brain. He smiled to himself, a little arrogant in his heart for knowing himself strong, hardy and unconquerable....

The telephone bell rang and Mac Donald sprang up with the alacrity of one accustomed to obeying bells. He went out into the hall; Hazeltine heard his cautious voice.

"Yes. He is here. This'll be for you, Hazeltine."

So Hazeltine went, took up the receiver, and a hoarse, fierce voice sounded in his ear.

"Mr. Basil! You're wanted!"

"But—what is it?" he asked, surprised.

"It's Mrs. Welley. There's been an accident and you'd better come to Mr. Lewis this very minute."

"But what sort of accident? What's happened?"

"Come and find out if you want to know!" cried Mrs. Welley, violently.

Ten o'clock was a latish hour in Manorgrange Park, with bedtime not far distant. But when Hazeltine reached the city at half-past eleven it was as if time had turned backward and it was no longer late. The streets were filled with people, the theatres had just emptied, and the restaurants and cabarets were filling; once when his taxi was held up in the traffic, he looked into a brightly lighted delicatessen shop and in there saw a respectable grey-haired woman buying eggs and butter, as if the day were just beginning.

Lewis's little house was quiet enough, though. A light shone through the glass of the door, but the windows were dark; the street was empty and quiet. Hazeltine felt a sort of embarrassment; it seemed unnecessarily dramatic to dash up here at half-past eleven and ring the bell; the haste of his journey appeared now a childish proceeding. Probably Mrs. Welley hadn't expected him to come tonight; the morning would have done quite as well. He hesitated, standing outside the door of the quiet little house; then his native effrontery came to his aid, and he pressed the bell.

He heard the sound go running through the house like a frightened little animal, burrowing down into the kitchen. He had a long wait, but he did not care to ring again, and at last, the door was opened. Mrs. Welley stood before him, wild as a witch.

"Well!" she said, with an air of triumph. "Now you've done it, among the lot of you!"

"Done what?" he asked. He came in, closing the door behind him, and something that there was in the house blew like a cold wind upon him.

"I saw it coming!" Mrs. Welley went on. "I knew! Harried and driven, he was, till it came to *this!* And now ..."

"What's happened?"

"What's happened?" she repeated. "You may well ask! Cut his throat, Mr. Lewis has, and he's lying dead upstairs. That's what's happened. Harried and driven ..."

"Shut up!" said Hazeltine, bluntly. "Who's here?"

"Oh *she's* here!" said Mrs. Welley. "And that's all you care about."

"Tell her I'm here—"

"I won't!" cried Mrs. Welley. "Go and tell her yourself! I'm here to wait on Mr. Lewis and I won't—I won't—I won't ...!"

He turned, and left Mrs. Welley in her most desperate mutiny, her woolly white hair pushed back from her sharp little face down which tears rolled without haste. It seemed to him that he had not really heard a single word she had spoken; he understood nothing except that Jocelyn was here, and menaced.

He went up the stairs, quietly, because, of course, it was necessary to be very, very quiet. And when he reached the first floor, he was startled to hear a soft murmur of voices. Who was there to speak in this house to-night? He frowned a little as he went toward that sound.

The door of a bedroom was ajar; he could look into it. It was filled with a warm, rosy light, and Mrs. Coons and Jocelyn were sitting in there, talking softly. Mrs. Coons was in dressing-gown and slippers; it was she who was at home; the fugitive Jocelyn had only strayed in. O most lovely wraith! There was on her face no new sorrow; had she not been born sorrowing for all her fellow-creatures? She sat in an attitude he knew so well, her arms extended on a table, hands clasped, her dark head bent; she was listening to Mrs. Coons, for she always listened to any voice that spoke. O most merciful and lovely wraith!

"Jocelyn!" he said.

Both the women turned toward him. Jocelyn rose; he went toward her; he would have taken her in his arms.

"Basil, my dear boy!" said Mrs. Coons, with a kind of sharpness.

He halted, obediently; he was still dazed, but he recognized the voice of the world. Despair seized him; was there always to be a barrier between them, so that he could never go to her, and she never come to him?

Mrs. Coons took him by the arm and drew him away, down the corridor.

"Basil!" she whispered. "Oh, isn't this horrible?"

"Yes ..." he said, absently. "Yes, of course ..."

"Why did he do such a thing?" she went on, her eyes filling with tears. "Just when it seemed as if ... We all hoped so that they'd be happy together.... Oh, poor, poor Jocelyn! What was it, do you think, Basil?"

A faint resentment moved him, because she was ranging him with herself and the rest of the world, and setting Jocelyn and Lewis by themselves.

"How do I know?" he said.

"She was with us, you know. A little dance ... And someone telephoned. Unfortunately, she overheard.... Poor Harold! He was at the telephone and he cried out—'My God! You mean Lewis Martinsburgh?' And then, of course, we had to tell her.... Oh, Basil! She *would* go.... Harold and I went with her.... A doctor was there, and two policemen—and that poor girl—"

"What girl?"

"Nobody seemed to know much about her. She said he'd come there, in a very strange state, and locked himself into a room—"

"But where? What girl?" he demanded, impatiently.

"I really don't know who she was, Basil. But she seemed a very nice girl. I'm sure she had nothing to do with it. And he was found with the door locked on the inside—"

"Where?"

"Somewhere on West Tenth Street. We all went—"

"It was Agnes!" he said.

Mrs. Coons looked at him uneasily.

"Will it be something—to hurt Jocelyn more?" she asked.

"Oh, no!" he reassured her. "But—just wait a minute, please! I don't understand. D'you mean he went there, to her flat, and killed himself?"

"Not so loud, Basil! Yes."

"And what happened to her?"

"The girl? Why, nothing. We left her there—"

"Alone?"

"I suppose so. I didn't see anyone else... And we couldn't think of anyone but Jocelyn then—"

"I'll have to go," he said.

Mrs. Coons was silent. There was light enough for her to see his face dimly, and dimly she saw and understood the look it wore.

"My dear boy ..." she said, unsteadily.

She fancied she heard him sigh, very softly.

He had to go to Agnes. It was a most obvious thing; there was no question about it.

"Do you want to see—Lewis?" Mrs. Coons asked, in a whisper.

This seemed to him preposterous. See Lewis? There was no Lewis. But he answered gravely, "Yes, thanks!" as if she had offered him a unique opportunity. She led the way to Lewis's room, opened the door for him, and he went in alone.

Lewis was Keeping Up Appearances.

And Hazeltine approaching him, could for the first time appreciate the value of that. He had seen enough of sudden death in France; now he could observe the gallant, immemorially ancient effort of man to conceal the horror of that. He had been appalled, too much shocked for any least regret, but now his heart turned to water at the pathetic decency of that quiet figure.

There he lay, in his neat dark jacket, with his necktie in a proper bow, his hair combed in his usual fashion; not a trace about him of his panic flight from life. Whatever had lain behind that locked door, the public was mercifully forbidden to see; there were doctors, nurses, undertakers, clergymen, organists, sextons, any number of persons trained and prepared to give to such tragedies an air of dignified usualness; because of their efforts, the majority could go through life and see nothing of death but this sublime and dignified masquerade. So that Hazeltine could look down at Lewis and feel, not horror, but pity.

There were flowers beside him, only a few, though, put there by Mrs. Welley, for Lewis was somewhat in disgrace. He was to have a very quiet funeral, as a punishment for so startling an end. He had made his bed, and now he was lying upon it; he had defied the social order and must pay the penalty of ostracism.

He seemed indifferent to that. You might have thought him still defiant, challenging by his decorum, his severe correctness, the suspicion that he had committed any deed of violence. There he lay, in all his awful candour, ready to welcome any scrutiny; stare as you would, he was not uneasy.

Hazeltine who looked at him, pale himself, his face impassive because of his great wonderment, did not know how like they were, and not only in body. He failed to draw the parallel; indeed, he could not. But the thought did come to him that here was a life ended in sterility, and that his own might end in that way—or in another, as he chose. He did see then that a man must choose, whether he will or not. Fate is no driver; she lies hidden at every crossroad; only when you have chosen do you see her face.

Hazeltine had chosen, long ago. He could not turn back now; he had to go on, to Agnes.

"Good-bye, Lewis!" he said, under his breath.

CHAPTER TWENTY-SEVEN

DAWN IN MANORGRANGE PARK

It was nearly one o'clock in the morning when Hazeltine rang the bell of the house on West Tenth Street, yet the landlady came promptly to open the door, and seemed neither surprised nor interested. Too much had happened that evening; she was just sick and tired of it all. A doctor, a policeman breaking in a door, an ambulance, and those newspaper men.... She recognized Hazeltine as a person in some way connected with the top floor; she didn't even bother to speak to him and he went by her with a careless nod.

As he passed the second floor a door opened and a head peered out; the house was not sleeping well that night. And even then he could see the light coming from the top storey, a river of light streaming down.

Agnes had heard his footstep and was waiting in the doorway of her room. Every light in the place was turned on, and the fierce illumination brought into high relief the strong lines of her cheek and jaw, gave to her a harsh and forbidding look.

"Agnes!" he said.

She shook her head mutely, and stood aside; he entered the room, closing the door behind him.

"Agnes!" he said, again, almost angrily, because her strangeness so troubled him. "I've come—"

"Yes, I know," she said, promptly. "I know. I'll tell you—I'll try to tell you all about it—"

"I don't want to hear. I've come—"

Her dark brows quivered, and fixed in a frown. "I've told all of them," she said. "So many times.... You see, I didn't know—"

"I don't care!" he cried, frowning himself. "I want you to come away—now—"

"But where?"

"Out to Mac Donald's house. I'm stopping there. He'll understand.... Come along, for God's sake!"

"But, you see," she said, "I can't get my hat."

"Can't get your hat?" he repeated, impatiently.

She shook her head again, and, like a child, pointed straight at the closed door across the room.

"Oh ...!" he said, blankly. "I see ..."

He realized very well what she had endured here in this brilliantly lighted room; he knew that he was horribly sorry for her, but he could not, at that moment, feel anything at all.

"I see ..." he said, again, and, in a tone of respectful curiosity— "What were you doing—when I came ...?"

"I don't know," she answered.

He wanted to tell her that he loved her and to say things about forgetting this and being happy, but it was simply impossible. Nor could he think of any solution whatever to the problem of her hat. There was nothing to be done; perhaps he could sit down for a bit and rest. There was nothing he wanted so much as that.

He realized, however, the extreme danger of that. If he once sat down, once let the tension slacken, he never could start again.

"Well, look here, Agnes," he said, plaintively, "let's go, anyhow. I'll get a taxi. It's not cold. Even if you've no hat, you know ..."

"All right!" she said. "I should like to—to—get away for a while."

"Wait here while I get a cab—"

"I'd rather not," she said.

So they went together, leaving all those lights blazing. She picked up a jersey and put it on, but she took nothing with her; she went bare-headed and empty-handed.

They picked up a cab on Sixth Avenue. At first the driver demurred at making so long a trip, but Hazeltine promised a double fare. And in they got.

He put his arm about her, and her head dropped on his shoulder. He sat very still, not to disturb her; she did not speak or stir, and he thought, from her quiet breathing, that she was asleep.

"Poor little kid!" he thought.

Her weight resting against him made his arm ache; he shifted his position cautiously, but he couldn't do much. And somehow that touched him beyond measure; the torpor of his fatigue was pierced by an overwhelming tenderness. He bent and kissed her soft hair.

"Poor little sweetheart!" he whispered.

She didn't hear. He took one of her limp hands and held it in his own, and something which he thought was a great sorrow came over him in a flood. Sorrow.... After all, he wasn't sure.... He couldn't think, just now. Only that a burden rested in his arms and that it was his pride and his pain to have it so.

"This the place?" asked a voice.

He opened his eyes and at once recognised the imposing entrance to Manorgrange Park.

"That's it!" he answered. "Straight ahead now."

His arm and shoulder were painfully cramped; he moved as much as he dared, but Agnes still slept. He looked out of the window. Manorgrange Park had the strangest look.... The little houses stood, all grey, in a vast grey desolation. The fields seemed to stretch beyond human vision; the little trees were frail, grey shadows; nothing was alive, nothing real. To his brain, still confused with sleep, this was twilight in a lost world; he was appalled by the silence.

The cab stopped; he withdrew his arm and shook Agnes gently.

"We're here!" he said.

She opened her eyes and looked at him; he smiled reassuringly, and got out. With the last bill he had on earth he paid the driver, and the cab drove off, and there they were.

"But—look!" she said, astounded. "The sun's coming up!"

He turned his head, and there in the east the splendour was coming, a light that grew and grew, so slow, so strong. The day was coming after the night.

"The sun ..." he repeated, awed as she was.

And then a lively little sparrow chirped; then all the birds waked up; the roosters shouted their braggart greeting; life was stirring with the sun.

"Oh, my God!" cried Hazeltine.

Agnes glanced at him anxiously, half-frightened by that note in his voice. She saw on his face the reflection of the sunrise and a look she could not comprehend.

"Basil ...!" she said.

He pulled her close to him, in a rough and hearty embrace, and for the first time since she had known him, he laughed aloud.

"I say! Isn't Manorgrange Park a beautiful place?" he demanded.

"Oh, it is!" she said. "I love it!"

So did he.

THE END

EARLY STORIES

by Elisabeth Sanxay Holding

Marie's View of It

The sisters were up-stairs in the cool, old-fashioned chamber leisurely making ready for bed. Amelia stood at the bureau, brushing her shining hair by the light of a dim lamp; Marie sat in a low arm-chair, unlacing her boots and talking vehemently. "I do despise that sort of talk," she cried. "'Melie, if you're *sensible* and *prudent* and *cautious*, as they want you to be, you'll simply miss *everything*. Being sensible means not wanting anything much, and being prudent means not trying to get what you want, and being cautious means not taking what you want even when you can get it. If you like him, 'Melie, and don't mind getting married, go ahead and take him."

"It isn't just what I want at this moment, Marie; it's a question of my whole future life."

"Darn the future!" cried Marie. "I'm not going to waste any of these years—these *good* years. After I'm thirty, I sha'n't care what happens. I'm going to spend *now*, and pay for it when I'm old."

It was a plan that did not appeal to the sleek and pretty Amelia, thrifty by nature, liking to savor life slowly, who was not greedy to swallow it whole at one meal, but who wanted rather to store it up on her neat little shelves and to use it, spread thin, through years and years. She was a gourmet, perhaps, but not a glutton, like the lean, fierce Marie. There were times, though, when she envied Marie her feast.

"I'm not in a hurry," she said. "I'm only nineteen; there's lots of time ahead of me. I'm going to give myself the rest of this summer to make up my mind."

"But aren't you afraid he'll go away or die—or something?" asked Marie. "I should be. If I liked a man, I'd marry him *instantly*."

"I'm not afraid of his going away," Amelia answered. "Anyway, if he wants to go, let him."

"You're really not a bit in love with him!" said Marie, reproachfully.

"I *could* be, if I wanted; but I'm not going to be until I'm sure I want to be."

"Well!" said Marie. "When *I* fall in love— Gosh!"

She leaned her head back against her clasped hands and stared up at the ceiling. A thin, dark young creature of eighteen, not pretty, but in her awkward immaturity giving promise of something rare to come; a sulky face with childish mouth and puzzled eyes, the face of an inquirer, an adventurer, that mingling of carelessness and earnestness that makes a Drake, a Parsifal, a Columbus.

"I don't believe you ever will fall in love," said Amelia. "You'd expect so much of a man that you couldn't help being angry with him all the time."

"Perhaps," said Marie, with a sigh. "It's very likely I'll never be suited. Or maybe no one will ever like me. I've never had any beaus, have I, 'Melie?"

"No," Amelia answered, not without a tinge of complacency because of the very many she had had. "Still, you're young yet; there's no hurry."

Who could convince Marie of that, though—Marie in such a panting hurry to live, to be born!

"Oh, Lord!" she sighed, beginning to braid her heavy, black hair. "No one seems to understand!"

"I try," said Amelia; "but we're very different; aren't we?"

Neither of them could see, though, how immeasurable the difference even at that instant, at that time in life when they were most alike, still bearing the impress of their identical training.

They had, definitely enough, "chosen" their futures, confident that what they had selected would be delivered. Amelia looked for a few years more of very agreeable maidenhood, and after that the extravagant and indulgent admiration of a husband with a good income. She pictured lovely clothes, a charming home of her own, a sort of perpetual holiday, which she would deserve by being good and pretty. There was already a promising applicant upon whom she was deliberating during this annual summer visit to their great-aunt's farm. She was glad of the opportunity for calm, untroubled meditation. Whereas to Marie the visit was, as usual, a painful infliction.

"I thought I could go on studying here," she told Amelia, "but I can't. It's *too* quiet, and I have *too much* time."

"The rest will do you good," Amelia had answered. She was never able to take Marie's studies very seriously, because the object of them changed so frequently and rapidly. Marie's ambition was simply to be illustrious. She was a student in a woman's college, a headstrong, ridiculous student who pounced greedily on half a dozen unrelated courses, who wanted to learn everything in the world and all at once, economics and church history and Romance languages, it didn't matter.

They were the motherless daughters of a business man who

reverenced woman, and never presumed to interfere with the two angels quartered under his roof. He provided them with what he believed to be their due, money to spend, clothes to wear, whatever education they wished, a home, and an unfaltering interest in their affairs, and otherwise let them alone. And they did very well under this system.

"Ready?" asked Amelia. "Shall I turn out the lamp?"

In a minute the room was dark. A cool breeze from the meadows fluttered the window curtains; little insects made their cheerful music in the summer night; the leaves of the old horse-chestnut rustled—all dear and familiar sounds, and sweet fragrances of climbing honeysuckle and exquisite night blooms. The sisters lay side by side, both wide-eyed and meditative.

"What's that?" asked Marie, suddenly.

"Nothing. A motor-car somewhere."

"But it's coming here, Amelia." They listened intently. The purring of a motor grew louder, wheels spun over the gravel, a blinding light flashed by their window, and in a minute the doorbell rang through the quiet old house.

"Who on *earth!*" cried Amelia, sitting up. "So late, and coming in a motor!"

Marie was already at the window.

"It's the station taxi," she announced. "I'm going down to see who it is."

"Not *that* way, Marie!"

Marie was struggling impatiently into her dressing-gown.

"Bother! The sleeves are inside out! There!"

Her bare feet padded across the room to the hall.

"I'll go, Auntie," she called to the old lady standing in her doorway.

"But don't catch cold, precious. Marie child, come back and put on your slippers!"

She was down-stairs already though, and running along the hall. There was a bolt to draw back, a chain to unfasten, and a key to turn; then she flung the door open boldly and looked out at the belated visitor. He took off his hat and smiled apologetically.

In romantic luminosity the moonlight revealed him a prince from the Arabian Nights, as dark and slim as herself, but far more beautiful; melancholy, lofty, victim of some outrageous fate.

"I know it's late," he said; "I'm sorry—but it's a matter of life and death. Would you be good enough to ask Miss Ellis if she will see Stanley for five minutes?"

"I will," cried Marie, and ran upstairs again eagerly.

"Auntie, it's a man named Stanley. He has to see you for five minutes about something important."

The old lady shivered a little.

"My dear," she answered, "put on your slippers and go down and tell the young man that I positively can*not* see him."

"But, Auntie, he says it's a matter of life and death!"

"I cannot see him, my dear. And I do not care to explain," the old lady replied with great dignity. "Please to tell him it is of no use coming to me again."

Marie was incredulous.

"How *can* you—" she began, but the old lady raised her hand.

"Hush, my dear! You know nothing about it. I cannot see him."

Marie went down-stairs again, indignant and amazed.

"I'm awfully sorry," she said, "but Miss Ellis—can't see you."

The young man stood in silence, looking at her with clear and fathomless blank eyes. The station taxi had gone, was humming down a distant road; he was quite alone in the night, surrounded by the wide fields, the woods, the vast and melancholy summer night.

"Thank you," he said at last, and was turning away when Marie touched his arm.

"Look here," she said bluntly, "what is the matter? If you'll tell me, perhaps I can do something."

He shook his head.

"Thank you," he said again in that gentle and immeasurably moving voice; "I don't think you could."

"Tell me, anyway!" she commanded.

"I came to borrow money," he said with utter simplicity. "My wife is ill, seriously ill. The doctor has ordered her to go out West at once. I haven't the money for such a trip, and I must get it somewhere. So, as Miss Ellis was once very kind to me, I tried here."

"Wait just a little longer!" cried Marie. "I want to tell auntie *that*—about your wife. I don't think she understood. Is it urgent? Ought she to go at once?"

"Every day counts," he answered.

She rushed up-stairs again, to argue passionately with the old lady.

"It's his *wife!*" she cried. "She's dying. Something must be done at once!"

She put all her ardent heart into her plea, so that tears sprang to the old lady's eyes; but they were tears not for him, but for Marie and her youth and her fervor. For was she not bringing to that withered and mild old spirit the breath of old days, of bewitching moonlight, of sublime and touching faith, of the mad generosity of youth?

"Nothing can be done, my dear child," she said. "You mustn't think me heartless, but, you see, I know Stanley and you don't. Trust in me, my dear."

"What have you got against him?" demanded Marie, fiercely.

"My dear, I have helped the young man several times before. It is always the same—something urgent. I cannot."

"And just because he's been in trouble before, you want to—to—turn him away like a dog!" cried Marie, with a sort of sob in her voice. She couldn't think of telling arguments, because, after all, the chief argument was the young man himself, the chief recommendation his beauty in the moonlight.

She gave her aunt one look of profound resentment and started toward the stairs, but directly the old lady had closed her door, she turned back, and ran into her own room. Amelia was sitting up in bed.

"Oh, do tell me who—" she began, but Marie cut her short.

"Do keep quiet!" she said.

With dignified curiosity Amelia watched her while she lighted the lamp and, opening a battered old writing-desk, began struggling with the twisted lock of a little drawer. It flew open suddenly, and a shower of bills came out. She gathered them up, stuffed them into an envelope, and without glance at Amelia hastened out of the room again.

"Here," she cried, "please take this! It may help you. It's fifty dollars of my own. Father said I could do as I pleased with it."

The young man pushed her hand back gently.

"No!" he said earnestly, "I couldn't."

"Oh, don't be *silly!*" she cried, frowning. "Think of your wife, and not of your own pride."

He said "Oh!" in an odd voice, and turned away his head.

"Take it quick, please! I can't stay here, you know. Please! It's really my own. I don't need it at all. And I'd like so awfully to be a little bit useful to someone."

"No," he said in great distress; "I can't! Never mind, please; it really doesn't matter."

"Your wife's health *doesn't matter!*"

"I mean—I don't want—"

She thrust the envelope into his hand, and he kept it and her hand with it.

"What am I to say," he cried, "and how am I ever to thank you?"

"Don't bother. I'd better hurry up stairs again, or auntie'll wonder what I'm doing."

But her hand still lay in his, and their eyes met in a long look, both so dark, so young, so ardent. She was aware of a new power and beauty in herself; she knew how she looked, her thin body as straight as a rod in the scant folds of her dressing-gown, that thick braid over her shoulder, her bare feet, the moonlight ennobling her, as it did him, softening her vivid face, her brilliant glance. They stood there, both lost, both enchanted and made helpless by that radiance, by the sweet breath from the fields, by the clasp of their warm hands.

"I must go," she murmured.

He bent and humbly kissed her fingers.

"Good-night," he said.

But it was quite fifteen minutes more before she went up-stairs, and all that time Amelia, leaning out of the window, heard their low voices. Marie entered the bedroom as rapt and aloof as a sleep walker.

"A man to see auntie," she explained to Amelia. "I'll tell you all about him in the morning."

Their aunt, too, had something to tell. She took it for granted that Marie had talked to her sister and that both were indignant, and she began, not without hesitation, as they sat at breakfast the next morning.

"I don't want you to think me heartless or unkind, children," she began, while she poured their coffee and carefully put in the cream and sugar they liked, "and yet I can't explain without saying more against the young man than I care to say, because he has many good points. I was at one time very much attached to him. But you know, my dear girls, that there are people in this world—it is often kinder to oblige them to help themselves."

She stopped for a minute. It was contrary to her code to speak ill of anyone,—she thought it ill bred and un-Christian—but it was contrary to her common sense to allow the young man to become or to remain at all a hero or a martyr in Marie's eyes; she knew that to be dangerous and stupid.

"Stanley came here," she went on, "two or three years ago at harvest-time. He wanted work, so I took him on to help in the fields. He didn't do well at it, but I saw at once that he was unsuited—most unsuited for any such work. I had a talk with him, and he told me a great deal about himself. He said he was a poet, and that he went tramping about from place to place, all over the world, doing any work he could find. I took a deep interest in the young man. I should never have—have refused any reasonable request of his if he had not proved—untrustworthy on more than one occasion. I am very sorry to say it, very. He was not—quite—frank. And he is undoubtedly a very careless and extravagant young man. He has appealed to me several times, but he has never—reimbursed me, as he promised."

She found it difficult to speak harshly of her old favorite despite a little quite justifiable resentment; but she was rather dismayed to see on the faces of both her nieces the most eager curiosity. They passed over his moral shortcomings as negligible; they wanted to know his age, his family, all sorts of personal details. She could not tell them, because she did not know. His talk had been almost invariably about his poems and what the good old lady called his "feelings." At least she knew how he regarded the universe.

Amelia certainly expected a long and explicit account from Marie of her conversation with this interesting young man the night before, but she was disappointed. Marie was gruff and taciturn, avoided Amelia as much as possible, and very reluctantly gave the barest outline of the amazing interview. At last, pursued by questions, she offered to weed the flower garden, and from the window Amelia caught tantalizing glimpses of her, working doggedly, in an old straw garden hat and a faded cotton frock, keeping, as Amelia put it, her secret locked in her breast.

She came in at noon, hot and tired and unsmiling. Amelia was dusting their crowded bureau-top when she entered; and flung herself down on the window-seat.

"Look here, 'Melie," she said, with a frown, "I've got to meet him this afternoon at the station, and I don't know how to arrange it."

"What is there to arrange? We'll just go out for a walk and not say where we're going."

Marie was rather annoyed at having the path of her intrigue made so smooth; she agreed, however, and said no more. They dressed with great care, Amelia in white, Marie in a plain brown linen that showed every angularity of her lank young form. They disputed over the parasol; Marie objected to it as too "dressed up," and a bore to carry, and, as usual, won her point.

Another dispute arose directly they closed the garden gate behind them.

"This is what you must do, Amelia," said Marie. "You can come with me to the station and see him, and then you must say you have an errand, and start slowly home, and I'll catch up with you."

Amelia objected very strongly.

"I don't see why you should have him alone," she protested. "He's a married man, you know."

"Can't you see that he'll want to talk to me privately? He mustn't know that you know anything about the money. Do have a little tact, Amelia!"

Again Amelia yielded.

He was waiting on the platform of the little station, and when he saw them, he came forward, his head bared, his soft, melancholy eyes fixed upon Marie, only Marie, with no interest at all in Amelia's prettiness.

Even in the glaring sunshine and the dust his rare charm remained. In a dark suit that fitted closely to his slender body, with a low collar and a soft bow tie, he looked every inch a poet and a hero. And his gentle voice, his innocent and mild manner, his courtesy, profoundly affected Amelia. She lingered, walked with them along the road, engrossed in observing them until Marie removed her.

"Amelia has an errand," she said, with an inexorable glance at her sister. "We can stroll up the road a bit, and meet her later at the cross-roads."

Poor Amelia, unable to devise any sort of errand, sat patiently on a grassy bank by the cross-roads for a long, long time. The sun had begun to sink when Marie came running along the road. She was in a very good humor and inclined to be confidential, which was rare, and to be encouraged.

"I'm sorry I kept you waiting so long, old 'Melie," she said, "but we were having *such* a nice talk!"

"Let's hear about it."

"Oh, he began about hating to take the money and all that, and I told him not to be silly. And then—oh, we told each other about our lives—just the interesting parts, you know. He's been everywhere; it's wonderful to hear him. O 'Melie, just the sort of life I'd like! He fought in the Boer War, he's been in revolutions in South America, he's hunted tigers in India. One day he'll have plenty of money, and the next day not a penny. No one to think of but himself; not a tie on earth—"

"But, Marie, his *wife!*"

Marie stopped short, and looked at her sister.

"Do you know, 'Melie, we both forgot all about her! Never mentioned her!"

"He shouldn't," Amelia answered sagely. "It was horrid. But, still, he's probably awfully unhappy with her. Poets make such awful mistakes about marrying."

Amelia, while a model of propriety, had an incurable softness for handsome young men. So much so that, after decent protest, she consented to go with Marie again the next day to say good-by to Stanley. This time she provided herself with a book, and sat comfortably under a tree while her sister and the poet wandered off into the woods.

She held out a friendly hand to him when they returned.

"Good-by," she said. "Good luck!"

He took her hand, but said nothing, and looked into her face with his soft, black eyes.

"I want," he said at last—"I really must see your sister once more before I go!"

He looked so miserable that Amelia found no courage to rebuke him, and the next day, against her scruples, she went once more to the meeting-place. She had talked it all over with Marie.

"This really must be the last time," she had said; "otherwise I'll have to tell auntie. It really isn't right, and you know it. A married man! And where's his wife all this time? Do you mean to say that he never talks about her?"

"No, he doesn't, and I'm not going to bring up the subject. It would look as if I were trying to remind him of the money. I suppose she's gone out West."

"Your fifty dollars wouldn't take her far," said Amelia.

"I don't know and I don't care. I only know I'm awfully sorry for him. He's lonely and wretched. No one takes any interest in his work except me. I love to hear him read his poems aloud."

"So should I."

"Well, you can't. He's too shy." Amelia had had a certain experience with affairs of the heart, enough, anyway, to warn and alarm her. She argued and reasoned all the way home, because she saw very clearly that this thing was not at an end.

"If you won't promise not to see him again, I'll tell auntie," she said sternly.

Marie looked at her with scorn.

"Tell her," she said, "and see what happens."

After that poor Amelia dared not say a word. She knew her sister to be capable of anything and everything. She tried pleading, weeping, exhorting.

"I'm going to meet him again tomorrow," said Marie. "Tell auntie if you like. It won't stop me."

"This once more, then," Amelia agreed, drying her eyes. "O Marie, you're such a terribly *difficult* girl!"

Pride forbade Amelia to countenance this meeting; she started out with her sister, but as soon as they were out of sight of the house, she stopped.

"Go on alone," she said; "I don't want to see that man again."

Triumphant and radiant, Marie hastened along the road; her sister watched her with forlorn tears in her eyes. Marie running toward her destiny!

Her poet was waiting for her, standing, somber and patient, under a tree. But no sooner did he see her face than his somberness left him. She was so lovely, so flushed, sparkling, irresistible! Their hands met in a fervent clasp, and a long one.

"I'm going to show you a new place to-day," she told him— "a place 'Melie and I discovered years ago."

She went on before him, along a little path that led downhill through a glade of silver birches. Ferns lined the way, and fragile little flowers; it was a sweet solitude, dim, cool, and fragrant. At last Marie stopped. They had come to a steep decline, where the path ended in a great boulder.

"The rest is a scramble," she said, "but it's worth it. Look! Isn't it lovely!"

He climbed on to the boulder beside her, and with her looked down upon a little pool, like a steel mirror, darkly clear, image of austere tranquility, a place of unaccountable fascination.

"I wish you'd never been here before," said Stanley; "I wish no one had ever seen this place before to-day." He had jumped down, and stood below her, at the foot of the boulder. "And after I've gone," he went on, "you'll come here and never think of me."

She didn't answer, but looked down at him, her eyes soft and luminous. Passion kindled in his. She gave a little sob, stretched out her arms, and slipped down into his embrace. They clung to each other with throbbing hearts.

"Darling Marie!" he whispered, "I love you so!"

"And I love you," she answered. Her arms tightened about his neck, and she buried her head in his coat, sobbing.

"Don't cry, my love!" he entreated. "Look up, won't you, my sweetheart? Don't cry; there's nothing to make you sad, surely."

"I'm not sad," she answered, but the tears would not stop, though she smiled at him. "It's only—I can't explain."

He kissed her again, straining her against him, looking down at her dark and ardent face. He was waiting no doubt for ardent words; but, drying her eyes, she spoke in a voice suddenly become matter-of-fact.

"It won't do to have my eyes red. 'Melia would be sure to notice. There'll be an awful row, anyway. She's going to tell auntie about my meeting you."

"But, Marie, does that mean we can't meet again?"

"Oh, no. They can't stop me. It only means—oh, an awful lot of unpleasantness, rows, you know, and crying. I do hate that sort of thing so."

"But you'd come just the same?" he asked. "You'd defy them—just for me?"

Something in his tone grated on Marie.

"Not 'defy,' exactly," she said, with a quick frown, "and it isn't especially for you. It's simply that I won't be interfered with—ever."

He looked at her with a more respectful admiration. Here was a girl able to hold her own with the most exacting, the most spoiled poet that ever lived.

"Marie," he said seriously, "I don't want you to endure any sort of unpleasantness on my account. I'm not worth a minute's discomfort to you. I haven't any claim, any merit, except that I love you so, my dear sweetheart."

She melted at once, and smiled at him. But he remained grave.

"I love you so much that I—don't think I can go on this way. Why should we, anyway, Marie? If we love each other—only, are you *quite* sure, *absolutely* sure, Marie, that you *do* love me?"

Her eyes met his, candidly and nobly.

"No," she said, "not absolutely sure, But sure enough to—to risk everything for it."

"But I don't understand, my darling girl—"

Her dusky cheeks turned slowly scarlet, but she would not lower her eyes.

"I mean," she said, "that you're right about not going on this way. I think—it ought to be—either not meeting at all, or—or—going away together. No! Please don't kiss me! Don't touch me at all! It disturbs me. I want to make up my mind."

"Whether you love me?"

"No; I know that. Whether I'll go with you or not. I thought I made up my mind last night that it would have to be settled one way or the other. But I haven't been able yet—"

"But if you know that you love me, sweetheart, isn't that enough?"

"No," she replied sternly, "it's not. No, Stanley, I want—just another day. I'll meet you here on Sunday, and I'll tell you then. I'll *know*."

"Marie," he said, "I'd like to go on my knees to you. You're the finest, bravest—"

She cut him short with a vigorous, boyish sort of hand-clasp.

"Good-by," she cried. "See you on Sunday. Don't come with me; I'd rather go back alone." She scrambled up the hillside, as awkward and swift as a young colt.

She was surprised and disappointed with herself because she slept that night quite as usual. She had intended to stay awake and think. But she waked up very early in the morning with a weary and confused mind, as if she had been thinking all night long in her sleep. Amelia lay tranquilly beside her, rosy and innocent. It was impossible that, in similar circumstances, Amelia would hesitate for an instant, would even contemplate the course which she contemplated.

With a leaden heart she watched the awful majesty of the dawn. It was the sort of sky one sees in old paintings. She had a confused, childish idea that those lofty, crimson-tinged clouds and the brilliant, spear-like shafts of light from the sun were a particularly fitting background to the sudden appearance of an offended Jehovah. She had never before felt so wicked or seen so clearly the depth of the abyss before her. The problem presented itself to her in stark simplicity; she saw it like some antique tragedy, a deadly struggle between love and virtue. She never attempted to justify the former; she unhesitatingly called the thing a sin. The question was, whether to sin or not, whether she should give up everything for love. She was not much of a reader. Modern fiction was unknown to her; in all the old-fashioned novels she had read the heroines who made this sacrifice accepted shame and misery as a necessary consequence, acknowledged themselves sinners.

Then there were those women whose very names enthralled her— dark Francesca in hell, Héloïse, Nicolette, Guinevere. She meditated on queens flinging away their majesty, proud women gladly humbled. She envisaged herself giving up her college course, her inheritance from her aunt, and Amelia's companionship, her equivalents. As much as any of these illustrious women, she would be giving up everything, beggaring herself for love, losing her soul.

And while she tried to deliberate this tremendous question, there was life going on as usual. She got up at the usual time, dull and wretched; there was no opportunity to adjust herself, not a quiet moment alone; she must dress and go down-stairs. When she didn't eat, there were kindly questions and insistence; when she became rebellious and sullen, her aunt and her sister were ingenuously conciliating. They tried to relieve her, suggested a tonic, followed her about, urging her to rest. She felt like a person who had a secret knowledge that the end of the world was near and who looked on at the activities of mankind with irritable despair.

The long day wore itself away, and Sunday came. They all went to church as usual in the morning, Marie driving the old surrey, Amelia and the old lady on the back seat. She sat through the service like a statue, heard the solemn commandment read, repeated it herself, clearly and firmly—God Himself telling her she *should not* run off with a married man.

She drove them home, but did not get out of the carriage herself.

"My head aches," she said. "If you don't mind, Auntie, I'll stay out in the air."

"Don't be gone too long, pet," the old lady answered, "and keep Billy out of the sun as much as you can."

So she left them at the front door and drove off down the road, sitting up stiff and straight in her Sunday dress of white linen. The old horse trotted along, the carriage bumped and rattled. They watched her out of sight, and then went into the dim, cool house.

Dinner was ready at two o'clock, but Marie had not come home. They waited half an hour, an hour. The old lady grew very anxious, although on Amelia's account she tried to hide it.

"Eat a little dinner, my dear child," she said, "and then afterward perhaps you'd better walk over to Clifford's and borrow their horse and buggy. Don't worry, my dear; you know how often she is late."

Amelia had her hat on, ready to start off on the long walk to Clifford's farm, when the carriage flashed by the window in the direction of the barn, and a few minutes later Marie walked into the dining-room.

"I went to meet Stanley," she said brusquely. "I'm going away with him tonight. There's no use talking to me. Amelia, you'd better tell auntie what you know." And without another word she went up-stairs.

When they followed, she was moving about the room, packing her things in an old valise. She was as indifferent to them as if the rooms were empty. She would not even answer when they spoke. The old lady talked to her gently, with a gallant effort to hide her frantic alarm. She urged religion, affection, worldly policy, the love of the dead mother, every argument she knew; entreated her to wait even for one day, and at last, all her patient love and wisdom ignored, sat and watched in silence. Amelia lay face downward on the bed, sobbing hysterically: "O Marie! you *can't!* you *can't!*"

Marie went on, folding ribbons, opening and closing drawers, walking back and forth from closet to valise. Then putting on her hat and coat, she picked up the bag and went out, pushing aside her sister, silently removing the trembling old hands that tried to detain her. She hurried along the road with eager feet that stumbled a little in the thick dust, her heart pounding, her breath fluttering in a tumult of excitement. She reached the cross-roads and turned off into the little woodland path, and, panting, leaned against a tree. The last rays of the sun were lying bright on the ferns and mosses and slim, white trunks of the birches; the sky above was pale and fair, and a little evening breeze came running through the leaves with a long whisper. The birds were chirping drowsily all about her: a low, reedy whistle sounded overhead, there was a plaintive cry from a cat-bird, and far off a distant trill, very sweet and clear.

She loitered now, for she was in advance of the appointed time; she was tired, too, and beginning to grow hungry. The bag was heavy. She left it behind a tree, to be picked up on the way back, and went on more comfortably down the steep hill to the lake.

She was startled at the change the dusk had made. What she saw now was a black and sinister pool, shut in by trees, edged by rank grasses, teeming with stealthy life. There were strange sounds, splashes, gurgles, lapping; night-birds began to call; the sunny peace of the afternoon had fled, and it was suddenly night. She sat down on a stone at some distance from the water to wait.

One star came out; she could see it, solemnly bright, through the branches. The breeze blew cooler, rustled in the leaves with a louder, longer sigh. She had a terrible, bitter feeling of loneliness; she felt cut off forever from her old friendly world, felt truly a sinner and an outcast.

Far off she heard Stanley whistle, and presently he came hurrying down the path.

"Dear sweetheart," he cried, "were you frightened here all alone? I tried—"

"No," she answered, squirming out of his embrace, "but I'm hungry. Do come on, Stanley! We'll miss that train."

She couldn't see his face, but his voice was profoundly disappointed.

"Marie, I didn't think you'd—I thought you'd be glad to see me!"

"I am," she cried remorsefully, for the curious pity she had always felt for him seized her now. She gave him a hasty kiss and patted his hair. "You poor old darling!" she said.

That encouraged him; he put his arm about her and held her closely.

"There's really no hurry," he said. "Let's sit down here, sweetheart; it's quiet and cool, and we can talk over our plans."

She agreed reluctantly.

"All right; but I'm tired to death of this place. I waited so long, you know."

"I only want to please you, darling. We'll go anywhere, do anything you like. If you'd rather—"

"I don't care, Stanley," she cried, "only—I suppose I'm irritable. It's been such a strain making up my mind!"

"Don't I know, dear girl? Do you think I don't realize all you're giving up? I only wish I were the greatest poet who ever lived, to put my heart into words. I'm so sorry, my Marie, that it must be this way, all alone, no kindly wishes, no wedding—"

"Oh, how *can* you!" she cried, jumping up—"how can you be so *stupid* as to speak of that!"

"But, dearest girl, I didn't know you cared so much for that sort of thing— ceremonies and so forth. Really, I didn't."

"You—you talk about 'realizing,'" she went on, with a sob, "but you don't. You—you don't seem to know that it's a—a tragedy!"

"A tragedy!" he repeated, "My dearest girl! A tragedy not to have a wedding! I didn't know. If you feel so strongly, hadn't we better wait?"

"Wait for what? I told you I'd made up my mind, and I have."

"Wait until we can have a real wedding, the sort you want."

"What are you talking about, Stanley? How can we have a wedding?"

"If you've set your dear heart on one, you shall have it. I'll make the money somehow—"

"What is the matter with you," she cried, "talking about *weddings!* Do you want to be a *bigamist!*"

He started violently.

"My God!" he cried, "I forgot!"

"Forgot your wife!"

"No! no! I—what will you think?— I mean—I forgot I'd said that— about being married. You see, I'm not —"

"Are you divorced, then?" she demanded in a curious tone.

"No, I never was married. I only said it—for your aunt—a—a sort of joke, do you see? Really, I'm terribly ashamed of it, Marie."

"I see," said Marie. "A joke—so that you could borrow more money from her."

"Please don't be too harsh. I know it was—very wrong. But, Marie, I've always been a careless, irresponsible sort of chap. I didn't see it in its true light. I was so desperately hard up! And, really, dear girl, I didn't know you believed it."

"Why did you think I lent you the money, then? For yourself? For— a joke?"

"Don't, darling! Please don't be so cruel! And please believe Marie, that, no matter what else I've done, I'd never have been blackguard enough to ask you to run away with me if I hadn't been able to marry you. I took it for granted that we were to be married directly we got to the city. I thought the only drawback was my poverty. Please, my dear girl, you know poets aren't to be judged quite as other men."

"Aren't they?" said Marie, grimly. "Come on! We'll miss our train."

Poor Amelia at home had found it impossible to sleep in the room left desolate by her sister. Forlorn and weeping, she lay beside her aunt, her head resting on the frail old shoulder, her smooth hair brushing the wrinkled cheek.

The shutters were all closed, and a night-light burned in a basin, shedding a feeble glimmer over the great, high-ceilinged room. She stared about her restlessly. Everything was peaceful, orderly, antique: the huge, old bureau; the horsehair sofa; the mantelpiece draped with a fringed, blue-velvet lambrequin; the little bedside table, with its bottle of cough mixture, spoon, glass, and jug of water; the crayon portraits on the walls. To Amelia, used to the breezy darkness of her own room, there was an oppressive, sick-room atmosphere, a stifling sense of being shut off from the great, calm universe. She sat up with a sob.

"I think I'll go back in my own room, Auntie," she said.

"Shall auntie go with you, pet?"

"No, thank you: I'm afraid I'd keep you awake. I'm so restless!"

They kissed each other tenderly.

"Good night, pet!"

"Good night, Auntie dear!"

The clock struck twelve.

"So late!" said the old lady. "Try to sleep a little, child. You're worn out."

She answered, "Yes, Auntie," dutifully, and started for her own room, when a sound from below made her stop in terror. Footsteps on the porch! The knob of the front door rattled, the prowling steps moved on to the French windows. Amelia came flying back.

"Auntie, what's that!"

"We'll soon see. Don't be frightened, dearie," the trembling old lady answered. "Raise the front window, and I'll call out. But stand well back. He might shoot."

Everything was quiet now. Amelia unbarred the shutters, and with a sudden burst of courage slammed them open.

"Who's there?" she called.

"Marie," answered a matter-of-fact voice. "Come down and let me in."

With a queer little scream, Amelia ran headlong down the stairs to unbolt the door. Marie was standing outside, bag in hand.

"Where's auntie?" she asked.

"In bed. O Marie!"

Marie pushed by her sister, and started up the stairs, closely followed by the fluttering, white-gowned Amelia.

The old lady was sitting up in bed in her dim, peaceful room, looking patiently toward the door.

"Well, I've come back," said Marie, putting down her dusty bag. "He wasn't married, after all."

They didn't understand; they looked at her with anxiety.

"It is—all right, then?" Amelia asked timidly. Marie looked at her scorn fully.

"I tell you, he was *not* married. He began to make plans for a wedding. He'd forgotten he'd pretended to have a wife. And at South Point I asked him to get off and send a telegram to you; there was a ten-minute stop there. And I jumped off while he was gone, and left a note for him, pinned on the seat." The matter-of-fact voice suddenly broke, and she began to cry passionately. "I just wrote: 'Keep the money for a wedding present. I despise you. You are a beast.'" She sobbed. "And I walked all the way back from South Point, miles and miles. I *never* was so tired!"

"Poor lamb! Poor Marie!" murmured the old lady. "Thank God we have you safe at home again! The pain will pass away in time, dear child—"

"Pain!" cried Marie. "There isn't any pain. I don't think I really liked him, anyway. I only wanted to do something—oh, noble and—and sacrificing. But just getting married! What is there in *that?*"

With Unbowed Head

Mr. Carr began the day by descending into the cellar, where he was "knocking together" a chair. It was a loud enough knocking together, but not an altogether well directed one; like many artists, however, he was satisfied with his accomplishment at the instant of completion. It was a sort of deck-chair, which would fold; it was made of white pine and covered with green rep, necessarily baggy, to allow for the folding. He carried it up the stairs and set it upon the veranda of his little house; then he called his wife to do her duty.

"Sit in it!" said he, majestically; but she was a woman and hampered by tradition. She remembered its predecessors and things they had done to her. She did sit in it, but with exasperating caution.

"Lean back!" he urged. "Now, isn't that comfortable? Don't get up! Rest!"

"I have things to do," she murmured. Suddenly the legs shifted and straddled farther apart, and she shrieked.

"Sit still!" said her husband. "It's meant to do that. Now you stay there and rest, and I'll attend to the dishes."

There was little he would not have done to keep her in that chair, and Mrs. Carr had long ago learned to submit to such desires for fear of hurting his feelings. She was a small, pleasant, pug-nosed woman of forty, with her hair in a girlish knot at the nape of her neck; never in life had she expressed any of her little emotions. She felt it wrong to trouble other people with her griefs and worries, though why she thought such knowledge would trouble them I can't say. She sat in the chair, concealing from Mr. Carr her sharp anxiety about the milkman.

He hadn't, however, her point of view about bills. He was hurt and angry because tradesmen were too greedy, and impatient to wait until he had made his fortune. He didn't see why he should share alone the burden of his temporary unproductivity; it ought to be shared by the community, as his wealth would be when he got it. But Mrs. Carr had been for a long time an independent spinster,—a school-teacher,—and it had been her unambitious idea that what you could not pay for, you could not have. She saw the splendor of her husband's theory—first get what you want and then try to pay for it. It was heroic, but alarming. She had never imagined how immorally easy it was to the get things you couldn't pay for; she felt less respect for tradespeople when she saw what they would do. She said all the time that she had "perfect faith in John," yet she despised other people who trusted him.

"If I could manage three dollars on the bill," she was thinking, looking with an anxious frown at the small patch of lawn between her and the street. It was the worst lawn in Rockdale Park, and she was the worst-dressed woman. She was high-minded, certainly, but she felt all this; it was painful to her to sit there on the veranda, exposed to the eyes of all the people in the houses across the way. Until her husband had made at least a part of his fortune, she had a well nigh irresistible desire to hide herself and all her activities; she went so far as to dry the washing in the cellar.

"Perhaps he'd take two," she thought, when suddenly the chair went dead beneath her, and flung her violently on her back. Only the girlish knot at the nape of her neck protected her unhappy head; her spine, not protected, received a shock that stunned her.

Her husband heard the impact, and came out, not hurrying, because he never moved quickly, but anxiously. His wife still lay flat on her back, on the ruin of the chair; he helped her up, a little alarmed at her limpness and pallor. But she knew it was her duty to dispel his alarm, and she sank into another chair, and smiled brightly.

"Are you hurt, Sweetheart?" he inquired in his dignified, sonorous voice. She said she was not, and he bent over his chair.

"Did you move suddenly?" he asked. "Did you kneel in the seat?"

Certainly this was not one of her habits, but disappointment made him a little unjust. He stroked his chin and frowned. He was a dusty, rumpled, brown-gray man, heavy, a little bald, with eye-glasses; it was obvious that he had not a good razor and very little personal vanity. He was four years younger than his wife; his great dignity and gravity added years to his outward appearance, but his optimism, his faith in himself, his beautiful trust in life, were such as rarely survive the twenties. Even the failure of this chair did not dismay him. He thought and thought, looking down at it; but he had already mentally rejected that chair and was planning another.

"I'll try oak," said he. "This pine's too soft."

Mrs. Carr, still weak and giddy, wondered if oak would cost more. All this lumber, these planes, saws, hammers, vises, and nails were so expensive! She was willing to believe it was cheaper to make chairs than to buy them, but she couldn't help feeling that they could do without more chairs of any sort. Of course she said nothing of all this, but smiled, kept smiling, until Mr. Carr went off, in his frayed overcoat and stained felt hat, brown-gray, like his face and his hair. Then she got up to go about her housework, but her back hurt her very much; tears came to her eyes as she crept into the house, quite unable to keep from groaning as she moved. It was a wonderful thing to have a man to take care of her; only it was hard work.

II

Mr. Carr had in the meantime just lost his train. He always allowed himself just the right number of minutes to reach the station and walked at his invariable pace, with firm and stately carriage. If the train was gone when he got there, it was obviously not his fault. He had thirty minutes to wait for the next one; the station was deserted, for the other men of Rockdale Park had gone much earlier. They were office men, chained to desks, slaves; Mr. Carr refused that sort of life. In the first place, it would ruin his health, and in the second place, there was nothing in it. As soon as he had got married, he had given up his despicable office job, with its insulting salary, and launched out. For five years, though, he had been deceived by the "propositions" he took up.

His latest proposition, a sample of which he carried with him in a tiny suitcase that aroused instant suspicion in every office boy, was a folding-lamp which could be put into your desk drawer, if such a singular desire should come to you. Any intelligent person, one would imagine, would at once discard and scrap all other lamps in favor of this, because this had all the good points of all other lamps yet made, in addition to its whimsical collapsibility. But until you have tried, you cannot believe the mulish obstinacy of the world. People won't even try a thing they don't want.

He picked out a good seat on the train, one on the river side and away from the sun; he put the tiny suitcase on his knees and laid out on it number of cards on which were type-written the names and addresses of "prospects"; and he had twenty persons that day predestined.

His working day was a short one account of psychology. It didn't do to see a man before ten, because of the morning mail; you must approach no man between twelve and two, because he was either out for lunch, hungry, or digesting lunch. And precisely at four o'clock, according to Mr. Carr, a sinister sort of fatigue descended like a cloud upon the offices, and it was wise to step away. All this made it necessary for him to spend a good deal of time at the "movies"; but although this cost a bit, good ideas often came to him there, and sometimes he fell asleep, which refreshed his brain.

This day went by in the usual way. He sold nothing, but that didn't discourage him. Slowly, subtly, he was creating a market, introducing into men's minds an ineradicable passion for folding-lamps. On each of his cards he wrote something: "Interested; return July 10." "Will need equipment Sept." And on one or two, "N. G." Be assured that a "prospect" had to be notably forcible to secure *that* rating; a less brave spirit than Mr. Carr's might have written instead in blood and tears of hideous humiliations. No one could humiliate Mr. Carr, no one on earth.

He went back to Rockdale Park as calm, dignified, and cheerful as he had left it in the morning. Even the sight of his chair still lying in ruins on the veranda didn't distress him; nor did the sight of his wife in bed, very much. She would soon be all right; everything would be. She didn't tell him that she was suffering cruelly, and of course she did not mention the chair; that would have hurt his feelings. She said she had a bad headache, which is good enough for any husband. He tied an apron about his portly form, cooked the dinner, and swept and garnished the house. He liked doing that. Then, after he had washed the dishes, he sat down beside his wife and read aloud to her; and while she listened to his resonant and manly voice, tears of gratitude rolled down her cheeks.

She tried to be better in the morning, as she had promised, but could not bring it off. She was unable to get up.

"Never mind, Sweetheart," said Mr. Carr. "Leave everything to me."

He did all the work of the house, cooked the meals, waited on her nicely; but still she grew no better. Three days went by, and he suggested a doctor.

"No, John dearest," she protested; "we can't afford it." She paused a moment. "I'd really like it better if you'd go back to business. I can lie here quietly till you come home—"

"Who'll cook your lunch?" he asked.

"But if you don't work, there'll be no lunch to cook," she cried.

"Leave it all to me," said Mr. Carr. On the fifth day he decided that it was rheumatism, and Mrs. Carr drank dutifully of the patent medicine for its cure. She did not suffer so much now, and she was afraid she knew why. She lay very quiet, staring at nothing, astounded at what she saw approaching. She was never guilty of the indelicacy of mentioning an elemental fact; the word "death" she never used. She preferred to say "passing away," and I think she had schooled herself to believe that she would actually do that, actually vanish, body and all, leaving nothing to trouble her courageous husband.

He was superb. He did everything; he brought her up the daintiest little meals, two portions of everything, for he ate at her bedside. Sometimes she asked him feebly how he managed, where the money came from.

"You leave it all to me," he said. "Don't you worry."

He was, as a matter of fact, doing something that would have broken her respectable little heart. He was pawning their wedding silver and everything else available. He slipped out in the evening with a newspaper bundle, and came back with cash. They had absolutely no other income, but that didn't discourage him.

In the course of time he deemed it necessary to call in a doctor. He thought it out, and decided that the sample electric lamp should pay the doctor; and it did. The lamp was not his, and he might get into trouble, but he faced that unperturbed.

The doctor told him the truth bluntly, because he mistook Mr. Carr's fortitude for something else. He told him his wife was dying, and was likely to be some months in doing so. Very well, Mr. Carr could handle that, too. He sat down at once and wrote to his wife's wealthy and aloof aunt in the city. He described his wife's illness in terms more medical than any doctor could have used, adding a human touch worthy of a poet or a salesman. True to his principles, he sent a "follow-up letter," and in the end he "got results." He kept up a regular correspondence with Aunt Kitty; his letters were beautiful, and were read aloud in the city. He concealed all this from his wife, which was kind and wise.

III

At last the gas was turned off in the house, and the water; the telephone was removed, the chattel mortgage on the furniture foreclosed. Mr. Carr was left alone with the wrecks of six homemade chairs. He expected momentarily to be turned out of the house, but until that should happen he existed gipsy fashion, and went about the neighborhood selling hand-knit washcloths. He saw a big future in that. He missed his wife, but he looked forward to rejoining her in the hereafter and of having a great deal to tell her. He was no longer dusty, but grimy, and his calm majesty had in it now something of mystic resignation. He said it was his duty to his wife's memory to justify the faith she had had in him. Perhaps he was doing so. He sat in the bare kitchen in the evening, with a candle for light, and meditated over a pipe. The washcloths were not appreciated, but that didn't discourage him.

One evening at twilight he was coming home carrying the sort of thing that once connoted beer; he was however, fetching water from a neighboring brook in which to wash. He had a bologna sandwich in his pocket, and a bag of tobacco, and he whistled sweetly as he came. He was surprised to see a motor-car standing before the house, but not dismayed. An elderly lady was sitting in it; she beckoned to him, and he approached.

"Are you John Carr?" she asked.

"I am, madame," he answered with courtly grace, removing his hat. In the dusk, and to old eyes, there was nothing to be perceived but his stately carriage, his serene and well modulated voice.

"I'm poor Janet's Aunt Kitty," said she. "Dear me! dear me! She was the last I had left, and now she's gone."

"Yes, she's gone," said Mr. Carr, and the tranquility of his tone startled the old lady.

"You don't take it very hard," she observed, with displeasure.

"No, I don't," said Mr. Carr. And in that moment came his apotheosis. "I have the great consolation of knowing I did everything possible for her while she was here. And I shall see her again. "Death," said he, "means little me."

"You 're not afraid of dying?" asked the old lady, who was.

"I'm not afraid of *anything*," said Mr. Carr. "Death is only a bridge." And he went on, and the old lady could have listened to him forever.

"I'll step inside," said she. "I like to hear a man talk like this."

"I cannot ask you to come in," said Mr. Carr, "because the gas has been turned off and the furniture taken away." Somehow he did not think of offering her one of his home-made chairs.

"Mercy me! You're living there with no lights and no furniture?" cried she.

"And no water," said Mr. Carr. "But I don't need them. I have my own thoughts and memories and a candle."

"You're a wonderful man!" said she.

He didn't deny it.

"But you can't be getting on very well in business," she added.

"I gave up my business when Janet fell ill, so that I might attend to her as she deserved," he answered. "I don't complain; she was worth any sacrifice."

The old lady drove away, weeping. She had materialized out of the dusk for the sole purpose of witnessing the apotheosis of Mr. Carr; her part in life was played, and she died the next month. She left all her money to him, as who would not?

He is now wealthy, and no longer makes folding-chairs of Georgia pine, but cabinets of lacquer-work. He is quite unspoiled by his fortune.

"I always had faith in life," he will tell you. "I never lost courage. I knew I'd work my way out of my troubles."

His Remarkable Future

"Haven't you any umbrella?" asked Hardy, with a frown.

"I have one," answered Miss Patterson, "but not here."

She was dignified, he was somewhat severe. Both were important, preoccupied, adult persons, full of business concerns; nevertheless, they did not quite know how to proceed with the conversation. They stood side by side in the lobby of the office building, looking not at all at each other, but at the steady and violent rain. Miss Patterson was reluctant to walk off in such a downpour, and Hardy was determined that she should not.

"Silly kid!" he thought. "In that flimsy suit and those fool shoes!"

Any number of other girls ran past, some with newspapers over their hats, some laughing, some gravely worried, but he was not perturbed by them. They could stand it. No other living girl was so peculiarly fragile as Miss Patterson, or beset with so many dangers.

"I think it will stop," said she.

This annoyed him. She was trying to make light of a most serious situation.

"Why?" he demanded.

"Because it always does stop," she said. "At least, it always has, in the past."

He turned his head to look at her, and he grew a little dizzy. In the bleak light of that dismal day, Miss Patterson seemed to glow with a strange radiance. Her light hair was like a nimbus under her hat, her blue eyes were lambent, and she chose just that moment to make the color deepen in her cheeks. It was not fair!

"I'll get a taxi," he said.

"Oh, no!" she protested. "Please don't! I live miles and miles uptown."

"Doesn't matter," said Hardy, and off he darted.

He stopped a cab with the air of a highwayman, and returned to Miss Patterson. As he put her into the vehicle, a curious change came over them. Hardy ceased to be masterful and severe, and Miss Patterson was no longer dignified. They looked at each other steadily, with a strange sort of despair.

"Look here!" said Hardy, in an uncertain voice. "Can't I come with you?"

"Oh, no!" cried she. "Oh, no! Oh, you'd better not!"

But they both knew that he was going with her, that he must, that the inevitable moment had come, the moment foreseen by both of them all through the winter.

"What's the address?" he asked.

That was the last thing needed. Now he knew where the human, unofficial Miss Patterson lived. She was disassociated from business now. She was not a typist, but a girl.

She seemed aware of all this, for, as he got into the cab beside her, she looked at him in a new way—a look so bright, so clear, so gentle!

"Look here!" he said. "I—I don't want to be a nuisance. If you'd really rather I didn't come—"

She only shook her head. If she had tried to speak, she would have ended in tears.

He didn't know that he, too, had a new look—that his young face had grown pale and strained, his eyes dark with his great fear and his great hope. And this was the splendid, vainglorious Mr. Hardy from the import department, the young man of whom great things were expected, who was to be made assistant buyer when Mr. Hallock left at the end of the year.

The other girls had talked about him a good deal, for he was a figure to capture the imagination—a handsome boy, swaggering a little in the honest pride of his young manhood; only twenty-three, and going to be made assistant buyer!

"You know," he said, "I've often wanted to—to have a little talk with you. I—I often noticed you."

"Did you?" said Miss Patterson, ready to laugh through her unshed tears, for he needn't have troubled to tell her that.

"But you see," he went on, "I didn't know—I couldn't tell whether you—"

She was very glad to hear that, because sometimes she had been afraid that he could tell, could read in her face what was in her heart.

"You know, you're so different from anyone else," he said. "Every time I saw you, I—whenever I saw you, it seemed—that is, I thought you were so different from anyone else."

He stopped, aware that he was doing very badly, and filled with horror at his own idiotic words. She would think he was a fool.

Yet how could he possibly convey to this ethereal, fragile, and unworldly creature any idea of his own tempestuous love without alarming and offending her? He had no business to love her. It was a gross impertinence. She was an angel, and he was nothing but a clumsy—

The taxi turned a corner sharply, and he was flung sidewise, so that his shoulder brushed hers.

"I'm sorry!" he cried earnestly. "I couldn't help it!"

"But you're soaking wet!" said Miss Patterson.

Her gloved hand rested on his shoulder, and her voice—no, impossible!

"You're not—crying?" he asked incredulously.

"Yes, I am," said Miss Patterson. "I am. I can't bear to—to think of your getting so wet and catching a cold—just to get me a—a taxi!"

"But I shan't catch cold," said Hardy. He was trying to bear in mind that her words, her tears, were nothing but an expression of her wonderful kindness and humanity. She would be sorry for anyone who got wet and caught a cold in her service. That was all that she meant—absolutely all. "I shan't catch cold," he went on. "I never do; but you—you see, you're so delicate—"

"I'm not!" said she. "Not a bit! But I remember perfectly well that last February you had the most—oh, the most awful cold!"

"Edith!" cried he, astounded, overwhelmed by this confession. "You remember *that?*"

Miss Patterson suddenly drew away, and ceased weeping.

"Well, yes," she admitted. "I—yes, I remember."

A silence.

"Then you must—must feel a little interested in me," said Hardy. Silence.

"I hope you do," added Hardy.

The worst silence of all.

"Why do you hope that?" she asked, in a blank, small voice.

"Because I—ever since the first time I saw you, I thought perhaps you'd noticed."

"Noticed what?" inquired Miss Patterson, and he fancied that there was a shade of coldness in her voice. He was in despair. Of course she had no idea what he was driving at, he was so appallingly clumsy and stupid about it. He must do better than this! He drew a long breath.

"My prospects are pretty good," he remarked. "They're going to make me assistant buyer at the end of the year."

"So I've heard," said she, and this time there was no mistaking the coldness in her tone.

"I didn't say that to boast," he assured her anxiously. "I only wanted to tell you because—I wanted you to know that I—"

"I shouldn't blame you for boasting," said Miss Patterson, in a polite, formal way. "Everyone says you have a remarkable future before you."

"Not without you!" he cried. "I don't want any future without you! Oh, Edith, I don't know how to tell you—"

The head of the auditing department, in which Miss Patterson worked, often praised her for the quickness with which she grasped new ideas. This praise seemed justified, for she understood Hardy without further explanation.

Nevertheless, they both had an enormous amount of explaining to do. All the way uptown they were engaged in explaining to each other, with the greatest earnestness, just how they felt, why they felt so, and when they had begun to feel so. When they reached the depressing West Side street where Edith lived, they hadn't half finished.

The taxi stopped, and the driver turned around, so that they couldn't go on explaining, or even say good-by; but Hardy went into the dingy little vestibule with his Edith.

"Darling girl!" he said. "Shan't I come upstairs with you and see your aunt?"

She turned away.

"I'd rather you didn't, Joe," she said. "Not just now, please!"

He was willing to do anything in the world she wanted, except to leave her; but that was almost impossible. She seemed to him so forlorn, so little and so young. The brightness had left her face now. She was downcast and pale.

"Edith!" he said. "Aren't you happy at home?"

"No, Joe, I'm not," she answered. "I'm wretched!"

When she saw what that did to him, how much it hurt him, she was overcome with remorse.

"Oh, but it doesn't matter—now!" she said. "Not now—when I have you. Really and truly, Joe, I don't care a bit!"

Her anxiety to reassure him, to send him away happy, touched Hardy almost beyond endurance. He had always been aware of something wistful, something a little sorrowful about her, like a shadow over her clear beauty. She had been the dearer to him for that. She was a thousand times dearer to him now because she was sad, and must look to him for her happiness. He meant to make her happy at any cost!

II

Those words, "at any cost," did not come consciously into Hardy's mind. He didn't really believe that happiness cost anything—or love, either. You found them, suddenly, on your way through life, and of course you had a right to keep what you found.

He did see difficulties, though. His prospects were good, but in his immediate present there were many things that troubled him.

His chief trouble was one which young fellows of twenty-three who want to get married have encountered before. It was money. His salary of twenty-five hundred a year was more than he needed for his own wants, and he had done a very sensible thing—he had begun buying stock in the company that employed him, turning in ten dollars of his salary every week for this purpose. He had four hundred dollars saved in that way, but no one ever repented a folly more heartily than young Hardy now regretted his prudence.

He couldn't touch that money. He knew very well that one of Mr. Plummer's strongest reasons for promoting him was that infernal stock he was buying. If he were to sell it, or to stop his payments, Mr. Plummer would want to know why, and Hardy's prospects would be in jeopardy. He couldn't marry without those prospects, nor could he very well get married without the money.

Well, any wise and experienced person could solve that difficulty for him. He must wait. Even Edith, who was neither wise nor experienced, told him that. They were having lunch together a few days after their great discovery of happiness, and Hardy had been explaining the situation in detail.

"We'll have to wait," said Edith. "Anyhow—"

"No," said he. "I can't stand seeing you so miserable!"

"But I'd be a hundred times more miserable if I thought I was doing you any harm!" said Edith.

As soon as the words were spoken, she realized that she had made a serious mistake, and tried hastily to remedy it.

"I'm really not miserable, Joe!" she cried. "Not a bit!"

He knew better, though. Without even having seen her, he was becoming acquainted with Edith's aunt, and learning to appreciate her talent for making people miserable. Edith never told him about it. It wasn't her habit to complain, but to anyone who watched her as Hardy did, the thing was obvious.

One evening, when he was walking to the Subway with her, she had to stop in the drug store to buy a bottle of "nerve tonic" at two dollars a bottle.

"You don't take that stuff, do you, Edith?" he had asked anxiously.

"Oh, no!" she replied. "It's for Aunt Bessie. She's in very poor health, you know."

"What's the matter with her?" Hardy bluntly inquired.

He did not fail to notice Edith's troubled face and rising color; and the answer that Aunt Bessie was "terribly nervous" seemed to him to explain a good deal.

Then he learned that Aunt Bessie was upset if Edith was a few minutes late in getting home, and that she would be still more painfully upset if Edith should even suggest going out in the evening.

"She's alone all day, you see," the girl explained, "and it does seem selfish to go out again."

"Oh, very selfish!" Hardy interrupted. "And what about Saturday afternoon and Sunday?"

"Well, you see, Joe, she's alone all week, and—and she hasn't anyone but me. Anyhow, Joe, we see each other every day in the office, and we can have lunch together, can't we?"

He said nothing more just then, for he could see that Edith was unhappy and anxious. For those first few days even having lunch with her was almost too good to be true; but the day when Edith said they must wait, and Hardy said he wouldn't, was Monday, after he had spent a horrible Sunday without a glimpse of her.

"No," he said again. "We can't go on like this. I can't, anyhow."

Again she pointed out that they saw each other every day in the office, and could have lunch together. She added that they had only been engaged five days.

"I know," said he. "It would be all right if I could see you, but you won't let me come to your house, and you won't go out with me."

"But we see each other—"

"Yes, and we can have lunch together, for the next ten years, I suppose!" Hardy interrupted.

"It won't be anything like ten years, you silly boy! At the end of the year, when you—"

"Yes, and do you know what's going to happen then? They're going to send me to Europe, with Preble, for two months."

"Oh!" cried Edith.

For a moment she was silent, overcome by this news. Then she made a gallant attempt at a reasonable, calm, businesslike manner.

"But, after all—two months!" she said.

Her smile was a very poor one, and her voice betrayed her. Instead of helping her, Hardy became unmanageable.

"Look here!" he said. "September, October, November—that's three months that we can have lunch together. Then I'll be away for December and January; so perhaps after five months I may have a chance to—kiss you once more, if your aunt doesn't mind. Five whole months, and you won't let me see you alone for five minutes!"

"Oh, Joe, darling! Do be reasonable!"

"You're a little too reasonable," said he. "If you really cared for me—"

There is no better way to begin a quarrel than with those classic words. Edith grew angry, but her anger was such a mild little thing compared to Hardy's that she took refuge in flight, and left him sitting alone in the restaurant. All was over!

That afternoon they had four hours to think over their words. When Edith came downstairs, Hardy was waiting for her in the lobby.

"Edith!" he said. "Edith! I don't know how I could have been such a brute! Edith, I can't—"

"Oh, Joe, you weren't! I know it must seem heartless to you for me to talk that way; but you don't understand, Joe!"

As they walked toward the Subway, she tried to tell him. It was the hottest hour of that sultry September day, and she looked so jaded, so pale, that he was frightened. He held her arm, his tall head bent, to catch every word, his eyes fixed on her face.

"You see," she said, "I owe so much to Aunt Bessie. She took me when I was a tiny girl, after mother died, and she gave up everything for me—everything, Joe! She used the little bit of money she had to send me to a good school, and when that was gone she went to work. That's what ruined her health—working in an office; and she did it for me, Joe. If she's a little—a little trying now, I—you do see, don't you, Joe?"

"Yes, my darling girl, I see," he answered, more gently than she had ever heard him speak before. "I think—see here, Edith! Could you spare time for a soda?"

She thought she could. They went into a shop nearby, and sat down at a little table in a dark corner. He stretched out his hand toward hers, which lay on the table, but he drew it back again. He wasn't going to do anything that might bother her, never again. He would be patient, he would do anything in the world she wanted. He was sick with remorse and alarm at her pallor and fatigue.

"I'll do whatever you want, Edith," he said. "Only—I love you so! If you would just tell me more about yourself! It's hard not to know."

It was her hand that grasped his.

"As if I didn't understand! Oh, Joe, I worried so awfully about you that time you got wet! If you had been sick, I couldn't have been with you. I didn't even know who there'd be to take care of you."

"Don't!" he said suddenly. "Please don't, little Edith! I don't need much taking care of. It's you! Do you mind telling me what—how you—how it is with you financially?"

She did tell him, readily and frankly, and he was appalled. She was supporting herself and her aunt on her meager salary. Two persons entirely dependent on this slip of a girl!

"Edith!" he said. "Won't you marry me now? My salary's enough for us to scrape along on."

Both her hands clasped his now.

"Joe, my own dearest, I can't!"

"We can take your aunt to live with us for a while, until I've got my raise."

"Joe, we can't!"

"I don't care how bad she is. If you can stand her, I can."

"You couldn't! Don't you see, Joe, that that would spoil everything? We couldn't start like that. But if you'd—"

"If I'd what?"

"Nothing!" she said hastily. "I'll tell you another time."

But instead of telling him, she left a note on his desk the next morning.

> DEAR JOE:
> I will marry you now, if you won't ask me to give up my job.

"I don't wonder you wrote it," said Hardy, when he met her for lunch.

"Joe, it's the only way!"

"It's not *my* way," said he.

She reminded him that he had promised her to do whatever she wanted, and he replied that he would do so—except in this instance.

"Well, I won't let you have the burden of taking care of Aunt Bessie," she told him. "It's bad enough for you to think of getting married, anyhow, when you're so young, and just at the beginning of a wonderful career—"

"Young, am I? Then what about you?" he asked. "No! When you marry me, you'll be done with offices. That's something I won't argue about."

She pretended to be angry, but in her heart she adored him when he was magnificent and arbitrary.

III

"It isn't really a lie," said Edith. "I really do go to the French class."

"It's too near a lie to suit me," said Hardy bluntly. "I'm sick of this hole-and-corner business. It's—can't you see for yourself that it's degrading to both of us? Edith, can't we be honest about this? Let me go and see your aunt, and tell her the whole thing. If she makes a row, I dare say I can live through it."

"I dare say *you* could," Edith answered briefly.

They were coming near to one of the gates of Central Park. Their walk together was almost at an end—a walk which only a few weeks ago would have been a delight almost unsupportable, a thing to lie awake at night remembering, to think of all through a busy day. Now that rapture, that glamour, was gone. With all their love, their hope, their blind tenderness for each other, they were bitter at heart.

It was a wild, bright October evening. The moon seemed rocking in the fitful clouds, the wind sprang like a kitten along the paths after the dry leaves, the bare trees creaked stiff and resistant. All the world was in motion, restless, hurried. All things were free—except themselves. It was intolerable to Hardy, an affront to his fine young pride in himself, his magnificent assurance. It was petty, base, shameful!

"Edith!" he said suddenly. "I won't go on like this!"

She stopped short in the middle of the path.

"I'm tired of hearing that," she replied, in a queer, unsteady voice. "You're always saying that—always blaming me; and you know we've got to go on like this—or not go on at all!"

"We haven't. That's what I'm always trying to tell you," he said stormily. "We don't have to meet this way—in this beastly, lying way—pretending to your aunt that your French lesson is for two hours instead of one, so that we can have one hour a week alone together. Tell her! Let her be upset! She'll have to know some time. Then at least I can come to see you in your own place, decently and honorably."

"I will not tell her now! You don't realize what it'll mean to Aunt Bessie. You don't care. She hasn't anyone but me. I *won't* tell her now, and let her have all that long time to think about—losing me. She's going to be happy as long as possible."

Hardy took her arm.

"Come on," he said, "or you'll be ten minutes late, and she'll have a nervous attack and keep you up all night, as usual!"

But when he felt how she was shivering in her thin jacket, a terrible compunction seized him.

"Oh, Edith!" he cried. "Edith, never mind all that! Darling little Edith, it's only *our* affair, after all! Let's get married now, before I go!"

"You know we can't," she said, with a sob. "Not when you're so obstinate and—and unkind. You know we couldn't manage for ourselves and Aunt Bessie, too, in any place where she'd be comfortable, just on your salary; and you're so unreasonable about my job!"

"Look here, Edith—I'll sell that blamed stock, and that'll provide for Aunt Bessie until I've got my raise."

"You won't! You shan't!" She pulled her arm away from him, and roughly wiped away the tears running down her cheeks. "Don't you dare to mention such a thing! I'm not going to ruin your whole life just for—"

"Well, you've ruined it!" said Hardy. "I can tell you that, if it's any satisfaction to you. I don't care now what happens to me, or whether I go on or not. You've shown me how little you care for me. You've—Edith!"

She had started running along the path, but he easily overtook her. All at once their arms were about each other, Edith's wet cheek against his, and all their pain, their bitterness, lost in a passion of tenderness and remorse.

IV

Still Hardy went about the office, magnificent as ever, very well aware of being a remarkable young fellow, who was to be made assistant buyer at twenty-three, a man talked about, admired, and envied. He was still proud of himself, still sure of himself, but some of the magic had gone out of it, some of the zest. He couldn't look forward to that trip to Europe with unmixed joy now.

Indeed, all the joys he had at this time were so mixed with anxiety and impatience that he could scarcely recognize them. He dreaded leaving Edith. He imagined all sorts of misfortunes that might befall her in his absence. Sometimes he even resented his splendid future, because it so burdened and harassed the present. He wanted to live *now*, not to wait.

Worst of all was the humiliation he endured from their furtive and hasty meetings. He had never before in his life been furtive, or even cautious. He had lived boldly and rashly, in the light of day, and it hurt and angered him to do otherwise. He wanted to love boldly and rashly. He wanted to be proud of his love.

Well, he wasn't proud; he was ashamed.

He couldn't understand Edith's viewpoint. Her life had been so repressed, so weighted down by unjust and inordinate demands upon her, that she was thankful for the briefest minutes of happiness. If she could meet Hardy for ten minutes on a street corner, she was joyous for those ten minutes—when he would let her be. He tried to let her. He would watch her coming toward him—such a gallant little figure!—and he would make up his mind to be tender and considerate; but when she was with him, when he saw her ill-dressed and ill-nourished, and couldn't help her, when he saw her glance at her watch even when he was speaking, his good resolutions only too often vanished, and he reproached her bitterly.

She didn't endure his reproaches meekly. He wouldn't have loved her, if she had. On the contrary, she replied to him vigorously, and so many, many times they had left each other in anger, to be paid for later by hours of remorse.

Neither of them was quarrelsome by nature, nor was there any lack of real harmony between them. They were both generous, quick to forgive, eager to understand, passionately loyal to each other. Every one of their disagreements would have been quickly adjusted and forgotten, if they had had time; but they never did have time, and neither did this fellow of twenty-three and this girl of twenty have any greater amount of patience and ripe wisdom than others of their age.

Sometimes a sort of panic seized them, and they felt it necessary to "explain." They had fallen into the habit of taking a little more than the allotted hour for lunch. Though Edith had been solemnly warned by her superior, she found it impossible to leave Joe in the middle of a speech. He was so unreasonable about her always being in a hurry.

So there was lunch almost every day, and the walk to the Subway, and that hour stolen from the French class once a week, all through October and November, until the trip to Europe was only a few weeks ahead of them. Mr. Plummer hadn't actually told Hardy he was to go, but the thing was understood. Mr. Loomis, the buyer, was taking pains to train him, and had once or twice said such things as:

"You'll see how that is for yourself, Hardy, when you're in France."

"It'll probably be before Christmas," said Hardy. "The idea is that I'm not to be told until Hallock is gone, because I might slack up on my present work. Silly, childish way to do—as if it was a treat for a good boy!"

"Well, it will be a treat, won't it?" said Edith. "You've always—"

He looked across the table at her. The cold air had brought no color into her cheeks. She looked weary, downcast. He could see that her smile was an effort, and in her eyes was the look that he couldn't bear.

"No!" he said. "I wish to Heaven I wasn't going! I mean it! If I have to leave you like this—"

"Joe," she began, and was silent for a minute. "I—I know it's selfish of me; but—oh, Joe, when I think of your going away—"

Mr. Plummer, who was also taking lunch in that restaurant, saw his promising young man lean across the table and lay his hand on that of Miss Patterson from the auditing department.

"Too bad!" thought Mr. Plummer. "A boy with a remarkable future before him—and getting himself entangled before he's begun! Too bad! Too bad!"

Fortunately, however, he could not hear what monstrous folly the boy spoke.

"I won't go, Edith! I'll stay here with you. Nothing else counts with me but you—only you. I'll—"

"I want you to go, Joe, darling," said she, with quivering lips; "but I thought—only I know you wouldn't! I—if we could just get married before you go, and not tell anyone till you come back—just so that we'd really belong to each other—then it wouldn't be so hard!"

And Hardy, the bold, the rash, the magnificent, who hated anything secret and furtive, looked only once at her dear face, and agreed.

V

"You're late again, Miss Patterson," said Mr. Dunne.

"I'm awfully sorry," said Edith. "I'll really try not to again."

But she didn't look sorry. She sat down at her desk, flushed and a little out of breath, and, to Mr. Dunne's great displeasure, there was a smile hovering about her lips.

"Miss Patterson," said he, "I'm afraid this is once too often."

Edith looked up in alarm.

"But, you see—" she began, and stopped.

She couldn't explain to Mr. Dunne that this was a most pardonable lateness, and not at all likely to happen again. Going to the City Hall for a marriage license wouldn't occupy much of her time in the future. Thinking of this, she smiled again—and lost her job. Mr.

Dunne didn't like people who smiled when they were late.

So it happened that just when she badly needed a smile she hadn't one. The wretched little imitation she gave to Hardy, an hour later, didn't deceive him for an instant. He stopped beside her desk—a thing he had never done before.

"What's the matter?" he demanded, and would not be put off.

No use to tell him that he shouldn't stand there and talk to her! He knew that very well, and he didn't care. A mighty rage filled him. Edith, his Edith, his own girl, to be discharged and humiliated like this!

"Get on your hat and jacket," he commanded, "and come on!"

"Joe! You mustn't—"

"Look here!" said he. "I won't have you here like this. If Dunne told you to go, then go now. Good Lord! Haven't you any pride?"

She was too wretched to be angry at him. She did get on her hat and jacket, and, in full view of everyone, Hardy walked out of the office with her at three o'clock on a busy afternoon.

"We'll go to the flat," he said, "and talk it over."

They had a flat of their own. Hardy had insisted upon this.

"We'll take it now," he had said; "and whenever we see anything especially good in the way of furniture, we'll buy it. Then, when I come back, we'll have a place of our own all ready for us."

It wasn't quite what they wanted, but Hardy had very little money just then, and their only time for house hunting was what they had been able to pilfer from their lunch hour; so they had taken the first one that seemed at all suitable. It consisted of three tiny rooms in a remodeled house west of Central Park.

They had already become inordinately fond of this future home. To be sure, there was nothing in it except a barrel containing a Limoges dinner set, which Hardy had bought from a shipment received at the office; but Edith had made a flying visit and measured the windows for curtains, and after that she could look upon the place as her own.

This afternoon, when Hardy opened the door with his latchkey, the place was obviously a *future* home. It was bare, bleak, and dusty, with slanting sun rays falling across the ill laid board floor of what was going to be the sitting room.

The door closed behind them, and there they were, alone, with plenty of time for talking now, and neither of them said one word. Hardy began walking about. His footsteps made a loud and somehow a melancholy sound. His voice in the empty little rooms was not at all his confident office voice, but boyish, and, to Edith, terribly touching.

She sat down on the barrel, struggling against her despair and misery, while he moved about in the kitchen, mocked by a gas stove with no gas in it, and water taps that gave forth no water. She knew how he felt; she knew what he would say.

"But I won't!" she thought. "I'll get another job. I won't let him take care of Aunt Bessie now. I won't! I won't! Not now, when he's just beginning."

If she were making resolves in the sitting room, so was Hardy in the kitchen. He hadn't been singled out by Mr. Plummer because of his gentleness and consideration. He had a remarkable future because he was remarkably persistent and clear-sighted about getting his own way, and Edith was no match for him.

"No!" said he. "No more jobs! We'll tell your aunt *now*, and we'll get married to-morrow, as we planned, and we'll move in here."

"We can't, Joe. We haven't any furniture, you know—"

"Then we'll get it."

"And Aunt Bessie—"

"We'll see Aunt Bessie now. Look here, little Edith! It's got to be this way. I couldn't have my wife running about looking for a job. I couldn't go away and leave you working in a strange office. It was bad enough in the old place. Look here, Edith, don't you think you can be happy with me? Don't you love me enough?"

"I love you too much, Joe! It's not fair to you. You'll—oh, Joe, you'll have to sell your stock, and Mr. Plummer—"

"Edith," he said, "I've been thinking lately—I don't know how to put it very well—but it seems to me that maybe it's a mistake to live so much in the future. Suppose there wasn't any future—for us? Suppose something happened to one of us? Edith, I can't stand thinking of that! Look here! Let's just live now, and not be afraid of what's going to happen. Let's start this thing"—he stopped for a moment—"with courage and confidence," he finished.

She put her hand on his cheek and turned his head so that she could look into his honest, steady eyes.

"Let's!" she said, with a very unsteady little smile. "I feel that way, too, Joe. We'll begin this minute, and unpack the china, just so that we'll—we'll feel at home!"

VI

Hardy turned his back upon Mr. Plummer, and looked out of the window. It was a cold, rainy day. The people far below on the street were hurrying by under umbrellas.

"In that case, Hardy," said Mr. Plummer, "I'm sorry, but—"

"Yes, sir," said Hardy.

He couldn't, at that moment, say anything more. Something had risen into his throat and silenced him. He would have liked to speak, to tell the man who had shown so kindly an interest in him that he regretted his hasty and violent words. He hadn't meant all that he said. He had come to tell Mr. Plummer that he wanted to sell his stock. He had listened, as patiently as he could, while his employer remonstrated with him. He had endured a pretty stiff lecture upon his recent slackness and lack of attention to work, because he knew he deserved it; but when Mr. Plummer undertook to warn him about "entangling" himself with that "young woman in the auditing department," all his genuine respect for his chief had vanished in an overwhelming anger. That "young woman" was his Edith!

He didn't like, now, to recall what he had said.

"I'm sorry, Hardy," said Mr. Plummer again. He was looking at the boy with an odd expression on his lined face, a look half respectful, half sorrowful. As a man, he liked Hardy the better for his outburst, but as a business man he deplored it.

"I wish you the best of luck, my boy," he said. "Refer to me at any time."

"Thank you, sir," said Hardy.

Off he went, with his words of apology unsaid, with five years of friendly interest unrewarded, and with his own heart like lead. He walked through the office for the last time, and into the corridor, leaving so much behind him.

Edith was waiting for him in the lobby.

"Oh, Joe!" she cried. "I found a place uptown where they promised to deliver the furniture this afternoon. Imagine! And I got the dearest material for curtains! I brought a sample to show you."

She was opening her hand bag, but he stopped her.

"No, don't," he said curtly. "Not just now."

Here she was, chattering about curtains, after all that had happened! He remembered how he had left her the evening before, after a horrible interview with her aunt. He remembered her pitiful attempts to soothe and comfort that hysterical old demon, and her anguish when she failed so utterly, and was told that if she married "that man" she would be cast off—except for the trifling communications necessary to continuing her support of the martyr.

"And I couldn't sleep for worrying about her!" he thought bitterly. "I thought she'd be ill, and look at her now—perfectly happy, talking about curtains!

"Come on!" he said aloud, and then stopped, with a frown. "Haven't you any umbrella?" he asked.

"I have one," she replied, "but not here. It wasn't raining when I started."

"Edith!" he said suddenly. "Don't you remember?"

How could he have imagined that she was happy, or that her mind was filled with thoughts of curtains? That small, gallant, smiling thing, so pale, so troubled, with the shadow of her suffering dark in her eyes!

"It's nearly twelve, Joe," she said, looking at her watch. "We haven't much time."

"Oh, yes, we have!" he told her. "We have any amount of time, for I'm never going back there."

"Joe!" she cried. "Oh, Joe! Oh, no, no! Don't tell me you've—"

He drew a long breath, and then looked down at her with a grin.

"You've got a young man with a remarkably uncertain future," he said. "Never mind—we'll start a new future. Anyhow, I shan't have to go to Europe now, and leave you."

"Oh, Joe! What have I done?"

"I did it myself," he said sturdily, "and I'm glad. Thank Heaven, we've got time, now, for a nice, peaceful wedding!"

Who Is This Impossible Person?

The up train stopped, a porter sprang down the steps with two heavy bags, assisted a lady to descend, climbed on board again, and he and the train went off, leaving the lady and the bags there. The platform was deserted, shining like a treacherous sheet of water beneath the dim lamps. The rain fell steadily. It was the blackest and most dismal night that ever was.

For some time the lady stood just where she had been left, with an annoyed, affronted expression upon her face, as if she was waiting for someone to come and remove this unpleasant weather. Nobody came, nothing stirred, and she herself was strangely inactive.

Did she look like a submissive or helpless creature? On the contrary, she was a portly, white-haired lady, dressed in black of a somewhat majestic style, and not only her face, but the set of her plump shoulders and even the jet ornament on her toque, seemed to be alive with energy and resolution.

Yet she did not move. She turned her head to the north—rain and darkness were there. She turned it to the south—the same thing. Behind her she knew there was nothing but the railway track; so, with a sigh, she picked up the bags and went on toward the waiting room.

Then, had there been anyone there to see, the secret of her reluctance to move would have been revealed. This imposing and dignified lady, whose very glance was a rebuke to frivolity, had nevertheless one outrageous vanity—she *would* wear shoes that were too small for her.

Setting down the bags, she turned the handle of the door, and it was locked. Through the glass she could see into the dimly lit room, where there were plenty of benches upon which a sufferer might rest. Exasperated, she rattled the knob and rapped upon the glass, but all in vain. Picking up the bags again, she made her way painfully to the end of the platform, to see what she could see.

The town of Binnersville, however, was one of those illogical towns which are almost invisible from their own proper railway stations. There lay before her a forlorn and lifeless street lined with small shops, all tight shut, and not a human being in sight.

Her sharp eyes, however, caught sight of something very welcome.

At the end of the street, standing before a faintly illuminated drug store, there was a real, civilized taxi. With all the speed possible to her she went toward it, to seize it before it could vanish.

The street was slippery, the bags were heavy, and the portly lady in her little high-heeled shoes made a dangerous progress. Nevertheless, she got there. Seeing no driver where a driver should have been, and being a woman of enterprise and resource, she set down her bags, leaned across the seat, and blew the horn three or four times—great, loud squawks that remanded startlingly through the night.

At once the door of the drug store opened, and a young man appeared on the threshold.

"Kindly take me to No. 93 Sloan Street," said the portly, white-haired lady.

"But I'm not the driver," said the young man.

"Then kindly call the driver!" said she. Opening the door of the cab, she managed, with considerable effort, to shove one of her bags inside. The young man was there to help her with the other.

"The driver's in the shop," he explained, "getting something taken out of his eye; but—"

"Be good enough to tell him I am waiting," said she.

"He'll be along in a minute, and then he can take us both to—"

"Pardon me!" said the portly lady, in a perfectly awful voice.

The young man seemed a little taken aback. She was now settled inside the cab, and he was standing outside in the rain. It was very dark, and they could not see each other; but so expressive was her voice that he fancied he knew how she looked. "I shall instruct the driver to return here for you, if you wish," said she.

"But, you see," said the young man, quite good-humoredly, "I had engaged this cab. It's late, and the weather's bad, and I'm going in your direction. We can—"

"Pardon me! I cannot consent to that."

"What?" persisted the young man. "Why not?"

"It is not my custom to encourage chance acquaintances," replied she. "If you insist upon getting in, I shall get out."

"But look here!" protested the young man. "I—"

She was already struggling with the handle of the door.

"Very well!" he said curtly. "I'll go!"

As he turned, he saw the driver coming out of the shop, holding a handkerchief to his eye.

"This lady wants to go to No. 93 Sloan Street," said he. "Oh, never mind *me!*"

And he set off on foot up the hilly street, in the pelting rain. The portly, white-haired lady watched him go.

"I cannot," she said, half aloud, "encourage chance acquaintances—especially on Lynn's account."

II

For years the house at 93 Sloan Street had displayed a sign announcing that it was "to let or for sale," and these words might as well have been followed by "take it or leave it," for that was the owner's attitude.

It was a hopeless house, dark, damp, and badly arranged, standing in a garden where enormous old trees cast so dense a shade over the front lawn that not even grass would thrive. As for the back garden, only the queerest, most obstinate, ancient shrubs were there, huddled against the side fence, because anything less tenacious was inevitably carried away by the river in its annual spring flood.

Just now the river was low, dolloping along dejectedly between its brown and uninteresting banks. Everything was brown—the water, the bare trees, the fields, the road in front, and No. 93 itself. Altogether the breath of life had gone out of Sloan Street, and to anyone coming down from the sunny, breezy hilltop it seemed a sorry spectacle.

Someone had come down from the hilltop this morning—a brisk, neat little red-haired lady. She came smartly along the road to No. 93, pushed open the gate, and walked up the garden path. She saw the portly, white-haired lady standing on the veranda, looking down the road.

"Good morning!" said the visitor. "I'm your neighbor, Mrs. Aldrich."

She waited at the foot of the steps, because she thought she would not go up on the veranda until she was invited. Well, she never was invited.

"Is there anything I can do for you?" she asked, with honest and neighborly good will.

The portly lady looked down at her as if doubtful whether such a creature could really exist.

"Thank you, there is not," she said.

Mrs. Aldrich was greatly taken aback.

"I thought perhaps—" she began, in a tone not quite so neighborly, but the other interrupted.

"Very good of you, I'm sure; but I shall do very well, thank you."

That last "thank you" seemed capable of lifting Mrs. Aldrich out of the garden all by itself.

"I wouldn't set foot in that place again," she declared, "if she begged me on her knees!"

This declaration was addressed to her nephew, Jerry Sargent. She had made it before, to her husband and to a neighbor or so, but she found special pleasure in telling things to Jerry, for the strange reason that he never agreed with her. She was a shrewd, sensible, rather peppery little woman. She had been his guardian when he was younger, and she still interfered pretty considerably in his affairs—which he good-humoredly permitted.

"If you could have seen the way she looked at me!" she went on. "As if I were a—a toad!"

"I know," replied Jerry. "I didn't see her, but I heard her, and I know the sort of look that would go with that tone. 'Who is that impossible person?' She told me she didn't encourage chance acquaintances, and it looks as if she meant it!"

"I should have made her get out of that taxi and walk—in the rain!" cried Mrs. Aldrich, who had been informed of the episode of the previous night.

"Of course you would," her nephew agreed, with a grin. "I know you! And you'd have called her names out of the window as you passed her, wouldn't you? But I'm much milder. I was ashamed of being a chance acquaintance, anyhow. It didn't seem respectable."

"I wish you wouldn't take everything so lightly!" complained Mrs. Aldrich, hut she didn't mean it. The thing she loved best in her nephew was his careless and generous good humor, his utter lack of malice or resentment. "You ought to have more pride, Gerald, than to allow yourself to be trampled on."

He rose to his feet, and stood looking down at her with an expression of great severity; and though his aunt knew it to be assumed, she thought it very becoming to his face. A big, handsome fellow he was, with the gray eyes and black hair and all the wit and charm and grace of his blessed mother, and all the energy and practical good sense of his father. A good man of business he was, but into the dullest matter of routine, into the most trifling details of everyday life, he brought his own sort of laughing romance.

"Very well, madam!" said he. "You're disappointed in me because I've let myself be trampled on. Now you'll see what I can do when my pride is roused!"

"Jerry, you ridiculous boy! Where are you going?"

"Down to No. 93," said he. "The turning worm! Good-by!"

And off he went, down the hill, whistling as he walked.

III

Without the slightest hesitation Jerry opened the garden gate, went up the path and up the steps, and rang the bell. At least, he imagined that he rang the bell, but as a matter of fact he did nothing except turn a handle which was connected with nothing. After two or three attempts he began to suspect this, and knocked instead, which soon brought someone running along the hall to open the door.

He was astounded—not because it was a girl, and not because she was pretty. He had met pretty girls before, and knew that they were likely to crop up anywhere; but this girl had exactly the sort of prettiness he had been looking for and waiting for so long that he had almost given up hope of finding it.

She was tall, slender, dark-browed, so gracious and serene, with lovely, fragile hands; and her eyes! They were black eyes, so clear, so quiet, so luminous and untroubled! It didn't make the least difference that she was wearing a gingham apron and carried a rolling pin under her arm. She was matchless, she was incomparable, in her was personified all the romance left in the world.

"Did you—" she began, and hesitated. "Are you—"

"I thought—" he answered, still a little dazzled. "That is, I thought maybe—" It was this tremendously important and significant conversation that the portly, white-haired lady interrupted. She appeared suddenly in the background, and regarded them with severe astonishment. "Are you the plumber?" she inquired of Jerry, raising her eyebrows. "Run away, Lynn!"

"I don't think so," he answered absently, because he was watching Lynn "run away" as slowly as any healthy human being could well move.

"Indeed!" said she. "The plumber should be here."

The inference evidently was that Jerry Sargent should have been the plumber. "No," he added, with a smothered sigh. "I just stopped in to see if there was anything you wanted done."

"There are several things that I want done," she replied; "but I trust I shall be able to find the proper workmen to do them. I need a plumber and a carpenter. Are you a carpenter?"

Now Jerry knew very well that she knew he wasn't a carpenter, and that she simply wished to be obnoxious. On the spur of the moment, looking steadily at her, he answered:

"Yes, I am. Any little odd jobs you'd like done?"

She returned his glance with one quite as steady.

"There are," she said.

With that, he promptly took off his coat, and she, equally determined to see the thing through, led him into the dismal front room.

"I want shelves put up," said she. "Three rows—on this wall. There are boards in the cellar for that purpose." Fortunately Jerry was by nature "handy," and in his younger days had had much experience in building chicken houses and rabbit hutches and such things. With the calmest air in the world he set to work, wondering for what possible reason she could want a triple row of enormous shelves. For some time the portly lady watched him, but that didn't worry him, for he felt sure that she knew even less than he did about putting up shelves; and at last she went away.

When he was alone, he couldn't help laughing. It might have ended that way, with Jerry thinking the whole thing a rather idiotic joke, in which he was getting somewhat the worst of it, if something had not happened to change the aspect of the situation.

He was hammering away at a bracket which would—he hoped— support one end of one of those monster shelves, when he heard a light footstep behind him, He turned and saw the incomparable girl.

She smiled in her serious way, and Jerry tried to look equally serious, but did not succeed very well. In the first place, it wasn't natural to him to be serious, and, in the second place, he was extraordinarily pleased to see the incomparable girl again. He couldn't help fancying that she shared at least a little in his delight.

Anyhow, she was very friendly toward this strange carpenter. She asked him if he needed anything else for his work. He thanked her earnestly and said that he did not. Then she advanced a little farther into the room, and laid one of her slender little hands on the boards standing against the wall.

"Is the work very hard?" she asked.

"No," said Sargent. "I like it—very much!"

There was a long silence. She was still standing beside the boards, running her delicate fingers along the edges, with her eyes thoughtfully downcast. The shifting sunshine, filtering through the leafy branches outside, threw a wondrous light upon her gleaming dark hair and her pale, clear features. Somehow it hurt Jerry to look at her. There was something about her, some intangible shadow over her young face, which made him feel sure that she had endured much, and had endured it with fortitude and courage.

"The poor little thing!" he thought. "Shut up here in this dismal hole, with that dragon! Oh, the poor, poor little thing!"

He suddenly realized that he was in his shirt sleeves. With a hasty apology, he put on his coat.

"You know," he said, "I'm not really a carpenter."

"I knew you weren't," said she. "I knew you were—well, I mean, I knew you weren't."

Another silence.

"Would you like a cup of tea?" she asked. "I'd be—oh!"

"What's the matter?" cried Jerry.

"Nothing," she answered, but he saw her pull a handkerchief out of her pocket and wrap her hand in it.

"Let me see!" he commanded.

"Really it's nothing," she protested; "only a splinter from those boards. I should have known better."

Well, splinters ought to be taken out, lest they fester; and it was the most natural thing in the world for Jerry to insist upon performing the operation. She fetched a needle, and he burned the point in the flame of a match, and grasped her injured hand firmly.

He hadn't realized what it would mean. The splinter was long and deeply embedded, and he could not help hurting her. She winced and bit her lip. When at last the heartbreaking job was done, his face was quite pale. He still held her hand, and was looking at her with the most miserable contrition; but she smiled.

"You mustn't be so silly!" she said. "It's really—"

"Lynn!" said an awful voice.

Lynn, suddenly growing very red, escaped at once, and Jerry saw her no more that day.

He would perfectly well endure being called a plumber, a carpenter, and a chance acquaintance, but he could not endure this. He no longer wished to laugh, he no longer saw this thing as a joke. On the contrary, he was immeasurably offended by the suspicious and scornful glare he got from the portly, white-haired lady.

IV

Next morning the postman delivered a letter at No. 93, addressed to Mrs. Nathaniel Journay, who was none other than the portly lady.

> DEAR MADAM:
> In order to avoid a misunderstanding which has often been a cause for dissatisfaction in our tenants, we beg to call your attention to that clause in your

lease which restrains the tenant from driving any nails into the walls, or in any way defacing or marring the walls or woodwork of the premises.

Trusting that you find the house entirely as represented,

Very truly,

COOPER & COOPER, Agents.

"Humph!" said she, very much taken aback.

Lynn looked up from her breakfast.

"What is it, auntie?" she asked.

"Nothing," said the other calmly. "Simply one of the necessary annoyances of a business career."

She was prepared to say a good deal more than that to a certain person. She was by no means stupid. She put two and two together, and chalked up a mighty black four against that fraudulent carpenter. He was the talebearer. Very well—only wait until he presented himself again! In the meantime the indomitable woman finished the carpentering herself. The noise of the hammering made her very nervous, but she made up her mind to defy Cooper & Cooper if they should appear. She had to have those shelves, and she would have them.

That afternoon a man came by, asking for work. He said he was a gardener; and after Mrs. Journay had cross-examined him until he was reduced to an abject condition, and she felt sure he was no spy, she set him to work.

The next morning she had another letter from Cooper & Cooper, pointing out to her that it was strictly prohibited to tenants to remove shrubs in the garden, to lop off branches from trees, or in any way to mar or deface the garden.

This time she wrote a tart answer, remarking that the garden was in a lamentable condition which no one could deface or mar, that the branches lopped away had been those which shut off light from the house, and that she would really be justified in sending the landlord a bill for this work. Nevertheless, she did not employ the gardener again.

For a few days she and her niece were invisibly busy within the house, but at last, one bright morning, they came out with a ladder, which Mrs. Journay held while Lynn climbed up it and hung out a glittering gilt signboard, lettered in black:

YE OLDE NEW ENGLAND BOX SHOPPE

The sign shone in the sun like a warrior's shield. The two women regarded it with pride and pleasure.

"I believe the customers will begin coming to-morrow," said the elder.

But the first thing to come the next day was a letter from Cooper & Cooper.

> DEAR MADAM:
> It has no doubt escaped your notice that the premises at No. 93 Sloan Street are upon highly restricted property, which restrictions forbid the use of the house or grounds for any business purpose. You will find this covered in the fifth section of your lease, any violation of which, if willfully persisted in, renders the contract null and void.
> Very truly yours,
> COOPER & COOPER, Agents.

"Let 'em!" she cried aloud, dismayed, but valiant as ever.

"What is it, auntie?" inquired Lynn.

"Never mind, my dear!" said the other. "You go on painting your boxes, and I'll attend to the business arrangements." Mrs. Journay spoke in her usual confident manner, but at heart she was alarmed and not at all certain as to what she ought to do. She was certain, however, that her niece must not be worried by these unexpected developments. To protect Lynn was her chief duty on earth, and her chief pleasure, too. Terrible as she might be to others, to Lynn she was never anything but kind and generous and affectionate, in her august fashion.

"I'd rather know, auntie," insisted Lynn. "I think I really ought to know. We're partners, aren't we?"

"Yes," said Mrs. Journay. "Yes, I know that, but—"

"We can't carry on our business," Lynn continued, "unless we both know everything about it—can we, darling?"

She was now standing behind her aunt's chair, resting her soft cheek against that imposing coiffure. Mrs. Journay frowned.

"It doesn't seem necessary," she said. She was already conquered, however. To tell the truth, her serious and quiet niece had always been able to wind Mrs. Journay around her little finger.

"Let me see the letter, auntie dear!" said Lynn.

She did see it, and the two former ones.

"It's that man!" deduced Mrs. Journay. "There's no possible doubt of it. He came here to spy. Someone sent him. My theory is that someone knew we were going to start this shop, and, fearing the competition, determined to drive us out!"

Lynn stood looking down at the letter with a curious expression. "I see!" she said.

From her face one might imagine that whatever it was she saw gave her very little pleasure.

They were both silent for a time, with their meager little breakfast forgotten between them. They had always been more or less poor, but never in this way. Until recently they had lacked neither dignity nor comfort. They had had their friends and their little diversions, and a cozy sort of existence, until something happened. It doesn't much matter what the catastrophe was. The important fact is that their small income vanished, and here they were, gallantly prepared to make a new one for themselves.

And was this enterprise, into which the very last of their savings had gone, to be wrecked by Cooper & Cooper? Mrs. Journay would not permit it. Often in the past, when she had coldly ignored people, such people had disappeared from her sight—beneath the surface of the earth, for all she knew; and she decided to try this on Cooper & Cooper. She would scornfully ignore them. The shop should go on—it must! She was about to say this aloud, when Lynn began to speak.

"Auntie dear," she said, "let's give it up!"

"Lynn! I am surprised!"

"Yes!" Lynn went on, with a sort of vehemence. "Let's give this up and go away from here."

"Lynn! Your boxes! The beautiful boxes you've painted!"

"I'd like," mid Lynn, "to see them all sailing down the river! Oh, auntie, do let's go away! I hate this house and this place and—we'll go back to Philadelphia, and I'll take a position in an office, and—"

The girl stopped short at the sight of her aunt's face.

"Oh, my dear!" she cried. "I didn't really mean that! No—we'll stay here, of course, and we'll make a wonderful success of the shop."

She sat on the arm of her aunt's chair, and they talked with enthusiasm of their dazzling future; but they didn't look at each other—not once. They talked, they even laughed, and after breakfast they went about busily preparing for customers; but all the time there lay over them the black shadow of this persecution. Why should anyone wish them ill?

"I'd really be glad to go," thought Mrs. Journay, "if it weren't for Lynn; but I can't and won't have Lynn working in an office. I'll make this—this disgusting shop a success!"

Lynn went on painting boxes all the morning.

"He was the only one who knew about the shelves," she said to herself. "Out of petty, despicable spite against poor auntie, he went off and told the agents; and after he'd been so—not that I care, though. I knew all the time that he was one of those men who always—who always pretend to—to like people!"

Stilt, in spite of not caring in the least, it seemed to her that this incident was harder to bear than all her other misfortunes—harder to bear than exile from her old home and her old friends, than her desperate anxiety about money, or than the frightful tedium of painting boxes.

"Because it's such a humiliation," she explained to herself.

The admiration of young men was certainly no new thing to Lynn, but that a man should look at her like that, should speak as he had spoken, and then so basely betray her aunt and herself

Her cheeks burned with just anger, or perhaps with shame, that even for a moment she should have thought so well of him.

V

No one came to molest them that day, or the next, or all that week, or that month, but this good fortune was counterbalanced by the fact that no customers came, either.

Mrs. Journay and her niece took turns in attending to the shop with the regularity of deck officers standing watch; and, having once arranged a schedule, they were afraid to depart from it, for fear of admitting in any way that trade was not brisk. Lynn went on and on painting boxes, because, in the first place, they had a large stock to be painted, and, in the second place, she had nothing else to do; but the dismalness of sitting in that big, dim room, to see the boxes piling up on the shelves, and to make calculations which showed that the money decreased even faster than the boxes increased, was not a life to give animation to a girl, or comfort to an elderly lady.

Indeed, the only thing that supported them was their splendid, ridiculous Journay fortitude and obstinacy. They had gone into this thing without help or advice. They wouldn't ask help or advice now, and they wouldn't complain.

It was Lynn's turn in the shop that afternoon. She sat there behind a long table on which were a tin cash box, wrapping paper, twine, and a pile of pretty little blue cards on which was printed:

YE OLDE NEW ENGLAND BOX SHOPPE—Hand-decorated gift boxes for all purposes—Chests made to order.

She was sewing, but when she heard a step on the veranda she hid the sewing in a drawer and began to write busily on a pad. The front door was open, and the customer entered the room. Lynn looked up with an alert, businesslike expression—and it was that man!

"I've been away," he began eagerly. "Otherwise—" He stopped short, looking at Lynn. "Is anything wrong?" he asked,

"No," she said evenly.

For an instant her clear eyes rested on his face, and then they glanced away, as if he wasn't worth regarding. She was not rude, or scornful, or awe-inspiring like her aunt, but her attitude was unmistakable.

"I'll have to ask you to excuse me," she said politely. "I'm busy this morning." Rising, she moved toward the door.

"No!" he cried. "Please wait! Please tell me what's the matter! Every minute I've been away, I've been thinking of getting back and seeing you again. I—please don't go! Just tell me!"

"I have nothing to tell you," said Lynn, with energy. "I have nothing to say to you at all, except that I'd appreciate it if you wouldn't come again."

Then she vanished. Before Jerry had recovered himself, he was confronted by his mortal enemy, Mrs. Journay.

"Kindly send your bill for the carpenter work you did," said she, "and it will be attended to promptly."

He tried a smile.

"That was just a little neighborly service—" he began.

"I prefer not to accept it as such," she interrupted.

"Well, I prefer not to send bills," said he, resolutely good-humored. "If you'll allow me, I'll introduce myself—"

"I do not allow you."

"I'm sorry," he replied firmly, "but it's time it was done. I'm Mr. Sargent, your landlord,"

This was a blow to stagger Mrs. Journay, but she rallied superbly.

"Indeed!" said she. "Now I see it all! Very well, call your Cooper & Cooper to put us out. Let them—"

"But there's no question of that!" he protested. "I'm only too glad—"

She really was magnificent!

"I refuse to be under obligations to you," she said. "Your agents may

forbid me to do such and such a thing, and I shall do it. I defy them.
I defy you. I intend to continue in this course until I am forcibly
ejected. Instruct your Cooper & Cooper to that effect. I do not
recognize you!"

VI

This was ordinary rain. From a sullen sky it came driving down
like a sheet of fine wires, digging into the sodden ground, dashing
on the roof, beating down the tiny new leaves on the trees, riddling
the muddy water of the now hurrying river. This was the worst of
three rainy days, and the house on Sloan Street was in a sad state.
There was water in the cellar, there were spots of mold on the
walls, and everywhere there was a most miserable, dank, bleak chill,
which even these two resolutely cheerful women could not ignore.
They did not appear to relish their breakfast.

"I—" began Mrs. Journay, and, for the first time since Lynn had
known her, she visibly hesitated. "If you can look after the shop
alone," she said, "I'd like to—to—attend to some business."

Now, if she had not been so intent upon her own duplicity, Mrs.
Journay would have observed that Lynn's conduct was unusual. The
girl showed no surprise at her aunt's singular decision to go out in
such weather. On the contrary, she seemed relieved and pleased.

"I don't mind at all," she replied. "Not a bit! I—not a bit!"

So Mrs. Journay put on an old raincoat with capes, and a hat that
was good enough for the rain, and her overshoes, and set off.

Lynn, watching that erect and imposing figure tramping through
the mud of Sloan Street, took out a handkerchief and cried into it
for a good ten minutes. She planned treachery that day. She had
made a secret appointment with a wholesaler who would, she
hoped, buy all those boxes for a lump sum, and thus put an end to
some of their financial difficulties—and also to the shop.

Fortunate that she did not suspect her aunt's errand! Even Mrs.
Journay, with her unconquerable spirit, was very, very unhappy that
morning.

"But," she said to herself, "there wouldn't have been enough to pay
that man his rent on the 1st of next month, and that I could *not*
bear!"

She, too, had renounced the shop, and intended to tell Lynn so in
the evening.

In the meantime, on she pressed. The mud was slippery, the rain
disconcerted her by beating in her face, and her shoes were even

more uncomfortable when worn with rubbers. What was worse, her way lay uphill, and up a mighty steep hill at that, and she had a heavy heart to carry with her. She turned her ankle rather painfully, the top button burst off her raincoat—she breathed so hard—and the rain ran down her neck. Still, as was her admirable way, she reached her goal. At last she stood upon the summit of the hill, and though to be sure she did not cry "Excelsior!" she felt a little like that.

She turned for a last glance behind her. There lay Sloan Street far below, and No. 93 was plainly visible in every detail. She sighed sternly, faced her destiny again, and turned in at the gate of a fine stone house before her. She rang the bell.

"Mrs. Aldrich?" said she to the maid, and presented her card.

She was asked to step into the music room, but would not. She was too wet. She would stand in the hall; and there Mrs. Aldrich found her when she descended.

Now Mrs. Aldrich, when she saw that card, had meant to treat Mrs. Journay as Mrs. Journay had treated her; but it was impossible. In the first place, Mrs. Aldrich was not capable of a majestic manner. She was peppery and sharp, sometimes, but never hoity-toity. In the second place, the caller looked so forlorn and tired and wet that all her rancor vanished. She held out her hand with a smile and a friendly greeting.

"Pardon me," replied Mrs. Journay, in the most frigid tone she had ever used. "I fear you mistake my purpose. I have come"— here she opened her purse and took out a bit torn from a newspaper—"I have come to apply for this position as cook."

"Oh!" cried Mrs. Aldrich.

"If the position is not filled, I believe I have at least some of the qualifications you desire. I understand cookery in all its branches. I am honest, clean, and strictly sober."

This was awful! This was intolerable! "Oh, but, my dear Mrs. Journay!" cried Mrs. Aldrich, immeasurably distressed. "I—don't you see? I can't! Let's sit down and

"Thank you," interrupted the other. "Then I must apply to the next place on my list."

"Oh, dear!" said Mrs. Aldrich, for she could not endure the thought of Mrs. Journay going out into the rain again, and tramping about, looking for a position as cook. She could not endure to see this magnificent creature so humbled. "Can't—something else be done?" she asked.

"Thank you, it cannot."

"Then," said Mrs. Aldrich, "if you really feel that you must, then please stay here with me."

"Thank you. I shall ask you to allow me to use the telephone for the purpose of sending a message to my niece. May I safely say that I shall return to her at ten o'clock this evening?"

"Oh, much earlier! Whenever you like!"

"Pardon me," said Mrs. Journay, "but I believe I understand the requirements of such a position."

VII

"The dam has burst," said old Mr. Cooper.

He made this melodramatic announcement with great calm, because it was a very unimportant dam, and not likely to evoke much excitement; but Jerry Sargent, his employer, sprang to his feet.

"What?" he cried. "Elliot's dam? Then Sloan Street must be under water!"

"I'm afraid so," said Cooper, somewhat startled; "but No. 93 is the only house there that's tenanted, and I didn't imagine you'd be much upset about *them*."

He was still more startled by the expression he now saw upon Sargent's usually good-humored face.

"What do you mean by supposing that?" thundered Jerry. "On the contrary, they're—they're *special* tenants. They—"

"Well," said Mr. Cooper, "you see, in view of the correspondence we had with them—"

"What correspondence?"

"Why, those letters that Mrs. Aldrich directed us to send while you were away. You distinctly said we were to take directions from her in your absence."

"Let me see those letters!"

Mr. Cooper produced them. Mr. Sargent read them.

"It's an outrage!" shouted Jerry. "It's persecution! It's—"

He flung himself into his overcoat, jammed a felt hat well down on his head, and started out, slamming the office door behind him. His roadster stood at the curb. He got in, started off with a jerk, and went down the street, around the corner, and out into the road that led to Sloan Street from the town. It was a good road, and he took advantage of it. He turned another corner, and Sloan Street lay before him at the foot of the hill.

Oh, Sloan Street was under water, sure enough! It was, in fact, a shallow stream, moving sluggishly. It was certainly not more than six inches deep, and there was no danger, visible or implied; yet to

Sargent it was horrible, that sullen, muddy stream, under the merciless downpour of rain, with stanch old No. 93 standing there among the bowing, dripping branches of the trees.

He left his car, ran down the hill, and splashed into the water, ankle deep. His feet sank into the mud, the rain beat in his face, but he bent his head and floundered on, the slowness of his progress putting him into a dogged fury. He wanted to get there at once, to explain.

He stumbled over something, fell to his knees, and lost his hat while regaining his feet. He wiped his rain-blurred eyes with muddy sleeve, and went on.

"Mr. Sargent! Mr. Sa-argent!"

He stopped, turned, and saw Lynn standing on the hill he had recently left.

"Oh, please come back!" she cried. "Please, Mr. Sargent!"

He did come back, and stood before her.

"I had to come," he said, "to tell you that I didn't know anything about those letters from Cooper & Cooper. I never heard of them till to-day."

Never in his life had he imagined that a girl could look like this. Her hair lay dank across her forehead, giving to her glowing face an adorably childlike look. Her dark lashes were wet, and were like rays about her clear eyes; and the kindness, the heavenly kindness of her regard! The poor fellow had positively no idea that she was a forlorn, bedraggled little object. There he stood, looking up at her, and she looked at him, and tears came into her eyes.

"Don't!" he cried.

"But you don't know!" she said.

She meant that he didn't know how splendid and gallant and handsome be appeared, bareheaded in the rain, with a great streak of mud across his face, and how deeply touched she was by his coming through a flood to explain about the letters; and of course she didn't wish him to know.

"I—my boxes!" she said, by way of explaining the tears. "I've been into the city to see a wholesaler, and he's bought them all. I had them all on the dining room floor, ready to pack, and I'm afraid—"

"I'll see what I can do," said Sargent.

"No! No! Mr. Sargent, come out of that water!" said she sternly. "It doesn't matter!"

"It does," said he. "Wait here!"

Off he splashed again.

No. 93 was built on the side of a little slope. The front door was reached by a flight of steps, but the back door was level with the garden, and Jerry knew very well that the house must be filled with water. He kicked open the gate, made his way along the path and up the steps to the veranda, and put the pass key he carried with him into the lock.

The key turned readily, but the door would not open. He pushed his hardest. At last he drew off a little and crashed against the door with his shoulder. Then it opened, and a great flood of water, dammed up inside, came rolling down the steps in a cascade. Suddenly something heavy, borne on the swift-moving current, struck Jerry on the shins, knocked him backward, and, sailing on, struck him violently on the head. The chill, muddy water rolled over him, but he was as indifferent to it as the fleet of hand-decorated boxes that went down the front steps with him.

VIII

Mrs. Aldrich and Mrs. Journay sat in the kitchen, side by side, on two straight-backed chairs. They had just had a quarrel, due to Mrs. Journay's obstinately refusing to eat her lunch with Mrs. Aldrich and insisting upon having it in the kitchen. In the course of this quarrel Mrs. Aldrich had explosively confessed that it was she who had ordered the Cooper & Cooper letters sent, and who had observed from her hilltop all that went on below.

"Because I didn't like the way you treated my nephew," she explained. "Can you forgive me for that?"

"I can," said Mrs. Journay, calmly. "I should have felt the same, if it had been my nephew."

"Then," said Mrs. Aldrich triumphantly, "if you really do forgive me, the least you can do is to come in and have lunch with me decently!"

But Mrs. Journay would not, so Mrs. Aldrich had sent away the two servants and eaten there in the kitchen with Mrs. Journay. In the beginning both of them were very angry, but they became more and more friendly every minute. They had a great deal to talk about— they had Lynn and Jerry to talk about.

"Jerry tells me that your niece is a charming girl," said Mrs. Aldrich. "He's talked about her incessantly ever since he first saw her; and it isn't like Jerry to be so enthusiastic."

"She is a charming girl," replied Mrs. Journay complacently; "and as for your nephew—"

The front doorbell rang, and Mrs. Aldrich went to open the door. Mrs. Journay sat where she was.

"Jerry!" she heard Mrs. Aldrich cry in a tone of fright.

"Don't worry!" answered a cheerful voice which Mrs. Journay recognized without difficulty. "It's only a scratch; but—this is Miss Journay. She saved my life!"

"Oh!" protested Lynn. "Really I didn't!"

Mrs. Journay then entirely forgot her position, and hurried into the hall. There she saw that man, with a bandage around his head, and Lynn standing beside him.

"Auntie!" cried Lynn, amazed. "You here?"

"Why not?" inquired Mrs. Journay. "I might ask why you are here!"

"Mr. Sargent got hurt trying to save my boxes," Lynn explained anxiously; "so you see, auntie—"

"What am I expected to see?" asked Mrs. Journay, with lifted eyebrows.

Mrs. Aldrich now intervened.

"Jerry," said she, "now that I've had an opportunity of knowing Mrs. Journay better, I see that I was wrong—altogether wrong. I want her and her niece to stay here with us until that horrible old barn is put in order for them again—if it ever is; and I want you—"

Jerry stepped forward and held out his hand, smiling. Lynn thought, with a flash of hope, that even her aunt could not resist him; but Mrs. Journay regarded him sternly.

"Lynn," said she, "introduce this young man to me. I do not know him."

"But, auntie!" protested Lynn. "You've seen him—"

"Not properly," said Mrs. Journay.

"Mrs. Journay, this is my nephew, Gerald Sargent," said Mrs. Aldrich.

Then Mrs. Journay took his outstretched hand and smiled, the jolliest sort of smile.

"I always liked that boy!" she observed aside to Mrs. Aldrich.

Nickie and Pem

"Pem, you're too darned good!" said Nickie.

"I don't call it being good," replied Miss Pembroke. "I call it simply being self-respecting."

This was the sort of thing her friends found objectionable, and Nickie began to object now.

"Lord!" said she. "Don't we work hard enough to deserve a little fun now and then? It won't hurt your precious self-respect to speak to a man now and then, will it? I can't—"

"Oh, that's all nonsense!" interrupted Miss Pembroke. "I see enough of men, and I put up with enough from them. When I'm off duty, I don't have to put up with anything, and I *won't!*"

"Nobody wants you to. The boys who are coming this evening are awfully nice boys. If you'd just come in and speak to them—"

Miss Pembroke closed her book sharply.

"Nickie," she said, "I'm very fond of you; but I don't like your friends—not any of them—and I wish you'd let me alone."

"Certainly," replied Nickie, in a haughty and offended tone.

She turned all her attention upon the process of manicuring, but neither the haughtiness nor the silence reassured Miss Pembroke, who knew that they wouldn't last. It was hardly worthwhile to open her book again, for Nickie would be sure to interrupt.

"It's getting to be too much of a good thing," she reflected. "I needed a good rest after that last case, but I'll never get it while Nickie's here. This whole thing was a mistake. I ought to have taken a room somewhere by myself, where I couldn't be bothered."

This was by no means the first time she had regretted her present domestic arrangements. It was all Nickie's fault, of course. Nickie had told her what a fine thing it would be to join with three other graduate nurses in taking a flat.

"A nice little home of our own," Nickie had said, "where we can rest when we want to, and entertain our friends, and keep all our things. The other girls are simply great. You'll like them."

Miss Pembroke had said that five girls were too many.

"But we'll never all be home at the same time," Nickie had assured her. "Lots of times you and I will have the place to ourselves."

In the course of a year this had happened only once. When Nickie was at home, Pem was off on a case. When Pem came home, instead of finding her faithful Nickie, one of the other girls would be there, or sometimes two of them; and Pem didn't like them. She didn't like their "parties," or their conversation, or their cheerful, careless style of housekeeping.

She herself was never careless, and, though she was even-tempered and polite, she wasn't often cheerful. As a nurse, she was matchless. Doctors wanted to send her to their most troublesome and exacting patients, because not only was she quick, capable, and intelligent, but she could hold her tongue and keep her temper, and she had a cool, quiet way with her that kept her patients in good order.

But this cool, quiet way of which doctors so highly approved was not at all pleasing to her housemates. Even Nickie thought it deplorable.

"Pem," she had said to her once, "you could be young and beautiful, if you'd only learn how!"

There was truth in that observation. Miss Pembroke had both youth and beauty, and somehow managed to disguise them, so that they often went unnoticed. People would say that she was "impressive," or "dignified," or something of that sort, because they never saw her off guard, as Nickie saw her now. She was a tall, slender, dark-haired girl, with an austere, fine-bred face—not the sort of face one would turn to look after in the street, but a face which patients—above all, male patients—found very, very hard to forget. Her slender hands were clasped about one knee, and her clear amber eyes were staring thoughtfully before her. She was, thought Nickie, engaged in daydreams of some mysterious and enchanting kind unknown to more ordinary girls. But in reality—

"Nickie's getting coarse," Miss Pembroke was reflecting.

There was no coarseness to be seen in Miss Nicholson's rosy, jolly face, nor to be observed in her manners and conversation. Indeed, no one but Miss Pembroke had yet seen any trace of it; but Pem was by nature critical, and just at this moment she was jaded and dispirited after six weeks of a ferocious typhoid patient, who had fallen in love with her in a very trying and ill-tempered way. Moreover, she was mortally weary of Nickie's persistence.

"I'm sick and tired of men," she thought. "All Nickie ever thinks of is men, and going to parties, and having what she calls a good time."

Now this was not quite doing justice to Nickie. When she was not working, she was undeniably very fond of playing; but when you consider how very short and infrequent were her play times, and how very hard and exhausting was her work; when you consider that this lively, warm-hearted young creature had to witness every sort of human agony and wretchedness; when you bear in mind the tremendous responsibilities she so faithfully accepted; her generous readiness to do more than she needed to do, her charity, her sympathy, her sturdy courage—when you think of all this, it is not difficult to forgive her for being somewhat frivolous during her little hours of freedom.

There were weeks at a time when men, parties, and having a good time gave her mighty little concern. Just now, however, her mind was entirely given to such matters; and, as Pem expected, she couldn't help trying again to persuade her friend.

"Oh, Pem!" she said coaxingly. "Just this once! Come in and speak to the boys, and if you don't like them—"

"No!" said Pem.

But she did, and, by doing so, she changed the course of three lives.

She had no intention of seeing Nickie's friends. In fact, she came nearer to quarreling with Nickie than she had ever yet come, and she retired to her own room with flushed cheeks and a frown on her calm brow. She was not in the habit of losing her temper, and this unusual annoyance disturbed her. She was restless, and couldn't settle down to read or sew.

Her neat little room seemed all at once too neat and too little, and she wanted to get out of it. It was a clear, fine night. A walk, even a solitary and aimless one, wouldn't be bad. She had put on her hat and coat, and was just about to open her door, when—when Nickie's party arrived.

Impossible to go out now! In order to reach the front door, she would have to pass by the sitting room, and Nickie would see her and stop her.

"Nickie has absolutely no pride!" she thought, angrier than ever. "Even after what I said to her, she'd try to drag me in there!"

She took off her hat and flung it on the bed.

"I'll read," she decided.

She couldn't read. The party disturbed her too much. They were laughing and talking, and presently someone began to play the piano and sing. It was an idiotic song, but it was delivered in a hearty, boyish voice that was somehow very touching.

There was violent applause when the singer finished, and after a few minutes he began again.

Pem came nearer to the door, her face grown very pale. "Keep the Home Fires Burning!" Someone else sang that—one night in Montreal—the night before the troop ship went out—a boy in a lieutenant's uniform. Pem snapped the light and stood listening in the dark, her hands clenched, her eyes closed.

> "So turn the dark clouds inside out,
> Till the boys come home."

"Oh, God!" whispered Pem; for that boy would never come home, and the Pem who had listened to his gallant young voice was gone, too.

The singing stopped, only not for Pem. It went on sounding in her ears. The voice that she would never hear again and the living voice mingled together until she could bear it no longer. She must go in and see this other one—see with her own eyes that he was a stranger, in no way like—anyone else.

II

Nickie welcomed her with a cry of joy.

"Here's my pal!" she said, triumphantly. "Now you'll all have to be good little boys. Pem, here's Mr. Brown and Mr. Caswell and Mr. Hadley. Look 'em over!"

But the only one Pem wanted to see was Caswell—the boy who had been singing, the boy who must not look like someone else. Well, he didn't. That one had been fair and this one was dark. There was no resemblance in a single feature; and yet the spell was not broken.

There was some quality in this man that stirred intolerable memories to life in Pem—something in his voice, in his smile, in the hearty grip of his hand. She looked and looked at him, trying in vain to catch that fugitive likeness.

She had never been so lovely, or so utterly careless of her own beauty. Her eyes were wonderfully luminous and soft in her pale face. Her hair, a little disordered by the hat she had pulled off, floated about her forehead in tiny, misty threads. She hadn't a trace of that cool, quiet manner now.

Under that look of hers young Caswell grew suddenly ardent.

"I say!" he began. "You know—you're simply—simply marvelous!"

"Didn't I tell you so?" said Nickie, delighted. "Now sing some more, Cas. That's what brought her to."

"No," said Pem. "Please don't."

The spell was slowly dissolving. She could see Caswell without illusions now—an ordinary nice-looking young fellow, unfortunately a little the worse for drink just now, like the others.

She had come in without any idea of staying, but for Nickie's sake she resigned herself to a wearisome half hour. This was Nickie's idea of a good time, and these were Nickie's "awfully nice boys"! One of them offered Pem his pocket flask, but she declined, civilly enough, and sat down on the piano stool, so that Caswell couldn't sing again.

She was quite aware that he was looking at her all the time. Very well, let him look! She felt a thousand miles away from him and the others, and somehow very lonely.

This sudden change disturbed Nickie. Now that she had got Pem here at last, it would never do to let the party prove a fizzle. She whispered to one of the men, and then called out:

"Pem, get your hat on! We're all going up to the Devon to dance!"

"No, thanks," said Pem firmly.

There was a chorus of protests.

"Oh, come on, Pem!" Nickie entreated. "I don't want to go alone with three fellows, and I'm dying for a dance. Please, Pem, just for an hour!"

"No, thanks," said Pem again. "I'm sorry, but I don't feel up to it. I'm tired."

And then, beside her, she heard a voice which, in spite of herself, she could not hear unmoved.

"I say, Miss Pembroke! Please!"

She shook her head, but she smiled, for once more she caught a glimpse of that curious likeness, and it made her gentle toward him. What was it? What could she see in this flushed, unsteady boy to put her in mind of that other, fine and stern, a young knight?

"Look here!" said Caswell, bending lower, so that only she could hear. "Please don't—don't judge me by this. I—I'm—I can't tell you how sorry I am for you to see me—like this. I—I don't do it, you know, I give you my word. You see, I've just come back from Melbourne, and this was my first night on shore, and—if you'd just give me another chance!"

"All right, I will," said Pem suddenly. "I'll see you again. I'll be glad to."

And she meant it. She no longer wanted to deny the unreasonable, half scornful liking she felt for this man. She did like him, and that was enough.

"Oh, but, look here!" he cried. "We're sailing to-morrow for Halifax. I've only got this one night!"

"But you'll come back to New York, won't you?"

"Oh, some day!" he answered bitterly. "God knows when—*I* don't.

We're running all over after cargoes. We may come back here from Halifax, and we may go anywhere. It may be months before I see you again."

"Would that be so awful?" asked Pem, with a smile.

But he didn't smile.

"Yes," he said. "It would—for me!"

Pem was annoyed at her own response to his emotion. She wanted to laugh at him, and she could not. This was the worst sort of nonsense—the sort of thing Nickie was always telling her about. Nickie would call this "thrilling." Well, Pem didn't.

"I'm sorry for you," she said ironically; but, as if there were magic in his eyes, the words turned to truth when she looked at him. "Please don't be silly!" she added, in a quite different voice—gentle, almost appealing.

"The only silly thing would be to pretend it wasn't like this," said he. "I didn't want it to be this way, but—it just happened. As soon as I saw you—"

Pem jumped up.

"All right, Nickie!" she called out. "I'll go with you!"

III

Caswell got into the taxi after her and slammed the door.

"Oh, Pem!" he said. "Pem, you wonderful girl!"

"You know you really are silly!" she protested.

"Then I hope to Heaven I'll never be anything else! I'd give all the common sense and prudence and so on in the world for one night like this. Hang being sensible, anyhow! Let's be silly, Pem!"

"I am—I have been—sillier than I ever was before in my life. Don't, Arthur!"

She felt obliged to object to his putting his arm about her shoulders and kissing her—a very unconvincing little objection, however, to which he paid no attention.

"You do love me, don't you, Pem?" he asked, and waited a long time. "Pem! I say, Pem! You do love me, don't you?"

"Oh, I really don't know!" she cried impatiently.

Was it love, she thought? It was not in any way the love she had felt before—not that strange and terrible thing, half pride, half humility, half anguish and half ecstasy.

"That couldn't ever come again," she thought.

It had been her consolation for so long, that never again would that intolerable emotion stir her heart. After she had lost that one man, there wasn't another walking the earth who could capture her interest—until this evening.

She couldn't understand the glamour that enveloped young Caswell, the inexplicable charm of him. He was neither very handsome nor very clever—just an ordinary nice-looking boy; and yet, when he said that he would give all the common sense and prudence and so on in the world for one night like this, she agreed with him in her heart.

They had gone to a restaurant and danced, they had taken a taxicab to another restaurant and danced again, they had had supper—that was all there was to it. It was simply one of those brainless "parties" so dear to Nickie—with too much drinking on the part of the men, too much smoking, the stupidest sort of talk and laughter. Then why had it been so beautiful? Because of that boy's glance which always followed her, that look on his face, his fervent, halting love-making?

Suddenly she stopped trying to reason about it. It *was* beautiful. She had been utterly happy again; she was happy now.

"Pem!" he said. "Oh, Pem! Can't you tell me? I'm going away, you know."

His voice broke, she felt the arm about her shoulders tremble a little, and her eyes filled with tears.

"I'm afraid I do love you," she said. She gave him one kiss, and then, with a little laugh, pushed him away.

"Don't talk anymore about it—not now," she said. "Look! The sky's getting light. It's morning."

"And I'm due on board at ten o'clock," he said. "I'll come back to you, Pem. Pem, you won't forget me? You won't—you couldn't, could you, Pem?"

"I don't think so," she answered.

The taxi had stopped before the apartment house, where Nickie and the two other boys, just arrived, were waiting for them in the street. A pallid light was spreading in the sky, and a strange quiet lay over the city. Trucks rumbled far away, but there wasn't a voice or a footstep. The street lamps still burned wanly.

"It's time for breakfast," suggested one of the boys. "Let's go to a beanery and have something to eat."

"No!" said Pem sharply. "We've had enough. Good-by! Come on, Nickie!"

For she had seen on Nickie's face something that hurt her—something that she had often seen in the mirror, reflected in her own eyes.

IV

Nickie was lying on the bed, flat on her back, without a pillow, her eyes resolutely closed, in a stern effort to rest. That morning, just as she was saying good-by—very willingly—to the cantankerous old lady with a broken arm whom she had been attending for three weeks, Dr. Lucas had telephoned and told her that he wanted her for night duty on a pneumonia case. It was a bad case, and she had a bad night ahead of her. She must rest now; but she couldn't. This wasn't rest.

She heard the key turned in the latch, and the front door opened quietly.

"Hello, Mac!" she called.

But it was not Miss McCarty who answered. It was Pem.

"You home, Nickie?" she said. "That's nice."

She came into the bedroom. Nickie sat up and stared at her with wide eyes.

"For Pete's sake!" she exclaimed. "What's the meaning of all this, Pem?"

"I don't know," replied Pem slowly. She had taken off her hat and coat, and was looking at herself in the glass—at her carefully dressed hair, the artful touch of color in her cheeks, the new frock of navy twill with red leather buttons. "I look rather nice, don't I, Nickie?"

"Yes," said Nickie, "stunning; but—well, I suppose I'm not used to it. But what's the reason, Pem?"

Pem's explanation did not satisfy her. Pem said that her patient was a wealthy young woman suffering from a mild form of melancholia. She had to be diverted, and—

"I had to look halfway decent, going about with her," said Pem. "She wanted me to."

"Finished now?" Nickie asked.

"No—it may last for months; but I often get an afternoon off when her sister comes to stay with her. She likes me to clear out sometimes, so that she can tell her sister how awful I am."

"Doesn't she like you, Pem?"

"Oh, pretty well; but she doesn't really like anybody but herself. That's what's the matter with her. She's got everything on earth—money, and friends, and a wonderful husband. Lend me some of your powder, Nickie?"

"Powder? Going out again now, Pem?"

Pem nodded.

"Who with?"

"With a man," said Pem, laughing. "Don't faint!"

"Of course it's not my business," observed Nickie, "but it—it isn't the husband, is it?"

She waited a long time for an answer.

"I wish you'd tell me, Pem. I always tell you things."

Pem turned and looked at her steadily.

"No, you don't, Nickie," she said; "not always."

Nickie looked back at her friend quite as steadily.

"I do," she said. "I tell you anything that really matters. You see, Pem, the reason I am asking this is because I thought you were rather gone on Arthur Caswell. You see, I've known him for a long while, so I—"

Pem turned to open the bureau drawer, and to take out a pair of white gloves and a handkerchief.

"I'll tell you something, Nickie," she said in a curt, cool voice. "He would never have looked at me that night if I had been my real self. I acted like a fool, and that's what he liked. That's what everyone likes. After he'd gone, everything seemed tame and flat, and I felt so lonely that I couldn't stand it. I'm going to keep on being a fool, Nickie. I'm going to make people like me. I'm going to live, and enjoy myself!"

"All right," said Nickie; "but what about Arthur Caswell?"

"He'll never come back."

"Yes, he will."

"If he does, then—but he won't. I'm not going to waste my life—or what's left of it."

"If I was going to waste any lives," said Nickie, "I'd rather waste my own than anyone else's."

Pem was astounded.

"What's the matter with you?" she demanded. "Are you trying to preach to me, Nickie? It was you who started the whole thing—always pestering me to go to parties."

"I never went out with a married man in my life," said Nickie; "and I never would, either."

"That's a little too much, after that last party!" returned Pem scornfully. "You wouldn't go out with a married man, but you don't mind three fellows who've been drinking!"

"How do you know I didn't mind?" cried Nickie, jumping up. "Just let me tell you, Pem—I knew Arthur Caswell's people in Halifax. His father's a strict Presbyterian. I know what he'd think about that, and

I'd have stopped Arthur, too, if—"

Pem was about to make a sharp retort, but she changed her mind in time. Going over to Nickie, she put her arms about her friend.

"I'm sorry, little pal," she said gently. "I didn't mean to."

Nickie gave her a rough little hug.

"All right, Pem," she said. "I know! But, Pem, for my sake, please don't go out with this man. You'll be sorry for it—awfully sorry. It's not like you. Don't do it, Pem!"

"You don't understand, Nickie. He's a wonderful man, so honorable—"

"He's not honorable if he goes out with you behind his wife's back."

"How can he help it, when she's turned her back on him for good? She's horrible to him. Nobody else would have put up with her as he has. He is honorable, Nickie; he's a gentleman through and through. He's so lonely—you don't know what that is, but I do. He's longing and longing for women to be nice and friendly to him. If his wife was ever halfway decent to him—"

She stopped short, because the doorbell had rung.

"There he is," she said. "Nickie, it's nothing to be ashamed of. I wish you'd see him and talk to him. Then you'd understand. Open the door and talk to him while I'm getting ready."

Nickie hesitated for a moment.

"All right!" she said, then. "I'll talk to him!"

Without even troubling to smooth her unruly hair, off she went, down the passage. In a moment she was back.

"Pem," she cried, "Arthur Caswell is here!"

They stared at each other in a sort of dismay, both speechless for a time.

"I'll take him out, quick," said Pem. "When Mr. Blanchard comes, tell him something—anything. I'll see you later, Nickie. I'll stop here before I go back to Mr. Blanchard's."

"All right," Nickie said again.

When Pem had gone, she closed the bedroom door after her; but she didn't even try to rest now.

V

Pem went down the passage with a lagging step and a heart strangely troubled and doubting.

"No," she said to herself. "Of course it can't be like that. I just imagined it. I've thought about it so much that—no, it couldn't really have been so wonderful. He couldn't have been so dear. When

I see him again I shall get over being so silly."

But that silliness was the best thing in her life. For weeks the glamour of that enchanted evening had colored all her days. The music they had danced to still sounded in her ears, faint and stirring. When she closed her eyes, she could see again the sparkle and glitter of that tinsel fairyland of Broadway, made true and fine by the boy's love.

"I won't be an idiot!" she told herself. "When I see him again, I'll find that he's—not really like that!"

So, with what fortitude she had, she entered the little sitting room. He didn't hear her. He was standing at the window, with his back toward the room, his hands in his pockets—such a straight, stalwart figure!

"Hello!" said Pem. "It's a surprise to see you here again!"

Then he turned, and it was true, all of it—that look she had remembered, that glamour, that enchantment.

"Oh, Pem!" he said. "Didn't you know I'd come?"

For a minute she was utterly content in his arms, as if her restless and disconsolate spirit had at last found peace; but not for long. She moved away, still holding his hand, and looking at him with a misty smile.

"You're so beautiful!" he said. "Sometimes I thought you couldn't be as lovely as I remembered, but you're a hundred times—"

The clock on the mantelpiece struck three.

"Let's go out!" she said hastily.

He was a little taken aback.

"Can't we stay here, Pem? I want a chance to talk to you."

"Not here. We can talk somewhere else. I know a nice little tea room where we can dance."

"I don't want to dance," said he; "and—look here, Pem! I'm a bit hard up, this trip."

She couldn't help kissing him for that.

"As if I cared! We'll take a bus ride, then."

"No, we won't do that, either," said he, half laughing. "We'll stay where we are. I want to talk to you. I—does this suit you, Pem?"

From his pocket he pulled out a ring, carried loose in there, without a box, without even a bit of paper, and laid it in her hand. There it was, honest and unashamed, like himself—the tiniest little diamond. She stared down at it through a veil of tears.

"Best I could do," he said a little forlornly. "You see, I never tried to save my pay, and it's darned small, Pem, old girl. I'm only third mate. I dare say I don't make as much as you do."

"Never mind! That doesn't matter," she answered, so low that he could scarcely hear.

It seemed to her the most touching and beautiful thing that had ever happened, that he should come to her with his poor little ring, so simply and loyally offering her all he had.

"But we can manage," he went on more cheerfully. "I've figured it out. We can take a little flat, you know, and if we're careful, we can get on. You won't mind a pretty quiet life, will you, Pem? Nickie told me you weren't keen on going out and all that. I'm not, either—at least, not now. I was, you know, but not now. We'll settle down—"

He stopped short, looking at her with a faint frown, but she did not meet his eyes. She was shocked, appalled, at her own traitorous thoughts. She glanced again at the ring, and tried in vain to recapture the tenderness and pity she had felt.

To settle down and marry this boy—not to dance with him, not to listen to his lovemaking to the accompaniment of music, in a bright dazzle of light, but to marry him and settle down to a deadly quiet life—she knew very well what that meant. She had often enough been in the sort of little flat they would have to live in. She went into such places when sickness was already there. She had seen all the makeshifts, all the sordid and pitiful anxieties of such existences—people who hadn't enough towels and sheets, who couldn't afford hot water bottles, who couldn't afford even the necessary sunlight.

The quiet life! What had he to do with a quiet life? He had come suddenly into her own chill, somber existence, startling her into youth and gayety—that was why she loved him. A dear, honest, silly boy, to dance with, to be happy with for an evening, but—

"Pem!" he said abruptly. "What's the matter?"

At his peremptory tone, she found it less difficult to speak. She put her hand on his shoulder and spoke as kindly as she could.

"I'm afraid you're going ahead a little too fast," she said. "After all, we've only seen each other once before, you know. Doesn't it seem—"

"Do you mean that you don't care for me?" he interrupted.

His bluntness disconcerted her.

"No," she said, with a trace of impatience; "but we don't really know each other. I think we ought to wait—until we're sure."

He was silent for a long time, searching her downcast face.

"You're sure now, aren't you?" he asked at last. "All right, Pem! All my fault! I might have known—"

And in the face of his sincerity, his honest and unresentful pain, she could give him no false hope, no false consolation, nothing but the truth revealed to him by her silence.

He took the ring from her hand and looked at it with a shadowy smile. Then, before she knew what he was about, he threw it out of the open window into the street.

She came to the window and looked down, but she couldn't see it in the street far below.

"Oh, why did you do that?" she cried. "Why, didn't—"

A sob rose in her throat. She turned away her head, so that he should not see her tears.

"Don't cry!" he said. "It's all my fault. I should have known better, of course. I say, Pem! Please don't cry! The whole thing isn't worth it. Just—let's say good-by, Pem!"

She held out both her hands. After a brief hesitation, he took them in his.

"I'll never forgive myself!" she said unsteadily. "Never!"

"Nothing to forgive," he assured her, with a gallant attempt at a smile. "I—anyhow, I'm glad I ever saw you. Good-by, Pem!"

If it could only have ended then! If he could have gone then, with that moment for them to remember! But it was their great misfortune that no such memory should be left to them.

The doorbell rang, and Nickie, came out of her room.

"Shall I go, Pem?" she asked. "Or—"

Pem looked at her helplessly. As the flat was arranged, the front door could not be opened without affording a plain view of the sitting room.

"I'll let it ring," said Nickie, with a fine effect of carelessness. "No one we want to see."

But that was not Pem's way. She came of an austere and stiff-necked family, living secluded on an exhausted little Vermont farm. They had nothing much but pride to keep them warm in winter, to feed, and clothe them. Pride was the only heritage that came down to Pem, and pride would not allow her to refuse admission to Mr. Blanchard, no matter what it cost her. As for the possible cost to Arthur Caswell and to Nickie, that didn't occur to her just then.

She opened the door herself.

"I'm afraid I'm a little late," said a courteous, apologetic voice. "Please—"

Then, as he followed Pem inside, he caught sight of the others, and made a general bow.

"This is Mr. Blanchard, Nickie," said Pem.

He looked altogether what Pem had called him—a gentleman through and through. He was a rather slight man in the middle forties, with a sensitive, harassed face, hair a little gray on the temples, and fine, dark eyes. He hadn't in the least a furtive or shamefaced air. Indeed, there was a quiet sort of straightforwardness about him that favorably impressed Nickie, in spite of her prejudice against the man.

"I've heard a great deal about you from Miss Pembroke," he said.

Nickie liked his smile, his voice, his well bred ease. She liked all this, and yet, when Pem presented Caswell to him, her liking was a pain. Arthur seemed so young, so awkward, such an immature and unimpressive creature, in contrast to his senior. She wanted to defend him against comparison. She wanted to force Pem to see, and Mr. Blanchard to see, the splendid qualities in the young sailor.

But she had no chance. Before she could interfere, Blanchard had mentioned that it was growing late. Pem had answered that she was ready, and off they went.

VI

"I would never have told you," said Blanchard. "I would have gone on the best way I could, without you; but now—"

Pem looked at him across the table. By the light of the gold-shaded electric candle his thin face was almost incredibly fine. He looked, she thought, a little inhuman, with his delicate features, his dark, glowing eyes, and the silvery gleam of white on his temples. His tremendous consideration for her, his squeamishness, had made his story such a long one!

After all, she wasn't a girl just out of school.

"I've seen more of life than he has," she reflected; "and yet it has taken him two hours to tell me that his wife is going to divorce him. I suppose it'll take another hour before he can tell me that he hopes I can marry him when he's free. I suppose it ought to take me a week to answer him!"

She stifled a sigh. It was nonsense for him to try to shield his wife from Pem, who had two months in which to observe her savage egotism. Such a dilemma for his chivalrous soul—to make it clear to Pem that his wife had no just cause for divorcing him, and yet to protect the woman against the implication of cruel unreasonableness. All things considered, he had done very well.

"A—a mutual agreement," he had called it. "I think you'd better not go back," he went on gently. "She's very much upset. Her sister and her mother are with her."

Silence fell between them. The orchestra was playing in a gallery behind them—a gay and delicate air. The rooms were filled with the sort of people Pem liked about her, with light, laughing voices, faint perfumes, and the smoke of cigarettes.

One of Blanchard's hands was extended on the table—a slender hand, beautifully tended. He was so fastidious in everything, so kind, so honorable, so appealing in his masculine assumption of her ignorance and helplessness. He wanted to take care of her and shelter her. He would have been horrified at the thought of her living in a little flat on a third mate's pay. He would have turned pale at the sight of that poor, poor little ring.

"You're very quiet," he said, a little anxiously. "I hope I haven't—"

Pem looked up with a smile.

"No!" she thought, as if defying a voice that had not spoken. "It's no use! I'm not like that. I couldn't stand it. I shall be happy with Everett. It's his kind of life that I want." Aloud she said, in the ladylike, noncommittal tone he expected of her: "I'd better be going back to Nickie now."

Blanchard took her back in a taxi, and all the way he talked of impersonal matters—not a word of love. She knew he wouldn't mention that until he was free to do so honorably.

He left her at the door. She turned as she entered, and saw him standing bareheaded in the street—a handsome and distinguished man, yet somehow pitiful to her, with that touch of white at the temples.

The flat was empty when she got in. Nickie, of course, had gone to her case. Arthur Caswell—she couldn't imagine his destination.

On the kitchen table were the disorderly remains of a tea for two. The sitting room, too, was very untidy, as Nickie always left it. Pem turned on the electric light and began to set it in order. She emptied the ash tray, full of the stubs of those horrible cheap cigarettes she had seen Caswell smoking. She picked up the magazines that lay on the floor, and straightened the chairs.

The piano was open, with music on the rack. She went to close it. The lid slipped from her hand, and, falling, jarred the strings with a queer, trembling discord. She could have imagined it the faint, distant echo of a voicea young voice.

Sometimes Things Do Happen

Mr. Samuel Pepys set down the happenings of his days with unique candor and spirit, and, by so doing, became immortal. Edward Cane also kept a diary. Like that of Mr. Pepys, it was written in cipher, and it had a good deal about the author's wife in it; but in other ways it was very different.

Edward was passionately concerned with the future. He made prophecies, and it displeased him that these prophecies were not fulfilled. His was a just and reasonable mind. He knew—none better—how things ought to be, and he was displeased that they were not so.

He had, indeed, given up looking through the earlier pages of his diary, because it hurt too much; but he remembered some of the things. He remembered, if not the actual words, at least the spirit in which he had prophesied about this marriage of his. It was going to be different from all other marriages. Why not, since he and his Mildred were different from all other persons? It was going to be a splendid adventure.

"We shall never become stodgy," he had written.

Well, as far as that went, they hadn't. Quite the contrary!

This evening he began his daily record:

I have shut myself up in my—

"In my own room," he was going to write, but that was not exact. It was Mildred's room, too. She could come in if she liked. He couldn't really shut himself up anywhere on earth. He crossed out the last two words, and leaned his head on his hands, struggling valiantly to be just, fair, and exact, and to crush down the extraordinary emotions that outrageous woman aroused in him.

Never, before his marriage, had he felt such fury, such unreasonable, ungovernable exasperation. He had had a well deserved reputation for being a strong, self-controlled, moderate young man. That was one reason why he had risen high in the credit department of a mammoth store—because he could handle angry, cajoling, or desperate customers so firmly and calmly; and here in his own home he was utterly defeated.

He raised his head and looked about him. He saw Mildred's things everywhere, crowding and jostling his things—even her silly white comb standing up in one of his military brushes.

"Well, what of it?" he asked himself. "I'm orderly and she's not. I always knew that."

No use—he could not be philosophic about it. He got up and removed the comb with a jerk. As he did so, he caught sight of his own face in the mirror. It startled him. It was a strained and haggard face.

"I can't stand this!" he said to himself. "This can't go on!"

And just at this moment the door burst open and she—the cause of all his exasperation—appeared in the doorway.

"Edward!" she said in a furious, trembling voice. "Will you get that ladder, or won't you?"

"I will not," he replied.

His own voice was not altogether steady, but he was much calmer than she. She had been crying—he could see that; and, as he faced her, she began to cry again.

"You beast!" she cried. "You selfish, heartless—"

"Look here!" said Edward. "I can't—I won't stand any more of this! I'm sick and tired—"

"And what about me?" she retorted. "After your promising to make me happy!"

That was too much. Edward could have reminded her of things she had promised, but he scorned to do so. Contempt overwhelmed him. She had no scruples. The only thing on earth she cared about was to get her own way; and she wasn't going to get it—not this time! Her monstrous unfairness, her ruthless egotism, appalled him. He felt anger mounting to his brain, destroying his fine moderation.

"Look here!" he began.

"I won't!" said she. "If I'd had any idea what you were really like, I'd never have married you, Edward Cane!"

"No doubt!" said Edward frigidly. "However, another woman—"

All he had been going to say was that another woman—any other woman in the world, indeed—would have considered him a fairly good husband; but Mildred chose to take his words in a different spirit.

"Another woman!" said she, and laughed.

"If things happened as they should," Edward went on, with heightened color, "I'd go away—now. I'd go off—"

"With another woman!" said she, and laughed again.

He was glad to hear the doorbell ring. If he hadn't gone out of the room just then, he felt that he would certainly have put himself in the wrong. His patience was exhausted.

"Oh, are you leaving me now, Edward?" Mildred called after him mockingly. "Hadn't you better take a clean collar—or a toothbrush, at least?"

Evidently she hadn't heard the bell, and he did not condescend to enlighten her. He made up his mind not to speak to her again, no matter what the provocation. He went on down the stairs to the front door, and opened it.

"Edward!" she cried.

Ha! She was giving herself away now! She was worried!

He opened the door wider, and, as he did so, he heard her start down the stairs. It was only a bill, left lying on the veranda. He stepped out to pick it up.

"Edward!" he heard her call. "*Eddie!*"

A sudden gust of wind blew the door to with a crash, and an equally sudden impulse made him go hastily down the steps and along the path.

The front door opened.

"Eddie!" she called. "Come back this instant!"

He strode up the road and turned the corner.

"Do her good!" he said grimly to himself. "Now I'm out, I'll just stay out for a while. I'll smoke, and take a stroll."

Unfortunately, however, he had changed into an old coat, and had nothing to smoke with him, and no money to buy anything. Also, he was hatless. He shrugged his shoulders with a fine gesture of indifference. He could stroll, anyhow, and think—think this thing out to the bitter end.

It was all bitter, beginning and middle as well as the end. Mildred wished to make a slave of him, to break his spirit, to destroy his manly pride. No—this should not be!

It was a strange, uneasy sort of night—blowing up for rain, he thought. Filmy black clouds went racing across a pallid sky, and the trees rocked and tossed. It was cool, too, for May. He quickened his steps a little.

"I'm upset," he thought. "I'm more upset than I realized."

Somehow, the familiar suburban street had a new and almost sinister aspect. The trim houses with their lighted windows looked like houses on the stage—delusions, with no backs to them. Faint and eerie music was coming through same one's radio. A dog howled, far away. Everything was different.

"This is a fool trick," he thought suddenly. "I can't stay out here. I'll go back and—and simply not answer her."

II

A taxi came round the corner. The wheels, spinning over the road, sounded like rain. He turned back.

"Sir!" cried a voice. "Please!"

The taxi had stopped, and a woman was leaning out of the window. Was she calling him? It must be so, for there was no one else in sight.

"Can you please tell me where Mrs. Rice lives?" said the woman.

"Er—no," said he. "I'm sorry, but I don't know anyone of that name here."

He spoke a little stiffly, because he did not *like* that voice. It was musical enough, but lacking in calm. She was not discouraged, however.

"If you'd just please look at this—card," she said. "Perhaps I've read the name wrong."

Now Edward was frankly suspicious. He did not want to approach that taxi, but he had not the moral courage to refuse. He would have preferred to be set upon by bandits, to be blackjacked and robbed, rather than show his reluctance. He stepped off the curb and crossed the road. He *knew* that something was going to happen.

The woman in the taxi handed him a card; and at the same moment she clutched his collar, and, leaning forward, whispered in his ear:

"Say that Mrs. Rice lives in that house! Pretend to read the card! Quick!"

What could he do? He didn't want to say anything, but he did not know how to refuse this agitated creature. He took the card, went around to the front of the taxi, and pretended to read the card by the fierce white glare of the headlights.

"Oh!" he said. "Mrs. *Bice!* I see! She lives there—in that house."

"Thank you!" said the woman in the taxi.

The instinct of self-preservation warned him to be off then, but he had also another instinct—that of helping other people who were in trouble. Something was obviously wrong here, and, prudent or not, he could not turn his back and walk off. The woman had got out, and stood beside him in the road.

"Please pay him and send him away!" she whispered.

So that was the game!

"I'm sorry," said Edward blandly, "but I've come out without a penny in my pockets."

"Here!" said she, and thrust a purse into his hand. "Only *please* get rid of him!"

He saw he had been wrong. With a certain compunction, he approached the driver.

"Five dollars!" said the man.

Edward leaned over and looked at the meter.

"Two forty," he said.

"She made a special rate with me—" the driver began.

"Two forty," said Edward briefly.

He opened the little purse, and found it crammed with bills—large bills, some of them—an extraordinary amount of cash. He was searching for change when the driver commenced.

Now Edward, as assistant credit manager, was not unaccustomed to remonstrances from persons who could not get what they wanted; nor was his nature a submissive or timid one. He felt quite able to withstand the driver's attack; but women are not like that. Bluster impresses them, and this woman was impressed.

"Oh, please!" she cried. "Give him the five dollars! Give him anything! Only do get rid of him!"

After all, it was her money. Edward gave the driver a five-dollar bill, with a low and forcible remark. The engine started up, and off went the taxi. It seemed extraordinarily quiet after it had gone.

"Drunk," observed Edward.

"I know!" said the woman. "He was perfectly awful!"

She was going to cry, if she had not already begun; and he wanted no more of *that*.

"Now, then!" he said, in a loud, cheerful voice. "Shall I get you another taxi?"

"Please!" said she.

She was crying now—no doubt about it. What was worse, she took his arm and clung to it.

"If you'll wait here for a few minutes—" suggested Edward.

"Oh, I can't!" she cried. "Oh, please don't go away and leave me all alone!"

He saw himself that it wouldn't do to leave her standing here in the street while he walked half a mile to the station for a taxi.

"I'll go into the Baxters' and telephone for one," he thought.

But Mrs. Baxter was a particular friend of Mildred's. She would bother him. She would ask questions. She would want to know what he was doing, wandering about at ten o'clock at night. She would suspect that there had been a quarrel.

The idea was intolerable. He would not go to the Baxters'; and, not having been long in the neighborhood, he knew no one else.

As he stood deliberating, the lights in the house behind them went out, leaving the world very dark. For the moment, he felt a thousand miles from home. He felt marooned, cut off. He couldn't believe that just around the corner was that six-room house of hollow tile, with all improvements—that house which was mystically more than a house because it was his home. He owned it. In his experience as assistant credit manager he had seen what fatal accidents could happen to defer deferred payments, and he would have none of them. His rule was to pay cash. Mildred had more than once protested against this rule, but in vain.

"You're always looking ahead and imagining that all sorts of queer, awful things are going to happen," she had said, only the day before; "but they never do!"

They didn't, didn't they? A lot she knew!

"Where *can* I get a taxi?" asked the voice at his side, and he came out of his reverie with a start.

"I'm afraid you'll have to walk to the station," he said; "unless you happen to pick one up on the way."

"Oh, dear!" said she. "Is it far? Half a mile? But if I've got to walk that far—isn't there some sort of hotel in the town?"

"Yes—there's the American House," Edward told her.

"Then I'll go there," said she. "If you'll just please tell me the way—"

He knew that he must go with her—that she was one of those women who can never go anywhere or do anything alone. Impossible to explain how he knew this, or how, in the dark, and without having even once looked squarely at her, he knew that she was young, pretty, and charmingly dressed. Stifling a sigh, he set off at her side. It had to be.

She thanked him very nicely. He assured her that it was no trouble at all, and then they both fell silent. She sounded as if she were walking quickly, her little high heels clacking smartly on the pavement; but as a matter of fact their progress was slow—a snail's pace, Edward thought. At this rate, he wouldn't get back to the house for an hour—that is, if he ever did go back. He said to himself that he had not made up his mind what he would do; but in his heart he knew that he couldn't help himself. He was a victim of destiny.

"But it is awfully nice of you!" said the fair unknown. "Were you just out taking a walk?"

"I wasn't going anywhere," Edward replied gloomily.

"That's like me," said she. "I'm not going anywhere. I don't care where I go, or what becomes of me!"

This alarmed Edward. After having been married to Mildred for nearly six months, he knew that such people were possible. They really didn't care where they went or what they did. They were incalculably dangerous and reckless.

"All women," he thought somberly, "are alike—all of them!"

Perhaps at this moment Mildred was not caring where she went or what became of her.

"I know you must wonder," the fair unknown continued. "I don't suppose anyone in the world could understand."

She paused, but Edward gave her no encouragement.

"I really did know a Mrs. Rice who lived somewhere in this neighborhood when I was a little girl," she resumed. "Such a dear old lady. And somehow, in my desperation, I thought of h-her." She was wiping her eyes with a small handkerchief. "You must think I'm so weak and s-silly!"

"Oh, no!" said Edward politely.

A fatalistic gloom enveloped him. He felt no curiosity at all. He knew not where he was going, or why; and what chiefly occupied his mind was a profound longing for a smoke and a hat. With a cigar, he felt, he could have regained his philosophic outlook. With a hat, he could have faced this situation more like a man of the world. He had neither, and he was walking off into the night, away from home.

The lights of the town made him anxious that the lady should dry her tears.

"I think it's going to rain," he observed in an easy, conversational tone. "Country needs rain badly."

He might have known that it wouldn't work. She paid no attention whatever to this remark.

"I only want to hide," she said. "If I could have found dear old Mrs. Rice! That driver—he was so awful! He was going to drive out into the country and murder me. I saw it in his face. And then *you* came!"

"I happened to be there," Edward corrected her.

"Isn't it strange, the way things happen?" she said in a low, intense voice. "Doesn't it seem like fate?"

It did. Edward said nothing. He was trying to invent some excuse for getting his arm away from her before they passed any shops where he was known. He failed to do so, however. The lights in all the shops on the main street shone upon him, hatless, with the desperate lady clinging to him.

The portico of the American House was in sight now. They drew nearer and nearer. Ten steps more—

"Quick!" she whispered. She pulled violently at his arm, and in an instant he found himself inside a jeweler's shop. "He was there—outside the hotel!" she whispered, "If he'd turned his head! He'd surely have killed you! Isn't that a *sweet* bracelet?"

This last remark was for the benefit of the young man who had come behind the counter. He seemed pleased, and brought out the bracelet in a velvet box.

"Sweet, isn't it?" she murmured.

She nudged Edward hard. He glanced at her, and a thrill of terror ran through him. She was smiling archly at him. Her tears had in no way marred a most lovely and piquant face. She was a beautiful and elegant woman, such as Edward had frequently seen in his office. He knew these pampered beings, and their naïve and exorbitant demands.

"Yes," he replied faintly.

"Get it for me, dear!" she said.

He was stupefied.

"I want it! Get it for me, dear!" she repeated, with the same arch smile; but her elbow dug sharply into his ribs.

"How much?" he asked in a hollow voice.

"Only twenty-five dollars," she said brightly.

He turned aside, and from her well filled purse took out the requisite amount. The young clerk wrapped up the bracelet and handed it to her. As he did so, she leaned across the counter.

"Is there a back way to get out?" she asked in a low and confidential voice. "They're out there, looking for us, and we want to give them the slip."

"Certainly, madam," said the clerk. "This way!"

He opened a door at the rear of the shop. They followed him along a dark passage, across a yard, through a gate in the fence, and out into another street.

"Er—good night!" said the clerk.

"No!" returned Edward. "Look here!"

But the fair unknown, still clinging to his arm, positively dragged him on.

"Stupid!" she hissed. "Hurry up! Do you want to be killed?"

They turned the corner into a dark alley, and here Edward stopped.

"Look here!" he said sternly. "This can't go on! I—"

"Don't you see? He thought we were a bride and groom, trying to get away."

Edward believed none of this. He did not believe that he was in any danger of being killed by any person whatsoever, or that the clerk had thought what the unknown imagined; but women, as he had noticed before, always believed what they wished to believe.

"I have to live in this town, you know," he observed.

Of course this observation did not move her. Women never considered the future. They lived, reckless and heedless, in the present moment.

"Where do you want to go now?" he pursued. "It's getting late."

"Leave me!" said she. "It doesn't matter. Thank you for all you've done. Go away and leave me!"

"I can't leave you here—in an alley," said Edward, repressing a violent irritation.

"What does it matter?" said she. "I don't care what becomes of me!"

"Well, I do!" said Edward.

"Oh, how sweet of you!" she cried, and began to weep again.

"I mean," Edward explained hastily, "that I couldn't leave *any* woman alone in a place like this."

"You're so ch-chivalrous!" she sobbed. "I knew it the moment I heard your voice!"

"I am not chivalrous," replied Edward firmly; "only—look here! I'll get a taxi and see you home."

"I have no home!" she wailed.

"You must live somewhere."

"I don't—not anymore. Oh, leave me! Leave me! I don't care!" She clutched his arm again, in that frenzied manner which so startled and annoyed him. "Oh, my hat!" she cried. "It's raining!"

She was right—the first heavy drops were beginning to fall.

"Oh, my *pretty* little hat!" she cried.

Now, Edward's was a just and logical mind, and yet even he had sometimes been illogically moved by trifles. This infantile plaint about a pretty little hat reminded him of certain things Mildred had said, and aroused in him a pity which the stranger's tragic and mysterious sorrows had hitherto failed to inspire.

"Come on!" he said.

III

Edward was now the leader of the enterprise; he did not know where they were going, but he led the way, down the alley and out into a street which was new to him. It was one of those streets that may so often be found lurking near neat little suburban railway stations—a mean street, dark and deserted. A light burned dimly in a cutthroat barber's, another light in a shoemaker's, revealing the shoemaker and his family of pale infants. There was a—what was that?

"The Palace Restaurant—never closed," a sign said.

They hurried into the Palace Restaurant just as the rain began in earnest.

"You can wait here till it's over," said Edward.

He purposely refrained from saying "we," but he knew that he could not desert the silly, helpless creature. They sat down at a little table near the window, and, when the proprietor came up to them, Edward ordered ham and eggs and coffee.

"I couldn't eat anything in this horrible place!" whispered his companion.

At first Edward was inclined to agree with her. It was not an appetizing place. The tablecloth was stained, and there was a stale and unpleasant aroma in the air. A glass case displayed a lemon meringue pie and a raisin cake which did not appeal to him.

When the food came, however, he ate it—to his regret, for, after having eaten, his desire for a smoke increased tenfold. He could think of little else. Stern and silent, he sat there thinking of the cigars in the pocket of his other coat, of the box of cigars in his office. He knew this to be a weakness, and he was struggling against it; but the struggle was difficult, and he was in no mood for his companion's words.

"You're unhappy—like me," she said softly.

"No," said Edward. "No—it's entirely different."

"Oh, I understand!" she said.

She went on, about life, and how hard it is when you really feel things, and how alone you are, even in the midst of crowds. He tried not to listen, but he had to hear some of it, and it infuriated him.

"Very likely," he said; "but I'd like to know your plans. What do you want me to do? Get you a cab, or what?"

She shrank back.

"Oh!" she said. "I see! You mean—I understand! You want to go. Leave me, then! Go! Why should you care what happens to me?"

"It's after eleven," was all that Edward answered.

There was a silence.

"Very well!" she said coldly. "I shall take the next train into the city."

There was another silence. The proprietor had retired, and they had the Palace Restaurant entirely to themselves. The rain was dashing against the windows. The street light outside showed only darkness.

What, Edward wondered, was Mildred doing now? She was capable of anything—of telephoning to the Baxters, to the police. Perhaps she had gone away herself. Perhaps she was wandering about in this storm, searching for her husband. It was a wild and fantastic notion, but that was the sort of thing women did. Look at this one! He did look at her, and she looked at him, with cold scorn.

"Will you be kind enough—" she began.

Just then the door opened and two men came in. They were the editor and the subeditor of the local paper, both of whom Edward knew.

"Hello, Cane!" said the editor. "Just put the paper to bed. What are you doing here?"

"Nothing much," Edward replied as casually as possible.

The editor turned to the fair unknown.

"How do you like our little town, Mrs. Cane?" he asked. "Once you get to know—"

"I am not Mrs. Cane," she interrupted

"Oh! I—er—yes," said the editor.

He waited a moment, but no one said anything. Then he and his colleague sat down at a table as far away as they could get.

"Why didn't you keep still?" said Edward in a low, fierce voice. "He's editor of the newspaper here."

"Did you imagine I was that sort of woman?" she returned. "Did you think I would pretend to be the wife of a perfect stranger?"

"No," said Edward; "but you didn't need to say anything. He'll talk—"

"Do you imagine I care?" said she.

Of course she didn't. Women care only for themselves. Edward could not trust himself to speak, but he thought. He thought.

"I'll find out who she is," he said to himself, "so that I can send her back for the money for her ham and eggs."

A dismal bellow pierced the night.

"The eleven forty pulling out," observed the editor to his companion. Edward heard this.

"When's the next train into the city?" he asked, across the room.

"Five-twenty to-morrow morning."

"Now you see what you've done!" said the fair unknown to Edward.

"What I've done?" said he, amazed and indignant; but she was far more indignant than he.

"Now what am I going to do?" she demanded. "The last train's gone. I can't go into the city, and there's nowhere here for me to stay."

"Are you blaming me for—"

"Yes," said she. "You're a man. You ought to have—"

"Just what ought I have done?" Edward inquired with biting irony.

"I don't care!" said she. "Very well! I'm going to stay here all night."

"You can't."

"I'm going to!" said she.

"And I thought Mildred was unreasonable!" Edward reflected.

The image of Mildred rose before him, remarkably vivid. With great justice and moderation he compared her with this unknown individual. All women were not alike. Mildred was different. There was something about her— Sometimes, of course, she was simply outrageous, but, even at that— That time when he had the flu—or when anything went wrong in the office—

"And she's very young," thought the just man. "She's nothing but a kid. Perhaps I should have made allowances."

"Won't you smoke?" said a voice.

Glancing up, he saw the fair unknown proffering a silver cigarette case. Edward did not smoke cigarettes, and he had pretty severe theories about people who did so, but this time he was weak. He took one and lighted it. It was a horrible perfumed thing, but it helped him. The fact that he had broken one of his rules helped him, too. He felt more tolerant.

"Don't you—er—smoke?" he asked his companion.

He thought she was just the sort of person who would; but she shook her head.

"Arthur doesn't like me to," she said. Her voice had changed, and her face, too. She was downcast and pale. "I made him get me that case," she went on. "He hated to, but I made him."

Tears had come into her eyes again, but this time Edward felt rather sorry for her.

"Don't cry!" he said kindly—the more so as the two editors had just gone out, in discreet silence.

"I can't help it!" said she. "My whole life is ruined. You don't know—oh, you don't know what a beast I've been! And now—now I've lost Arthur!"

"Who is Arthur?" Edward asked sympathetically.

"My husband," said she. The tears were raining down her cheeks. "My dear, kind, wonderful, darling husband! I wanted to punish him, and frighten him, and I ran away. We had a quarrel. My life is ruined, and all because of a penny!"

"A penny?"

"Yes. Arthur said the two sides were called heads and tails, and I said they were called odds and evens. I know he was wrong, but why didn't I give in? Oh, why didn't I give in? Both our lives ruined! He's frightfully jealous. He'll never forgive this—and for a trifle like that!"

"I—" said Edward, and stopped. His face, too, had grown pale. "Ours was about a cat—Mildred's cat," he went on. "It got up a tree, and she wanted me to go next door and get a ladder and get it down. I told her it could get down by itself when it was ready. She—"

"How cruel of you!" interrupted his companion.

"It was not cruel," asserted Edward.

"It was! If you loved Mildred, you'd get dozens of ladders for her."

"If she loved me, she wouldn't ask me to make such a monkey of myself," retorted Edward. "I did it once, and the people next door laughed at me. I heard them."

"You shouldn't care," said the fair unknown severely. "You were entirely in the wrong."

"As a matter of fact," said Edward, "you were entirely in the wrong yourself, about that penny."

"What?" said she.

She rose and faced him with flashing eyes. Edward rose, too. His eyes did not flash, but they were steely. They regarded each other steadily, with magnificent pride.

Suddenly she began to laugh.

"I am glad," said Edward, "that you find this amusing."

"Oh, dear!" she said, sinking back into her chair. "Aren't we pig-headed, both of us?"

"Kindly don't—" Edward began, but she did not heed him.

"Oh! A penny—and a cat!"

"Well," said Edward, "perhaps—"

"Come on!" said she, rising again.

"Let's go back and start all over again!"

"I—" Edward began.

"Oh, do come on!" she cried impatiently. "It was Arthur I saw outside the American House—when I pulled you into the jeweler's, you know. Oh, do hurry! He's traced me that far—perhaps we'll find him still there!"

"We?"

"Of course!" she said. "You've got to explain everything to Arthur. Come on!"

"But your hat!" Edward reminded her, as a last desperate plea.

"My hat!" she replied with supreme scorn.

So they went out of the Palace Restaurant into the driving rain.

IV

"Whew!" said Edward to himself, wiping his moist brow with a still moister handkerchief. "Whew!"

Arthur had been found in the American House, and he had been difficult to handle. If Edward had not had such a thorough training in his business, he could never have handled the situation in so masterly a fashion. Arthur was a rich young man, and accustomed to being kotowed to. Edward, however, was accustomed to rich people who were accustomed to being kotowed to. Many times he had explained to wealthy and indignant customers facts which they had not cared to consider—that, for instance, the mere possession of enough money to pay one's bills did not suffice for a credit department; that there must be a certain willingness to use the money for that purpose.

Edward had not kotowed to Arthur. He had been mighty firm with him, though kind, for he had felt sorry for the man. It had been a bad night for Arthur. He had been desperately worried about his wife. Patiently, inexorably, Edward had made him listen to reason, and in the end there was a touching and beautiful reconciliation. Arthur's wife, with truly admirable unselfishness, had said that it did not matter who was right about the penny. Both of them had declared that they owed everything to Edward and would be his lifelong friends.

He was now at liberty to attend to his own little affair. Having no money to pay for a taxi, he set off on foot in the direction of his home. It was still raining, and as black as the pit, yet he fancied he could feel dawn in the air. Taking out his watch, he saw that it was half past four. He had been away all night. He remembered his last words to Mildred:

"If things happened as they should—"

She had said that they never did, but they had. He was strangely justified, yet he felt no triumph. The rain fell cold upon his uncovered head, and his spirit was cold within him.

"She must have been worrying," thought Edward.

Indeed, that was an inadequate word for what he knew she must have felt. He thought about Mildred, not in her outrageous moments, but as she was at other times, when she was her unique and incomparable self. He thought about marriage, in a large, general way. He also thought about his own marriage, and what he had intended it to be.

At last he thought about himself. Soaked through to the skin, cold and weary, Edward groped after justice. It was a creditable performance—the more so because he was unaware of it. He groped, and he found a new and startling piece of wisdom.

He quickened his pace. The wind had died down and the rain had stopped, but he did not know that, for the drops still pattered thickly from the trees. As he turned the corner of his own street, he saw in the sky the first streak of dawn—a pale gray creeping up into the black.

His reasonable mind told him that there was no cause here for wonder, yet he did wonder. He stopped for a moment and watched the marvelous dawn—watched it make a fresh and utterly new day and a new world. His own house seemed to grow before his eyes, turning from a shadowy mass into something familiar and yet strange. He had come home—after what extraordinary wanderings!

He advanced, walking on the sodden grass, so that his steps should be noiseless. He entered his neighbor's garden, thankful that they kept no dog. He took a ladder from the unlocked tool shed, and, carrying it with some difficulty, set it up against a certain tree on his own front lawn.

Then, still noiselessly, he stole up on the veranda, and, stooping, examined the doormat and the darkest corners. Unsatisfied, he went around to the back of the house; and there, against the kitchen door, he found that which he sought—a cat. He wished to tell Mildred that he had brought her cat down from the tree, and he would not lie. It should be true.

The cat was mutinous. She struggled as he held her under his arm, and it was difficult to ascend the ladder. However, he did so. He put the cat on a branch, and let go of her for an instant, in order to get a better hold on her for the descent. She began climbing higher up. He clutched at her, but she eluded him. She was a heavy cat, but she went up a slender branch, which bent perilously beneath her.

"Kitty! Kitty!" whispered Edward. "Oh, you fool!"

Her hind legs had slipped off, and for an instant they were kicking desperately in the air, reminding him of a Zouave in white gaiters.

"Come, kitty!" murmured Edward. "Come on, kitty!"

The creature clawed and clutched desperately, swung under the bending branch, came up on the other side, and began to come down, facing him with wild yellow eyes. He caught her as she came within reach. He thought the touch of a firm human hand would reassure the terrified animal, but it was not so. She appeared to be suspicious and resentful.

As the cat's claws pierced his shoulder, Edward recoiled, and very nearly fell from the ladder. Probably he uttered some sort of exclamation, as almost anybody would. Anyhow, Mildred's head appeared at an upper window.

"I'm getting your cat down," Edward explained.

By the time he had reached the foot of the ladder, with the cat, Mildred had opened the front door. She was carrying something in her arms, which she set down in the shadow of the veranda. She gave it a gentle push with her foot, and it ran off, unseen by Edward.

Edward set down his cat, and she also ran off.

"There you are!" he said.

Mildred came down the steps.

"Oh, Eddie!" she cried.

It was quite light now in the open. He could see her face, and it seemed to him rather wonderful.

"Eddie!" she said. "You're soaking wet! Oh, Eddie, it was all my fault!"

"I don't know that it was," replied Edward meditatively. "Some of it was my fault, I think."

She came nearer to him.

"Oh, Eddie!" she cried. "It really doesn't matter one bit whose fault things are, does it?"

He was startled, for that was his own particular bit of wisdom, painfully arrived at. Mildred *was* a remarkable girl!

THE END

Elisabeth Sanxay Holding Bibliography
(1889-1955)

NOVELS

Invincible Minnie (1920)
Rosaleen Among the Artists (1921)
Angelica (1921)
The Unlit Lamp (1922)
The Shoals of Honour (1926)
The Silk Purse (1928)
Miasma (1929)
Dark Power (1930)
The Death Wish (1934)
The Unfinished Crime (1935)
The Strange Crime in Bermuda (1937)
The Obstinate Murderer (1938; reprinted as No Harm Intended, 1939)
Who's Afraid? (1940; reprinted as Trial by Murder, 1940)
The Girl Who Had to Die (1940)
Speak of the Devil (1941; reprinted as Hostess to Murder, 1943)
Kill Joy (1942; reprinted as Murder is a Kill-Joy, 1946)
Lady Killer (1942)
The Old Battle-Ax (1943)
Net of Cobwebs (1945)
The Innocent Mrs. Duff (1946)
The Blank Wall (1947)
Miss Kelly (1947)
Too Many Bottles (1951; reprinted as The Party Was the Pay-Off, 1951)
The Virgin Huntress (1951)
Widow's Mite (1953)

STORIES/NOVELETTES

Patrick on the Mountain (*The Smart Set*, July 1920)
The Problem that Perplexed Nicholson (*The Smart Set*, Aug 1920)
Marie's View of It (*The Century Magazine*, Dec 1920)
Mollie: The Ideal Nurse (*The Century Magazine*, Jan 1921)

Angelica (*Munsey's*, May-Oct 1921)
The Married Man (*Munsey's*, Dec 1921)
The Foreign Woman (*Munsey's*, July 1922)
Hanging's Too Good for Him (*Munsey's*, Sept 1922)
Like a Leopard (*Munsey's*, Nov 1922)
Lost Luck (*The Bookman*, Dec 1922)
The Girl He Picked Up at Coney (*Metropolitan Magazine*, Feb/Mar 1923)
The Aforementioned Infant (*Munsey's*, Mar 1923)
It Seemed Reasonable (*Munsey's*, Apr 1923)
Unless Experience Be a Jewel (*The Sovereign Magazine*, Apr 1923)
Horseshoe Over the Door: Stories (*Woman's Home Companion*, May, June, July, Aug 1923)
Old Dog Tray (*Munsey's*, May 1923)
The Matador (*Munsey's*, June 1923)
A Hesitating Cinderella (*Munsey's*, July 1923)
The Postponed Wedding (*Munsey's*, Aug 1923)
With Unbowed Head (*The Century Magazine*, Aug 1923)
This is Life (*The Nation*, Aug 15 1923)
The Marquis of Carabas (*Munsey's*, Sept 1923)
Out of the Woods (*Munsey's*, Oct 1923)
Miss Flotsam and Mr. Jetsann (*The Dial*, Nov 1923)
Benedicta (*Munsey's*, Dec 1923)
Keeping the Boy at Home (*Woman's Home Companion*, Dec 1923)
Nickie and Pem (*Munsey's*, Feb 1924)
His Remarkable Future (*Munsey's*, Apr 1924)
His Own People (*Munsey's*, July 1924)
Who Is This Impossible Person? (*Munsey's*, Aug 1924)
Ye Gods and Little Fishes (*The American Magazine*, Aug 1924)
Mr. Martin Swallows the Anchor (*Munsey's*, Sept 1924)
Too French (*Munsey's*, Jan 1925)
The Good Little Pal (*Munsey's*, Apr 1925)
Flowers for Miss Riordan (*Munsey's*, May 1925)
Mrs. Prunes (*Woman's Home Companion*, May 1925)
Marionette (*The Century Magazine*, June 1925)
Sometimes Things Do Happen (*Munsey's*, June 1925)
Miss What's-Her-Name (*Munsey's*, July 1925)
The Long Night (*Ladies Home Journal*, Sept 1925)
The Wonderful Little Woman (*Munsey's*, Sept 1925)
As Patrick Henry Said (*Munsey's*, Oct 1925)
The Worst Joke in the World (*Munsey's*, Nov 1925)

As Is (*Munsey's*, Dec 1925)
That's Not Love (*Munsey's*, Jan 1926)
Rosalie Gets Out of the Cage (*The American Magazine*, Feb 1926)
The Thing Beyond Reason (*Munsey's*, Feb 1926)
Dogs Always Know (*Munsey's*, Mar 1926)
Highfalutin' (*Munsey's*, Apr 1926)
Bonnie Wee Thing (*Munsey's*, May 1926)
Memory of a May Night (*Pictorial Review*, May 1926)
Vanity (*Munsey's*, Jun 1926)
The Compromising Letter (*Munsey's*, July 1926)
Miss Cigale (*Munsey's*, Aug 1926)
Blotted Out (*Munsey's,* Sept 1926)
Pale Pink Crime (*Woman's Home Companion*, Sept 1926)
Human Nature Unmasked (*Munsey's*, Oct 1926)
Chris Had Gone (*Ladies' Home Journal*, Nov 1926)
Home Fires (*Munsey's*, Dec 1926)
Totally Broken Reed (*Woman's Home Companion*, Mar 1927)
The Grateful Lunella (*The American Magazine*, May 1927)
The Old Ways (*Munsey's*, July 1927)
By the Light of Day (*Munsey's*, Aug 1927)
Out for a Good Time (*Woman's Home Companion*, Oct 1927)
For Granted (*Munsey's*, Nov 1927)
Incompatibility (*Munsey's*, Dec 1927)
In Chains (*McCall's*, Dec 1927)
One Misty Night, (*The American Magazine*, Feb 1928)
Derelict (*Munsey's*, Mar 1928)
Half an Hour Late (*Woman's Home Companion*, Mar 1928)
This Road Is Closed (*The American Magazine*, Apr 1928)
Inches and Ells (*Munsey's*, June 1928)
It Is a Two-Edged Sword (*McCall's*, June 1928)
Too Late (*Liberty*, July 21 1928)
Proud and Pig-Headed (*Pictorial Review*, July 1928)
Outside the Door (*The Elks Magazine*, Oct 1928)
Hard as Nails (*Liberty*, Oct 20 1928)
Important Things (*Liberty*, Nov 17 1928)
A Dinner Date (*The American Magazine*, Jan 1929)
Vera's Superior Smile (*Pictorial Review*, Jan 1929)
Saving Up (*Liberty*, Jan 5 1929)
Flow and Ebb (*Liberty*, Jan 26 1929)
Without Benefit of Police (*Complete Stories*, Feb 1929)
The Sin of Angels (*The American Magazine*, Apr 1929; *The Grand Magazine*, Jan 1939)

Dare-Devil (*The American Magazine*, June 1929)
Little Deeds of Kindness (*Liberty*, July 6 1929)
Broken Faith (*The American Magazine*, Oct 1929; *Cassell's Magazine of Fiction*, July 1930)
Prelude (*The Delineator*, Sept 1929)
Carline (*Liberty*, Oct 12, 1929)
Rose-Leaves (*Liberty*, Jan 18 1930)
The Chain of Death (*Liberty*, May 24, May 31, Jun 7, Jun 14, Jun 21 1930)
On Condition (*The Elks Magazine*, Sept 1930)
Mrs. Herbert's Notion (*The Delineator*, Nov 1930)
The Girl in Armor (*Street & Smith's Detective Story Magazine*, Aug 8, Aug 15, Aug 22, Aug 29 1931)
Porthos (*Maclean's*, Sept 15 1931)
It's All Right for Men (*Liberty*, Oct 10 1931)
Humility (*Maclean's,* Nov 15 1931)
Brides of Crime (*Street & Smith's Detective Story Magazine*, Nov 7, Nov 14, Nov 21, Nov 28, Dec 5 1931)
The Preposterous Mrs. Manders (*Woman's Home Companion*, Mar 1932)
Hound's Bay (*Street & Smith's Detective Story Magazine*, Mar 5, Mar 12, Mar 19, Mar 26, Apr 2 1932)
Wonderful Day (*Good Housekeeping*, Jan 1933)
If It Hadn't Been for Laurel (*Liberty*, Jan 28 1933)
No Personal Calls (*Maclean's*, July 15 1933)
That Woman (*The Delineator*, Oct 1933)
Like Father, Like Son (*The Novel Magazine*, Jan 1934)
A Man Can Take It (*Collier's Weekly*, May 12 1934)
The Green Bathtub (*Collier's Weekly*, June 16 1934)
Vital Interlude (*Redbook Magazine*, July 1934)
The Last Night (*The Passing Show*, July 14 1934)
All She Could Get (*Collier's Weekly*, Sept 15 1934)
The Unfinished Crime (*Street & Smith's Detective Story Magazine*, Nov 10 1934)
"I Could Brighten Your Life!" (*The American Magazine*, Jan 1935)
The Bride Comes Home (*Cosmopolitan*, Feb 1935)
Dawn Smile (*The Strand Magazine*, Apr 1935)
The Root of Evil (*Collier's Weekly*, Apr 27 1935)
Nobody Would Listen (*Mystery*, Aug 1935)
Somebody's Cynthia (*Collier's Weekly*, Aug 3 1935; *The Passing Show*, Nov 2 1935)
It's Time Life Began! (*Redbook Magazine*, Dec 1935)

You Never Can Tell (*Collier's Weekly*, Dec 14 1935; *Grit*, June 1936)

Bermuda Murder (*Street & Smith's Detective Story Magazine*, July 1936)

Unscathed (*Ladies Home Journal*, Jan 1936)

Lost (*Redbook*, Feb 1936)

Cross Purposes (*Collier's Weekly*, May 30, 1936)

Can Do! (*Pictorial Review*, July 1936)

Scandal (*Woman's Home Companion*, July 1936)

Background (*Redbook Magazine*, Aug 1936)

Intent to Kill (*Street & Smith's Detective Story Magazine*, Sept 1936)

Night Life (*Redbook*, Sept 1936)

Murder Solicited (*Street & Smith's Detective Story Magazine*, Nov 1936)

Third Act (*Pictorial Review*, Apr 1937)

Drifting (*McCall's*, May 1937)

Wedding Day (*Cosmopolitan*, Sept 1937)

The Nicest Little Lunch (*Cosmopolitan*, Nov 1937)

Echo of a Careless Voice (*McCall's*, Jan 1938)

Illusion (*Good Housekeeping*, Aug 1938)

They Take It So Lightly! (*Cosmopolitan*, Oct 1938)

Two Passes for the Show (*Liberty*, Nov 5 1938)

So Sort of Proud (*Good Housekeeping*, Mar 1939)

Money Can't Buy It (*Liberty*, Aug 5 1939)

Open That Door (*Liberty*, Aug 26 1939)

Blonde on a Boat (*The American Magazine*, Dec 1939)

Late Date (*Cosmopolitan*, May 1940)

Proposal (*McCall's,* May 1940)

On Yonder Lea (*Good Housekeeping*, Aug 1940)

Tropical Secretary (*The American Magazine*, Feb 1941)

Tomorrow's Not Soon Enough (*McCall's*, Mar 1941)

What It Takes (*Grit*, Mar 9 1941)

Loved I Not Honor More (*Liberty*, Apr 12 1941)

The Fearful Night (*The American Magazine*, June 1941; expanded to *The Obstinate Murderer*)

Another Baby (*Woman's Home Companion*, Nov 1941)

I'll Never Forgive You (*The American Magazine*, May 1942)

Not Goodbye But Au Revoir (*McCall's,* Oct 1942)

The Kiskadee Bird (*Cosmopolitan*, 1944)

The Old Battle-Ax (1943; abridged, *Liberty,* Mar 18 1944)

Mrs. Henry Gibson (*Cosmopolitan*, Aug 1944)

Bait for a Killer (*Collier's Weekly*, Sep 30 1944, as "The Blue Envelope"; *The Saint Mystery Magazine*, Mar 1959; *The Saint Detective Magazine* [Australia], Nov 1959; *The Saint Mystery Magazine* [UK], Oct 1960)

The Unbelievable Baroness (*The American Magazine*, 1945)

The Net of Cobwebs (*Collier's Weekly*, Jan 6, 13 & 20, 1945)

Ten-Cent Wedding Ring (Cosmopolitan, Feb 1945)

Funny Kind of Love (as by Elizabeth Saxanay Holding, *Boston Sunday Globe Magazine*, Nov 11 1945)

Farewell to a Corpse (*Mystery Book Magazine*, Oct 1946)

The Other Mrs. Minor (*Cosmopolitan*, Sept, Oct, Nov 1946)

"Be Careful, Mrs. Williams" (*Cosmopolitan*, July 1947)

Second Marriage (*Cosmopolitan*, Apr 1948)

The Bird of Time (*Cosmopolitan*, May 1948)

The Stranger in the Car (*American Magazine*, July 1949)

People Do Fall Downstairs (*Ellery Queen's Mystery Magazine*, Aug 1947; *Ellery Queen's Mystery Magazine* [Australia], Aug 1949)

Friday, the Nineteenth (*The Magazine of Fantasy and Science Fiction*, Summer 1950)

The Legacy (*Liberty*, Dec 1950)

La Signora from Brooklyn (*Cosmopolitan*, Dec 1951)

Farewell, Big Sister (*Ellery Queen's Mystery Magazine*, July 1952; hardboiled satire)

The Death Wish (*Cosmopolitan*, Feb 1953)

Most Audacious Crime (*Nero Wolfe Mystery Magazine*, Jan 1954)

Shadow of Wings (*The Magazine of Fantasy and Science Fiction*, July 1954)

Glitter of Diamonds (*Ellery Queen's Mystery Magazine*, Mar 1955; *Ellery Queen's Mystery Magazine* [Australia], May 1955)

The Strange Children (*The Magazine of Fantasy and Science Fiction*, Aug 1955)

Very, Very Dark Mink (*The Saint Detective Magazine*, Dec 1956; *The Saint Detective Magazine* [UK], Oct 1957)

The Darling Doctor (*Alfred Hitchcock's Mystery Magazine*, Mar 1957)

Game for Four Players (*Alfred Hitchcock's Mystery Magazine*, June 1958)

The Blank Wall (*Alfred Hitchcock Presents: My Favorites in Suspense*, 1959)

THE SHOALS OF HONOUR

Basil Hazeltine has learned to live by his wits. As elegant and educated as he is, his only real talent lies in survival. He relies on his friends and relatives to supply him with spending money. Hazeltine himself has no interest in earning a living. His lack of ambition has already lost him the love of his life, Jocelyn, to his cousin Lewis Martinsburgh. Now Martinsburgh wants him to help him out with a young lady who holds some rather compromising letters he wrote her.

It's all spending cash to Hazeltine. He is happy to help his volatile cousin. But Hazeltine has to make a decision. He can't go on like this forever. So when Miss Huested, an older woman with a small fortune, comes to him with a proposal of marriage, he is faced with a dilemma—whether to maintain his self-respect and steer clear of the shoals of honor, or live a life of compromise and expediency. And then Jocelyn comes back into his life…

The Shoals of Honour is a story of New York City in the mid-1920s, filled with the contrary characters that Holding wrote about so well in her many mystery novels. Also included are six short stories from this period from the pages of *The Century* and *Munsey Magazines*.